GREGORY A. Dc
2006). A man of r
man, novelist, pla_____, _____p____, artist and poet. He studied
philosophy at New York University and earned a law degree from
Harvard before getting his professional start in the legal department at CBS Television. While working there, he began to pursue
a writing career, winning the O'Brien Short Story Award in 1940
and publishing his work in *Esquire*, *Atlantic Monthly*, the *Saturday
Review* and other publications. His other novels include *Enemy in
the Mirror* (1977) and *Love Letters* (1979). His lone horror novel, *The
Nest* (1980), was the basis for a 1988 cult classic film.

THE
NEST

GREGORY A. DOUGLAS

With a new introduction by
WILL ERRICKSON

VALANCOURT BOOKS

The Nest by Gregory A. Douglas
Originally published by Zebra Books in 1980
First Valancourt Books edition 2019

Published by Valancourt Books, Richmond, Virginia
http://www.valancourtbooks.com

ISBN 978-1-948405-30-0 (*trade paperback*)

Also available as an electronic book.

All Valancourt Books publications are printed on acid free paper
that meets all ANSI standards for archival quality paper.

*The Publisher has pursued every conceivable line of investigation and
inquiry in an attempt to trace the identity of the cover artist and/or
copyright holder of the cover illustration. Anyone with information is
requested to please contact the Publisher.*

Set in Dante MT

INTRODUCTION

Horror paperbacks published by Zebra Books in the 1980s are some of the most highly sought-after collectibles for genre fans who crave the tacky, lurid, ridiculously creepy—in other words, totally awesome—cover art. But what lies within, many a vintage horror reader will tell you, is quite often less than awesome. Zebra saw a buck could be made, and as long as the cover art—usually by artist unknown, as Zebra left out artists' credits on the copyright page—struck the potential buyer's eye, that was all that mattered; the story and the style within were simply an afterthought. They went all in on imagery: Skeleton sniffing a flower? Check. Skeleton in slippers and robe? Check. Satanic hologram faces? Check. Fruit sliced up by knives and razors in a crude visual pun? Check. A lone, precisely rendered cockroach beneath a full moon in a dark forest? Oh check. Like those fly-by-night film producers of yore, who had a movie title and poster prepackaged long before some poor soul was hired to write the script, it was all about that image.

But back to that lone cockroach. This moody, eerie landscape is featured on the cover of Zebra's 1980 previously unheralded offering, *The Nest*. This novel is in the grand tradition of "animal attack" fiction, best exemplified by of course the 1974 publication of both *Jaws* and *The Rats*, and continued through two more decades. For visceral, unrestrained thrills and chills, I'd put *The Nest* right up there with those two classic creature horrors. This is one case in which story and cover align in unholy matrimony; it's the kind of paperback pulp horror that I wish there were more of.

Written under the pseudonym Gregory A. Douglas by one Eli Cantor, there is a conviction and a dedication to horror, disgust, and despair that one doesn't often find in the genre, believe it or not. Recall what Stephen King said about *Rats* author James Herbert in *Danse Macabre* (1981): "He does not just write, he puts on his combat boots and goes out to assault the reader with horror." That's precisely what Douglas/Cantor does in *The Nest*. No one is spared: not pets, not children, not innocents, not lovers, not the goodhearted. A pall of doom, hinted at in the sickly blue-green of that unholy cover, hovers over the entire tale. This is a good thing.

Reading Cantor's obituary in the *Sarasota Herald-Tribune* (he died aged 93 in 2006), it's easy to see why *The Nest* has a satisfying quality so many other paperback horrors do not. "He was the ultimate renaissance man," his daughter stated. An award-winning writer going back to the 1940s, Bronx-born Cantor wrote plays, stories, poetry, and musical compositions, studied law and journalism, worked in the First Golden Age of Television, and ran a printing press, and was highly successful and well-recognized in all these fields for decades before he wrote *The Nest*. In other words, Cantor lived, and loved, the creative process, and was committed to it. This is not always true of paperback writers, for whom the term "hack" is a bit above the pay-grade. Cantor was simply over-qualified, and his dipping into the sleaze is something we should be thankful for.

All of these attributes contribute to the success of *The Nest*, purple prose and all. Like the pulp writers of yore, who wrote for a penny a word, or sometimes probably even less, Cantor goes all out. He works for those pennies, skimping on no detail (like how the insects eat through the victim's eyes into the brain). Early on, he gives a picture-postcard tour of his Cape Cod town of Yarkie, describing history, houses, buildings, and citizens to ground his tale in the everyday. Does that mean the story is padded and perhaps overlong at 448 pages? Maybe, but the scenes of cockroach horror are so powerful, so merciless, so unforgiving, that they more than make up for Cantor's overzealousness in other areas.

And overzealous describes Cantor's creatures too: if everyday roaches are disgusting, six-inch-long roaches with mandibles of chewing death are immeasurably more disgusting! A swarm of mutated cockroaches has somehow "organized" themselves by some unknowable miracle of evolution into a thinking organism, each individual creature a cell in the larger mass. As a biologist explains to the townspeople who have thus far avoided being roach fodder, "the Yarkie roaches are being directed by what I can only describe as a brain." Iiiick. (On the attribution page Cantor thanks famed sociobiologist E.O. Wilson for his insights into insect behavior; do you think Cantor sent him an autographed copy of the book? In a perfect world: yes).

I mentioned purple prose; there are so many amazing passages in *The Nest*, I will only give you a taste of this ripe and rotting fruit:

Having partaken of human meat and drunk human blood, the new cockroach breed was ravenous for more... they could not get enough of the human taste and would seek it endlessly, implacably, and with many more victories... She had to live with the inconceivable sight of great cockroaches coating her husband's face, a vicious, quivering crust of filth... It was intolerable to watch his companion choking to death because cockroaches were crammed in her nose and throat... to see these scurfy roaches drill into the body of his dear and cherished friend...

How did I discover *The Nest*, you ask. Why, through the internet, of course, where I stumbled upon its glorious cover art and knew I had to own it (and maybe even read it!) About four years ago I found myself in a Salt Lake City used bookstore, one of those really spectacular ones crammed full of not just used books but also all the dusty ephemera of our pop culture past. Their horror section was overloaded with paperback goodies, and lo and behold, a copy of *The Nest* was burrowed back in the shelves. When I placed my selections on the counter, the grizzled old owner tapped one nicotine-yellow fingertip on its cover and in his grizzled old smoker's voice gleefully said, "This book? Scare the shit outta ya!" (I do hope the Valancourt guys see fit to put that blurb on this new edition). He was not wrong, I was delighted to discover, and I am delighted again to present it to you in this reprint line of horror novels under the banner of *Paperbacks from Hell*.

With its delirious lapses in good taste, *The Nest* is a shuddering, creepy-crawly scarefest that attacks the reader with one revolting sensation after another. In vintage 1980s schlock-horror, you can't ask for more than that. So thank you, Mr. Cantor, for your commitment to scaring the shit outta us.

WILL ERRICKSON

Will Errickson is a lifelong horror enthusiast. Born in southern New Jersey, he first encountered the paperback horrors of Lovecraft and Stephen King in the early 1980s. After high school he worked in a used bookstore during the horror boom of the '80s and early '90s, which deepened his appreciation for horror fiction. Many years later, in 2010, he revisited that era when he began his blog *Too Much Horror Fiction*, rereading old favorites, rediscovering forgotten titles and writers, and celebrating the genre's resplendent cover art. With Grady Hendrix in 2017, he co-wrote the Bram Stoker Award-winning *Paperbacks from Hell*, which featured many books from his personal collection. Today Will resides in Portland, OR, with his wife Ashley and his ever-growing library of vintage horror paperbacks.

Thanks are due to novelist Eli Cantor for suggesting that an island could be as terrorized by an invasion of mutant insects as by killer sharks off its beaches.

The author gratefully acknowledges the studies in animal behavior of Dr. B. Faber of the American Museum of Natural History and Columbia University; and the publications on insect sociobiology of Professor E. O. Wilson of Harvard University. Any errors of science are the author's own, as is the fictional hypothesis of the insect mutation imagined in these pages.

—G.A.D.

TREMORS

ONE

Under a luminous moon, the garbage dump on Yarkie Island off Cape Cod began to shudder and vibrate grotesquely. It might have seemed an illusion of the moonlight on the quiet Atlantic that serene summer night, but the strange phenomenon near the beach was no mirage. It was as unmistakable as it was mysterious and ominous.

The thin topsoil over the island's refuse was trembling with an eerie drift. It was a sluggish and sickly motion, as if the mounds had turned into a viscous muck, or were mucidly floating on a hermetic current oozing from the depths. Without seeming reason, the slimy flux would stop and then pulse again. Sometimes an unearthly bulge appeared, like a tumor or festering pustule that seemed ready to split open, almost as if a buried-alive victim were straining to push out of a mouldy grave. A viewer might, with stopped heart, expect to see the excrescence burst, and a cadaverous hand lift a bony claw into the night.

But there were no witnesses to the shifting motion, or to the maddened rats that began to fling themselves wildly out of the garbage piles.

The vermin were squealing with agony as they sprang into the night air. Their writhing bodies were as bizarre as their gyrations and screaking; they were covered not with fur but with what seemed to be shells, scintillating in the moonlight. The pinpricks of fire on their rodent bodies flashed crazily over the dump with a metallic sheen until there was a quick change to the crimson of blood. The rats were cloaked in sequins of death; a nightmare scene out of an animal hell.

Routine poisons normally controlled the noxious creatures everyone knew and tacitly accepted as living in the dump. Wafarins held the inevitable rat population in check, and the cockroach broods were standardly contained by pyrethrum and sodium fluoride. Since the prevailing southwest winds carried the stench conveniently out to sea, it was easy for the dump—out of the sight and smell of Yarkie's homes—to remain out of mind.

Thus, no one marked, suspected, or theorized about the slithering mass of preternatural life seething through the stinking intercises. No one considered or remarked that conditions were ideal for breeding in geometric multiplication. For cockroaches, particularly, the ever-enlarging dump was a great progenitive womb—warm, fetid, moist, with food so cornucopianly plentiful that everything crawling, creeping, and scurrying through the foulness could gorge to satiation.

Until the change in Yarkie's poison controls by unwitting health officials upset the balance Nature had contrived, and unleashed a new appetite that bloodless garbage could not satisfy.

Aside from the dump's ugly acre at the northeast tip of Yarkie, the island was travelogue-picturesque. It sat "like a bowler hat" in the sea off the Cape some ten miles eastward of Chatham. It was about two miles wide, and four miles long, running south-north; with a central, forested dome—the "bowler"—bordered with beaches broken sharply by steep cliffs and ridges.

The village of Yarkie rose on the west side, facing

toward the Cape, above a deep-water harbor crowded with working fishing boats. The small town made a tidy New England grid of prim lawns and white spires amid tree-lined, red-bricked sidewalks. The old homes of long ago whaling captains stood doughtily behind boxwood hedges and whitewashed fences "making good neighbors." Outside the town, the Yarkie houses were scattered on a lace of lanes, once cart and wagon roads and a challenge to the few cars that used them. Bikes and shank's mare were more common on the island.

Most of the buildings were crisp white or gray shingles on hewn oak, what Thoreau had described as "sober-looking, and reflecting the (Cape Cod) virtues of thrift, neatness and independence." Almost all were topped with widow walks from which Yarkie wives and children had, as long ago as the late 1600s, scanned the surrounding waters for the first sign of sail of husband, son, brother, lover.

The four hundred-odd inhabitants of Yarkie were no-nonsense. They pretty much held with what one long-faded Cape newspaper had noted for posterity: A person would be "warned out of town" if he were not "twenty-one years old, of sober peaceable conversation, orthodox in religion, and possessed of saleable estate to the value of twenty pounds." In modern Yarkie, this proscription took the form of discouraging tourists and all publicity about the island's very existence. One ferry a day served more than adequately between Chatham and Yarkie even in midsummer.

It was not so much that the people were unfriendly as that they were self-satisfied; not so much uncharitable as parochial. They were quietly proud of their wealth and their heritage as whaling men, mariners, jack tars and fishermen (if not pirates and buccaneers), and they preferred to keep their island free of the vacationists who flooded Martha's Vineyard and Nantucket.

The Yarkie-ites continued to be "... of sober peace-able conversation." The redoubtable Johnson clan had produced one firebrand, a daughter named Jessica, now married to a Harvard biology professor, Richard Carr. But their daughter, Elizabeth Carr, visiting her grandfather, Elias, was more like the conservative old man than her activist mother. Captain Elias Johnson's view, expressed with some force, was that women, modern or old-fashioned, had enough to do making a home and raising children.

This summer, Elizabeth was clearly a child no longer. At twenty, she was to start her senior year at Radcliffe in the fall, and not even her deep love for Yarkie and her grandfather would keep her returning to the island many more years. On this visit she had displayed some of her mother's independence by bringing a black classmate as her companion. The islanders were standoffish at first, but the young woman was warm, honest, and dusky beautiful. She won over the people, and they won her over. Elizabeth was delighted. She had feared a fuss, at just the time she herself wanted the island's quiet perspective "to get her own act together." She had barely passed her junior-year classes, and was restless without any clear idea of a career ahead. There seemed an embarrassment of choices and a poverty of inner conviction.

For her friend's part, Bonnie Taylor was in love with Yarkie at first sight. She had expected to find the island as charming as Elizabeth had promised, but nothing had prepared her for the eighteenth century world she entered when she stepped off the small ferry. It was hard to believe that many homes used only kerosene lamps and candles for lighting, and wood and coal stoves for cooking. It was both enchanting and refreshing. She was amazed to find how quickly one learned to rise at dawn, wash with gasps of incredibility in cold water, warm one's hands (and rear

4

end) thankfully at the kitchen stove, and feel a steaming breakfast mug of coffee washing down to heat the stomach and the cockles of one's heart.

She was half sorry to learn that these experiences had only been due to a temporary problem with Captain Johnson's generator, which otherwise supplied modern lights, heat, and hot water.

Bonnie's regret on this summer day of a planned picnic in the woods on Yarkie's High Ridge was that Elizabeth could not join her. The captain had celebrated his seventy-fifth birthday too enthusiastically the night before, and was resting a bruised toe and frayed temper. Elizabeth had insisted that Bonnie take the lunch basket, and—though there was nothing to be saved from on the island—the captain's dog, Sharky. The small, frisky animal was as brave as his breed was nondescript. Two years before, when an imprudent youngster plunged from the captain's fishing boat for an unscheduled swim, it was Sharky who had catapulted into the water to savage the Mako shark attracted by the boy's splashing. It was the day the dog's name was changed from Pooch.

"Just stay on the path," Elizabeth told Bonnie as she started her off at the edge of the Yarkie woods. "Don't go past the pine grove. You'll recognize it by a little waterfall there and the picnic tables. The path beyond goes to the town dump. You don't want that one."

"No way," Bonnie agreed, laughing. Dumps were what she was spending her life leaving behind.

Bonnie found the grove a sylvan setting out of a Maxfield Parrish painting. The morning sun was slatting down between high tree branches, striping golden bars on a carpet of leaves and pine needles inches thick. The air's freshness seemed almost tangible to Bonnie, as if she could rub it like a lotion between her palms and smooth it over her body. Being alone, she considered stripping, but thought it would be imprudent in case anyone else appeared.

As she spread her blanket, the woman noticed that the dog was sniffing nervously where an opening in the trees led out of the circle of the grove. That was the way to the dump, she remembered. Sharky's sharp nose was probably picking up the odor. Smiling, Bonnie considered this was one time it was better to have duller senses. Let Sharky romp his own way.

She paid no attention to the dog's soft growling that turned suddenly into little yipping barks. It was Sharky's way of enjoying the outing, Bonnie thought as she lay down comfortably amid the pine fragrance. The hushing trickle of the small waterfall was a magic of its own. It brought to her mind quiet Japanese gardens and Zen koans, the settling peace of the simple acknowledgments of nature—the sky she could see vaulting above the treetops, the delightful bird songs all about. Boston was another planet. She called pleasantly to Sharky. He came to her slowly. She wondered why his little body was trembling under her stroking fingers. He was panting as if he had been running hard. He continued to turn his head toward the path, growling again. Bonnie considered it was probably the dog's asking why Elizabeth wasn't with them. She kept stroking the soft coat, but the trembling did not stop. On the contrary, the woman felt the animal's heart beat faster under her hand.

"What's wrong, Sharky?" she asked casually. "Something bothering you?"

The dog's answer was to startle her by leaping away. At the path, his body went rigid, his head up, his ears high, his nose forward, his left front leg lifted. He stopped growling, and it was then Bonnie Taylor heard the other, unfamiliar sound. It came out of the forest, a rustling susurration somehow inimical and threatening. She told herself quickly it was only a rustling of leaves, but there was no breeze and no motion as far as she could peer down the shadowed aisle outside the grove. Probably a snake, she decided. But not dangerous, or Elizabeth would have cautioned her. The woman turned calmly back to her blanket.

Sharky did not come when she called again. She saw his ears quivering, straining. She heard the sound once more, louder and clearer now. It was a hissing that sent sudden electric chills up her spine. She had known coon-hissing back home in Mississippi, but this was not the same. And the dog was acting crazily. He had begun to hop about, as if the ground was hot. He was bobbing his head, yipping and whining in a way that would have been called hysterical in a human.

The sibilance was clearly coming closer. Bonnie jumped to her feet and hurried to collar Sharky. If there was some danger stirring such instinctual dread in the dog, she was not going to linger in the place. There might be animals in the woods Elizabeth had not thought to mention.

At the same moment, she became aware of a strange odor, as if a foul-smelling acid had been vaporized in the air nearby. Sharky had sensed it before she did! It was making him cower and cringe now, in a way she had never seen. The dog was pressing his shaking body against her legs, whining pitifully. She lifted his body to hug and comfort him, but to her shock, he bared his teeth, snapped at her, and raked her forearm with his claws.

Crying out in surprise and pain, Bonnie dropped Sharky to the ground. "What's got into you?" The dog faced her viciously. From the friendly, docile pet she had known, he became a snarling, ferocious-looking beast. Seriously frightened, Bonnie backed away slowly. The beads of blood on her arm might be evoking some primitive instinct of attack. Dogs were descendants of wolves. With genuine alarm, Bonnie grabbed up the aluminum picnic box and held it in front of her breast for protection.

But Sharky transformed again. With quick, rough barks of furious challenge, he launched himself away from Bonnie into the deep woods toward the hissing noise.

Moments later, Bonnie was riveted by a change in Sharky's barking. There was an abrupt high yelping, then a cry of acute agony. Bonnie shivered, trying to see the dog through the heavy growth. She stepped out of the grove gingerly. If there was an animal out there that could hurt Sharky, it could hurt her. But she had to know what had happened. The dog could simply have gotten into a patch of burrs, though that wouldn't account for his erratic conduct earlier.

One careful step after another led Bonnie Taylor along the umbrageous path that went toward the dump. The way was through great mounds of springy leaves, the residue of scores of Yarkie autumns, undisturbed through the years except by occasional deer and the smaller denizens of the woods, raccoons, muskrats and the like.

Bonnie halted to listen. There was only silence now. Even the birds were quiet, she observed. No leaf rustled; there was no hissing sound, no dog noise, no motion anywhere that she could detect.

Then she heard the whimpering, a gasping for breath. It sounded almost human, but it was Sharky, certainly, somewhere near. Bonnie took a determined step in the direction of the soft cries, only to be stopped by the loud hissing. It was like an angry warning, a command for her to stay back.

With all her voice, Bonnie called, "Sharky! Sharky! Here, Sharky!" She bent for a fallen branch. Her mouth tightened with purpose. She would find Captain Johnson's dog, and she would protect herself against whatever was lurking in the dark copses into which he had disappeared.

Moving forward again, Bonnie kept looking about alertly, feeling an idiot, not knowing what kind of danger

8

she should be anticipating, and whether it might come at her from in front, or the sides, or even from above. She swung her branch grimly, as if to show that she was not afraid, though she was quaking inwardly.

Walking alone in the thickening woods, beginning to get a faint smell of the garbage stench, frightened of the mysterious hissing that stopped and started so disturbingly, Bonnie wanted desperately to turn back. She gritted her teeth harder. She'd be damned if she'd show yellow. The strange sibilant sound, she told herself firmly, was obviously just some kind of snake she was unfamiliar with, and Sharky had probably killed it by now.

It was then that Bonnie Taylor stepped sickeningly on the white body almost entirely buried in leaves that were stained crimson with blood. It was obvious that a thrashing battle had taken place. When she knelt to brush the leaves away, she found Sharky lying on his side. The dog's coat was pocked with fresh blood. His legs were kicking in a palsy of animal pain. In Bonnie's presence, his whimpering sounds became louder. He looked up at her with a piteous whine for help. Bonnie vomited. The dog had only empty sockets where his eyes had been.

TWO

"I couldn't bring him back," Bonnie wept in Elizabeth's arms. "I wanted to, but I just couldn't bear it! I'm so sorry."

Elizabeth Carr embraced her friend. "We understand, Bonnie."

"No, you don't. You can't imagine how horrible it was!"

From his couch, Captain Elias Johnson asked, "Just his eyes, you say?"

Bonnie sobbed, "I don't know, Elias. He was bloody all over . . ."

"No more now," Elizabeth said firmly. She looked over at her grandfather. "I'm going down to the sheriff's. If we've got rabid animals in the woods, Amos Tarlell needs to know."

A command from Johnson stopped his granddaughter at the door. "Slow down, Liz! It could have been birds, you know."

"Birds?" Both women repeated the word incredulously.

The old man nodded. "Sharky might have found a nest. You get a herring gull mad, you'll find how sharp and deep its bill can dig." The captain heard the lack of conviction in his own voice, but he wanted time to think without Sheriff Amos Tarbell bolting around the island, upsetting people needlessly.

Bonnie Taylor ventured, drying her cheeks, "There didn't seem to be a nest or anything like that . . ."

Elias Johnson held to his theory stubbornly. "We get snowy egrets that pass this way, too. They've got beaks can drill to China!"

Elizabeth countered, "Egrets stay on the beach, don't they?" She knew Yarkie Island birds quite as well as her grandfather did.

"Might get a stray in the woods, maybe a sick one, which'd make it meaner." The old man sucked his teeth. If Sharky was dead, nothing could bring him back. But he needed to know it was no mystery. There had to be a sensible explanation, and birds were probably it, from what Bonnie reported.

Elizabeth voiced a new thought. "Were there any men up there?"

Bonnie told them she had seen no one.

Elizabeth prompted, "Those fellows who came across the ferry yesterday?" There had been an unkempt group of three "punks," dressed outlandishly in Nazi caps, torn army pants, and ripped shirts. On the pier, they had eyed

Elizabeth and Bonnie lewdly, making suggestive gestures the women had turned from with disgust.

Bonnie shook her head, swallowing hard. It was too horrible even to contemplate that any man, no matter how brutish, would put out a dog's eyes. What would he use? A sharpened branch? A walking stick? She fought to keep her stomach from turning over again.

An urgent knocking on the front door interrupted the three. Captain Johnson called irascibly, "Come on in before you break the damn thing down! You know the door's open!"

A tall man of about twenty-five entered in a hurry. The sea was in his lean, weathered face, with its black Portuguese eyes, long nose, and a heavy mustache that curved down on both sides of a strong mouth. Craig Soaras was the mate of Johnson's fishing-charter boat, the *Jessica*, and a childhood friend of Elizabeth. Children loved him. They tugged at his large mustache knowing its piratical fierceness masked warmth and shyness. They rode his back, they clung to his shoulders when he sailed them across to Chatham for the annual visiting circus.

To Craig Soaras, the *Jessica* was like his own boat. To him, the long hours at sea passed in the best way a man could live his life—caring so ardently for what he did that he was scarcely aware of doing it. His sailing and fishing were no more "work" than breathing or eating, or lying on a beach watching fiddler crabs scuttling about and pipers dance on the wet sand with the ebb and flow of the waves.

Now the man panted anxiously to the captain, "Can we talk alone, Elias!"

Knowing these men, Elizabeth quickly led Bonnie out, but she could not help wondering what needed to be private between them.

In the living room, Craig moved quickly to the captain's side. Johnson paid hard attention. Craig wasn't a man easily upset, and he was sure blowing a conch now.

"Elias, I was around the north side going for bluefish—" Soaras couldn't help interrupting himself with a fisherman's enthusiasm. "Caught a nice one, twenty-seven pounds!"

"Fair . . ." Elias Johnson teased and waited to hear about the worry he saw in the man's eyes. Had the price of their fuel gone up again?

He was told more than he ever bargained for.

"I was opposite the dump, off the rocks there, when I saw Russell Homer waving at me from the bulldozer, where he was spreading some new soil on the garbage. He was signaling with his shirt, seemed like some kind of trouble. I rowed on in. Russ came zigzagging down the beach; I figured he was dodging mosquitos or something."

"What'd he want?"

"For me to get him out of the dump on the boat."

"Didn't he have his jalopy there like always?"

"Yes, but it was full of—rats."

"*Rats?*—What the hell!"

"That's what I said."

"Since when is Russ afraid of a couple of measly rats?"

"Hundreds of them! I saw them myself! Something loco is happening at the dump, Elias! Weird and awful. I got Russ on board and watched with my glasses. Like he told me, I saw rats jumping up out of the garbage there as if they were damn birds! And dropping back *dead!*"

Elias Johnson rubbed his nose, thinking hard. "We put new poison out there last week," he said, "the way those Public Health people told us, to keep the vermin from getting used to one kind. Must be killing the rats now . . ."

Craig Soaras clenched his leathery fists. "That wasn't any poison, Elias! Those rats were dead from having their eyes put out! I saw it plain as day!"

The captain's head snapped up. "*What?*" Eyes gone! *Like Sharky's?*

Craig scowled. "What in the name of the saints could

12

do a thing like that? Hundreds of those rats, every one without eyes!"

The captain rubbed his nose harder. It sure as hell wasn't any herring gulls. And even he had known his talk of egrets was phony. Something here just damned didn't add up. He'd heard every crazy damn thing in his life, at sea and ashore, but never anything like this.

Craig added, "That's not all. Seems like the rats are going nuts. They thrash around like something's driving them wild. I could hear them squealing all the way to the boat. They flop around, like dizzy, climb on each other, gash at each other—and then drop dead like that!" He snapped his calloused fingers. "You think it's rabies?"

"Where's Russell?"

"I dropped him off to tell Amos. If those crazy rats head for town, this island is in for a helluva mess."

The old man stood up vigorously, disregarding the pain in his foot. "Let's get to Amos ourselves, Craig. Pronto!" As he followed his mate out of the house, Elias Johnson muttered to himself with new understanding. Rats! Yes, rats crazed by the new poison might go for the dog's eyes. So that's what had happened to poor Sharky! Lucky that Bonnie had got away with a whole skin. People had better stay out of the woods for a while! Russell Homer had better stay off the dump, for that matter, until they learned what the hell was happening out there.

Hobbling to the town hall downhill on Main Street, Elias Johnson took in the quietness of the harbor below. The Atlantic was lying low today. Didn't fool anyone on Yarkie Island. It would probably storm tomorrow, but meantime the people were enjoying the spell of good weather. Too dry for the woods, but on every Yarkie beach this noon young and old were having a good time, swimming carefree, sunning themselves, picnicking.

His own plan for the island was already formed in Johnson's clicking mind. Decision One: He would phone his son-in-law at Harvard and explain about the new poisons causing rat trouble at the dump. Richard Carr could hurry one of his assistants to Yarkie to check it out. No doubt they could correct the problem with their modern chemicals. Decision Two: The sheriff's office would officially announce that the woods were being sprayed. Starting at once. Everyone had to keep out. That would give the Harvard fellow the time he needed.

Maybe Richard Carr would come over himself, with Jessica, if she wasn't too busy. With Elizabeth already on the island, they could have a nice family reunion. There was a silver lining even to the clouds over the village dump. The captain smiled faintly to himself as he limped up the brick steps under the sheriff's sign. To the familiar faces greeting him on the hilly street, he turned an unrevealing, unworried smile—old Elias Johnson just going about one of his ordinary chores as Yarkie selectman.

The only unfamiliar note on the street was the "punks" about whom Elizabeth had remarked earlier. The three were not only ragged, they were literally dirty, and they seemed to take pride in their offensiveness as they lounged in front of Elvira Soaras' Cafe near the pier. Their eyes were insolent, following people who passed by as if daring anyone to comment or protest.

One of the men stirred. "It's getting hot, man. Let's hit the beach we found yesterday!"

The others nodded. Swaggering abreast, the three moved along Main Street, heading up the hill toward High Ridge. Purposely they gave no way, so that everyone approaching had to step into the gutter to let them pass. They laughed aloud at the discomfort they imposed. "Bunch of hicks," one sneered. "Some pretty chicks," another added. "Fuck 'em later," their companion urged impatiently. "I want to wrap one up!"

He was talking about the marijuana they had in their jeans, of course.

THREE

Across the island, on Yarkie's east shore, Reed Brockshaw was waving his two children out of the ocean. "Chow time, kids!" Six-year-old Kim and nine-year-old David came splashing and giggling out of the slapping waves in the noon sun. They shook themselves like puppy dogs and pounded up the sand to Doreen Brockshaw, waiting for them with large bath towels. Her embrace was fierce in its intensity. It was almost a year since fire—an ever-present island hazard—had consumed the house Reed had built. Only the man's heroism had saved the children. Before the volunteer trucks arrived, he had plunged heedlessly through the wall of flame. Miraculously, none had suffered more than minor burns.

It was a miracle Doreen Brockshaw daily held in her mind beneath her long red hair. Each morning she went quietly down to the kitchen at dawn. In her white nightgown she brushed her hair back, lifted her green eyes to the coming day and sent up the meditations of her thankful heart.

Reed Brockshaw once came upon his wife in her praying. He withdrew silently, comprehending her need to be private in this. It was a measure of the couple's devotion that no words were needed. Reed and Doreen Brockshaw had an other-century marriage appropriate to an old-fashioned island.

Reed himself had sailed with Elias Johnson on many charters but now he was working as a carpenter on a marina being built by another selectman of the island, Stephen Scott. Reed missed the ocean trips, but the land pay was better, and building his new house was costing more than even he had planned for.

Doreen was saying, "We need more firewood, kids." Reed had carefully built the small cooking fire on the side of the dunes away from the forest. The trees came close to the shore at this spot, and he knew they were tinder. He half rose to go himself, but remembered his father's saying: Shared chores mean shared family. The Yarkie way. In the winter they called gathering firewood "going wooding." Let David and Kim go wooding now.

Something made the father turn to look after the two small figures stamping gaily into the trees. On impulse he got to his feet and started to follow.

His wife laughed at him. "Don't be such a fusspot, Reed. We know every inch of this place and there isn't a blessed thing in there that can hurt them."

Brockshaw didn't answer his wife, and he didn't stop. Doreen held her peace. She knew the constant anxiety for the children her husband harbored. If her own answer was her morning prayers, his was this special vigilance. He was tactful, she appreciated. She didn't think the children were aware how closely he kept them in view.

In the forest, David, as the older child, took charge. He pointed to a thicket on the right, in the direction of the distant village dump. "You go that way," he commanded his sister. He himself had spotted a pile of broken branches on the opposite side and intended to gather its riches alone.

The little girl went obediently into the thick copse, though she could see nothing but the crowding bushes. She had trouble getting through even with her small and agile body, but she was intent on bringing back as much wood as any old officious brother. Kim dropped to her knees and wiggled on. She heard her father calling and flattened herself in the leaves so he would not spy her.

In the quiet she heard an unfamiliar sound. It was

16

coming from behind a heavily leafed bush before her. It was a rustling of leaves accompanied by a hissing Kim had never known before. With curiosity, the girl spread the bush apart with her hands, wincing at sharp thorns that drew spots of blood.

Kim peered into the gloom. The noise might be a baby bird fallen from its nest, or a baby rabbit, or a chipmunk caught in a crevice—though she had never heard such hissing from any of those friendly animals.

She decided she would go back and tell her father when she heard her brother calling triumphantly through the trees, "Hey, Dad, betcha Kim can't beat *this* load!"

The bravado of it stung Kim with an anger that steeled her purpose. She lowered her head and butted her way obstinately toward the sibilant sound. She came to a half clearing where there was a little more light. It fell on a gleaming jewel lying in the leaves before the child's astonished eyes. Directly on top of a heap of leaves there was an iridescent shell, longer than her longest finger, which scintillated like treasure in a ray of sunlight.

It was unlike any shell she had ever seen on the beaches. The delighted girl leaned over, her face near the object. Her lustrous eyes, wide with guileless curiosity, were scarcely an inch above the shining shell when she sensed that it was alive. She bent more closely, studying it intently. It was hard to make out in the shifting light, but from the front of the thing there emerged two antennae, like those she'd seen on crabs and lobsters, though smaller.

The shell shifted slightly in the leaves, and the antennae, thrust in her direction, seemed to be reaching up toward her eyes. She moved her head back quickly.

What kind of creature was under the pretty shell, Kim wondered. As she reached her fingers out to turn it over a sharp hiss issued from whatever it was. Her hand jerked away. Fear prickled her spine. "I just want to *see*," the child murmured indignantly. "I'm not going to hurt you, you know!" She reached for the shell obstinately. This time something flashed out so quickly she hardly saw it. But she felt the sting, and tumbled away. Lying in the leaves, she stared at her hand and saw blood running along her finger.

Angry now, Kim crawled forward once more. The tarnation thing had dared to bite her! She bent to examine it again, but more cautiously now, ready to hop back if it pulled any more tricks. Then she realized that another "whatever-it-was" had appeared through the leaves. And another, and another. There were antennae waving all about, encircling her.

At once, the child was tingling with a primal fear. This wasn't a game she liked! She started away, then decided to go back. She *would* take one of the things to show her parents, and put David in his place. She reached down determinedly with the hand that had not been stung.

When she lifted the thing into the ray of sunlight to observe it more closely, it seemed to go dead.

With her small fingers, Kim gently stroked the shiny shell, and saw the iridescent color came from the folded wings. This creature didn't look like a beetle at all. It was —she couldn't believe her eyes—a roach! She said it aloud: *"Cock-a-roach!"*

But so big!

Nobody in the world had ever seen a cock-a-roach this size! It was a giant! It was a cock-a-roach from the kitchen of the giant in *Jack and the Beanstalk!*

Kim began to giggle as she made up a story about the strange bug climbing down the beanstalk and getting lost in the Yarkie woods.

She wondered why it was so still: Had she stunned it picking it up? Was it afraid of the sunlight? She knew that cock-a-roaches liked to stay in the dark cracks at home.

The girl looked at the great insect with growing curiosity. Had this bug bitten her? It looked so nice, not at all anything to be afraid of. She lifted it higher, closer to her eyes to see it better.

"Kim!" It was her father, angry-sounding. His voice startled her and the bug dropped out of her grasp.

"I found something, Daddy! Come and see!"

Reed Brockshaw grabbed his daughter in his arms. "Are you all right?"

Kim pointed at the leaves. "Look at the shells there!" But before her father could turn his eyes, the girl saw the glinting surfaces vanish. She pouted. "They're down in the *leaves!*" She didn't want her father to think she hadn't told the truth. "Cock-a-roaches! Look at my finger!" She lifted her incontrovertible evidence. "It even bit me. See the blood?"

The man started away with the girl against his chest. "We'll put something on that. Does it hurt, honey?"

"No." Her father smelled of sun and tanning lotion, and love, and she hugged him hard.

To his wife, Reed Brockshaw said, "Kim stuck her finger on a thorn. Put a Band-Aid on it . . ."

Kim spoke indignantly. "It wasn't any thorn! A cock-a-roach as big as a house *bit* me!"

"Oh, you," her brother said predictably, "always making things up!"

FOUR

Captain Elias Johnson was on the sheriff's official phone, finishing his call to his son-in-law in Cambridge. The circle of men was waiting respectfully. At the ancient, worn oak desk sat Amos Tarbell, sheriff of Yarkie Island. He was a self-contained man of forty-two, of medium height, but with the stocky strength of a man who had sailed freighters around the world. His face was like his body, strong and solid. His eyes were sharp with looking into distances and into people. Few on Yarkie fooled with Amos Tarbell.

The noon whistle was blowing at the volunteer firehouse across the street when Johnson finished on the phone. Aside from Craig and Amos, two others were present. Russell Homer was a slight fellow, with a narrow, bony face but a quick and willing smile. His life had been uphill on Yarkie, his ineffectual mother dead when he was an infant, his father the scorned town drunk. He had been brought up by an aunt who was strict even by island standards. He wore an Ahab-type beard to look older, respectable. He knew his was the dirtiest job in town, except for the fish-cleaning shed. Russell didn't mind. Riding the yellow bulldozer at the dump, he dreamed his dream, oblivious of the stink, the screaming gulls, the scurrying rats, the streaming roaches. He was saving for the day he would put a payment down for a machine of his own and hire it out on Yarkie. He would be his own boss, his young wife and son would be invited to any home on the island, even Hildie Cannon's on High Ridge, the cream of the cream.

Right now Russell Homer sat hunched over, feeling guilty for the mess at the dump. Maybe he didn't spread the new chemicals correctly. He kept repeating a private prayer that the Harvard people could fix things fast. It was lucky they had Elias Johnson who could put them in touch with that kind of help and authority.

Stephen Scott, seated next to Homer, was a fat man who always seemed to be puffing for breath even when he was still. He was the Yankee entrepreneur of Yarkie, a selectman like Johnson, and persuasive enough even to get the votes for his marina project. He could be greedy, but people also knew he often helped poor families anonymously. It was a typical Yankee contradiction.

Ben Dorset entered the office just as Elias Johnson

began his report. Dorset, a lanky, blond man of thirty, was the first deputy sheriff and assistant fire chief under Craig Soaras. He had come from the firehouse where, following Johnson's instructions, the pumper truck was now leaving to crisscross Yarkie with a warning that High Ridge Woods were out of bounds, being sprayed.

Elias Johnson spoke crisply, "Richard says he can't tell us anything till he knows more, but he agrees the new poisons may be the trouble. He thinks that the rats may try to get out of the dump, so, Amos, we'd better put some men with guns at the spit out there, where it narrows, and have them shoot any buggers they see. At night we'll set up flares."

"Right!" the sheriff agreed promptly.

"Meantime, we're in luck. Richard's top assistant, a Dr. Peter Hubbard, is free to come out pronto. Hubbard is on his way to Logan right now to catch the plane for Chatham, he'll be here early this afternoon. We need someone to go over to Chatham for him . . ."

Stephen Scott said at once, "Reed can take my Bertram!" Everyone understood the spirit of the offer. The Bertram craft was "the gold-plated yacht," Scott's pride. It was the fastest boat around, could make the ten miles in less than half an hour even in rough water. "Where *is* Reed?" Scott thought to ask.

Craig Soaras remembered it was Brockshaw's day off, and that his family had planned to picnic around East Beach. "I'll find him," Craig volunteered. He himself would have enjoyed the rare opportunity to sail the Bertram, but he knew that Scott would prefer to have his own man at the wheel.

Johnson said impatiently, "Okay! Whoever goes to Chatham, have him ask for Dr. Peter Hubbard." He stood up abruptly, clearing his throat. "Now Craig and I will go find Sharky and bury him."

"Damn shame!" the sheriff murmured. "That was a real nice pup."

Scott spoke to the group quietly but with power. "And we all keep this on the quiet side, fellows, right?" The men comprehended his concern without further explanation; their grim faces told him so around the room.

Craig Soaras was opening the door for Elias Johnson to leave when a middle-aged woman with two girls swept into the office, fuming with outrage. Hilda Cannon was a widow, the doyen of one of the oldest of the old Yarkie families, and she considered the sheriff's office an extension of her own home. She and her twin daughters, fifteen-year-old Rebecca and Ruth, filled the room with their bulk and wrath. The woman was in mid-shout before the door closed, and Johnson turned back to hear her complaint.

Mrs. Cannon shook a sausage-like finger under the sheriff's nose. She vociferated, "I warned you, Amos, but would you listen to me?" The woman pivoted to Johnson as her oldest friend. "Elias, I told him to run those hoodlums off the first day! We don't need layabouts and drifters on this island!"

Amos Tarbell's neck swelled against the tight collar of his starched tan uniform. "And I told you Yarkie is still under the United States Constitution!" It was now the sheriff who looked to Johnson for confirmation. "We may not like those three fellows, but they have their civil rights too, you know."

Hilda Cannon's eyes bulged. "What about my girls' constitutional rights?"

Amos Tarbell addressed the two girls directly. "Those men touch you, Ruth? They talk out of the way to you, Rebecca?"

The girls started to giggle, and their mother herded them behind her back. "They are embarrassed enough! I'll tell you what those hooligans dared to do! They *exposed* themselves to my girls! They are out there right now in the cove by Rock Cliff stark naked!"

The old captain said dryly, "Well, the girls didn't have to look, did they?"

The woman was taken aback. "Are you standing up for those bums?"

The man continued. "It's a steep hike up to where you can see that cove, Hildie . . ."

Mrs. Cannon whirled on the sheriff. "You put those hoodlums in jail where they belong!"

The sheriff looked to Johnson and Scott. "Do we have an ordinance against nude bathing?"

Both village officials had to recall. Johnson said, "Don't think we ever got around to that."

"Never had that particular problem come up," Scott allowed.

Amos Tarbell soothed Hilda Cannon's ruffled feathers. "I'll go down there and get them dressed."

"Off this island!" she insisted, huffing out with her daughters.

FIVE

While Elias Johnson and Craig Soaras were startling into the woods to get Sharky's body for burial, three nude men were taking their ease on the secluded beach they had discovered below one of Yarkie's cliffs. The rocks formed a wall on one side, and the forest was protective on the other.

The noon sun was baking their skin and Angel Dust was baking their brains. One of the three suddenly jumped to his feet. His young naked male body was handsome though his face was puffy and slack. At eighteen, he looked thirty and more. He was gasping wildly for air and shouting, "I'm a *fish!* No wonder I can't breathe! Come on, Bo! Come on, Tony!" His mouth gulped as he pounded across the sand and plunged beneath the waves before his companions could take in what was happening.

The man named Bo opened one eye. "What's the shit, Tony?" His speech was drug-slurred and muffled by the heavy black beard he wore.

His companion grunted out of his own fog, "Alex gone to take a piss."

Bo smirked. "My ass. He gone to whack off."

The two eased back into their cradle of sun, drowsiness, and sea sounds. Neither one noted that no head broke the surface where their friend had dived.

Looking down at the men from the top of the rise, Amos Tarbell found it hard to accept that the zombie-like forms were probably of good families, with rewarding careers open to them. They were the results of modern permissiveness, he thought—at home, in school, in a world of eroded values. It had pithed their characters as surely as something evil had pithed the eyes of Elias Johnson's dog that morning.

Amos Tarbell and Ben Dorset slid down the rocks and raced into the water past the two prone bodies. The sheriff yelled, "Don't you bastards realize your buddy is drowning!"

The two sat up in the sand, blinking vaguely at the disturbance. Bo laughed to Tony, the younger, slighter figure. "Wild shit here, man."

But the two displayed a befuddled interest when the sheriff and his deputy came ashore with the inert body of their friend. Amos Tarbell began artificial respiration. The man named Tony protested, "Hey, this guy is reaming Alex!"

The two started angrily for the sheriff, but Ben Dorset

24

pulled his gun. "Just quiet down, and nobody'll get hurt." He put Bo's hands behind his back and slipped handcuffs on.

"Hey, man, we ain't done nothing!"

The younger one started to run, but Dorset tripped him and handcuffed him as well.

Bo complained, "How the fuck we supposed to get dressed with our hands behind our back?"

Amos Tarbell called to Dorset. "This one's coming around. Radio the office for a boat—"

Tony whispered to Bo, "They're *fuzz*, man! I can't take another bust!" With that, while Ben Dorset was preparing his walkie-talkie, the man darted away into the forest. His bearded friend lumbered after him.

Ben Dorset started to follow, but Tarbell stopped him. "Don't worry about them." Working on the near-drowned figure, the sheriff couldn't help smiling at the picture of two naked fellows, with their hands locked behind, trying to climb up to the ridge through the tangled thickets. He said, "We'll pick them up later."

There was a crash from the trees and a sharp cry. It was Tony's voice, alarmed. "Bo! I can't get up!"

There was no answer.

"Bo! Where the hell are you?"

The only sound was a loud hissing noise. Both the sheriff and his deputy looked toward the woods. "What the hell was that?" Dorset said.

The cry behind them became a scream. "Bo, come back!"

The scream turned to a burst of horror. "My foot! Christ, something is eating my *foot!*"

Ben Dorset said uneasily, "Hey, Amos, you think—"

"The rats? No. We're too far from the dump. He's just having a bad trip."

The voice in the woods soared into an inhuman

screech. "My cock! Holy Jesus God! It's biting my *cock!*"

Ben Dorset nodded to the sheriff. "Bad trip." He'd learned about drugs in police school. It was the fellow on the beach who needed their help—he looked like he'd swallowed the ocean.

The screeching exploded into a staccato of agony. "My eyes, Bo! I can't see!"

The deputy got up. "I better go take a look in there, Amos."

The sheriff shrugged. "If it'll make you feel better."

Sprawled where he had tripped in the Yarkie trees, Tony Carlucci was anguishedly telling himself it was just an evil trip—the flitting shapes on his body were unreal, like the d.t.'s. The nails driving into his ears, the teeth tearing his flesh, they were the hallucinations of bad shit.

The stinging *up his rectum*—how could that be *real!*

The man flung himself about, legs flailing. He bucked and twisted and squirmed. Without the use of his hands, he was helpless. But he groaned to himself that he was tough stuff—whatever this shit was, he would beat it!

Then Tony Carlucci could swear some feathery things were touching his lips, almost like tiny kisses. For a moment it was pleasant, but then there were sharp pins stabbing his mouth, and he could feel bugs crawling between his lips. The man gagged and clamped his teeth against them, until the pain of flesh being eaten from his bones made him cry out. In that instant, his open mouth was crammed with hissing insects. In another instant, his throat was invaded with a vibrating mass of huge, evil-smelling bugs he could not make out. The man gulped reflexively, swallowed against his will, and spewed out, all at once, it seemed. He felt hot blood spilling from his throat, pouring through his lips which were being chewed away to the bone of his jaws. He cried, soundlessly now, "Oh, *God*, please help me!"

In the depths of his addled brain, the man was only too aware that this was no bad dream. Searing irons had burned out his eyes. Spikes were splitting his skull. His brain itself was being chewed from within by razor teeth. This was a "trip" from which he would never return.

Tony Carlucci knew he was dying, and it was not his past that flashed before him but the future he would never have. He wanted to plead that the drugs had only been kid stuff, his quitting school only macho wild oats, he had always intended to be straight, join his father's grocery, marry, have kids.

Have kids? His cock and his balls had been chewed away on this crazy island!

Nerves in the man's head were jangling like fireworks. He felt lightning forking out of the blackness of his eyes. Bugs were burrowing through his brain. Their bites were like flints striking fire in his skull. The edges of his brain were browning and curling up, frying in pain. And buzz saws below were cutting his body apart, separating his limbs, slicing away chunks of his organs.

Tony Carlucci's final sob of helplessness was that of a small child falling into a bottomless black abyss. "Mama —Mama, mia!"

The teeming cockroaches ate steadily, voraciously, stripping the body like piranha, and worse—chewing the bones to powder.

SIX

On the beach, the rescued man was breathing steadily, though still in a stupor. The sheriff called toward the woods, "Ben, what's up?"

His deputy came out of the trees, shaking his head. "Dunno. It's the damndest thing. Those two guys must have had one hell of a fight. There's blood all over, but not a sign of where they went."

Amos Tarbell followed Ben Dorset back into the woods. Dorset pointed to a place where a body had plainly pressed the leaves into a mat. "He made a track to just about here." Signs of a struggle were clear. Low branches were snapped off. There were fresh tangles of leaves smeared with blood.

The sheriff found himself swallowing hard. "How the hell could they have had this kind of a fight with their hands locked?"

Ben Dorset was pointing up through the trees. "One of them went up that way, looks like. But there's only one track, right?"

The sheriff made his inspection and agreed.

"Then where the hell is this other guy?" Ben Dorset asked both the sheriff and the forest.

There was no answer from either.

Finally the sheriff shook his head. There were no other clues than the ones that made no sense. He said hoarsely, "We have to get back out. The boat will be here soon. We'll send some men to check this later."

The deputy hung back. "Amos," he asked in a whisper, "do you think this fellow—*might it be like what happened to Elias Johnson's dog?*"

The sheriff spoke sharply. "It was a bad trip, like I said! We'll find both those creeps on top, bet you a month's pay!"

Amos Tarbell plowed out of the forest back to the beach, angry and confused. He did not really believe he would find the men on the ridge, but whatever else was happening was beyond his experience and comprehension. Where could two naked men have got to? How could they have bloodied each other as savagely as the scene suggested? It was inexplicable—unless.

Unless.

Sheriff Amos Tarbell was compelled to let the odious thought take form in his troubled mind. *Crazed rats might be running the woods.* Packs of wild rats with festering rabies! That would be worse for Yarkie than even the sharks some years back.

This was more than he could handle alone. He glanced at his watch. Twelve-thirty. Reed Brockshaw should be on the Bertram to Chatham by now. The scientist from Harvard would be on the island soon.

The sheriff shook his head unhappily. It looked like they could use all the help they could get. And it had started out such a quiet, sunny day on Yarkie this morning.

SUSPICIONS

ONE

When Hilda Cannon left her house for a lunch date at twelve-forty-five, her daughters grabbed their field glasses and hurried through High Ridge Woods toward the cliff from which the cove could be viewed.

"Momma'll kill us if she ever finds out," Ruth said nervously.

Rebecca put on a studious expression. "We're allowed to go bird-watching, aren't we?"

Ruth flushed. "Not for these kinds of birds." She held back. "Becky, the fire truck said to stay out for the spraying."

Rebecca sniffed the air. "They haven't reached here yet." She went faster through the trees. "I hope old Amos Tarbell doesn't chase those fellows before we get there!"

"We should have had the goshdarn glasses before!"

"I got a good look anyway. Did you ever *see* the one with the beard?"

"I wasn't looking at his *beard* . . ."

The girls' exchange tinkled through the trees as they plunged on, breathing hard with both their exertion and their anticipation.

Ruth stopped abruptly. "Hey, wait! What's that?"

Rebecca pushed ahead impatiently. "You're gonna make us miss them!"

Ruth called after her sister with fear shaking her voice. "Becky, stop!"

Rebecca shouted back through the trees, "Amos is going to chase them *away!*" But she skidded to a halt at the sight to which her sister was pointing in horror.

In this elevated section of the woods, the ridge was only sparsely covered. On a stony ledge before the girls, the wind-blown pines were dwarf-size and twisted like Japanese bonsai. The open platform was swarming with rats. They were large, fat brutes, disgusting with their swollen bellies, narrow rodent faces, and snaking tails. That was revolting enough, but the freakish spectacle was the dance the rats seemed to be doing.

One after another, rats leaped into the air. Their thin legs kicked wildly, their long tails whipped madly, their heads jerked from side to side. In the macabre ballet, scores of rats were in the air at one time, colliding, snarling, snapping with squeals of fury.

In their berserk acrobatics, many rats flung themselves off the cliff, as if their maddened brains imagined they could fly like birds. They plummeted to their death in the sea below, to be scavenged by quickly gathering fish and birds.

"Let's get out of here!" Ruth trembled.

Rebecca had her binoculars up. She screamed in surprise and horror. "It's *roaches!*"

"Roaches?" Ruth was incredulous.

"*Cockroaches!* Millions of them! Great big King King cockroaches!"

"What are you *talking* about?"

"Big cockroaches all over the rats!"

Ruth had trouble focusing her glasses. Her sister was all too horribly right! Every writhing, "dancing" rat was literally coated with cockroaches. The brown color of the rats was not their fur, but the shells of the insects. And, as the glasses showed in their amplification, the roaches were clearly eating at the rats as they clung to them. The girls could make out the dark spots on the rocks now—pools of red rat blood dripping from the mayhemed animals. The girls could see clearly, too—all too terribly clearly—that heavy roaches were gouging out the rats' eyes, crawling up the rats' nostrils, and disappearing into their ears.

The girls' revulsion could not help but be tinged with something akin to pity. The rats, loathsome as they might be, were still living creatures that could feel pain. It was beyond human capacity to watch them being eaten alive this nightmare way.

Held mesmerized by the view enclosed in their field lenses, the girls did not observe that some frantic rats, still free of the roaches, were streaking into the trees. Their racing line of terror headed them blindly to where the two were standing.

Too late, Ruth and Rebecca heard the chittering noise of the pack. In an instant, sharp rodent mouths were gashing the girls' feet, gulping the quick human blood. The frenzied jaws of leaping rats were tearing the white throats before the panicked girls realized what was occurring. The binoculars went flying. Without even time to scream, the Cannon girls were rolling on the ground, punching and tugging at the assaulters. Streams of blood now poured from the young faces, arms, their gnawed fingers. Chunks of flesh were ripped from their breasts, bellies, and thighs. Narrow raping snouts shoved hungrily into their genitals, in a terrible mockery of the girls' careful innocence.

Neither the expiring Cannon daughters nor their rat attackers saw the swelling legions of great roaches that were advancing toward them. The roaches moved across the ground like a monstrous organism. Each roach was like a single tooth in a huge maw. In minutes, the myriad of insects had stripped the flesh of both rats and girls to bone—and then razored the skeletons to powder. Then the huge mass rested, pulsing quietly as with one communal breath, before disappearing en masse in a single wavelike motion beneath the heavy leaves.

Stillness and silence remained in the forest.

TWO

Amos Tarbell had just returned from the jail infirmary where the near-drowned man was recovering when Hilda Cannon rocketed into his office again. She was more distraught than earlier, and had trouble speaking through her fresh anger. "I came home from lunch and saw that man in my garden! Without a stitch on his filthy body! Not down on the beach, but in front of me in my garden! *And . . .*" she let her voice peak to the height of her new anxiety, ". . . I can't find Ruth or Becky anywhere! That man has raped them and killed them, Amos!" She was trying not to break into tears.

The sheriff came around his desk and held the woman's shoulders. "Hildie, how could a man rape someone with his hands locked behind his back?"

Hope appeared in the woman's twitching face. "He was *handcuffed?*"

"Handcuffed," the sheriff repeated.

"But where are my girls, then? It's almost two o'clock!"

Amos Tarbell sat down to the papers on his desk. "Visiting some friends, or out fishing, or bird-watching."

"I told them strictly to wait home till I got back from Beatrice Scott's!"

The man said soothingly, "We'll pick that fellow up. Don't worry. Incidentally, did he talk to you or anything?"

"Come to think of it, yes, he did!"

The sheriff looked up. "What was that?"

"He said—" The woman thought for a moment to get it exact. "He said, 'Take me to your sheriff.'"

Her words echoed in the office before they both burst into laughter. The creature from outer space had spoken.

Tarbell asked, "Well, why didn't you bring him in?"

The woman coughed. "Me? A naked man?"

"You could have given him a blanket or a robe . . ."

"I suppose it was foolish," the woman added. "I was just too upset." She managed a dry smile. "It isn't every day I find something like that in my garden . . ."

"I guess not," the sheriff smiled back sympathetically.

Mrs. Cannon started out, her lips working with inner confusions. "I'll ask around after Ruth and Becky."

"I'm sure you'll find them safe and sound," Tarbell said.

When the door closed, he let out another blurt of laughter. That must have been the funniest damn most hilarious spectacle anywhere, anytime—that bearded fellow in front of none other than Mrs. Hilda Digges Cannon in his birthday suit. "Take me to your sheriff!" Tarbell slapped his desk in a paroxysm of delight and relief. If the one man had showed up, the other would. Ben Dorset had been foolish to bring up the question of the rats . . .

But when Amos Tarbell answered his ringing telephone, his laughter and his assurance faded fast.

THREE

In the woods around the picnic grove, Elias Johnson and Craig Soaras were baffled. They had faithfully searched the area described by Bonnie Taylor, and there was no dog body or sign of one.

"I'd think Bonnie was mistaken, except she's so dang bright," Johnson muttered. "She said to the left of the path, which should be just about here." The old man went to his knees with a grunt of stiffness. "Nothing. She must have got the place wrong in her excitement."

Craig shook his head strongly. "That's one lady knows her right from her left, as you say."

Johnson gave his friend an approving smile. "There are still some folks are surprised that blacks think and talk as if they were human." The old man knew Craig Soaras wasn't one of them. Craig's own people were *bravas*, from the Cape Verde Islands back many generations, a place where the Portuguese and Africans had intermarried freely.

The old man realized he had been yattering to himself to cloak the doubts piling up in a sinister way. Sharky was a brave dog but not a stupid one. If there had been an attacker in the woods, he would have stalked it carefully before exposing himself to danger. Yet, there was no indication of a struggle, and no track suggesting Sharky had followed some spoor and was now perhaps asleep himself in one of the island's many caves.

A whoop from Craig Soaras startled Johnson out of his thoughts. His mate was pointing up a tree. The old man wondered why. Craig of all people knew dogs don't climb trees. This whole damned business was full of mysteries. The captain made his way to the elm where Soaras was standing. The tree was considerably to the left of the trail the men had searched earlier, and it stood in a knee-high stack of old leaves. Johnson still heard the crackling sound with pleasure. Way, way back when he himself was a kid he had tumbled and bounced in leaf heaps like this.

He stopped suddenly, brought up by a sound strange to his Yarkie-tuned ears.

Craig called, "Over *here*, Elias!"

"Quiet!" Johnson commanded. His hand was cupped to his head. His friend understood at once. Old Elias had heard something he had missed. And there it was! A rustling in the leaves around a stand of white birches. Both men squinted in that direction.

"Mice," Craig decided. Then impatiently, "Look here, Elias!"

The old man stood rigidly, listening hard. "No mice till night!"

"Might be the poison at the dump has got everything upside-down."

"Might be." The rustling had stopped. Johnson gave his attention to his friend. "What've you got there?" He moved to the tree and looked up where the man was pointing.

Craig asked, "Think that's bird feathers?"

Johnson said, "Looks more like, I dunno, rabbit fur, maybe." On a branch above there was something like a piece of stained cloth.

"What the hell would a rabbit be doing up a tree?"

Johnson again made his abrupt motion demanding silence. Now both men heard the hissing sound, more distinct and persistent. It was somehow menacing, the way the clicking of a rattlesnake's coils is chilling even to someone who does not know the threat.

"What the hell is that?" Craig whispered.

"Not any damn mouse I ever heard of," the captain observed sharply.

The young man took a step toward the unusual sound. "Let's go see."

"Get that thing off the tree first," Johnson directed.

It wasn't easy. For all his strength and agility, Soaras had to make several attempts before he caught a branch and could swing himself up. He stretched and reached for the white object.

"God Almighty!" he cried.

"What did you find?"

"Catch this!"

One of his dog Sharky's ears dropped into the stunned hands of Elias Johnson.

At the same moment, a huge rat, almost two feet long, sprang with a blood-curdling squeal from a nearby leaf mound.

Craig Soaras yelled, "Up anchor!" and tumbled from the tree. "Let's get out of here!"

But Elias Johnson was mesmerized by the rat's arabesque. It whirled and contorted its body in the air again and again, and neither man saw the large insect form that dropped like a shadow from the rat's flank, to scuttle away into the leaves.

Weaving drunkenly on the ground, the rat spied the men. Its eyes malevolently took them in as its tormenters. The animal lowered itself to spring at Elias Johnson's throat. Its lips were drawn back in a venomous snarl, its dripping fangs livid for human flesh.

Craig jumped in front of Johnson, sweeping up a branch to use as a club. The rat launched itself at him. Craig brought the club back like a bat and swung with all his muscled might. He caught the leaping rat squarely on the head. The men heard the animal's skull splinter, its back break. The rat, with an expression of almost human amazement, went sailing away through the air, a grotesque home run for Craig Soaras.

When the animal fell, its legs still clawing the air, the whole pile of leaves heaved.

Craig yelled at Johnson urgently, "There's more of them in there!" He pulled the old man around unceremoniously, and they took off.

Had they looked back, they would have seen the rat's broken body suddenly disappear, yanked down into the leaves by something waiting beneath, something invisible but a force of power. A force that hissed hungrily over the rat's body, letting the promise of the other prey go this time.

Captain Elias Johnson cursed to himself as he ran alongside Craig Soaras. So it *was* rats had got Sharky!

His foot hurt, but he wasn't about to slow down. His head hurt, but he wasn't about to give up on Yarkie. Mad rats like this one, obviously rabid, were hellishly dangerous. Where there was one, there would be more. Thank God Craig had batted that bastard away. Those leaves were full of them, that was plain. Russ Homer was right, dammit!—a new kind of rat was loose on Yarkie. They could only hope the young scientist, Dr. Peter Hubbard, would know what to do.

There wasn't time as Johnson ran painfully away from the once-tranquil picnic grove to ponder how Sharky's ear had gotten up on a tree. Or where the rest of his dog was.

The balance at the village dump had indeed been upset. Insects and rodents that had lived peacefully amidst the plentiful garbage were suddenly at odds. Massive doses of pyrethrum had imposed a paradoxic effect on the mutated roach population.

A temporary excitant even in ordinary situations, the pyrethrum jolted the new roach breed into a frenzy of new activity and, more important, new hungers.

The Yarkie rats were the first victims. When chance brought larger prey to the crawling mandibles and jaws, an even stronger taste and relish developed. At the same time, The Nest was throbbing with new vigor, as if the fresh nutrition was itself speeding and amplifying the mutation. Warriors and foragers had multiplied to the many millions. Soon the Colony would be ready for the necrotic raids that would make them masters of all that their swift legions could reach, encompass, engulf.

FOUR

By two-thirty, a meeting was in progress at Elias Johnson's home. Elizabeth and Bonnie had served sandwiches for a late lunch. Elizabeth was glad she could busy herself. It was disquieting to be in the same room with Peter Hubbard. She had tried to keep her greeting casual. She never wanted him to know of the sixteen-year-old crush she had on him when he had appeared in Cambridge to be her father's laboratory chief.

The man was lost to her in two ways, she had quickly realized and accepted. It wasn't just her youth; he was then twenty-two, later on the six years' difference would scarcely matter. But he was buried in his work, had already published an acclaimed thesis on animal behavior. His second devotion was obviously Dr. Wanda Lindstrom, another assistant in her father's department. The woman biologist was Peter Hubbard's age, like him a prodigy with an early doctorate. At twenty-six now, she was a leading expert in the field of *Entomology*, insects in layman's language. And, contrarily, she was beautiful, with silken blond hair down to her shoulders and a walk like Marilyn Monroe. Unfair! the young Elizabeth had jealously thought. But a handsome pair Peter Hubbard and Wanda Lindstrom had made, young Elizabeth conceded. She had turned to her own interests—music and literature—and had taken care to be otherwise engaged when her father invited the two for dinner.

Now, with Peter Hubbard in her grandfather's house, Elizabeth was looking at the man not only through her own, older eyes, but through the interest of the Yarkie men. She saw first the sensitivity of Hubbard's broad mouth, as she remembered it. The others marked first the honest, strong light of the scientist's blue eyes, which reflected quick intelligence and hard-earned knowledge. Elizabeth saw the sensitivity of Hubbard's hands, as she had once fantasized they might embrace her. The Yarkie men were taking in the squareness of the scientist's shoulders, the jut of his chin that said he would not be put off by difficulties. They reserved judgment, in their way, but they liked what they saw.

Actually, Elizabeth considered, there was much of her father about Peter Hubbard. He was as tall, and had the same appealing gangling posture. She supposed the biologists got it from their constant bending over laboratory apparatus, the cages, dissecting tables, microscopes and their endless log books.

Peter Hubbard, in his turn, was taking in the people in the room. He showed a profound interest that was flattering and a profound curiosity that was unnerving. Elizabeth felt his eyes turn to her, and she fought again not to blush. She was twenty now, not sixteen; he was twenty-six, not twenty-two. On Yarkie, with a common problem, it would be impossible to avoid him as she had done in Cambridge. But the last thing she wanted was more complication in her life. She turned her attention to the coffee tray.

Elizabeth saw Craig Soaras studying Peter Hubbard out of the corner of his sharp eye. For her the difference between the two men was the dramatic difference between Yarkie and Cambridge—"Cambridge" being the whole outside world. Craig was content with the sea, which held its own complexities and challenges. Peter was content with nothing, because the truths he sought could never be final. If Craig hooked a fish, it was there on his line. If he steered a boat through a gale, it was there safely tied up at the pier. But that wasn't so with the scientists like Peter Hubbard and her father. Every answer Peter caught taunted him with new questions—some of them very terrible and urgent to Yarkie right now, as her grandfather, putting down his cup, was about to inform all of them.

As the captain described his and Craig Soaras' experience, the mood of the group turned increasingly somber. Johnson spared no words, and now he did not hesitate to have everyone hear the news Russell Homer had brought that morning about rats going crazy at the village dump.

Peter Hubbard listened intently. When Elias Johnson emphasized the phenomenon of the blind eye sockets, the biologist's head came up thoughtfully.

Amos Tarbell and Ben Dorset were listening with their own newly sharpened suspicions. Craig Soaras kept nodding numbly at Johnson's recital. He still had difficulty believing what he was hearing, even though he had been attacked by one of the crazed rats himself.

Bonnie Taylor could not sit still. She left her chair to stand at the Johnson fireplace, gripping the mantel. Her premonition that she had lost Sharky to some terrible fate was turning out to be too atrociously true, though no one fully understood what had taken place. Her own lingering guilt was not diminished by the obvious fact that something extraordinary—for which she could in no way be blamed—was afoot on Yarkie Island.

Like Bonnie Taylor, Russell Homer could not shake the sense of responsibility he had carried since the morning. It did not help that he was hearing now of other harrowing incidents. Maybe he had concentrated too much poison in one place, shorted another. He hung his head. Maybe the Harvard man would find he was indeed accountable and denounce him to the whole island. All his hopes would be smashed.

Reed Brockshaw was listening with his own horror. Just hours before he had allowed his children to wander among the trees. The blood on Kim's finger—what if it had not been a thorn! What if the "shell" had been the nose of one

41

of the sick rats Elias Johnson was describing! Lucky he had found Kim in time! The man was ashen beneath his sunburned skin.

Stephen Scott's face set into a gelid frown. This should not be happening to Yarkie, he thought angrily. These were good people, good families. The men worked hard, on the water, or making sails, building boats, caulking, rigging, fishing. Honest men. There was pride here, the pride of self-sufficiency. The island had to bring in things like furniture and hardware and building supplies, but mostly they made and grew what they needed. No one here was soft, and no one too dependent.

Despite the grimness of Elias Johnson's report, Stephen Scott could not help but smile as his mind went back to a family story of a great-great-grandfather who was a whaling captain. It seemed that old Ezekial returned from a two-year voyage with one seaman lost to a sickness. At the inquiry, Ezekial produced the drug cabinet with which a ship's master practiced medicine on board. The chest contained numbered bottles, along with a list of symptoms to be treated. Ezekial was asked by the officials, "Didn't you give this sailor the prescribed bottle?" The captain explained, "I did, indeed. But I was all out of Bottle 13, so I gave the man some of Bottle 6 and some of Bottle 7."

It was still the Scott family's best tale.

How the generations change, and yet persist, the fat man thought as he looked across the room at Elizabeth Carr. Elias' granddaughter was another of the self-reliant ones, a girl without airs. Tall, and a looker, her skin like fresh cream, and her brown hair with strawberry glints in it that set off her friendly gray eyes. Bad-worried now.

Not wanting to accept the threat Elias Johnson was describing, Stephen Scott focused on a mental picture of his store instead. No rats could upset Yarkie's solid

42

foundations! "Scott & Sons" sold every kind of gear for boating, fishing, building, what-have-you. Half-closing his eyes, Scott could visualize his stocks of oilskins, netcorks, cleats, clam rakes, waders, diving equipment of every type. In what had been a sail loft above, there were trap floats of every color, piled up anchors and tubs, coils of rope, lines for trawling, pails for bait, traps and weirpoles, straps and tackle. To make the strongest hand-sewn sails, he even supplied the traditional three-sided needles.

But Stephen Scott's wandering thoughts could not keep Elias Johnson's message at bay for long. *Yarkie was in trouble!* If Yarkie was in trouble, he was in trouble. The marina had taken most of his capital. If people and money didn't start coming in, he would lose everything. There had always been rats at the waterfront, but nothing like what he was hearing now.

The fat man shook his head, took a sighing breath, and finally opened his ears to the captain's words. Johnson was talking directly at Dr. Peter Hubbard.

Scott regarded the Harvard scientist with some skepticism. The man looked almost too much like a picture of a professor. He had on a worn tweed jacket with leather elbow patches. His gray slacks showed wear at the cuffs. His moccasin-type shoes were scuffed and unpolished. But as the man knocked his pipe out and unwound from his chair, it was with a sense of confidence that made Scott lift his own head hopefully.

The hopefulness did not last beyond Peter Hubbard's first comment. "I can't tell you anything useful at this point, obviously," the man told the group gravely. "Just as obviously, you may have caught a severe problem here. The fact is that some sections of the country have reported unusual rat infestation this year. Until this morning I hadn't heard of it in Cape areas, but rats could have come in by any boat, and they breed quickly. I came out fast today because if you do have a rat problem, we need to identify it in the shortest possible time frame.

"My first priority is to set up a temporary lab." He turned to Johnson. "Where will I be working, sir?"

"How about the attic right here? You can look it over—"

Despite herself, Elizabeth interrupted, "Grandpa, you're not going to bring those *rats* into the *house?*" For a moment she thought Peter Hubbard resented her interfering, but instead she gratefully heard him support her. "It might not be wise, captain," he said. "I'm not going to have all the precautions of a solid lab arrangement, you know."

Elizabeth saw the man's eyes on hers, and read friendship in them, an offer to start anew. She was not mistaken about it. Peter Hubbard had forgotten how charming a smile Elizabeth Carr had, and he was taking her in as a captivating, grown woman for the first time.

The sheriff suggested, "We have a room over the jail. It's got water faucets, some tables . . ."

Craig Soaras observed reasonably, "But that's in the center of town. If anything got loose, there could be hell to pay, couldn't there?"

"I'm afraid so," Hubbard agreed.

Stephen Scott spoke for the first time. "Also, we don't want everybody in Yarkie hearing about this until we know what it's all about. Right?" He gave them all his best smile, the one he used when he rapped his gavel to adjourn a town hall meeting.

Heads nodded around the room.

Ben Dorset reminded them, "There's the old light-house, up northside."

"Good man, Ben!" Scott endorsed.

Elias Johnson thought it over. "Makes sense to me," he told the scientist. "We'll run you over for a look-see. You tell us what you need, we'll put it in."

Amos Tarbell added, "It's far enough out of the village

so nobody will bother you, and close enough to Harbor Road so you can get in and out."

Scott heaved himself up. "Good! I'll lend one of my jeeps. Just let's all remember that gossip travels faster than the wind."

Elias Johnson informed Hubbard, "Doctor, I'm already keeping folks out of the woods, told them the trees are being sprayed. The sheriff's deputies and the volunteer firemen are taking care of that. But what about those rats? Will they stay *in* there?"

The scientist spoke between puffs, lighting his pipe. "On the basis of what we know about rat behavior generally, I'd say your breed prefers to keep hidden."

"Good, then!" Reed Brockshaw exclaimed. He needed badly to grab onto any promise that there would be no general danger.

The scientist finished lighting up and addressed them soberly. *"Unless,"* he added, "there's something in your woods that is driving the rats out."

"How's that?" Stephen Scott challenged quickly.

"From what I've heard this afternoon, I'd have to suspect that something is attacking the rats seen this morning. A quick theory is that they've been hit with some kind of virus. It might affect the inner ear, which would account for the dizziness we've been told about. Or it might be some form of rabies that is driving the rats at each other, and at people . . ." He hesitated a moment. "Though frankly I must say I have no idea how the dog's eyes would be put out the way Miss Taylor described."

Bonnie shuddered, and moved to a corner of the room. She was afraid tears might come again, and she did not want the men to see her cry.

Johnson took charge. "We'll get your lab set up at the lighthouse. Pronto."

"The first thing I'll need is some specimens," Peter

Hubbard said quietly. "Can you get me at least a couple of the rats?"

Craig Soaras and Russell Homer were on their feet. "I'll go right back in! I'll get you the stuff you want from the dump!"

Amos Tarbell rose, with his hands held wide and his fingers wiggling urgently at the men. "Hold it, hold it! This may be dangerous. We'll do what we can, but first we'll get some guns. If we're going into the woods, we need to cover each other . . ."

Elizabeth heard the sheriff with growing horror. It was hard to believe it was only hours since she had sent Bonnie off to the picnic grove with Sharky for a pleasant, serene afternoon. Poor dog. Poor Yarkie, it seemed, if Peter Hubbard couldn't help them!

Peter Hubbard was saying to her grandfather, "From what I've gathered so far, captain, I won't be able to handle this problem alone. I'd like you to call Dr. Carr, please, and ask him to send over my associate, Wanda Lindstrom."

Elias Johnson gave a quick nod. "I'll get on the phone right now!"

Elizabeth's jaw quivered at the sound of the woman's name. Immediately she chided herself: *I should be ashamed of myself!* With all of Yarkie Island in some unknown danger, how could she be concerned about an old jealousy —one she had never had any right to feel in the first place! She forced a noncommittal smile, and went quickly to Bonnie. She saw how disturbed her friend was, and spoke to her quietly. It helped her get control of herself. She was not going to forget that Peter Hubbard and Wanda Lindstrom were outside the circle of her life!

The Yarkie men started out of the Johnson house on their assignments.

Peter Hubbard turned to Elizabeth. "Could I trouble you for another cup of coffee, Elizabeth?" he asked pleasantly.

It was Bonnie who hurried to the kitchen. She wanted a chance to be alone, if only for minutes.

Elizabeth heard herself saying, in a restrained tone, "It's too bad you have to come to Yarkie under these circumstances, doctor."

He nodded, keeping his eyes straight on hers. "I can see that," he smiled slightly. "Please don't be formal with me, Elizabeth. We're old acquaintances, after all." He held his hand out to her. Elizabeth touched it coolly with her fingertips. She was past a girlish infatuation now. She would remain at arm's length with Dr. Peter Hubbard —she would be an agreeable and proper hostess to her grandfather's guests, including Wanda Lindstrom. Nothing more.

"You've certainly changed," Peter Hubbard was saying, his eyes unwavering on hers.

Before Elizabeth could respond, Elias Johnson interrupted them from across the room. "Peter, I have Doctor Lindstrom on the line now. She can come out on the first plane tomorrow, but she wants to talk to you . . ."

Hubbard turned for the phone at once. Elizabeth could not help noticing the change in his voice, the intimate way in which he began to discuss with his colleague the chemicals and scientific apparatus they would need for their work on Yarkie.

Yes, Peter Hubbard should indeed be talking in that manner to Wanda Lindstrom and not to her, Elizabeth Carr thought as she stalked to the kitchen after Bonnie. That was exactly the way it should be and exactly the way she wanted it, she told herself sternly, closing the door against the telephone conversation with a bang.

The noise brought the man's head around. A small smile formed on his lips. Even while he was speaking earnestly to his colleague in Cambridge, the thought was in Peter Hubbard's mind that there were more than bio-

47

logical misunderstandings to clear up on Yarkie. He would try to have a talk with Elizabeth Carr, but it was plain that tact was called for.

The scientist returned all of his attention to the telephone, continuing with the list of the analytical apparatus he wanted Wanda Lindstrom to prepare for the required laboratory. The workroom would have to be makeshift but it would get them started, at least. Hopefully, they wouldn't have to go further . . .

FIVE

By twilight, Dr. Peter Hubbard was settled in at the abandoned lighthouse on Yarkie's north shore. Over the years, the unpredictable ocean had stranded the building on a long sand bar, and a new light had been constructed on a higher point.

With the scientist was the nucleus of what was to become Yarkie's laboratory team. Craig Soaras was to do whatever carpentry work was needed. Elizabeth and Bonnie had volunteered for the house and kitchen chores.

Johnson and Scott, as the elders, agreed that whatever meetings were required should be held at the lighthouse, so that people in town wouldn't begin to wonder at the group's frequent convening.

As darkness spread over the island, the men who had been searching the woods came in. Elizabeth was relieved to see them all apparently unharmed—Reed Brockshaw who had insisted on scouting with Johnson, and Russell Homer who had teamed with Ben Dorset and Amos Tarbell. Stephen Scott did not appear. He was hosting a long-scheduled "social do" at his home, and to call it off would have aroused the very suspicions he wanted to avoid.

The men put their guns away, and fell to the supper

Elizabeth and Bonnie had prepared. There was tacit agreement that reports would he tabled until after the meal. The men were hungry after a long day, and it was clear that there was nothing urgent to tell.

There was praise for Elizabeth's fish chowder, and such praise from the islanders was an accolade indeed. Elias Johnson smiled with pleasure and pride. It was his recipe, handed down to Elizabeth, but he wasn't about to take anything away from the satisfaction he saw on his granddaughter's face. She reddened most becomingly, he thought, when Peter Hubbard of Harvard requested a second helping. He watched approvingly as Elizabeth stirred the bottom of the pot to get a ladle full of "the good of it" for the man. His eyebrows lifted a little. They didn't make an unhandsome couple, at that, though he noticed that his granddaughter was obviously keeping a distance from the scientist. Well, they were all on edge, considering the hectic day.

Elias Johnson liked the feeling of family all around the big kitchen table. It wasn't only the common danger drawing them all together. Dr. Peter Hubbard fit right in. The Yarkie men liked the fact that he had no airs as might be expected of a Harvard professor in the midst of simple fishermen. On his part, Hubbard felt the offer of friendship from all of them, along with their confidence that his specialized knowledge would aid them. He could only hope they were right.

After supper, they moved from the kitchen into the large room taking shape as a laboratory. Craig had already set up several counterlike tables borrowed from the summer-closed school cafeteria.

Amos Tarbell brought out a small envelope. "We did spot some track," he told Hubbard, starting the session off. "There may have been a lot of it, but the leaves were so messed up that we couldn't tell." He tapped a small pellet onto the table. "Doesn't look like any rat dropping to me, though."

Hubbard said at once, firmly, "That's cockroach!"

"Cockroach?" The word went around the table with inflections of surprise.

Elias Johnson asked, "Isn't that pretty darn big for a *roach?*"

Hubbard replied, "Yes, if you're thinking of the usual house variety. These droppings are from what you call water bugs. And unusually large ones at that, I'd say."

Russell Homer contributed, "Lots of them crawl around the dump all the time!"

Hubbard asked, "How big, Mr. Homer?"

The man answered as if he were a Harvard student in class. The professor had called him *Mr.* Homer! "Some are about an inch and a half, but they run to two inches . . ."

"Normal," the scientist nodded. He nudged the dropping aside. "That's not your problem, gentlemen. Roaches can be a nuisance, but they don't fit what we've been hearing today."

Elias Johnson thought of his dog's ear, which Craig had given to the scientist earlier that afternoon. No roach could be big enough or strong enough to chew off Sharky's ear.

As if reading the man's mind, Hubbard reported, "I've been studying the dog's ear. I have to wait for the equipment Dr. Lindstrom will bring tomorrow morning, but I can tell you right off—rats do not bite the way the ear seems to have been torn off."

Bonnie felt the nausea again, though with less sense of personal guilt.

Hubbard was going on, "At least not any rats I've ever seen or heard of before."

Craig Soaras asked with surprise, "You mean our rats might be different?"

Hubbard replied, "It's possible. There may be some

50

kind of mutation out there. I seriously doubt it, but it's one of the things we need to consider." The scientist turned to Russell Homer. "You said before that there were dead rats all over the dump. Did you get any specimens?"

The man shook his head, miserable. "I tried, but it's the damndest thing, Doctor Hubbard! *There isn't a one of them to be seen now!*"

Elias Johnson supported the young man. "When Russ told me that, I went out to look for myself." He slapped the table. "Something or somebody has cleared off every damn rat these fellows saw before."

Craig Soaras confirmed it too. "I went back. I couldn't believe it."

Russell Homer added, "And not a one in my car, either! Craig saw them this morning, piled in there like it was a hearse!"

"What could go after dead rats that way?" Johnson asked the scientist with open anxiety.

In Peter Hubbard's scientifically moving mind, the Harvard man was scanning his memory for parallels in the realm of animal behavior. It was common knowledge that many vertebrate predators dragged prey back to hidden caves and burrows to feed themselves and their young. In the insect world there were also many examples. The classical case of the *Polyergus refusens* was one. This was the species of ants that enslaved other ants, specifically the *Formica*. The way they went about it made a fascinating pattern even to a scientist whose business was the amazing variations of natural conduct.

If a scout of a *Polyergus* colony came on a nest of the genus *Formica*, she would hurry back to her home nest. Along the trail the scout would deposit on the ground the specific odor that signaled the presence of the *Formica*. Promptly, a phalanx of *Polyergus* workers would go slave hunting. After they overcame the defenders, they would seize the *Formica* pupae in which young were developing, and bring them back to the *Polyergus* nest. There they would hatch into the slave workers.

Hubbard tapped his pipe on the table thoughtfully. There were hundreds of similar instances in biology. Few people other than trained biologists, he considered, had any real notion of the complicated adjustments Nature used to accomplish her purposes. Sometimes they seemed like exquisite clockwork parts all fitted together with fantastic precision.

The ability of insects to move objects many times their own weight was remarkable, to be sure, but it was a relatively undramatic example of Nature's inventiveness. Peter Hubbard reflected on what his students called *The Case of the Dichocheles*.

This insect was a mite that lived in the ears of moths. The trick was that one moth ear had to be left open, so that the infested insect could still have enough hearing to detect the sonar of the bats that came after moths for food.

If both of a moth's ears were infected, it would be deafened and soon fall prey to a bat—and the mite would perish along with its host.

The ingenious answer was the laying down of a chemical scent in the moth's second ear by the first mite intruder. This chemical successfully kept other mites out. In this way, the host moth could fly to live another day, and the mite could survive with it.

The relevance to Yarkie of the myriad examples like this in the natural realm was that a scientist found it hard to label a development "unnatural" or even "abnormal," except in the strictest statistical sense. Nature made its own rules. From one point of view, Peter Hubbard could argue, there was no such thing as a "freak," except by *man's* definitions; everything that happened had to be deemed natural just because it had simply happened.

It was only when man interfered that terms like "artificial" should properly be used, Hubbard observed to himself. One question confronting him on Yarkie was precisely this: whether what was happening was "natural" or induced. Upon the answer might depend his course of action.

Hubbard realized that his thoughts had preoccupied him while the people were impatient for him to continue.

He questioned the waiting group, "Do you have any special trouble with ants here?" It was a wild shot. No ants he had ever heard of could move a *dog*, even though some species had the capacity to transport many times their own weight.

The men looked at each other puzzled, and shook their heads. They could see that Peter Hubbard was as unsure as they were, and it increased their distress.

Amos Tarbell spoke his own concern to Hubbard, "You said before it wasn't roaches that got Sharky, and not rats that cut his ear off. If it isn't roaches and it isn't rats, what the hell *is* out there, and what the hell has cleaned off all the dead ones?"

Hubbard shook his head. "At this point, I don't know what we're dealing with any more than I know why all of you found everything so quiet in the woods and at the dump."

To the group, Elizabeth voiced her own new puzzlement. "First I was afraid you might be attacked, now I'm scared that you weren't. I mean, with nothing at all out there now, it's certainly mysterious, isn't it?"

"To put it mildly," Peter Hubbard said to her wryly.

Elias Johnson said, "Well, I'm grateful for small favors. Hildie Cannon has been wandering around looking for her daughters, and if those rats had been rampaging, she'd be a goner."

Bonnie asked with genuine concern, "Has she found the girls, Elias?"

The captain's head turned negatively. "I told her they likely sailed over to Chatham to visit their aunt. They do that sometimes. Must have left her a note she missed. Hildie was going to phone her sister as soon as she got back home."

"Which reminds me," Peter Hubbard interjected, "can we get a phone out here?"

Amos Tarbell told him there had once been a connection, and they could have it in service by the morning. The sheriff went on, after a deep breath, "And speaking of missing persons, we still haven't found the fellow with the beard or his friend. Even if the woods are quiet, I hope they're out of there." He couldn't restrain a little smile. "Though I hope they don't show up in Hildie's garden again! She's upset enough as it is."

What none of them knew was that a kind of nature's truce had occurred in the Yarkie forest. The cockroach attackers were sated after their gorging on fresh meat and hot blood. The rats, reprieved, were in their own nests. All was quiet on the forest front . . . for the night.

DREAD

ONE

Coming from Stephen Scott's party at about eleven-thirty that night, summer resident Harvey Tinton was driving alone on High Ridge Road. He had disregarded his wife's warning and taken the one drink too much that always pushed him past discretion; after that, he kept holding out his glass for refills. Hell, he told himself, a man needs to relax on vacation. All year he worked uptight as an investment analyst. Millions rode on his calculations and predictions. It was an onerous burden, because he had the responsibility for people who were seeing inflation burn up their hard-earned money.

His wife refused to understand him, Harvey Tinton fumed. She didn't realize how lucky they were to be renting on Yarkie. It was only because he handled Stephen Scott's account. No, Blanche kept complaining about how primitive it was. She hated what he loved—the steady putt-putt of the little generator that kept their house lit, and the vacation-camp look of the propane gas tank for their cooking fuel, and most of all the way the woods came right to their front door. In fact, you had to walk through an isle of beautiful birches to get to the house.

Aside from Blanche's bitching, he was relaxing better this summer than anytime he could remember. The people were friendlier than he had been led to believe, and the beaches even cleaner and more beautiful. The days were flowing as peacefully as the Garden of Eden—better, because there were no snakes on Yarkie. But Blanche was after him to leave before their month was up. Their quarrel that afternoon was another reason he had let himself go at the Scotts. Hell with Blanche.

Leave Blanche and move out here for good! Go in with Scott on the marina, and do some fishing. Harvey Tinton laughed aloud in the car, relishing again a fishing story told at the party, so typically Cape Cod. Seems a native was instructing a vacationer like himself. "You get some molasses and put it on your hook instead of bait, see? That will attract bees. The bees will stick in the molasses and go into the water when you cast. Now, bees don't like water, so they'll get sore, and soon as a fish comes near they'll sting it to death!"

Fishing and easy living, what could be sweeter! Come home at night to woods like these, the fresh air—in his drunken state he forgot the warning about a spraying—take a nice walk with a drink of rum in your hand before bed. That's how God meant a man to live, not crowded on sidewalks with muggers and graffiti and blaring radios!

As Harvey Tinton's car swerved on the winding road, he was glad he had got away from his wife. She'd get her own ride home okay. Let Blanche come after him in the woods. He smiled and wet his lips. Maybe they'd get to do it under the trees. He had fantasized that and it had been super. But fat chance to get Blanche to lift her skirts in a bed of leaves and pine needles. She, the silk-sheet cunt of all times!

It was the curving road that made the car scrape trees now, he told himself, not his lax driving. It was his clear eyes that were seeing the man in the middle of the road.

What the hell! Maybe he was drunker than he believed. Could that be a real person jumping up and down in the

56

headlights, a man balls naked with his prick flopping around like a misplaced white tail?

Harvey Tinton went for the brake automatically. If the guy was for real, he was in some kind of trouble. If he wasn't for real, Harvey *Tinton* was in trouble, and he'd better stop driving before he wracked up the car and himself.

As Tinton slowed down, the man charged the car, crying, "Take me to your sheriff!"

Tinton spied handcuffs. The man was a criminal. A crazy! Rapist! Sodomist!

Tinton's foot hit the accelerator. The man fell to his knees on the road. Tears were streaming into his black beard. "Please, please," Bo Leslie wailed miserably, "take me to your sheriff!"

By then the car was too far away for his words to be heard. The bearded man staggered to his feet. His chin went down to his hairy chest in his desolation. He headed back into the woods. He had to get some sleep. What a day this had been. What a predicament he was in! He had lost Tony. He was lost himself. He was scratched, bitten, bleeding, and exhausted. He staggered to a bed of leaves and let himself down thankfully. The sharp, dry edges stuck his skin but he was too weary to care. Clumsily without the use of his hands, he rolled over on his stomach and let his eyes close. He thought, that fucking driver could have helped me—and then laughed despite himself. He must have been one mean apparition in the night, enough to scare the shit out of anyone, much less a drunk like that jerk.

As Bo Leslie burrowed into the leaves for warmth, the prickliness began to soften under the weight of his body. The man pressed deeper down. It began to feel good, he'd be damned if his cock hadn't found itself a place like the old butter groove. Hey, this wasn't bad! he smiled, licking his lips. Funny habit, to lick his lips as soon as he felt an erection coming on, like the way he always spit into the toilet to help himself pee . . .

Hey, this wasn't pussy but not bad at all, man! He began to heave up and down. Pretty okay. Good. Okay. Okay, okay, okay good good good! Why not?

The moonshafts through the trees struck the man's faster-pumping buttocks.

TWO

Mrs. Hilda Cannon, driving High Ridge slowly because she was bone-tired, was worried sick. The girls were not at her sister's in Chatham. She couldn't find the sheriff. He wasn't in his office or at home, and by the time she finally learned he was at the old lighthouse—for some reason she couldn't fathom—there was no way to phone him. Well, she couldn't go chasing him all over Yarkie. He was probably in the woods looking for the drifters. She had no choice but to wait until morning.

If her girls weren't in Chatham, where, where, where in the name of Old Scratch could they be?

Her sputtering thoughts were snapped off by a movement in the trees that caught the corner of her eye. Might that white fluttering be Rebecca's dress? The girl had worn white today! She stopped the car, and sat for a moment considering. She never much liked going into the woods alone at night, and they said they sprayed today, though she'd smelled nothing. But there was something there, in the trees, ahead to the right, bobbing around. What would Rebecca and Ruth be doing there? Helping some animal out of a trap? Hunting was against the law, but some of the summer kids were tempted.

Hilda Cannon got out of her car purposefully. With her

eyes glued to the moving white object, she missed a hole and twisted her ankle a little. She sat on a rock at the edge of the woods to rub the pain out. In the quiet of the night, she thought she heard a rustling noise behind her. She got up with a start. It came to her that there was no sound of the crickets that usually made a commotion in the Yarkie air at this hour, no hoot of an owl. She listened harder. The rustling sound was distinct. She sat down again, relieved. It was mice, she nodded, or the muskrats she knew lived in this part of the forest. But then it was almost as if her ears rather than her nose picked up the faint, foreign odor. It wrinkled her nose with both its strangeness and its pungent unpleasantness.

She rose again, and followed her new curiosity toward the movement in the trees. She wondered whether the bitterish taint in the air might be the new poisons at the dump, or the stuff the town had sprayed on the trees. Strange they would do that on such short notice, but she was glad she remembered. It was another reason not to go too far into the woods. The heavy woman's mind kept circling as she walked on, sniffing. The foreign smell couldn't be from the dump because the wind was southwest, as usual, she knew that very well. It might be some dead animal rotting in the forest.

As Hilda Cannon neared the target of her inquisitiveness, she thought she heard a human sound ahead. As if someone couldn't catch his breath. She quickened her pace. It might be one of her girls, at that! Maybe a foot caught in a trap! She was running now.

There *was* a human body in those trees! It was covered with a blanket of leaves except for what appeared to be— oh, impossible!—appeared to be the back of a man. A man thrusting up and down as if in the act of—!

Mrs. Cannon's mind shut off. Branches hit at her face as she withdrew from the bushes she had parted. She didn't notice the little whips, or the small cuts they made on her cheek. That could not possibly be a human being! But the sounds now coming all too clearly from the forest mound were explicit.

The woman turned, but could not leave. The image was a magnet she could not resist. She scolded herself for a wanton, but her hands moved of their own accord to part the bushes again and let her look in with burning eyes. Quick glances at the road assured her she was alone. The man did not know she was watching. Oh, what an abysmal act! How outrageous for him to be doing this thing! In *her* woods! She wanted to scream at the pervert to stop, to get out, but her voice was imprisoned by her own undeniable if unbidden excitement. She wanted to run back to her car, but her feet were rooted by an inner wish she did not suspect she owned, beyond her conscious control.

Suddenly, as the man heaved up in his own excitement, moonlight gleamed on metal handcuffs. Now it was plain to her who the man was. A scream flared in her throat, but she stifled it. The last thing in the world was to let this beast know she had seen him in his obscene act. He would vent his lust and brutality on her.

Hilda Cannon fled to her car, while Bo Leslie, blissfully unaware that he had had a visitor, continued his unanticipated satyric tryst. He plunged harder and harder in his mounting lust. He did not know that the vibrations of his act were reaching nearby creatures. Their antennae were lifting, rising, dipping as his signals told them of his presence. This swarm of roaches had been pleasantly ensconced in an old snake burrow, had not been called back to the Central Nest. They had fulfilled their mission for this day, but if there was new food now—or possibly new danger, as from the dump rats that had suddenly become Enemy—then they were ready to move again, at once.

Restlessness passed from great roach to great roach

as the vibrations came over the forest floor stronger and heavier. As Peter Hubbard would explain in the Yarkie laboratory later, people didn't understand that when they saw household roaches scurrying for the kitchen cracks, it wasn't so much that the light had been turned on. True, roaches preferred the dark, but their first alarm system was their sensitivity to vibration. It was the approaching footsteps that sent them fleeing long before a light switch was ever touched.

Bo was approaching his orgasm. Without his hands to lift him, he reared back and thudded down, sending clearer and clearer tremors along the ground.

The aroused roaches formed into wide columns and platoons, and began to march hungrily. They were handsome, even elegant, in their way, a burnished mahogany color that blended into the leaves. Their segmented exoskeletons formed the flexible shields that, with their folded wings, gave a jewel-like appearance in the light, the iridescence that had attracted Reed Brockshaw's little girl.

These were not the common house cockroaches, which Peter Hubbard would describe as *Bratella germanica*. Nor were they what he would first suppose—the familiar "water bugs," called by scientists *Periplaneta americana*, well-named as "wanderers."

The Yarkie Island roaches bellying toward Bo Leslie through the leaves were three, four and five inches long, some almost an inch around. The size was unusual for the climate, though five-inch roaches—*Blabbearus*—are seen commonly in the tropics. Peter Hubbard and Wanda Lindstrom would wonder, later, at the mandibular development that had provided Yarkie roaches with mouths much wider than any normal species, together with jaw muscles so powerful and teeth so razored that nothing would be left of a skeleton. The two biologists ascertained that these unusual cockroaches on Yarkie could indeed attack as viciously on land as the legended piranha fish in water. Swarming by the thousands, as now at Bo Leslie, they could consume a prey with lightning speed.

The seeming delicacy of their legs belied the roaches' strength and speed, except for the bulge of extraordinary muscle where the limbs—hairy in this section—joined the body. Working as a colony, in the way of insects like termites and ants, these roaches managed amazing feats for their size. Their speed, too, was remarkable. Even the ordinary house roach could travel at a rate of three-four miles an hour. These were even faster—the equivalent speed for a man would be well over two hundred miles per hour.

It was such creatures, incited and electrified by the violence of Bo Leslie's thumping, that were coming at the man fast. He had tried to prolong his pleasure as long as possible, but now he was done. The roaches raced nearer, spreading into a crescent, to engulf the man before he had time to respond. In his shivering ecstasy, still gasping for breath, the man did not for a moment even feel the unexpected new caress—the feather-touch of thousands of soughing antennae exploring his hot body. He was hardly aware of the first needle-like bites that began to taste his skin. It was the searing fire in his eyes that was Bo Leslie's first consciousness that he was being attacked—assailed in some way he did not understand. But he knew at once, deeply, that he was a goner.

His thrashing about was in vain. His skin, his muscles, his organs, his brains, his limbs, were being carved. Beneath the pulsating streams of blood carrying his life out of him, the man felt as if metal saws were ripping across his body, not so much devouring him as a jungle animal might, but slicing him apart.

Dimly, Bo Leslie saw himself in a mad magician's crate, with sharpened swords slashing his viscera. Or, he was a side of beef on a butcher hook, and cleavers were hacking his carcass into small chunks. The man wanted to curse and howl, but there was no sound except hissing air because his throat was gone. It happened so quickly that the man's body was still shuddering with his orgasm when his final breath issued, a crimson foam out of his decapitated torso. There was one last glimmer inside the man's skull before his brainlight went out forever. It was a flashing black humor: This was like dying in the saddle —he had always joked that that was the only way to go.

The Yarkie cockroaches, in obedience to commands encoded in their preternatural genes, mounted the new food supply Nature had bounteously furnished again. After they satisfied their own hunger, much prey was left. Their reflex now was to apply their teeth and mandibles to splitting the carcass and its bones into pieces that could be handled by the worker roaches their scouts had already raced to the Nest to summon.

Pulling, pushing, tugging, rolling, the multitude of roaches carried away the remaining fragments of Bo Leslie's flesh—as they had carried away the dog Sharky and the day's bonanza of slaughtered rats—to the larder chambers that digger roaches had prepared surrounding their new Home Nest on Yarkie.

The only thing left of the man when the insects were done was the metal handcuffs. With an inner organic compulsion like that of magpies, some of the roaches pushed these, too, along with the food, although it was plain that this hard shining substance was not meat nor bone nor blood, was not edible like the rest.

Then, in a coda that Nature enforced upon them each time, squads of roaches remained behind the transport forces to push at the forest leaves with their bodies. Using their legs, wings, and mandibles much as dogs use their hind legs after defecating, the insects spread leaves and soil over the scene of their own saturnalia. In short order, the rustling and bustling movements ended, the last of the monstrous cockroaches vanished into the leaves, and no disarray was to be seen in that part of the forest.

Heavy with food and their burdens, this foraging cadre returned slowly to the Nest. Arriving, the individual roaches rested sluggishly while worker roaches took the new food supplies to the storage areas. A few strays crawled home late, but the Nest was for all purposes, quiet —including the mysterious, shadowy Dome that rose in the center of the cave.

Yet night was the normal time of activity for these roaches as for others, and there was an undercurrent of pulsing energy—as if it would take only a plugging into a socket to electrify the whole community into wild action.

THREE

About a mile distant in the woods surrounding the Tinton house that same night, another roach family was resting. When the vibrations of Harvey Tinton's car first reached them, a few antennae responded alertly. Others joined when the man slammed doors in the house, and still others when the man's uneven steps outside began to disturb the quiet in the trees.

Tinton decided to go for a walk. The path through the trees was familiar, but he kept stumbling in his intoxicated state. Each unsteady bump brought more cockroach antennae fluttering. The whole group of the insect troop bristled when the man fell to the ground heavily.

Harvey Tinton lay happily where he tripped. The pine cushions and the leaves made a comfortable mattress. Half-dozing, he heard a car driving up to the house. That would be somebody bringing Blanche home. He heard the car grind away. Good! Blanche wouldn't find him inside, would realize he had gone for a walk. She'd come after him. But wait a minute—she would remember the warning about spray. He'd forgotten, damn it. Hope nothing poisonous is getting in my lungs, he thought dimly. He tried to stand, but his legs buckled.

The man laughed to himself as he lay back in the leaf mattress again. He'd surprise her when she came out, ambush her! Ha, she'd think she was being raped by one of those punks they had seen in town that morning. She might enjoy that—what the hell, hadn't their sex therapist advised them to use fantasies?

Harvey Tinton fell into a drunken sleep.

The vibration stopped. Antennae lowered. The Nest signals they detected in the air were not for these roaches near the Tinton house. Other groups were active somewhere, these insects sensed, but they themselves were not being ordered to scout or forage or defend or return. So they waited, though uncertainly.

Unwittingly, Harvey Tinton aroused them to action again. The man heaved out of his sleep sick to his stomach. Cursing himself for having drunk too much, he coughed up the misery of his insides. The rum tasted bitter and foul now, coarse as sandpaper in his throat.

Spewed and spattered on the leaves, Tinton's sickness issued a caustic odor on the air like a signal—almost like the pheromonic chemical signals by which many species of insects are known to communicate.

When Tinton finally finished, feeling better but disgusted with himself, the roach column halted. When the man lay still on the ground, logy, so that no new vibrations reached them, the insects grew uncertain again. And waited. They had the patience of Nature itself—unless pressed by some need—to rest and conserve energy.

FOUR

It was midnight when the sheriff, with Reed Brockshaw, Ben Dorset and Russell Homer, left the lighthouse for their homes. They took Elias Johnson with them, to drop at his house. Craig Soaras stayed; he and Peter Hubbard would use cots next to the laboratory they had established.

The first floor of the lighthouse was of generous proportions and lent itself to the emergency. The building provided a pie shape of which the kitchen was one wedge. On one side, the big laboratory space waited for the apparatus that would accompany Dr. Lindstrom. On the other side of the kitchen, a rickety staircase spiraled to the unused second story. Beyond it, there was a good-sized chamber where Elizabeth and Bonnie would sleep on cots this night, with room for Wanda Lindstrom when she joined the team the next morning. The last portion, completing the circle, was a cubicle Hubbard and Johnson's mate were sharing. Beds for all would be brought out the next day to replace the temporary cots.

Only a dent had been made in the accumulated junk accreted in the old building over the years. Elias Johnson broached bringing some village women out to help, but Elizabeth reminded him they wanted as few people as possible to know anything at all about the laboratory. The old man was proud when she declared, simply, that she and Bonnie would get the job done.

Spirits were high with the thought that at least some preparations were under way to solve the Yarkie quandary.

The first assignment was Craig Soaras's. He was to sail to Chatham to bring Dr. Lindstrom across to Yarkie. Considering the number of crates ordered by Peter Hubbard, and the delicacy of some of the apparatus, all agreed that the work boat, the *Jessica*, was a more suitable craft than Stephen Scott's yacht, though it would be less comfortable for the woman scientist.

Elizabeth wondered whether the crossing might not be rough. She had noticed that gulls in the harbor had flown high that evening—a sure sign to islanders that a "no'theaster" was on the way.

Craig and Johnson had sniffed the air and glanced at the sky. The captain promised, "She'll be a big blast, but she won't start till afternoon anyway."

Craig said laconically, "We'll manage."

Elizabeth heard herself saying, without knowing exactly why, "I hope Wanda Lindstrom has a strong stomach."

When all the others left the lighthouse for the night, the "crew" of four adjourned to the kitchen for a beer. It was pleasant sitting around the table talking casually, but Hubbard pointed to the moonlight streaming through the cracked, dusty window. "How about a walk before we turn in?"

Outside, Elizabeth hesitated, but let him take her elbow and steer her away from Craig and Bonnie, who headed toward a bank of sand dunes fringed with salt spray, roses, and plume grass. Elizabeth noticed approvingly that Bonnie seemed to be enjoying Craig's company. And vice versa. A summer romance could be pleasant, she thought, recalling how Craig had been her vacation companion when she was just becoming aware of boys. Craig had grown into a fine, strong man, as she always knew he would. Maybe it was too bad that Bonnie Taylor was so clearly headed for a law career and not marriage to a Portuguese fisherman. It was hard to know where the best chances for happiness really existed these days.

Meanwhile, Peter Hubbard brought her back to her own interests. He was asking her about Yarkie, and that

67

was eminently safe for conversation. Just because the moonlight was invitingly romantic on the sand and the waves, Elizabeth was glad there was Yarkie to talk about. Hubbard was saying he needed to know details of the island's flora and fauna before he started his work.

She answered enthusiastically, starting with the formation of the Cape by glacial moraines. The glacier had left a fairly flat surface of meadows and green marshes into which fingers of ocean reached on the eastward side and fingers of blue water on the bay side. "On Yarkie," Elizabeth added, "we have a lot of what Cape Codders call 'kettle holes.' Some of them are shallow, but the glacier dug some very deep." She mentioned one near Woods Hole that dropped one hundred twenty feet.

Hubbard nodded. "I've heard of that one, but I didn't know that's what they called it." He repeated, "Kettle holes." He smiled. "People think we Californians have colorful language, but it's nowhere near yours in New England."

Without warning, he dropped to the sand and tugged Elizabeth down beside him. For a moment, she thought he was about to put his arm around her, and she was prepared to pull away, but the man was only reaching for his pipe. When he motioned to the moon and the sea it was to talk about the weather, not romance. "It's so calm and clear," Peter Hubbard said. "Is it really going to storm tomorrow?"

Elizabeth was relieved to talk weather. She pointed up to some very high clouds, just a few, but the harbingers. "That's the start, right there."

"Hard to believe." His eyes dropped from the starlit sky to her face. "Like the way you *have* changed, Elizabeth," he said as he had earlier that day.

Elizabeth got to her feet quickly. "I was telling you about Yarkie," she spoke in a guide's neutral voice. She pointed eastward toward Bonnie and Craig now sitting atop a distant dune, outlined against the light sky. "Past Bonnie and Craig there, about a mile due east along this north shore, we have a whopper of a kettle. It was covered over years ago, like the Yarkie pirate caves people talk about."

"Interesting," Hubbard allowed. There probably had been pirates on Yarkie, he considered. It was a swashbuckling thought for a Californian sitting on this New England shore with this lovely New England young woman so obviously avoiding anything personal between them. Her perfume mixed tantalizingly with the salty air of the sea. From this strand, Peter Hubbard thought, the Atlantic would be stretching north, past Newfoundland to the arctic, if he remembered his geography. To the east, the waves would be rolling in non-stop from Europe. It brought home again the vastness of the sea and land, and the inseparability of everything on the planet, inorganic and organic alike. As a biologist, this break in his university routine was doubly welcome, Peter Hubbard considered. It was good to get out of the classrooms and museums and into the air—this air, this moonlight, with this beautiful woman. But he had better not think of that. He was on Yarkie Island for other reasons.

To turn his mind, he asked, "What's a lighthouse doing so far back from the water?" The sand spit before them did indeed run a good quarter of a mile out into the sea.

Elizabeth answered with the assurance of a local. "Everything keeps shifting all over the Cape shores. You can have a beach one year, and nothing the next. Over at Nauset, they had to build four lighthouses to keep ahead of the ocean."

"So this light was once at the edge of the island?"

"It was once hundreds of feet out there on rocks you can't see anymore."

The man turned to look back at the building. It seemed

69

haloed in the moon, tapering gracefully upward to the walkway with its spidery platform circling the old glass.

"It's so beautiful, isn't it?" Elizabeth said. "When I'm on Yarkie, I sometimes think I never want to go back to Cambridge . . ."

He nodded. "I can understand the peace and quiet." Then he asked, "But isn't it fierce in the winter?"

She shook her head. "The Gulf Stream runs along here not far off the east shore. It keeps the weather quite moderate. We hardly ever get much snow."

The man noticed her identification with the "we" of the Yarkie residents. "I suppose that's why your trees and vegetation are so thick."

Elizabeth chuckled. A typical Cape Cod tale had come to her mind. "I don't mean it can't get bad. You'll probably see a tree twister tomorrow. There's a weather story my grandfather once showed me in an old New Bedford paper. It seems a man named Al Higgins was being interviewed about an unusual storm. Higgins told it this way: He had no sooner got to his hen house when the wind blew the door open and his best rooster hopped out. Next came a gust so fierce it whipped off all the bird's feathers and bounced the rooster up against the chopping block—which the bird hit so hard that the axe dropped down and cut off its head. So there the rooster was—killed, picked, and ready to clean for eating. And Mr. Higgins wound up saying, 'I don't believe there ever was such a gale before!' "

Elizabeth enjoyed Peter Hubbard's explosion of hearty young laughter. "Great characters, your Cape Cod people!" he said.

"They must be doing something right. Did you know that more people live to eighty or ninety in these parts than anywhere? Stephen Scott wants to can Yarkie air so people can take it home. They do that on Nantucket and Martha's Vineyard, you know."

"It's sort of fun, I suppose." Hubbard had been trying to light his pipe, but the breeze was too much for his matches, and he gave up.

"We can go back in if you like," Elizabeth said.

He shook his head. "Much too nice out here, Liz."

Her heart bumped despite herself. It was the first time Peter Hubbard had ever called her "Liz." She wasn't at all sure she wanted him to, especially with Wanda Lindstrom soon to appear. She said, "It's late, Dr. Hubbard," and started back to the lighthouse.

Hubbard stopped her before she reached the door. "I don't really have a clear picture of how Yarkie lies. Please fill me in."

With some stiffness, Elizabeth halted and acquiesced. "Well, to orient you, we're standing on the northwest corner. Think of the island as sort of a rectangle. If we go straight east along this north shore, in about two miles we come to the northeast corner. There's a point of land there that runs out a way into the ocean. It's where Yarkie has the garbage dump we've been talking about all day."

Hubbard nodded grimly. "I see."

Elizabeth went on. "Turning south from that corner, we run along the eastern shore. That's a mixed bag. It's mostly woods and cliffs until you get down to the southern part—where the best beaches are.

"Moving around the south end in a westward direction, you start picking up a lot of the Yarkie houses. The houses get pretty thick as you come up the west side of the rectangle, because the big harbor and the village are on this side, just about in the middle between the south end and where we are at the north end."

"Got it, and thanks." The scientist's voice asked, "You say the forest is heaviest around the northeast section?"

"Yes, and then up across the center of the island. That's the 'bowler hat,' the section called 'High Ridge.' "

71

"So the houses along High Ridge are close to the forest?"

"Mostly they're in cleared land, but the trees do edge in very close on some, yes."

"And where does the forest begin in relation to the dump?"

"The trees come right down to the place."

"So if rats are coming out of the dump, they could pass right into the woods?"

"Yes. But as you know, the sheriff has men out there tonight with flares and guns." Being with Peter Hubbard on the beach, Elizabeth had almost forgotten the sick feeling the talk of the rats now evoked with fresh impact.

He was going on. "What about the island roads?"

"There aren't many. Most houses are just off sort of dead ends. The main driving is Harbor Road. That runs the western length of the island, north-south. It goes from this lighthouse down through the village and the south end where it turns eastward and loops to join High Ridge Road. That runs along the top of the bowler, with the woods to the east. To the west; of the road, the island slopes down toward the village."

"Got the picture."

"At the north end of High Ridge Road, there's just a dirt track." Elizabeth pointed beyond the lighthouse. "It picks up right here, as you see, and runs along the north shore. It's the access to the dump, the way Russell Homer gets over there."

"I see."

"That's it," Elizabeth said. "No mighty road map needed."

"I'll try to drive around tomorrow."

Elizabeth's hand went halfway to her cheek. "Oh, I forgot. It'll be terribly messy. They just freshly tarred High Ridge the other day, and the sun still keeps melting it. There have been a lot of complaints. Some summer people by the name of Tinton, especially."

Peter Hubbard shrugged. "It'll keep. I'll be busy with Wanda tomorrow anyway . . ."

Elizabeth turned from him quickly and hurried inside. He took a step after her, then thought better of it. He was on Yarkie Island for one thing only—a mission that could mean life or death for these people, for the entire future of the community. It might turn out not that serious, but if there was any possibility of such a danger, he needed to keep all his concentration and attention on the job. Whatever he was finding he felt about Elizabeth Carr in this rediscovery of the girl—the woman, he corrected himself—would and should wait.

Peter Hubbard knocked his pipe out, being careful that the wind blew no sparks toward the lighthouse. Walking along the beach in the moonlight alone, he told himself there was time to know what, if anything, he wanted to do about Elizabeth Carr.

FIVE

Harvey Tinton's ears felt plugged with the same cotton that was filling his mouth, but he thought he heard a voice calling his name. Blanche? He jerked to a sitting position, expecting his head to protest with hangover pain, but the ardor of his returning fantasy swept everything else away. Hearing his wife's footsteps almost upon him, he swallowed with sexual agitation. Oh, she was going to get a screw to remember!

He chortled to himself. He realized he was still drunk, but the stiffness between his legs said the alcohol wasn't cheating him this time and he had a full-blown erection when his wife halted a step away. "Harvey? You shouldn't

73

be out here! You heard they've sprayed the forest!" He heard more concern than anger in her voice. Ah, at heart she was a dear woman. He did love her always. He wanted her more than he had ever wanted anything in life.

But he held himself quiet. It was a luscious game! In the silence of the forest he heard only a hazy sound, leaves rustling a little. Breeze in the leaves, yes. Pleasant. Romantic. Suitable background for a rendezvous with his love . . .

Harvey Tinton reached out from the shadows and grabbed his wife's leg.

The woman screamed in terror and tumbled to the ground, shaking pine needles and leaves all about.

It was just as the man fantasized, except that his wife recovered herself at once and slapped his groping hands away. Understanding his intent, she scolded, "Not here! Come in the house, Harvey!"

But he was not about to be circumvented or deprived of his dream sex. He pulled her down again roughly, shaking the ground.

"Oh, Harvey!" But her protest held half a submissive laugh. What the devil, the woman thought, it might be fun at that. It hadn't been fun for so long! She'd be darned if her husband's hot fingers spreading her thighs weren't turning her on. She could feel the unfamiliar wetness, and it made her squirm in anticipation. He was panting with whiskey and lust. She began to moan with her own images of pleasure. Let him. Let him, let him, let him do it!

But in their mutual heat, neither of the Tintons heard the rustling and hissing coming rapidly closer. Under the magnificent juniper red cedar where Harvey Tinton had hid, husband and wife grasped each other in the starry night in the pine-scented island paradise, moaning with their play and pleasure, until Blanche Tinton commanded sharply, "Harvey, stop doing that!"

Her husband's voice was innocent, totally without guile. "Doing what?"

"You know I don't like you touching me there!"

His voice, bewildered: "Touching you where?"

Hers, reprimanding: "That place!"

"I don't know what you're talking about!"

"You stop it this instant!"

"But I'm not doing anything!"

"Harvey Tinton, you take your finger away from there right now!"

The man sat up, grievously wounded. Drunkenly he lifted both hands in the air and waved his fingers before his wife's eyes.

Blanche Tinton shrieked in horror. "My God, what is it then?"

The man scrambled to his feet, pants open, his sex shrinking, furious at the interruption that was stealing his pleasure. "What the holy hell is with you? Are *you* drunk?"

The woman began to roll on the earth, scissoring her thighs. She seemed to be in the throes of sexual climaxing, but her screams were of shock and anguish. "Ouch! Harvey, what's *at* me?"

The man peered at his wife's tortured face doubtfully, not comprehending. For a moment he thought it was her game, her way of punishing him for drinking too much this night. But a moment later his eyes were blinking at the impossible sight of a million huge cockroaches spreading over her body. Up from between her now bleeding thighs, roaches were blanketing her entire undressed flesh. They made a cloak of crawling death, a cloak sequined loathsomely with their roach carapaces and folded wings that glinted evilly in the shafts of moonlight on the struggling, bleeding woman.

The man reeled on his feet. He smiled at what he was seeing, knowing at once the incontrovertible truth: He was still drunk as a pig, and imagining it all! He'd had his share of worse nightmares. What about the time he had fallen out of the airplane and kept tumbling head over heels over head over heels in time with the screams of Blanche looking out of the plane at him tumbling to hell, as she was screaming at him now in this tumbled air that was thick with a rotten smell of something acid? His own bile coming up. Good, if he vomited his head would clear, Blanche would stop screaming, and his feet wouldn't be sliding out from under him on the slippery pools of blood trickling from the jerking body beside which he thumped, losing his balance. Without her eyes, Blanche Tinton could not see the quick ravaging of her husband's face, his own blinding, and the quick, precise stripping of his flesh. She was screaming so loud in her own agony that she could not hear, even without the roaches eating through her ears to her tender brain, the cries of the sobered man realizing his incomprehensible doom and hers.

The distant screams of Blanche and Harvey Tinton reached Hilda Cannon only faintly. She was nearly asleep at the wheel. She needed to get some sleep, badly. The foul episode from which she had finally run was the last straw. She had been prancing around the island like a harpooned whale all day and night. She had to guess the girls had simply taken one of the Cannon boats and gone fishing, deciding to spend the night on the water. Meantime not to worry. The girls knew the sea and handling boats. The weather would hold until late afternoon. As for the beast in the woods, she could set Amos Tarbell after him first thing in the morning.

Mrs. Cannon was glad she could now see the start of her own new white picket fence. It was spanking fresh, had cost a bundle, like everything else these inflation days, but the old one hadn't been mended for fifty years, and had been broken down all around the Cannon family graves.

Beyond the plot, the woman could make out the high chicken wire that protected her precious herb garden. She particularly liked the Cape Cod custom of dropping herbs on the kitchen floor for people to walk on. It sent a fresh sachet fragrance through the whole house. This year she had santolina and dill, lavender and fennel, basil and sage, savory and thyme. Next season she planned tarragon and bee balm, with more varieties of thyme for the prettiness of the border they made.

For now she wanted not herbs or herb tea, but a solid drink of rum—the black rum tonight, to settle her stomach and unaddle her brain after all the strange happenings. There was nothing more she could do, she said silently again just before the shouting penetrated her consciousness.

Hilda Cannon's car jerked to a screeching stop even before she realized she had slammed her foot on the brake.

She backed up slowly, wide awake. What in the devil *was* Yarkie coming to!

Yes! Some kind of groaning, a strangling kind of sound, was issuing from the woods beside the Tinton house.

That man she had seen awhile ago!

That miserable no-good had come out of the woods after his abominable act, and he had got at Blanche Tinton!

Grimly, Hilda Cannon snapped open her glove compartment and grabbed her gun. She was licensed after her constant complaints to the sheriff and selectmen about the rabbits and other nuisances in her gardens. She shot only occasionally, and then less to kill than to scare away with the noise, but now she was glad that the pistol was fully loaded. She would teach that despicable character to assault decent folks!

The woman hopped out of her car and moved cautiously into the shadows of the trees, gun extended. She half hoped the degenerate would come at her. She wouldn't shoot to kill, no, she'd aim for his family jewels and hope he'd live a long life without them! Castration was the fate all rapists deserved!

She halted to listen for sounds of struggling. There was total quiet in the trees, except for a kind of sighing sound she couldn't identify. To her ears, it was more a strange puffing noise than a hissing, and then it was what she could only think of as a sibilance. It was like the sound she had heard earlier, but no animal she ever knew made such a disturbance. The woman hid behind a great bay-leaved willow her ancestors had planted. She could see that the Tintons had their house lights on, but there was no movement through any of the windows. If she knew Harvey Tinton, the man was sprawled drunk asleep upstairs after Stephen's party. She had been invited, of course, but was too upset about her girls to go. But the scream had been a woman's, and where was Blanche?

The disturbing noise became clearer, combined with a raking of leaves. It was exactly like a rake, she thought with amazement. Who would be in the woods cleaning at this hour? She moved forward stealthily, her jowls quivering over her gun.

Hilda Cannon's eyes fell upon what they could not deal with, could not accept for translation to her brain.

In the paralysis of her shock and revulsion, the gun dropped unnoticed from her hand. The scene before her, too plain in the flickering moonlight, was beyond the worst imaginings of even an Hieronymus Bosch, fouler than the most infernal depths of satanic demons.

On the forest path just yards away she saw a floor of seething malignancy. Roaches enormous beyond all experience were a livid carpet of putrefaction, exuding a sharp stink that curdled the air. The insects seemed not individual creatures but connected organs of a huge, reaching, blotchy beast. They flowed over the torn bodies of Blanche and Harvey Tinton like a living lava. A lava of clicking teeth and mandibles and grasping legs. A lava erupting from some maggoty, satanic pit.

But the unbelievable was real. The spiky-legged roaches were devouring everything, everything. Incredibly, the woman saw that they were gobbling not just the flesh and bone and blood but the very clothes of the ravished couple. Hilda Cannon saw giant insects ripping at the man's rubber sneakers, eating at his leather belt, the woman's sandals.

The bodies themselves, soaked in their own blood, were maimed and mangled almost beyond recognition by now. The putrid horde of insects was slashing and cutting the flesh into pieces that a squad of even larger roaches was carrying away. Hilda Cannon tasted bile. *Pieces of the Tinton bodies were being carted off*, there was no other phrase for it. More unbelievably, hundreds of the larger roaches had somehow bound themselves together, as if by some gluey secretion, to form a kind of platform, sordidly like the bed of a truck. Gruesomely, pieces of flesh were being loaded onto it! Fingers were recognizable, toes, ears, small bones and larger, splintered ones. In obscene sumps of darkening blood all around lay flesh and whitish bone and soaked pink gristle and recognizable organs—mangled liver, torn heart. A whole ankle was being dismembered from one leg by a cluster of great roaches gnawing away at the bone with loud clicking noises that sounded to Hilda Cannon like fiendish knitting needles.

In a climax of the staggering, repellent horror, Hilda Cannon made out one band of insects picking clean a skull that had been severed from the neck. She couldn't tell whether it was Harvey or Blanche. The head was a stark bloodstained bowl of death lying accusingly on blood-red leaves. It was the ghastly centerpiece of the unholy feast. As more roaches climbed over the skull and ate away the last of the face muscles and tissue, the jaw fell open. The gaping skull seemed to be beseeching heaven for help, for justice, for reprieve from this vandalization of everything human.

Then an even more sickening image wracked Hilda Cannon's heart. What appeared to be another type of creeping animal was moving among the roaches, inching slowly up the path away from the massacre. It seemed at first to be an unusually bloated centipede, a bizarre remnant of the dinosaur past. It was a yard long, with thousands of legs on each side of its disgusting body—legs scurrying like frantic cilia beneath the pallid, slimy thing.

It took a minute before Hilda Cannon realized she was watching a gang of cockroaches moving off a dismembered section of the intestine of one of the Tintons.

She wanted to faint, but instinctively knew that would be stupid as well as cowardly. It would allow the cockroach demons to turn on her. She had to remain silent, steady, and try to see the end of this living malediction on her island.

Despite her resolution, the scene of the hideous butchery was too much for her. Vomit rushed up her throat and exploded from her mouth, and she saw in an instant that she had drawn the vermin. A band of the giants was already racing to her hot stinking mess. Their relish at the new feast kept them momentarily from her, and she turned to plow through the trees toward her auto. Now it was doubly imperative that she find Amos Tarbell! Never mind her own nausea, the smell of vomit on her clothes, her disgust and abhorrence. There was an unspeakable terror loose on Yarkie that no one suspected! In her sickened heart, Hilda Cannon was miserably sure now that her own daughters had somehow been caught in the woods and destroyed by the unbelievable monster roaches. No one knew how many others had already been killed, but it had to be stopped. She would waken Tarbell and Johnson and Scott and—

The woman stumbled, grabbed for a tree to steady herself, and felt her skin scrape. Her hand was quickly wet with blood. And just as quickly she felt a sting and a needle-like bite on her palm. She went faster. In the dim light she made out a roach biting the back of her hand. She swung her fist against a tree, not caring how much it hurt her, wanting only to mash the insect. The mess dripped from her skin, and she impatiently brushed the blood off on her dress as she ran. She kept praying that the great body of roaches in the woods were still too busy with the Tintons—long beyond hope or help—to come after her. She had no idea how fast they might be though she had once heard that some roaches could fly. Those might reach her . . .

The stout woman fled with a speed she did not know she possessed, driven by more than fear. A sigh of relief burst from her lips as she saw her car just ahead. But the few paces to the open road and safety seemed like miles. Her lungs burned with each gasping breath; her throat was on fire; her lips were bleeding from where her own teeth had bitten through. But she would make it now!

Just steps from the road, Hilda Cannon felt a fluttering around her head. Instinctively, she threw her hands up, circling them wildly. If these were bats, she didn't want them in her hair. She knew bats didn't really do that, but she was hysterical with fright. And the more so with the realization that the fluttering wings were not of bats but belonged to flying roaches seeking her blood.

Forms of giant cockroaches were sweeping the air all around her now. It flashed in her head that they resembled the plagues of locusts she had seen in movies so thick they darkened the sky.

In the same way that Tony Carlucci had known his

doom, and Bo Leslie too, Hilda Cannon understood she would never take the last few steps to the road and the waiting car.

She went down helplessly under the terrible assault, blinded immediately by the avidly seeking mandibles. Even as she fell, two small rivers of blood came from the emptying eye sockets, tears of defeat, loss, disaster, death rolling down what was left of her cheeks.

The nerves behind the woman's eyes and ears exploded with internal fireworks, and as had happened with the others, an aurora borealis flared within. Her hands moved spastically over the ground seeking some weapon, out of an indomitable spirit that refused to concede. As with sailor kin of old, stubbornly holding breath in their lungs while drowning until the overpowering sea claimed what they could no longer withhold, Hilda Cannon had no weapon, no hope. The waves of roaches were the lashing seas of wild storm, the boat breached, the winds ripping the hair out of one's head, forcing open the clenched mouth and funneling the water of death into the unwilling chest. Except that Hilda Cannon was drowning not in salt water of the ocean but in the froth of her own sluicing blood.

Blind and deaf, she still struggled, with a thrust for life that came from the deepest spirit. She felt the thousands of knife-teeth having their way at her face, her neck, her breasts. She felt the thousands of mandibles tugging and clinging, ripping her living skin from her sinking, sweating body. She knew horribly the sensation of the cockroaches crawling into every orifice, her nostrils, and unthinkably, her privates, front and rear.

Hilda Cannon's prayer for a quick death, her giving up at last, was granted by the organized fierceness of her assailants.

Even before she had perished, swift scout roaches were

off to the Great Nest to signal another capture of the new prey the Colony now voraciously sought. Having partaken of human meat and drunk human blood, the new cockroach breed was ravenous for more. No longer would they eat of the dump's garbage or of Yarkie rat carcasses, or the vegetation, or other Yarkie animals. They could not get enough of the human taste and would seek it endlessly, implacably, and with many more victories.

Meantime, there was peace and contentment all around the Dome. Only the Warrior Guard roaches surrounding the center were in motion, and even they moved listlessly. All were well-fed, and there were no alarm signals of any kind coming into the Nest.

A few of the drab females were laying their egg sacs. This could be a time of delicate balance. When eggs were deposited in a disturbance, the mothers would almost certainly eat them. But in the quietude reigning now there was no cannibalism. The paludal, marsh-like odor made a kind of comforting atmospheric blanket for all, young roach and old.

"Cozy" was the anthropomorphic word humans would use to describe the insect home. The mood extended even to the many bands of roaches still out in pockets through the Yarkie forest—roaches not summoned back. These had made comfortable waiting places in their own camps, from which they could respond at a moment's signal— chemical or physical—in rampaging hordes.

SIX

Stephen Scott couldn't help laughing aloud as he drove home after dropping Tom and Deirdre Laidlaw at the house they rented on High Ridge a mile before the Tintons. It was a sign of his party's success, he supposed, that they were playing this game of automobile chairs. First, Harvey had left half-smashed, taking the Tinton car. Then his wife, Blanche, borrowed the Laidlaw jeep to drive home and check on Harvey. She wasn't back when the party broke up, so it fell to Scott to drive the Laidlaws in his Cadillac. They'd get their jeep from the Tintons the next day.

Scott was humming in a satisfied way. Both Tinton and Tom Laidlaw had shaken hands with him on a new deal he planned near Chatham. Yarkie's possibilities had been just about exhausted, he figured. The way to stay young was to plan ahead. Meantime, the marina here had better pay off or he'd be the laughing stock from Buzzard's Bay to Provincetown.

Everything would turn out all right, Scott assured himself, including this creepy business out at the dump. They should have stayed with the old poisons, but Big Brother had to keep meddling. Damn Boston, damn Washington! Yarkie could manage its own affairs without those knuckleheads, batterbrains, and blowhards.

He was taking the long way home, enjoyed driving the island by himself at night. In the bright moon, the High Ridge woodland was as beautiful now as he remembered from boyhood. He could recall the very trees where he and his friends had played. Approaching the Tinton house, he admired again the juniper red cedars planted by old Cannons in generations past. The trees in their height, girth, and dark foliage always seemed formal to him—trees wearing black tie and tuxedo. He wondered at the same time why the lights were still on at the Tintons. He'd have thought both Blanche and Harvey were fast asleep by now.

Scott drove with a proprietary sense along the stands of pitch pine and pin oak, the clumps of birches, and the elms like sentries guarding a king's preserve. He went slowly, aware of the gravel pelting up on the bottom of the car. He shouldn't have taken the big car, he thought, but he had forgotten about the tarring of the road up here. Had a couple of drinks too many himself, he chuckled.

Sometimes, like tonight, he felt as if he owned all of what he saw. In a way he did, because he loved it all and he could enjoy it all. And the Harvard fellow would help them get rid of the Yarkie contamination that had sprung up out of nowhere.

Scott turned his attention to the wide bay-leaved willow tree he was driving by. Its trunk was as weather-beaten as the Yarkie houses, and the broad circle of its branches made a crown of delicate leaves that hung in the night like the golden hair of the princesses he had loved in his childhood fairy tales—books he had hidden in these very woods to devour.

But when the man stopped his car with a grunt of surprise, it wasn't to admire the willow tree or any other. It was because he was flabbergasted to see Hilda Cannon's station wagon sitting in the Tinton driveway.

Damned funny! Hildie hadn't come to his party because she was so worried about her girls. His mind flashed: Had she found them at the Tintons? What would they be doing there?

Stephen Scott pulled his car up behind the station wagon and heaved his weight from behind the wheel. Riffraff were coming over to Yarkie, like those three bums yesterday. Couldn't tell what they might be up to.

The situation required caution, clearly.

Scott tiptoed distrustfully to the house. The door opened to his hand. No disorder, good. But also no people, downstairs or, puffingly he found, upstairs. If Hildie was visiting Harvey and Blanche, where the hell were they? Taking a walk in the woods? They didn't know the warning to stay out was phony. Maybe Hildie was helping

Blanche help Harvey walk off the rum he had guzzled.

Scott waddled to his car for a flashlight and moved with it into the trees. He beamed the light ahead, right and left. No Tintons. No Hildie. No nothing except his familiar woods.

The leaves along the path did look as if a wind had disturbed them, but that wasn't untypical up here, especially when the weather was near a big change. Gusts could blow up suddenly and puff themselves out. The only thing unusual was a bitter-sharp odor he detected. A fire somewhere? No. It was more fetid, piercing. Scott sniffed, grimacing with distaste. A decaying mouse under the leaves? The man bent over heavily, taking short breaths and frowning deeply with the sharp unpleasantness. He tilted his large head. Had he heard something in the leaves? Strange, unfamiliar? A whirring sound? A rustling? Like *hissing*? What *the hell* could that be? It was up the path ahead of him. Hadn't that black girl said something about a hissing noise? Scott switched his light out and listened sharply. Nothing. His ears must be ringing, he thought. He was panting from just his short walk. His fat body was sweating.

Switching the flashlight on again, Stephen Scott stepped forward into the leaves. He had an itchy feeling that something ahead was watching him come, waiting for him. He wiped perspiration from his cheeks. He could almost imagine beady eyes glinting at him from a copse in front. *The rats?* Scott's skin goose-pimpled. He had an animal sense that an animal was hunting him, not the other way around at all. Treacherous! He could almost see a lifted rat head sniffing with its thin snout to catch his scent. The rustling noise came again, suddenly from many directions! There was more than one rat! How could he have forgotten they roamed in packs? The man's spine went icy. He felt under water, with sharks circling silently in tighter and tighter moves, smelling blood, coming inexorably closer, maws open, jaws ready to slash . . .

Stephen Scott turned in the leaves as quietly as his bulk permitted, and started to tiptoe away. Then he stopped, his lips working. He was no coward. If there were rats out here, the Tintons and Hildie might have been attacked. He ought to check it out, unlikely though it was. He chided himself. It was the damned foreign smell that was making him as nervous as a horse with a burr under the saddle. He quieted himself. It occurred to him that he ought to take a sample of the leaves to the Harvard man. The odor might be a clue for the biologist. Now he was thinking sensibly!

Scott bent over to pick up a handful of leaves. He flinched. Something hard and cold was under his fingers. He withdrew his hand and straightened up, kicking the leaves apart to see what they were hiding. He was astonished. At the tip of his open-toed sandal there was the last thing he might have expected—a pistol.

The man bent down again to lift the gun, taking care not to mark it with too many of his own fingerprints. It seemed that something very much out of the ordinary was happening in these woods this night. He recognized the gun at once. All of Hildie Cannon's friends knew she owned it, and her initials were plain on the handle. As a selectman, he himself had been one of those approving her permit. No question, no question at all.

But what the tarnation hell was Hildie's gun doing here?

The disturbed man stood in the deep leaves staring at the weapon. His attention did not take in the hissing that was suddenly louder behind him. He was unaware that the "sharks" of his imagination were deadly real and close to his bare ankles, though in a form he could never conceive.

From the house, the Tinton phone jangled in the night. Scott was galvanized at the sharp, demanding ringing. He hurried to the summons without thought, and did not hear the hissing that rose in the trees like a cry of frustration. An especially inviting feast had gotten away.

The phone call was from the Laidlaws, wanting to arrange with the Tintons about picking up their jeep. Scott put them off, saying Blanche had gone to bed and Harvey was fixing a nightcap. He would deliver their message.

Going thoughtfully back to his car, Scott knew his decision. It was right not to start a gossip prairie fire by telling the Laidlaws that the Tintons and Hildie Cannon seemed to be missing. And if that was right, so was his conclusion not to call in Amos Tarbell until later. Everything might be completely innocent and harmless. The gun in his pocket was a disturbing element, but that might have a simple explanation, too.

Getting behind the wheel, Scott felt the leaves in his pocket. He tossed them out the car window with distaste. They were stinking up his clothes.

He started his engine, only to shut it again. He stared dubiously at the Tinton house and at the Cannon wagon. Anyone driving by now would wonder about it, as he had wondered. No sense having people snooping about, tongues wagging. The man eased himself out of his car again, went into the house to shut the lights, and decided he would drive the Cannon station wagon to the Cannon house where it belonged. If Hildie was out somewhere with the Tintons—he laughed silently at the thought that the three might have gone skinny-dipping—Blanche Tinton could drive her home.

After parking the station wagon in the Cannon garage, Scott walked back to his own car at the Tinton's. It was really musical chairs—and a good half-mile now, but he enjoyed it and the hiking was good for him. He resolved to do more walking and to start a diet. His breath was too short. His own huffing was like the sounds coming from

88

the woods. He stopped. It was that curious, alien mixture of rustling and hissing that had upset him in the Tinton trees. It was almost like a call, somehow inviting, yet repelling and, yes, frightening, at the same time.

Did rats hiss? Cats hissed. Raccoons hissed. What else hissed and would be scuffling through the leaves at night? Should he try again to enter the forest and see? He didn't have the flashlight now, and clouds were beginning to cover the moon. Still, he knew his way over every inch. The hissing was louder, pricking his curiosity more and more. He faced the trees and stepped off the road. The hissing increased, and a wave of pure fear swept over the man. He felt cold, bone cold, the way chill got into the marrow some winter days when the wind cut one's lungs. The hell with it! It was way past time to be home and in bed. The man slapped his palms resoundingly against his flabby thighs and turned from the trees.

Some sections of the road were sticky to walk on, though the cool evening air had largely hardened the tar. When he got to his car, Scott noticed that some large bug had got on the steering wheel through the open window. He could not see it clearly and didn't want to. It seemed torpid, a kind of beetle. He grimaced picking it up. Always hated things that crawled. He flipped the bug out. His finger felt sticky. Had the damn thing bitten him? He hadn't felt any sting. He looked at his hand, half-expecting to find blood. But what he saw was only a small black smear. He wiped at it with a tissue. Tar. He smiled with a new thought. For rats, the whole damn road along the forest would be like a giant flypaper, wouldn't it? Especially during the day in the hot sun. Good!

Stephen Scott started the car and drove safely home, never aware of the fate he had unwittingly thwarted.

WITNESS

ONE

The sea was running higher the next morning, but not yet threatening. Down at the harbor, Craig Soaras started the powerful engines of Elias Johnson's workhorse boat—husky twins of 250 horsepower each. The *Jessica* could take any weather that might blow up sooner than expected.

Craig had asked Bonnie Taylor—and hastily included Elizabeth Carr in his invitation—to sail to Chatham with him, but both women said there was still too much mess to clean up at the lighthouse. Elizabeth, particularly, wanted to have the building spic and span before Wanda Lindstrom arrived.

Craig had no difficulty recognizing Dr. Lindstrom on the Chatham dock. Other women were in shorts and halters, tanned and informal. She was pale, and wearing an elegant tan linen dress, with her hair combed severely back over a sculptured face. She needed no rimmed glasses to appear the academic she was. Her no-nonsense, brisk air projected her total self-assurance.

After an impersonal greeting and some confusion with loading the laboratory crates, Craig headed the *Jessica* back to Yarkie Island. His own innate shyness matched the woman's formal reserve. From the wheel, he watched the ramrod stiffness with which she stood holding the rail. He took her manner to discourage conversation. He felt like a schoolboy with a teacher; you didn't speak until spoken to.

Dr. Wanda Lindstrom was a good sailor, though, he had to give her that. The boat was heading into the wind, and landlubbers could be forgiven if the spanking motion made their stomachs "bilgey," as Cape Cod sailors put it.

Craig regarded the straight back with an open curiosity on his weather-creased face. The wind was draping the woman's dress closely around her body. She really was a looker, like the slim models in the magazines. Observing the biologist's femininity, Craig realized he had been expecting someone like his old teachers on Yarkie, plain as grocery bags. There was a spice in this woman's combination of academic frostiness and the looks of a movie star. He couldn't put his finger on which actress she reminded him of—it was the one with the high cheekbones, straightforward eyes, and wide mouth that could show a charming smile as well as the slight frown with which Wanda Lindstrom was turning to him now.

The man could not know it, but he was accurately sensing the two aspects of the woman's personality. She was of Polish descent on her mother's side, which accounted for her given name and the intriguing modeling of her face. It also gave her a passionate nature hidden beneath the stern exterior, but quick to flare into either anger or love. She kept the latter well hidden under the constraints of her father's blood. He was Swedish of the old school, class-conscious and stiff-upper-lip.

Whatever the combination, Craig thought, he preferred Bonnie Taylor's sunny smile and her flowing good nature. His regret was that Bonnie was so deeply upset by Sharky's end. He was sharply disturbed, himself. He could only hope, with the others, that Peter Hubbard and this woman scientist would come up with the answer quickly.

Last night on the beach with Bonnie, he had been the one to try to put Yarkie's problem in perspective. Big fish eat little fish eat little fish eat little fish, down to the plankton—on Yarkie, something had gone wrong with the chain. It was reckless for men to forget that Nature was always a primal shark. She might seem to be swimming placidly, half-asleep, but you always had to be wary. She could always turn and tear you to pieces, as the brewing storm might do in these waters later this very day.

"A little rough, isn't it?" the Harvard woman was asking.

Craig Soaras smiled broadly at her, almost an apology, wanting her to know that he and the others on Yarkie appreciated her assistance and wanted to be friendly. "Not yet," he said. "But it looks to be a bad one by tonight."

Her small frown held. "How long to Yarkie?"

The bowler shape was already rising out of the sea to the east. "Ten minutes, about." Craig asked anxiously, "You feeling all right, m'am?"

She surprised him with a light laugh. "No problem." Then she added in an open, friendly tone, "Please don't call me 'm'am'."

Craig Soaras's mustache twitched amiably. "Okay, doctor."

"Just Wanda does it," she told him pleasantly. "I understand we'll all be working together for a while, Mr. Soaras."

He responded, "Just Craig will do," and they laughed together.

With that, the man tied the wheel and went to stand at the rail. He noticed her hands. The left one was beautiful, with soft skin and long, sensitive fingers. The right hand shocked him. It was brute red, with crooked scar tissue in a leathery pattern. The woman saw his eyes. "A lab accident," she explained. And stopped. No need to talk of the image in her head every time she looked at her crippled hand. The mishap had been over in a flash. An experimental mouse had squirmed away and leaped into the beaker of nitric acid. Her reflex act had been so stupid, so fruitless. The animal was dead before her plunging hand hit the acid. Yet she supposed she would do the same thing again. An instinct to save life? Sometimes she thought she ought to have been a medical doctor rather than a research biologist.

The husky boat rose and fell, bumped and kicked up spray in the rising sea. Craig returned to the wheel. Dr. Lindstrom watched his easy, sure motions, his handsome eyes alert on the compass. The woman wished she could free her lab-cramped feelings, unfurl them to fly like the gulls to which the Yarkie sailor was pointing. The birds were wheeling over a roiling circle of sea to their left.

"School of blues over there," he called from the wheel. "There'll be a traffic jam here in five minutes." He would have liked to slow and show her the fishing, but it was no time for side excursions.

The woman's thoughts were elsewhere. Maybe if she could ever let her emotions show, Peter Hubbard would be less a stickler in their relationship. Thinking of her colleague brought her mind back to her business here. She moved over to Craig Soaras, steadying herself on the tilting deck with feet wide apart. The wind was blowing her hair out of its knot and she held her head tightly in her hands. "Craig, do you know the problem in the island? All Dr. Hubbard told me was the equipment he wanted to check on insecticides, something about rats and roaches behaving strangely . . ."

Soaras told her briefly everything he had seen himself and heard about from others.

Dr. Wanda Lindstrom said, "Well, it does sound like a mix-up of poisons. Shouldn't be too much trouble to correct." Craig Soaras was elated to hear it.

TWO

That morning, Stephen Scott purposely drove across High Ridge on his way to the meeting Elias Johnson had called at the lighthouse. Passing Hilda Cannon's place, Scott's worry deepened. The station wagon was just as he had left it. There was no sign of life, no Hildie, no Ruth, no Rebecca. He was tempted to stop, but held his foot steady on the gas pedal. If Hildie was in, he wouldn't know how to talk to her—the gun was the sheriff's business. If she wasn't home, he wouldn't know more than he did.

It was the same at the Tinton place. No sign of life. Best for him to go right on to meet the woman from Harvard.

Though the wind was up a little, the day was still sunny, and as Scott pulled up at the lighthouse he found the people outdoors on the beach. In a circle on the sand, there were Amos Tartell, Ben Dorset, Reed Brockshaw, Craig Soaras, and Russell Homer, and Elias, hunkered on a lobster trap. On folding chairs sat Elizabeth, her friend Bonnie, with Dr. Hubbard and the new woman. His first impression was that she was too beautiful to be any kind of professor, but if she was at Harvard she must know her stuff. When the introduction was done, Stephen Scott considered that he ought to report at once about the night before, but he argued with himself that it would only muddy the waters until he heard the scientists.

Dr. Peter Hubbard had already taken over. "Our first priority is to bring in specimens of the rats seen by Russell and Craig." The island informality had carried the younger men to a first-name basis quickly and easily. "The rats can't *all* have vanished. I suggest we set up a bait. Use a rabbit, perhaps." The scientist addressed Johnson. "If rats did get your dog, captain, they'll go for a rabbit."

"Makes sense," Johnson concurred.

Peter Hubbard continued, "We have to consider that this may be more dangerous than we've so far thought. There can be big packs of rats roving the woods. They can easily kill a man, especially if they are sick, as I suspect here."

The sheriff said quietly, "We all have guns now."

Stephen Scott spoke up. "Right, Amos! You deputize anyone you need!"

Elias Johnson suggested, "We can wear our foul weather gear—rubber boots, oilskins."

The scientist nodded. "That would be some protection."

The old man stood up. "Any volunteers?"

All the young men got to their feet. The sheriff said, "Too many, we'd only get in each other's way." He tapped Ben Dorset and Russell Homer. "Come on back to the office. We'll get the gear, and pick up a live rabbit at Julio's place."

Stephen Scott brushed sand from his slacks. If he was going to say anything, this was the time. But once again he silently asked himself what there was to report except the gun, and that might have slipped unnoticed from Hildie Cannon's bag any time she had walked in the forest. There were enough unanswered questions floating around without adding more. Right now, the sheriff had a clear-cut job to do. Let him go on, then, and bring in those rats, and let the Harvard people start their investigation. It suddenly occurred to Scott that he ought to ask Elias Johnson how much money the scientists were getting and who was paying, but he hurried after the sheriff with another thought.

"Hey, Amos, should we have the fire trucks go around town again about spraying?"

The sheriff nodded. "Good idea. Keep people away. Especially if we're going to have to shoot."

Craig said, "I'll call the boys right out."

"Phone working here?" Scott asked. "Good!"

Peter Hubbard joined the group. "Amos, if you catch anything, bring it right in. Make a note of *everything* you see—how the rat moves, how it holds its head, its tail. Everything. We can get important clues that way . . ."

The sheriff threw the scientist half a salute—one professional to another. "Got it!" As fishermen, they were used to the importance of reading small signs that others would hardly notice—a meager cloud appearing, a tiny shift in the wind, a momentary shadow in the water.

The three men piled into the sheriff's blue and white car.

Elizabeth stood beside her grandfather, gripping his hand. "I hope they don't get hurt!"

The captain said gravely, "They are good men, Liz."

That was just it, Elizabeth Carr considered, watching the car shoot away. They were all estimable people on Yarkie Island. It was unthinkable that evil animals were putting the place in peril.

Behind her, Elizabeth heard Peter Hubbard calling Wanda Lindstrom. "Let's unpack the microscopes first, Wanda. We want to take a real look at the dog's ear . . ."

THREE

Sheriff Amos Tarbell and his two companions made a zany appearance as they came into the pine grove where Bonnie Taylor had picnicked and lost Sharky. The glade was an incongruous background for their storm attire, heavy boots, yellow slickers and wide-brimmed hoods.

Tarbell stopped and spoke softly. "Bonnie said she found Sharky just off the trail there, to the left." They decided that spot was as good as any for the trap, in which a contented brown rabbit was nibbling on a large carrot.

The sheriff placed the cage softly and deployed the men. "Russ, you get up that tree." He couldn't help but grin. "If you can make it with those boots on . . ."

Russell Homer didn't like being laughed at, even in a friendly jest. He grated, "I've climbed higher masts in lots worse!" He swung up onto a pitch pine much as Craig Soaras had done when he discovered Sharky's ear.

"You got the camera?" the sheriff checked.

"Yup."

"Good."

Ben Dorset was calling from near the small waterfall. "Now what the hell is this?" He was lifting a good-sized aluminum container.

The sheriff glanced at it. "Bonnie must have left her picnic box." He looked back up to Russell Homer. "If it comes to trouble, Russ, use the gun first, the camera after."

"Right." The young man looked down appraisingly. Clouds were covering the sun, making it doubly shadowy in the forest—he wanted enough light for pictures. He prided himself on the photographic skills he had taught himself.

The sheriff stationed himself to one side of the trap, with Ben Dorset covering him from behind a tree. Birds sang in the branches, but the wind was beginning to whistle in a foreboding song of its own. Elias Johnson had timed the storm just about perfectly. These winds were the forerunners—the real blow would not hit for three-four hours. They had plenty of time. Tarbell called to his men, "Better get the goggles on, too."

Russell Homer fretted, "Amos, I won't be able to work the camera if I wear this damn thing."

"Okay," the sheriff assented. The man should be safe enough on his perch in the tree.

Settled in their places, with the rabbit quiet in the trap, the three men waited silently, uncertain, and uneasy. The

97

forest revealed nothing except an occasional trill of a bird, and the new sound of the wind in the branches above their heads.

Long minutes passed. Ben Dorset stamped his foot. "Cramp, damn it!" He stamped harder and harder.

"For crying out loud, Ben," the sheriff laughed, "you'll start an earthquake!"

Silence again. From his tree, Russell Homer said disgustedly, "This criminal doesn't return to the scene of the crime . . ."

"Quiet!" Amos Tarbell ordered abruptly. He thought he had detected a movement. Slight. But out there some way in front of the rabbit in the trap, the way he sensed the first touch of a small fish exploring a baited hook.

The men tensed. Dorset leveled his revolver. No rat was going to live a split second unless he went into the trap.

Russell Homer had the camera aimed.

The sheriff was leaning forward, with his own gun cocked.

They did not see the leaves move, but they heard the sound distinctly. It was a soft skittering, as if fingers were playing in the piles of leaves, the way children sift sand.

Suddenly there was a flutter of the leafy surface. A rat was coming!

But the next instant the men were guffawing to each other, with guns lowered and sheepish looks on their faces. The ferocious rat pack turned out to be a few lousy cockroaches! Big bastards, to be sure, but just overgrown bugs, fat from the dump.

"Big sons of bitches!" Ben Dorset observed.

Russell Homer said, "I've been seeing them the last week or so. Damn water bugs, eaten too much for their own good."

"Ugly suckers!" the deputy sheriff commented.

The sheriff quieted the men with a finger to his lips. It

occurred to him that the harmless roaches might be useful in attracting the rats. There certainly was an unusual scent around, musky-acid, sort of set your teeth on edge. If it was from the bugs, any rats in the vicinity would get it and hopefully come to where they'd see the rabbit.

The men watched indifferently as the three roaches moved slowly around the old lobster trap. The lingering odor of fish and bait undoubtedly had drawn them. Everyone knew roaches loved the stinky stuff, the more rotten the better.

The sheriff felt a chill up his spine, though he didn't know why. He sure as hell wasn't squeamish about the cockroaches, enormous as these might be. But he muttered a curse to himself as he saw the largest one—it must be a full five inches and damn near an inch around! —halt in front of the trap and vibrate its antennae toward the rabbit as if the damn wiry extensions were actual fingers reaching out to touch the animal. The miserable insect looked for all the world as if it were deliberately prowling around the trap, the way a hunting animal might do.

The sheriff dismissed his next thought: It was almost as if the roach was looking over the situation and making a decision about going after the rabbit *itself*. Absurd! How could a cockroach, no matter how unnaturally immense, figure to kill a rabbit?

The two other bulky roaches seemed to be playing follow-the-leader. Their head wires were all looping around the same way. If a man didn't know better, he'd swear the three insects were like science-fiction creatures communicating silently through ESP or some damn airwaves. Amos Tarbell saw the expressions of disgust on the faces of his companions. They matched his own. Those swollen cockroaches were nasty looking, no two ways about it. Now their antennae were suddenly beating the air a mile a minute, like egg whisks. Their heads began to jerk from side to side. A man would swear they were sensing the rabbit exactly like wolves or coyotes sniffing the air for unsuspecting prey.

And a man would swear they caught a scent, as three things happened at once. The first roach leaped into the cage. A second roach spread wings so wide it looked like a small bat. It whizzed inside and landed on the rabbit's back. The third roach turned and raced away, as if afraid, or as if it wanted no part of the massacre that started.

Gagging with nausea, the three Yarkie stalwarts watched the fantastic, repugnant sight. The first roach went directly for the rabbit's eyes. The men heard the click of the breaking cornea as the insect mandibles pressed in. They saw the gush of liquid from the eyeball as the panicked rabbit chittered with the pain. They watched what they could not believe: The great cockroach insinuated itself quickly into the rabbit's eye socket, obviously eating its way through, right on into the brain. Then the insect body vanished entirely while the men looked on.

The second roach was at the rabbit's neck. It moved exactly as if it knew the jugular vein, the way a leopard or lioness breaks a prey's neck or hyenas bite at hamstring muscles to bring a victim down.

Incredible was too mild a word. The sheriff could see the disbelief in Ben Dorset and Russell Homer. He was glad they were witnesses. To describe this scene without corroboration would be to invite the men in white jackets.

But it was happening, terribly happening, beyond any doubt. The rabbit was flinging its bloodied body about in agonized terror. Blood spurted from its torn throat and ran out of the trap onto the leaves. The savage roach had chewed through to the blood vessel it wanted. Those mandibles must be powerful to rip a rabbit's skin, the sheriff thought. Those teeth must be razor-edged to cut the wounds killing the rabbit. The men were almost glad when the bewildered animal twitched violently and fell on its side, dead in moments, out of its suffering.

"Jesus God!" Ben Dorset breathed.

The sheriff shouted across to him, "Gimme that damn box!" As Dorset tossed him the picnic basket, Tarbell yelled up to Russell Homer, "Come the hell down! We're taking the trap and leaving!"

Homer's face contorted. "We want the pictures, don't we?"

Amos Tarbell flung the trap into the aluminum box and slammed the cover shut. "Come *on*, Russ!"

"Jesus Christ!" It was a sudden cry of open alarm from Ben Dorset. The other men looked where he was pointing. An *army* of the giant roaches was advancing on them, literally thousands of the insects. To Russell Homer in the tree, their carapaces and wings looked like the shining armor of toy soldiers, little robots, wound up and coming mechanically through the leaves. But it was plain they were anything but toys. Their antennae were flailing above their heads. Homer thought of tanks with cannon circling in moving turrets. It was unreal, and it was the most terrifying experience he had ever known. He kept clicking his camera, desperately adjusting for shutter speed and available light. The Harvard people had to have this incredible record!

Amos Tarbell was screaming, "Russ! *No more time!*"

Homer kept taking shot after shot.

The sheriff and Ben Dorset emptied their revolvers at the insects. Earth and leaves and roaches sprayed into the air. But nothing deflected the column. The advancing cockroaches calmly crawled over the dead bugs. Some paused to chew at the bodies, but the main group kept coming.

Amos Tarbell tugged at Russell Homer's feet. A boot came off in his hand. "Dammit!" he cried, "we're in trouble, Russ! *Get!*" He flung the boot at the oncoming cockroach force and, banging into Ben Dorset, whirled for the road and the police car, much as Hildie Cannon had done the night before.

Russell Homer seemed suddenly to comprehend his peril. He jumped down from the tree, but in his effort to protect the camera he landed on his back, not his feet. Without his goggles, and missing a boot, Homer lay stunned. The roach column paused momentarily as the ground shook with the man's fall. Then it shifted of one accord in his direction.

"Jesus, damn!" Amos Tarbell yelled violently. He handed the cage with the rabbit to Dorset and raced back to Russell Homer. The man was thrashing on the ground now, realizing his danger, trying to get up and run. The front of the roach column was hissing steadily toward him. The sheriff's one thought was that Russell wore no goggles. Impelled by the awful image of the roach eating into the rabbit's eye, Tarbell leaped across the grove and yanked Homer to his feet. Dazed, the young man started to follow the sheriff, but in his confusion he dropped the camera. When he turned to fumble for it, hissing insects immediately lunged for his bare face. The sheriff jerked the man away just before their mandibles touched his skin. "The hell with the camera!" With a mighty shove, Tarbell sent Homer headlong up the path in Dorset's footsteps.

In turning to help his friend, the sheriff had lost his own lead over the roaches. Now they were only feet away from him. His boots and storm clothes made it hard for Tarbell to move quickly, but his adrenalin was pumping as it had done only once before in his life, when a Mako had abruptly attacked when he was swimming off the east shore with his family. He had stayed to battle the shark then, to give his wife and children time to escape the ravening jaws. Fortunately, he had gotten his fist on the

Mako's nose from above and pounded his own fear into it. He had been lucky. It was one of those times when a shark withdrew. The Mako had probably eaten not long before.

But the cockroach sharks, as Tarbell thought of the crawling column now, were not to be turned. There was no nose to punch, no mass to fight against. The sheriff knew in his gut that these bugs were killers relentlessly coming after his eyes, his flesh, his bones. He ran for his life with every gulp of acid-stinking air he sucked into his heaving lungs. It came to him that he was running not only for his own life, but possibly the lives of everyone on Yarkie! The scientists had to be told! They *had* to see the specimen roaches caught inside the dead rabbit . . .

Tarbell saw Ben Dorset nearing the road. It occurred to the sheriff that if he stopped and let the roaches take him, Dorset and Homer could get away. But in the pinch, he found he did not have the ultimate courage to sacrifice himself. Not, at least, while he was still a step ahead of the creeping doom. He raced with fire under his ribs now, not daring to look back. But he had seen how swiftly those impossible insects could move. He didn't have to remember how fast a kitchen roach skittered away, a damn streak of brown lightning, gone almost before the eye could spot it. He had long legs, but the bugs would keep gaining if he faltered for even a moment.

In front of him he saw Ben Dorset reach the road. Hope skyrocketed in his heaving chest. But at the same moment, Russell Homer went sprawling. The sheriff tripped over him and both men lay tangled in the leaves. Fumbling frantically to regain their feet, they slipped and skidded against each other clumsily. Russell kept crying, "Sorry, sorry!" Amos Tarbell saved his breath, shoving at the man with a silent vehemence.

A roach landed on Homer's cheek and folded its wings. Without thinking, the sheriff brought his gloved fist against the young man's face. The roach was mashed, but Homer bellowed angrily, "What the hell you doing?"

Another roach landed, moving straight for Russell Homer's eyes, and Amos Tarbell swatted the reddened, perplexed face again. The man raised his own fists, but at the same moment a roach flew onto the sheriff's cheek, and the light dawned. Homer used his own gloved hand to flick the insect off, but its mandibles had already drawn blood. The young man had no choice but to do as Tarbell had done. He slapped hard, and squashed the roach against the sheriff's jaw.

Both men heard the deputy sheriff bawling for them to hurry, but more roaches were hitting the men's open faces, and, while they headed for the road, they had to stop at every step to brush away or squash the marauders.

The roaches were winning, sliding all over the men, too many to be dealt with. Russell Homer cried out in protest and panic against the implacable killers. The sheriff fought silently, knowing in his heart that he was losing, that this was the last battle of his life—against an inconceivable enemy.

Until all at once the men were blinded by a searing light that scorched their eyes.

Russell Homer froze as if hit with a hammer, but Amos Tarbell understood immediately that his deputy had swung the police car's powerful spotlight down the forest path. He saw the roaches on Homer's cheeks let go and fall away to the ground. The nipping stopped on his own cheek. He wanted to stay and grind the miserable insects into the earth, but he stumbled on toward the light. Thank God they needed that great light to power through the mists and fogs that often covered Yarkie.

Tarbell pushed Homer, staggering, onto the road, and dared to look back for a moment. *Yes!* and praise Almighty God, the roaches were in disarray. The spotlight was anathema to them. He had wondered right from the start why even the first roaches had come out during the day, but the trap had been in a dim area. And these cockroaches were obviously all too different from what people expected, in all too many terrible ways. Thank God the searchlight had stopped them. He could see the column breaking up faster and faster, with roaches skittering crazily down into the leaves, seeking darkness now.

They might regroup and attack again, but the men had their chance to escape.

Ben Dorset had placed the aluminum box on the back seat, and the three men rode in front as the police car accelerated to over sixty in split seconds. Russell Homer hardly had time to close the door and was nearly thrown out as Dorset went screeching around a curve. Fortunately, Amos Tarbell had solid hold of his young friend. At the wheel, Dorset hit the siren in a crescendo of warning to anyone who might be ahead.

The sheriff could not help turning to see whether the roach army had reformed. Dorset was speeding too fast for a good look, but the road behind seemed empty.

The man's eyes lowered from the rear window to the picnic case bouncing and sliding on the rear seat as the car swerved left and right with the speedometer climbing to eighty, ninety, one hundred. They hit a bump and the box flew off the seat and bounced on the floor. Horrified that the lock might spring, the sheriff reached back to press the lid down. He uttered another silent prayer of thanks when he saw that the cover had held. It seemed to him he could see right through the metal to the evil antennae inside, reaching, reaching, reaching for them all. He shuddered with the feel of the livid mandibles clamping on his cheek and the sting of the insect teeth biting for his blood. He knew too well now what was happening on Yarkie. And knowing it, he still could not bring himself to believe that it was roaches—just *cockroaches!*—no matter how vicious and huge a breed—that could be so infernally powerful.

Yarkie could only trust that the two Harvard scientists could deal with the distorted insects and their unspeakable appetites.

Now Amos Tarbell could admit to himself that he had privately deemed Elias Johnson's phone call to Harvard too quick on the trigger. But now he was more than grateful. The cockroaches they had just so narrowly eluded were more formidable than any rats he had ever seen! If those bastards, those "crawling sharks," ever got out of the woods into Yarkie's homes the carnage would create a ghost island.

For that matter, it occurred to the sheriff, if those monstrosities ever hid on a boat and got over to the mainland, they could make a ghost land of the Cape itself. And hadn't somebody predicted it was insects that would take over the entire world in the end?

For all his experience and ruggedness, the sheriff shivered like a child.

The biologists would have to tackle the tumbling questions in his mind. They were in for a hellish surprise. It was the damnedest "rats" they'd find when they opened the picnic box he was still pressing firmly shut.

At the thought of the mangled rabbit and the grisly autopsy ahead in the laboratory, Sheriff Amos Tarbell of Yarkie shouted for Ben Dorset to stop the car. He didn't want to be sick all over everybody.

ALERT

ONE

The two scientists, their crisp white lab coats now stained with red flecks, came into the kitchen. They faced the anxious Yarkie group, pale and unsettled themselves. In all their years of scalpels and dissections, neither one had come upon a gory abhorrence like the sacrificed rabbit. The giant roaches had tunneled through the corpse erratically, apparently tasting and sampling this organ and that. The body was a ruptured blob with flaps of shredded gristle and bone curdled in a vile bloody soup on the bottom of the picnic box, disgustingly mixed with the remains of Bonnie Taylor's uneaten lunch.

The two roaches had been recovered. Peter Hubbard had found them lying torpid in the rabbit's torn lungs after their glut. One of the insects had been dissected immediately; the other was placed alive in a covered glass flask so its activity could be studied. Even in its lethargic state and in the undimmed laboratory lights, the roach showed signs of restlessness. Its antennae wafted about ceaselessly, and it moved steadily if slowly around the bottom of the jar, seeming to the scientists to be seeking its partner or the main column from which it had attacked the rabbit.

Peter Hubbard stood at the head of the kitchen table rubbing his cheek as if checking whether he needed a shave. It would become a familiar gesture to the group.

He measured his words, turning his head often to Wanda Lindstrom for corroboration. His report, spoken as emotionlessly as possible, sounded improbable even to his own ears. The woman biologist nodded her confirmation earnestly with each point he brought out. The room was charged with the kind of strain pervading a surgeon's office when a family is receiving the results of a biopsy for cancer. What kind of cancer was afflicting Yarkie?

Hubbard came to the point directly. "To start with," he began, "you ought to know that I told Dr. Lindstrom of certain suspicions in my mind from the moment I examined Captain Johnson's dog's ear." Bonnie winced visibly. "I didn't want to disturb the rest of you prematurely, but even without a microscope it was clear to me that something other than rats had attacked the dog.

"Now under the microscope we see plainly that the tissue was cut by sawteeth, *and*—" Hubbard paused for emphasis "—we have now confirmed that the shearing action is not up and down, the way most animals bite, but *side to side*."

The scientist spaced the last words, looking squarely into the eyes of his worried listeners, and added meaningfully, *"Side to side is the way insects like cockroaches chew!"* He paused again. "I had considered that possibility right away, but I was put off and puzzled by the size of the bites on the ear. You see, normally, cockroaches cannot open their mouths very wide. We do have cases, especially in the tropics, where roaches have attacked animals and even humans, but it has been only a small nibbling action, like small nips on the earlobes or lips of a sleeping child. Very small bites. Tiny, in fact. Nothing like the rips I discovered on the dog's ear."

Bonnie could not control the cold the man's words stirred in her body. Elizabeth tightened her grasp around the slight shoulders.

"Now that we have studied the two specimens the sheriff and his men brought back—" Hubbard interrupted himself to observe, "We haven't heard that story, but I'm sure it wasn't easy." He paused another moment. The three men exchanged pale looks. Their mouths were grim. It was the scientist's time to speak, not theirs.

Hubbard resumed, but his voice lost its scientific tone and became almost grating in his own clear perplexity. "I must tell you that these cockroaches we have examined here are decidedly, and very dangerously, unlike anything ever seen or heard of."

Stephen Scott asked, argumentatively, "You mean they're not just big water bugs?"

"Decidedly not! They differ in many ways. Just to start with, they apparently have the ability to attack and kill an animal like a dog or a rabbit. These cockroaches not only have bigger mouths than would be normal relative to their size, but their jaw muscles are absolutely enormous. You may not know it, but your ordinary household roach has much more efficient muscles than we humans do, relatively speaking." Hubbard put his fingers to his own jaw just below his ears. "Typically, the household cockroach shows no significant protrusion here. But on our specimens there are decided muscle bulges. This means the mandibles and the mouth are hooked to extremely powerful muscles, so that they can inflict the kind of damage we have seen on the dog and the rabbit."

The man turned to Stephen Scott, who was still eyeing him skeptically. "Mr. Scott, I wish these *were* just the garden variety water bug you mention. Their size alone tells a different story. The common water bug doesn't grow to more than about two inches. Only in the tropics do we find any cockroaches approaching four-five inches, like our specimens. Some have wing spreads of over five inches . . ."

Elizabeth asked with a little gasp, "You mean cockroaches can *fly*, Peter?"

He nodded. "When they want to. Actually, in biological terms, roaches are the most primitive form of winged insects."

Elizabeth whispered to Bonnie, "I never knew that!"

Bonnie mumbled, "I'm learning a lot of things I'd rather not know!"

Wanda Lindstrom rose. Eyes shifted expectantly to the woman as she leaned forward with her hands pressed flat on the kitchen table. She projected a sense of authority that made her seem taller than she was and, for the first time at least, put her feminine attractiveness in the shadow. It came to Elizabeth, admiringly, that the person addressing them with her sober words was not "a beautiful blond female ..."or "... attractive." She was a renowned biologist, a person of accomplishment and service, with a brilliant future. Elizabeth understood a new meaning in women's lib. When Peter Hubbard spoke, everyone listened to him as a scientist not a man. When Wanda Lindstrom spoke, she should be heard as a scientist in exactly the same way, not as a woman.

And her voice now held an objective, almost sterile tone. She was saying, "Dr. Hubbard and I have speculated that some ship brought in the ancestors of the cockroaches you have here. It could have been many, many years ago. These cockroaches may have been living on Yarkie for many roach generations, most likely out in the dump. They breed awfully fast, and I mean 'awfully' in every sense of the word. Let me explain that. Fertilization takes place when the male roach inserts the rear of his body—called the cercum—into the rear of the female. He deposits a sac of sperm." The woman's voice was that of a lecturer emphasizing a significant detail not to be overlooked. "The female holds this sac in her body *intact*, sometimes for several months. In other words, she can 'give birth' pretty much any time during that period. Out of the egg case, which we call oöthecae, the female can lay ten-sixteen eggs every five days or so. Perhaps in this Yarkie roach group there are more eggs and quicker hatchings, but even in the common ordinary roach you can see that one mother may mean over a thousand new roaches a year. Given a thousand mothers—and that's not many at all—you get a million roaches a year just from one group. And so on geometrically."

Elizabeth put in, respectfully, "But they don't all survive, of course."

The other woman nodded. "We'd be overrun everywhere, of course. Normally, many of the young die because the environment is unfavorable—not enough food or moisture, which in turn leads adult roaches, including the parents, to eat the babies. But on this island where the dump provides endless food and shelter, cockroaches like these would thrive."

Elizabeth had another question, vaguely recalled from a biology course in her sophomore year. "Don't they have natural enemies that might hold them down?"

The woman inclined her head again. "Yes. For example, certain wasps lay eggs in adult cockroaches. The hatching eggs feed on them and kill them. Then there are symbionts that kill, like the *Clostridium botulinium*, a form that lives only where there is no oxygen. It develops in the hind gut of the roach . . ."

Elizabeth noted with admiration the easy use of the scientific names and labels. Although she, better than anyone in the room but Peter Hubbard, knew the woman's professional status, it still seemed unusual for a mouth as lovely as Wanda Lindstrom's to be uttering the stiff designations. Unusual, impressive, and articulate, Elizabeth acknowledged.

Wanda Lindstrom wasn't finished. "We can't draw any final conclusions from just two specimens, but we haven't seen any sign of a natural enemy here, not so far. We have to suppose that the population of these brute roaches has simply been exploding on your island in a kind of organic flashpoint, and has now spilled out visibly." She added, "Perhaps as a result of the new poisons you have mentioned. We will be investigating that, of course."

Russell Homer exclaimed shakily. "From the tree, it looked like a zillion of them coming on at us! The whole damn ground was just cockroaches!"

Peter Hubbard answered quickly, "We're still just guessing, mostly. But in fairness I have to tell you what we do now know. It seems plain that these roaches can attack any body opening, including the ears. I told Dr. Lindstrom what Russell and Craig said about the dump rats running around dizzily. Now I think that roaches ate their way through the middle ear which, as you know, controls balance. I have to say it," the man went on with a scowl of his own revulsion, "these confounded creatures can kill in many ways. They can get up an animal's nostrils and down its throat, causing suffocation. They can get at the brain, as we've said already. Their mandibles are so strong and their teeth so sharp they can needle through skin to veins and arteries, causing death by hemorrhage."

Everyone was grimacing. The thought of slimy cockroaches sliding into every opening of a living animal shook them with more than disgust.

Ben Dorset said, unexpectedly, "Just seeing that roach get into the rabbit's eye was the most awful thing . . ."

Reed Brockshaw was listening with a blank expression, a look of incomprehension. His ears heard what was being said, but the enormity of it was too great for his mind to accept.

Elias Johnson voiced a question on everyone's mind.

"Why didn't we find anything of Sharky except the ear? I mean, all right, say these roaches killed him, but how did he *vanish?* Craig and I looked over every inch. Even say these bastards—" the old man did not stop to apologize to the ladies "—even say these bastards came at Sharky by the thousands like the piranha fish we all know about—we'd at least find the skeleton, wouldn't we?" His voice rose with the ire of his bafflement.

Peter Hubbard had to tell the man, "Elias, there are insects that leave no skeletons."

Johnson's widened eyes showed he couldn't believe it. "What? These roaches eat the bones?"

"They have teeth so sharp, and appetites so ravenous, that they can grind bones to powder and ingest them. Any bone and all bone." Hubbard added with an expression of his own disgust, "Including the skull, when they want to."

New murmurs of horror went around the table.

Stephen Scott could not contain his fearful question any longer. Almost stuttering in his premonition of the answer, he said, "You've been talking about these roaches killing Sharky, and the rabbit, and rats ..." He stopped, then could no longer hold the words in. "Are you saying these cockroaches can kill *people?*"

Hubbard answered, "Yes," bluntly, without hesitation or concealment.

Elias Johnson slapped the table. "No! That's impossible! Just *roaches?*"

Wanda Lindstrom backed up Peter Hubbard. "I'm afraid Dr. Hubbard is right. Especially if the insects attack in swarms, as we have to suspect."

"My God!" Scott whispered to himself.

"What'd you say, Stephen?" Elias Johnson asked roughly out of his own mounting trepidation. "What'd you say? Speak up, dammit!"

"Nothing!" Scott sputtered. He simply could not

permit his forebodings to assume the reality that words would impart to them. The possibility was too inhuman to contemplate. But in his mind's eye he was again in the empty Tinton house the night before, again flashing his light in the woods looking for the Tintons and for Hilda Cannon—and now totally unable to keep his concern from leaping to the question of the missing Cannon girls as well.

He was glad when a question from Craig diverted attention away from him. "How would Sharky's ear get up in a tree?"

"Roaches climb easily," Hubbard told him. "They might have been disturbed before they finished . . ."

"Lay anchor here just a minute!" Elias Johnson called out. "I just barely got it through my head that these damn things could be like piranha. Okay. Now you're telling us they—they lug away parts of what they kill?" His eyes were hot with the challenge of the impossible.

It was Wanda Lindstrom who gave him the gristly answer, in a tone so quiet it could barely be heard through the kitchen. "It's not any different from the way jungle animals drag prey back to their caves, for their young, or to feed on later. Conceivably, these insects have a central nest . . ."

Now Elias Johnson sputtered, "*Cockroaches* could drag a *dog?*"

The woman kept her voice clinical. "Not in one piece," she said steadily to the disbelieving faces around the kitchen.

"Oh, come on!" Amos Tarbell protested. "Ben, Russ and I saw the damn things just an hour ago. There were zillions of them, all right, and they did try to get at us, but you're saying they could drag *us* somewhere . . . ?"

The woman repeated, understanding their resistance, "I said, not in one piece." She sat down. The facade of the scientist was cracking. Despite her self-control, the image of a body being cut apart by mutant roaches sickened her, too.

Hubbard said sympathetically to them all, "This is tough, but none of us can afford to be squeamish. I must repeat what you already know, that there are many insects capable of moving weights many times their own, especially when individuals combine. You have probably seen ants doing this with your own eyes. Given the size and muscle of these roaches here, they could handle very large loads, especially if they have developed some kind of organization that is *not* common among the roach species."

Craig protested again. "I can see it with maybe an ear, a paw. But a whole body?"

Hubbard answered slowly, "Based on the behavior of related insects, like termites, I have to tell you that bands of roaches could, yes, chew and gnaw through tissue and cartilage and bone like a butcher's saw or cleaver. Yes, they could separate pieces small enough to be handled by gangs that would join together for the purpose."

Bonnie cried out, "Oh, please!" She ran from the room out to the beach with her hands to her cheeks.

Hubbard heard the expressions of consternation and continuing disbelief. His face hardened. These were seamen, used to the stink of bait and chum and the blood and guts of the big fish they disemboweled, the tuna, the sharks. It was no time for delicate stomachs. He gave Elizabeth a way out before he continued, "Elizabeth, do you want to check on Bonnie?"

The woman looked up at him and shook her head. Bonnie could take care of herself. She was staying to hear the worst.

Hubbard was unrelenting then, "Yes, roaches like these might well be able to cut through even a human body!" he certified.

Stephen Scott went paler.

"We have seen such behavior, I repeat," Hubbard stressed. "As I said, it's entirely possible that these insects can circle the limb, biting down as they go—"

"Good God!" Amos Tarbell groaned. "Like a bloody chain saw!"

"Exactly," Wanda Lindstrom sighed.

"Until they cut right through. Bone and all."

When the scientist stopped, the room was silent. Elizabeth and all the men were stunned. Peter Hubbard and Wanda Lindstrom had moved them into a world so alien, ogreish, and alarming that they had no way to formulate their reaction. The ghastliness was in the blood, beyond the reach of words or horror or comradely comfort. A strange, raw wind was blowing up from a biological nether world of phantasmagoric claws, fangs, and mindlessness. It would have seemed impossible anywhere; it was beyond all comprehension on Yarkie Island.

TWO

Elizabeth was no biologist, no scientist of any kind, but the awful logic of what Peter Hubbard had said must lead to another question, insane as it might sound. "Peter, what you and Wanda are describing—doesn't that take a kind of, er, *brains?* I mean, all the insects working together in such an organized way . . . ?"

"Roaches don't have brains!" Russell Homer made bold to scoff. A person didn't have to go to Harvard to know that!

Hubbard corrected the man quietly, "Of course the individual roaches do have brains. Rudimentary, but brains. The question here is whether there may be a larger center, controlling a *colony* of individuals."

"That's my question," Elizabeth nodded—aghast at her own thought.

"Such colonies are not unusual in nature," Hubbard resumed. "We all know the groups formed by ants and termites. Still, Russ is right in a way. The social organization of insects doesn't take place through a 'brain.' It works through a kind of community instinct. Each individual fits into the overall social pattern, something like robots running on a central computer program."

Russell Homer ejaculated, "That's what I said they looked like! Robots!"

Wanda Lindstrom contributed, "Peter, they ought to know that we did find an unusual and advanced nervous development in the specimen we dissected. Ordinarily, given the size of this roach, the brain should be no bigger than a small pea, sitting just behind the juncture of the antennae with the head. But in our specimen, the brain was at least twice as large. Also, the ganglia, which normally are only slight swellings in the insect's ventral nerve —that's a primitive chord that runs along the ventral side the way the vertebrate spine runs up the back—these ganglia are double the normal number, and they form more distinct nerve centers than I have ever seen in any insect species. So whatever signals these roaches are exchanging, they seem well-equipped to work together, whether in hunting down prey or disposing of it once they've killed it."

Hubbard took the ball again. He addressed the sheriff. "Now, have you told us everything you observed when the roaches went after the rabbit? Everything exactly as you saw it?"

He sounded like a district attorney, he knew, but this cross-examination could be important. The laymen would not understand the significance of subtle behavior that might be key points to the biologists.

The three men who had escaped with the rabbit trap concentrated. Russell Homer, especially, had his eyes screwed up, trying to replay every detail. He was thinking that if it was his fault the camera was lost, he would retake every exposure in his mind. He started to report aloud as the images followed upon each other. *Click:* "The rabbit stopped eating the carrot all of a sudden. It looked around, scared. That's when I heard the noise, the way we told you. Like a puffing sound, a kettle letting off steam. Not a whistle, just a hiss."

Wanda Lindstrom nodded emphatically.

"We thought it was mice."

Bonnie, who had come in quietly and was leaning against the doorpost, said softly, "I heard that, too, just before Sharky ran away."

Homer's eyes tightened harder. *Click:* "There were *three* of those cockroaches!" His eyes came open with his sharpened recollection. He turned to Tarbell and Dorset. *Click:* "Remember how one of them didn't follow the others into the trap . . ."

Wanda Lindstrom slapped the table. "One roach turned around and raced off," she anticipated.

The three men were startled by how she had guessed the fact.

She said strongly, "That third roach had a different job to do, you see! He went back to tell his friends that the scouts had found more food!"

Reed Brockshaw cut in, "*Roaches* do that? I know about bees flying back to the hive to show the way to flowers, but I never heard it about cockroaches!"

Peter Hubbard said somberly, "These roaches are full of surprises. Unpleasant ones."

Elizabeth asked him slowly, "You think we're dealing with a definite mutation, then?"

The scientist's answer was again upsetting. He eyed

the room frankly. "Dr. Lindstrom and I have been speculating about that possibility. You see, one of the classic cases of social organization among insects happens to be the termite colony, and—" he paused again for effect—"it happens that termites and cockroaches are related."

Amos Tarbell's surprise echoed the others'. "Termites and roaches?"

"We don't want to sound like a textbook, but you need to have this background if you're to understand what may be happening and how to protect against it." Hubbard knocked his pipe out and turned to his associate. "This is Dr. Lindstrom's specialty," he said. "Wanda, why don't you explain . . . ?"

Elizabeth admired the way the two tossed the biological ball back and forth, with total respect for each other's competence and no touch of self-importance. Marriage should be like that, she mused. She found herself half-wondering why they had not married in the six years of their obvious mutual esteem.

THREE

Obligingly, the blond scientist picked up where Peter Hubbard had left off. She understood exactly what he wanted her to explain: "It *may* be relevant," she began, "that termites and cockroaches evolved from a common ancestor. They are two branches of a root that is off by itself in the basic classification of the 'phyla.' Interestingly, one biologist has called termites the 'social cockroaches.' So it might not be too surprising if cockroaches displayed what might be called a 'phylogenetic drive' toward a social colonization that we find in termites."

Stephen Scott asked straightforwardly, "What's that 'phylogenetic,' please?" The man was blinking the way he had done as a student when he was trying hard to understand. It occurred to him that he had never tried harder in his life, or about anything more crucial.

Elizabeth answered, wanting to show again that she wasn't a scientific illiterate. "It means the development of the different species, the steps in the evolutionary process."

Wanda Lindstrom acknowledged her with an honest smile, and resumed, "Let's consider the termites for a minute—they may teach us something about these roaches. The first fact is that termites are amazingly adaptable. Especially in what they eat. Everyone knows they eat wood, and some people know they eat wool and paper, too." Dr. Lindstrom tapped the table firmly. "But hardly anyone realizes that termites *also* eat the plastic linings of electric cables, and have even destroyed horn and ivory, and—though you won't believe this—billiard balls! The *Mastotermes darwiniensis* of Australia!"

This time there were no rasps of disbelief. The listeners were getting used to their strange journey through the convoluted world of biology and the variegated forms of life.

The woman repeated, "Yes, termites eat plastic *and* leather *and—*"

Stephen Scott felt sicker with each word spoken. He echoed feebly, "Leather and rubber?" His one consolation was gone! He had thought it could not possibly be the giant roaches that had taken the Tintons and Hilda Cannon—and maybe Ruth and Rebecca—because he would have found shoes, leather belts, handbags.

He didn't want to hear Wanda Lindstrom's confirmation of his nightmarish fear, but the woman was saying, plainly and terribly, "If these roaches have mutated in the direction of the termite, they would not be leaving much evidence of their attacks, you see—whether they killed an animal or a human being."

Stephen Scott saw all too well. Although it was cool in the room, he was sweating as if it were a steam bath. "Maybe leather belts and stuff," he cried out desperately, "but what about a wrist watch, a pair of glasses! For God's sake, don't tell us they eat those too!"

"No, they're not that tough." Dr. Lindstrom permitted herself a sad smile. "At least not yet, to our knowledge. But what they can't eat, they might take back to their nest—like magpies. You know that's not unique animal behavior."

FOUR

In Amos Tarbell's investigative mind, blotchy thoughts were racing parallel to Stephen Scott's. Ruth and Rebecca Cannon! Had they gone back into the woods to spy on the naked men and been overtaken by the killer roaches? And what about the handcuffed fellows? Only one had shown up at all, with no news of the other anywhere this morning. And why was Stephen Scott asking his questions with his face all crumpled looking? And what was he taking out of his pocket now—?

"What the hell!" the sheriff exclaimed as Scott put Hilda Cannon's pistol on the kitchen table. With it, his story came spilling out. The group grew deathly white as they gathered the implications. There was the silence of a shared trauma when he finished.

Elias Johnson broke the silence. "So we have got ourselves one *hell* of a problem, looks like!"

Peter Hubbard said, "I am afraid so, Elias." The change from his previous formal address seemed indicated. The group was going to war together, and war made quick companions and intimates.

Amos Tarbell voiced his new concern. "Maybe I ought

to send some men out to look for Hildie and the others."

Johnson challenged, "And get the men chomped up, too? Sit down and let's hear what we're really up against!"

Peter Hubbard said, "Well, right now, all this is mostly conjecture on our part . . ."

Johnson clipped, "Conjecture away, damn it! If these consarned bugs are into a colony, we need to know it! We may have to get everybody off the island!"

Stephen Scott pounded a hammy fist into his palm. "Now wait just a goshdarn minute here! There's no need to panic the whole town!" His vehemence was inflamed by his personal uncertainty and secret alarm. "Dr. Hubbard says *conjecture!* We aren't going stampede everybody off Yarkie for a confounded *possibility!*" He turned on the biologists, seeking assurance. "That's all it is, isn't it, possibilities?"

Both scientists nodded. Peter Hubbard felt it was up to him to maintain perspective for the understandably nervous group. He said, "You are right, Mr. Scott."

Scott persisted at Elias Johnson. "For all we know, this'll be cleared up in no time when the lab really gets going here. Whole thing'll blow over! Why rouse up the town needlessly!"

Johnson answered back. "I wouldn't say needlessly from what we've been hearing!"

The fat man rejoined, "You want reporters all over the place? Don't you realize the bad name you'd give Yarkie! Who'd ever come back here if they heard we have—" he spit out the incredible words—*"killer cockroaches!"*

Elias Johnson asked the biologists, "How much time have we got?"

Peter Hubbard gauged the situation: "Evacuation *is* a big responsibility." His eyes sought Wanda Lindstrom. "I think it would be premature at this point."

His colleague's appraisal was the same. "The kind of

mutation we're guessing about would be very rare and unusual."

Scott loudly repeated *"very rare and unusual"* in Elias Johnson's ear. The old man growled, "I heard her! I ain't deaf, you know!"

Feeling more secure, Scott thrust another demand at the scientists in a militant manner. "What's this 'mutation' thing you keep talking about? Seems to me all we have here are some cockroaches and rats going nuts from new chemicals in the dump." He finished with satisfaction. "You just double check it, and we'll have this settled in no time!"

It was Wanda Lindstrom who answered the selectman, with her quiet authority. "Dr. Hubbard and I hope you are exactly right, Mr. Scott. And I agree it may not be necessary to take drastic action like clearing people out . . ." Her gray eyes bore into the man's as she added a signal word, *"Yet."* Then she said to the others, "But we had all better recognize that evacuation may become necessary if our surmise about a mutation should prove correct."

"There it goes again!" Scott muttered. Aloud he complained; "I'd still like to know what you mean by that."

Peter Hubbard intervened. To Elizabeth, it seemed he wanted to shield Wanda Lindstrom from harassment by Stephen Scott. She was embarrassed, herself, at the belligerence the man was displaying. Why, Scott was almost making it sound as if Yarkie's trouble was Wanda Lindstrom's fault. Elizabeth's admiration of the woman had been growing throughout the difficult session. She could only respect her self-possession.

Peter Hubbard was being patient with Stephen Scott. "I'm sorry if we seem to be getting ahead of ourselves, sir. I'm glad you asked about mutation, because it may not be clear to others as well." He did not wait for a response. "The word, of course, means a change. In biology it means a sudden variation in a form of life—in this case possibly the cockroaches—usually when something abnormal happens in the basic genes. Then a new form of the species is created. It might just die out—as happens with freaks such as you sometimes see in circuses. Or it sometimes persists and gives birth to more individuals with the new characteristics until a new species is, in effect, established . . ."

It was Elizabeth who interrupted, raising her hand as if she were attending a schoolroom lecture. "What causes the genes to change?"

"I don't want to get technical," Hubbard answered, "but we do know that chemicals can start a mutation chain going. We call them 'mutagens.' They work by interfering with the normal DNA bases that ordinarily control development. . . ."

Elizabeth responded thoughtfully, "And some chemical combinations in the dump may have caused 'mutagens' affecting the cockroaches?"

"That's one possibility, yes," Wanda Lindstrom answered her.

Russell Homer, following in sheer fascination, expressed an immediate thought, "But I only changed the poisons a couple of weeks ago. Could the 'mutation' happen that fast?"

Hubbard declared, "Good point. The process would have to be going on for a long time. I mean, although the first mutation would have been a sudden variation, it would have taken years for the mutated group to prevail and multiply in the numbers your reports indicate."

Almost with relief, Homer said, "Then it probably wasn't the new stuff I spread out there?"

Hubbard said, "Probably not, though it might have helped. We just don't know enough yet about what we're dealing with. Wanda and I are going to work on the hypothesis—just our guess, as we've said—that these cockroaches *have* taken a phylogenetic turn. We think they may be more like the *Hymenoptera*—that's the class of insects with strong social insects, like the ants, the bees, the wasps, the termites. There could be many causes. Maybe some radioactive material got into your dump over the years. Or some ship waste ... I can tell you that just lately at the Oak Ridge Laboratory there has been a study of a chemical called ethylnitrosourea, or 'ENU' for convenience. It's been shown to be five times more potent than radiation in causing mutations, in both plants and animals. Conceivably, we may be in a parallel situation."

Elias Johnson was leaning forward, his sea-weathered elbows bare and rough on the cedar table. The windows were beginning to rattle with a modestly rising wind, but no one in the kitchen was giving any attention to the darkening of the clouds becoming noticeable over the swelling waves outside. All eyes and ears were for Peter Hubbard and Wanda Lindstrom.

The woman now said, with force, "If these roaches have developed a social colony, then we would expect there to be a nest, a home base from which 'commands' are given. We should find a separation of activities much like termites and ants—such as worker roaches, and scout roaches, and foraging bands, all interconnected and communicating with each other constantly."

"How would they do that?" Amos Tarbell asked with a curiosity as acute as his growing dismay. He was thinking that the roach chase he and the other two men had barely escaped was devilish proof that the damn bugs were acting in concert and knew what they were doing!

His answer came from the woman biologist with an undertone of her sympathy for the group. She knew that these people were being sledgehammered by a horror they could not come to terms with. "Cockroaches" sounded so *minor* an annoyance, it was hard to accept that they might destroy an island like Yarkie.

FIVE

"Before I go on," Wanda Lindstrom said, "please understand that when I use a word like 'commands,' I don't mean it in a human sense. I dislike anthropomorphism —which assigns human-like emotions, purposes, values, and thinking to non-humans. Creatures like these roaches are sentient, of course, in that they receive and respond to stimuli. But they don't have 'emotions.' For example, people in cockroach research may say they are 'nasty' little beasts, 'aggressive,' 'hostile,' 'ugly,' 'foul.'

"All that name-calling is irrelevant, really inapplicable. Roaches are 'mean' not out of hostility but because their stomachs crave food. If nothing else is around, they'll eat another roach, even their own babies, as I said before. That doesn't make them 'cannibals.' Roaches hide, but they're not 'sly.' They conceal themselves, but it isn't 'guile.' They attack, but it's not 'anger.' The poet Tennyson said it very well: 'Nature is neither red in tooth nor claw.'"

Hubbard, who had seemed absorbed in cleaning his pipe, interposed, "We're simply talking about animals making the most efficient responses to different environments. There's solid research showing that *plants* put on courtship displays, and, as one botanist tells us, they show promiscuity, and fickleness, and even rape . . ."

Bonnie protested, *"Plants?"*

"That's right," both biologists said at the same time.

Wanda Lindstrom picked up her theme. "It only emphasizes what I've been saying. We have to keep in mind that the insects don't 'know' anything, no matter how purposeful their conduct may seem to be. They are driven by the purposes and urges of survival and propagation of the species, nothing more. Russell Homer wasn't far wrong in seeing them as robots . . ."

The young man blushed behind his Ahab beard, pleased to be singled out by this authority from Harvard.

"I myself once wrote of termites as mechanical toys wound up by a God at play. Except that too often Nature is not playing any childish game. Certainly not here!"

"Darn right!" Reed Brockshaw coughed.

Peter Hubbard expanded on Wanda Lindstrom's theme: "To put it another way, insects like these cockroaches are living out ancient, primitive compulsions, perhaps modified by mutation in certain particulars. Their activity may seem the result of 'planning,' or even of 'thinking' and 'feeling.' But there is absolutely no mental calculation as we know it. Dr. Lindstrom is right in seeing termites and their ilk as just traveling biological machines. I can think of these roaches as nothing, really, except mouths on legs. Mouths on legs," he repeated. "Which doesn't make them less dangerous!"

Wanda Lindstrom completed the thought-provoking image. "Just add sex organs, and a rudimentary nervous system, and you have Nature's whole truth about a roach."

"Makes it easier to squash them!" Bonnie Taylor muttered balefully.

Elias Johnson stayed on one track. "You both say something about their coming from a home base. If there's billions, and new eggs all the time, that nest would have to be a damn big place, wouldn't it?"

Hubbard could see the old man was thinking ahead to tracking down the source of the invasion. "Possibly, but not necessarily very big," he replied. "These cockroaches might live in layers on top of each other. That's not typical of cockroaches and I could be wrong, but we needn't necessarily look for a terribly large nest." He stopped and turned to Elizabeth. "Last night, you did tell me about some kettle holes on the island. We should certainly look into that."

Before Elizabeth could respond, Amos Tarbell was inquiring, "Would these cockroaches have something like a queen bee, then?"

Hubbard nodded. "Probably more like termites, who have a king and queen—if there's a central nest at all," he cautioned.

Johnson remained alert and inquisitive. "Okay, we know how fish school together, and the way sharks can sense vibrations a long way, and how dolphins and whales actually talk to each other. But how in Old Scratch can *bugs* do all the communicating you're talking about?"

Elizabeth said at once, "Everyone who's seen the roaches says something about their hissing noises. Could that be it?"

Hubbard shook his head. "In the species that we know do hiss—like the Madagascar roaches—it's a sign of disturbance. Actually, it's more a puffing of air out of their bodies through the spiracles, certainly not the kind of communication the captain is asking about." Hubbard stepped back. "That's another of Dr. Lindstrom's fields."

Wanda Lindstrom picked up at once, explaining, "A main way these roaches could be contacting each other would be through some specific chemicals we call phero-mones." She pronounced the last word slowly—"*pher-o-mones.*" It was a key to their understanding of what must otherwise be incomprehensible. She saw they were all attention. She could wish her college students were always as alert. But then, students' lives and livelihoods were not at stake . . .

"Pheromones are absolutely basic to insect communi-cation in cases of species social grouping," she resumed. "Mostly, the chemicals travel through the air as odors. They can be very specific. For example, one chemical pheromone can be the signal for food, another for danger, and so on. Among the termites, interestingly enough, the queen and king of a nest produce a substance that inhibits reproduction by the other insects of the group. In this way, the royal couple maintains solid control of the generations —Nature's way of continuing the specific characteristics it apparently wants to go on."

"Interesting kind of dictatorship," Reed Brockshaw mentioned.

"Nature doesn't provide many models of democracy," Hubbard commented blandly.

His observation brought to Elizabeth's mind a Churchill quote from her political science course: "Democracy is the worst of all systems, except for the alternatives . . ." It seemed true in the animal kingdom as well!

Wanda Lindstrom underscored, "The pheromones are a key method of controlling and maintaining the specialization the colony requires—the workers, the nurses, and so on.

"The chemicals are often laid down on trails, too. We mentioned the insect problem of handling food too large for an individual. Well, believe it or not, there is an insect, the fire ant, called *Solenopsis*, with a special gland to secrete a pheromone that summons its fellows to help move food it can't manage alone. This chemical happens to function by evaporation, and the workers can easily follow its smell in the air right to the prey."

"Fascinating," Bonnie said to Elizabeth, her eyes bright with interest. "I'm beginning to wish I'd taken biology!"

Hubbard disengaged his pipe. "Tell them about trophallaxis, Wanda."

She laughed at the blank looks the scientific word evoked. "Don't let that scare you. Trophallaxis happens to be a most dramatic aspect of insect communication. It means that one insect of a nest feeds another one by means of regurgitation, so whatever one insect eats travels through the colony in this form from one individual to another. In one experiment, individuals were fed a radio-active syrup outside the nest. When the brood was later examined, the stomach contents were found to be the same in every one of the insects. The radioactivity had been spread through all the members!"

Ben Dorset slapped his thigh. "Never heard a fish story to beat that in my life!"

"It's wild!" Elizabeth shook her head in wonder. New vistas of Nature and its marvelous mechanisms were opening up absorbingly, though the occasion was dismal.

Wanda Lindstrom was not through. "You can see that this process can control a colony in several ways. When one worker feels hunger or thirst, he is feeling pretty much what every other member of the society is feeling, and vice versa. Also, this common feeding helps transfer the various pheromones, meaning that all the individuals keep getting the same message."

Hubbard laughed from his seat. "Without room for misunderstanding!"

Amos Tarbell did not laugh. "My God, we're not up against cockroaches, we're up against a monster!"

Hubbard grew serious at once. "You're right, Amos! When the insects all get to doing their automatic jobs, you're talking about a fearsome machine. The fact is that insects do form superorganisms even more cunning—to be anthropomorphic for a moment—even more cunning than larger, vertebrate animals. You may be surprised to learn that termite nests are much more intricate than mammals make or even birds design. I myself have seen ant hills in the Serengeti as high as a man. For air-conditioning in the African climate, the termites or ants build two towers, one to draw cool air down into the nest, the other to discharge the warm air. And they have specialized workers whose only job is to beat their wings to keep the air circulating!"

"Man!" exclaimed Russell Homer, "I'd have got down off that tree a helluva lot faster if I'd known half of this before!"

"That's why it's important for you to know it now!" Hubbard warned. "Conceivably, these roaches can be organized like wolf packs, or worse. You know, when army ants go on their raids, they do more intricate maneuvers than wolves, and wolves are wily enough!"

Amos Tarbell nervously fingered his large belt buckle with the official county insignia. "Which leads to the obvious question. What do we do about it?"

Peter Hubbard frowned again. "We can't lose anything by going on the assumption that our theory about a mutation is correct. So let's figure there is a roach gathering place somewhere in the woods up on High Ridge, or near the dump. We try to find it."

The sheriff stood up briskly. "At the dump! Let's get out there and fire it!"

His friends were on their feet, glad again for action. "Right!"

"Good idea!"

"Let's *move!*"

"Not yet, please!" Peter Hubbard was waving his pipe at them.

They waited, wondering why Hubbard would delay the obvious.

"First of all, the new poisons have apparently changed the dump—if a nest was ever there in the first place. Second, a fire wouldn't do the job anyway. A nest would be deep in the garbage. Before fire or even smoke could reach it, every insect and animal in the dump would be out of there."

"Even with gasoline?" Amos Tarbell wanted to know.

"The top layer would burn, the rest would smolder. I'm afraid all you'd accomplish is to chase the cockroaches and rats out of the woods entirely!"

Scott blurted. "Hell, that's the last thing we want!"

"Obviously," Hubbard said.

The sheriff shifted impatiently. "Then what *do* we do?"

Johnson intervened and said, to Hubbard, "I want to get this clear. You're saying the nest wouldn't be at the dump?"

"Odds are it would be someplace else," the scientist repeated.

Johnson said to the others, "Well, we know where the kettle holes are . . ."

Tarbell made a sound of frustration, "Hell, Elias, they're all over the island. Take us a month of Sundays . . ."

Wanda Lindstrom suggested, "Why don't we start by mapping where roaches have been seen so far?"

The table buzzed agreement.

Ben Dorset voiced a common reservation. "Suppose we decide on places to look, what do we use for protection?"

Russell Homer offered, "Flashlights?"

Hubbard shook his head, "Nowhere near strong enough."

Amos Tarbell said, "Guns are no damn good, I can tell you that." His bullets and Ben's might as well have been water pistols. It was funny to be wishing the cockroaches *were* wolves! You'd have something to shoot at, something you could use your own power on! Insects, it turned out, were a hell of a bigger challenge.

Wanda Lindstrom inquired, "Do you have things like flares? Fire would keep the roaches away, I'm sure."

Craig Soaras answered, "The woods are too dry to chance fire, m'am!"

"I may have a thought," Peter Hubbard said. "Craig, you're the fire chief, I understand. Do you ever use dry-ice extinguishers?"

Craig nodded quickly. "Sure do! It's the only thing for

some kinds of fires." His voice rose with hopefulness. "You mean, we do a search carrying the tanks . . ."

"Yes. All the kettle holes, for instance."

"We'd have to get a lot more tanks."

"Is that possible?"

"I guess. From Chatham and towns around."

"Check that as soon as you can!"

"I'll phone up . . ."

Reed interrupted Craig. "Let me call Doreen a minute first. I want to be sure she keeps the kids out of the woods." The two went out quickly together.

Ben Dorset, at Peter Hubbard's side, asked anxiously, "What do we do if we find a nest?"

"Let's take one step at a time," Hubbard said. He called across to Amos Tarbell. "Are there any houses on High Ridge that may be in danger? I mean, any places sitting close to the woods without clear spaces around them?"

The sheriff needed only a moment to think. "The Laidlaws, maybe, and the Tintons for sure. I can phone them right now. Tell them we need to do more spraying around there . . ."

Elias Johnson said, "Good idea, but I think you might just be driving by, more casual, Amos. Seem like less of a fuss, and tell them Scott will put them up at his hotel until we get the all-clear. Right, Stephen?"

The fat man nodded at once. It was far better than a general evacuation.

Russell Homer came forward. "Peter," he said to Dr. Hubbard, very conscious of the first-name liberty he was taking, "you said you need more specimens. I'm sure I can get you some out at the dump."

"That may be too dangerous now," Johnson worried.

Homer had already figured he could come at the dump safely by boat, shovel some garbage into a metal can, and get back out fast. He told his plan with pride. Ben Dorset, looking out the window, shook his head. "It's getting on to blow now, Russ. I think this'll be a real bad one, and it can turn tricky up there . . ."

"I'll manage!" Russell wished he could show the two from Harvard the little lobster craft he had built himself— look, ma, no degrees! He had drawn the plans, shaped the planks, hammered the dowels, planed the boat, caulked it, engined it, and lovingly painted it bright blue with yellow stripes, like "a Portugee." The boat was underpowered, but Russell Homer knew to the last degree what it would and would not do in any wind and any sea. "You'll have your garbage!" he promised Wanda Lindstrom, not without a touch of swagger as he left the room.

His opening the kitchen door brought a blast of wind and sent flying the papers on which the sheriff had drawn a rough map to mark the roach sightings so far.

Elias Johnson pinched his nose and nodded toward the sky. "She'll be nasty in another hour or two."

Craig Soaras returned from the phone, moving fast. "Chatham'll give us all the tanks we need."

"Use my boat!" Stephen Scott said loud, wanting to be part of the action. Craig ran out to his car.

"Need any help?" Johnson called.

"Nope!"

Bonnie was at the door, tense. "Take care, Craig!"

Johnson told her, smiling, "He's the best sailor on the island."

Stephen Scott was asking the scientists, "How does dry ice stop them?"

Hubbard replied, "Like other insects, cockroaches breathe through spiracles, the little holes along their bodies. The dry ice will suffocate them and freeze them to death."

"Ha! *Good!*"

Reed Brockshaw rushed into the room from the telephone in an obvious state of panic.

Amos Tarbell asked, "Hey! What's wrong, Reed?"

"You can't believe it!" the man choked out in misery. "Doreen reminded me the Sunday School kids were supposed to have a picnic up in the woods today. Because of the 'spraying,' the new minister took them on a boating party in the *Tub* instead!"

The sheriff said encouragingly, "Well, she's a good sailor." The *Tub* was an old harbor boat-of-all work, stout and seaworthy, and the coming storm wasn't looking to be one of the *big* blows. But Tarbell understood the solicitude for his children that made Brockshaw shout furiously, "He doesn't know spit about sailing a storm!"

Elias Johnson tried to lighten the atmosphere. "Well, he's new and he didn't want to disappoint the children. We're lucky to have got George Kinray here, Reed. They might have sent us one of those ministers who try to stop the gulls from flying on Sundays . . ."

Brockshaw was in no mood for even mild levity. He shouted again, "There are times to listen to the Lord, and times to listen to the weatherman!"

ENCOUNTER

ONE

In the lighthouse kitchen, cleaning up after the lunch they had prepared for the group, Elizabeth and Bonnie were preoccupied with their own thoughts. Uppermost for Elizabeth Carr was the way Wanda Lindstrom and Peter Hubbard—alone in the laboratory again—moved in a private fraternity of their work. It was clearer than ever that she was out of her depth against Wanda Lindstrom. Fortunately, Elizabeth told herself, she had no special reason to be involved.

She forced herself to pay attention to what Bonnie, at the sink, was saying. "Do you think that really happens, Liz?" Elizabeth stopped drying dishes and looked up. Was Bonnie going to tell her it had been love at first sight with Craig Soaras?

But Bonnie's mind was not on her feelings for the handsome Portuguese. She was saying in a subdued way, "That those roaches could actually eat *people?*"

Without meaning it to be, Elizabeth's response was sharp. "How do I know? I'm not Wanda Lindstrom!"

Bonnie desisted, with understanding, only to split the kitchen air with a searing scream. A plate crashed from her hands and shattered to pieces.

"*What!*" Elizabeth cried out in alarm.

Elias Johnson and Stephen Scott burst into the kitchen. "You girls all right?"

Bonnie Taylor pointed a trembling finger at the corner of the sink and sobbed, "I thought I saw one!"

But the moving shadow was not a cockroach, large or small. A small cleaning rag had stirred in a draft coming through the warped window.

"Sorry." The woman went into her friend's arms shaking with embarrassment and relief. "I really thought—" she apologized.

Captain Johnson patted both women heartily on the backside. "We're all jittery as hell. What's the menu for dinner tonight? The men'll be hungry when they get back."

Elizabeth disentangled from Bonnie. "Reed Brockshaw brought in a nice blue this morning . . ."

"First-rate." Her grandfather tried to sound normal, "Put the pork to the beans, girls!"

TWO

Leaving the lighthouse, Sheriff Amos Tarbell belched sourly as he drove to the village. The girls had made a nice-tasting shrimp salad, but his lunch felt like lead in his middle. He was in a hurry to reach High Ridge and get the Laidlaws and Tintons out of their houses—diplomatically and tactfully—but he had to stop at the jail first. Stephen Scott, as Justice of the Peace, had ordered the release of the hoodlum jailed for nudity and drugs. The ferry for Chatham was delayed by the weather but they wanted the man on it, with a stern warning not to exercise his constitutional right to come back to Yarkie.

After releasing the prisoner, Amos Tarbell turned to the piled-up papers on his desk. Thus, he did not see the freed man turn up Main Street heading for High Ridge instead of going downhill to the ferry dock. Tarbell did not know that the three sunbathers had spotted jimson weed growing wild down at the cove. Indeed, the sheriff was not familiar with what the three experts gleefully recognized at once. Jimson weed was the latest discovery on the drug scene, better than marijuana because it was free to hand when found and—to the best of their knowledge—not even illegal, though it produced a similar high. But men like these were beyond caring about jimson's side effects, which included frightening hallucinations and irrational, dangerous conduct.

All Alex Matthews knew was that he wanted the open air after the lock-up. He was sure his friends would be hanging out at what they had jubilantly labeled their private Paw-Paw Patch. He had wondered for a while why Bo and Tony hadn't shown up at the jail. He decided they had gotten away from the fuzz and hidden in the woods. He was hazy about the whole thing. The sheriff told him he had nearly drowned, but he didn't remember anything. He'd had a great dream—like flying, only better. Being an actual fish! He could have swum under water forever. Still, some part of his head suggested he should be thankful that the sheriff had come along. It was one thing to dream a great trip like being a fish—it was another to make it real. Well, hell, everyone knew hallucinogens could be dangerous. The risk was part of the fun. Like Russian roulette, in a way. You really never did know when the shit might turn on you instead of turning you on.

He shouldn't be worrying about it, the man frowned at himself. He knew what he was doing, all the way. If there was danger, it was worth it to him. Hopheads of the world, unite! You have nothing to lose but the chains of the fools of convention!

The man broke into a run as he reached the tarred road bordering the woods. He remembered the path to the cliff and the cove. His excitement grew as he thought of the stash of Acapulco Gold his main men had waiting down there.

For a fleeting moment, he had considered stopping in the village and phoning his parents, but the hell with them, with college, with practicing Beethoven. *This* music was what he wanted—the loud rustling of the leaves in the forest, the songs of nature, like that hissing some neat animal was welcoming him with, the sound of the wind in the trees. Ah, here his gut and his head and his soul came together as he wanted! This was what he had come to Cape Cod for! He leaped on the path, coming down hard on the ground. He kicked his heels and cavorted at being out of the crumby cell. He stamped and scattered leaves as he bounded along. "God's dandruff!" he laughed at the leaves flying in the wind. The hissing, louder now, was like the whistling call of his friends.

Alex Matthews plunged into the thick of the darkening woods with a near-hysterical cry of joy: "Hey, you dudes! Ready or not, here I come!"

The roaches were ready. Suddenly, an ice pick stabbed the man in one eye, then the other, so that he never saw what it was he had been calling to in the woods. He crashed down with an expression of amazement and stupefaction that was soon the grin of a skull on a deathbed of crimson leaves.

THREE

Amos Tarbell drove north from the village, to pass the lighthouse on his way to High Ridge. Everything seemed to be in order and he did not stop. He continued eastward on the small road along the shore, which would have led him to the dump if he were not turning onto High Ridge Road at the junction.

The road climbed steeply after the southward turn to the ridge, and the sheriff could see the ocean clearly. Russell Homer's small boat was pitching and yawing in seas that were running visibly heavier now. But the craft was making steadily for the beach fringing the dump. Good boy, Russell, the sheriff considered. He might not be the brightest fellow on Yarkie, but he was a damned dependable one to have on any team.

Good team for a crisis all round, the sheriff contemplated. He'd take sailors for a tough job anytime, men who knew how to keep cool when things got hot. Take Craig Soaras. Hard to beat Portugee blood on the water, and a top-notch bunkie anywhere. He seemed to have calf eyes for Liz Carr's black friend, and that might not be too good. There was more than water between Yarkie Island and Cambridge. But it was none of anyone else's business, if that's what was simmering.

Reed Brockshaw, another winner. He was doing all the work on the marina, everyone knew. Scott ought to give him an interest. Probably would, too, before they were through. If they ever got through anything again after this spooky cockroach affair.

Ben Dorset. Ben was the one no one would have predicted good of. He had run to Boston with his family inheritance and blown it. But he'd come to his senses and back to Yarkie, and now a good right-hand police officer. Couldn't tell how people would turn out. Take Liz and her friend—who'd ever dream two Radcliffe seniors would get down on their knees scrubbing those filthy lighthouse floors. They had everything spick and shining, never pulled rank. The Johnson blood showed. The other girl? Bonnie Taylor sure had a sunny disposition—until Sharky, anyway. He'd seldom seen anyone so ruffled.

Well, they all had plenty to be upset about, didn't they? Lucky there was Elias Johnson, solid as rock. Simply his presence always made a difference anywhere in town. People thought and spoke differently when he was around. That was the real definition of leadership. America's unsung heroes, men like Elias.

Gravel, not yet settled into the road's tar, spit up at his car, making a kind of castanet rhythm to his jiggling thoughts.

Luckiest of all right now was that Elias had that professor son-in-law, able to snap fingers and send two expert biologists to Yarkie so fast. Right now, nobody would know which way to turn without them.

Not that he knew yet what to do, really. Amos Tarbell let out another sour belch. Sure learned a lot about "The Strange Universe of Insects," as one of those TV shows might put it. It *was* a whole different universe, at that. There was an unreal, outer-space feeling to the entire scene on Yarkie now. "Invasion of Space Ships"—hell, that wouldn't hold a candle to what was really, actually, in damn true fact *happening!* "Invasion of Cockroaches!" "The Crawling Killers!" It would sound giddy-pated if it wasn't so swear-on-the-Bible true!

The police car came up higher where the trees were thin, and the sheriff could see out to the ocean and the dump again. Homer's craft was almost at the dump spit now—but far out to sea behind it there was another boat. Tarbell stopped the car to look through his binoculars. The Sunday School picnic! The wind was coming at the old *Tub* dangerously. She seemed to be wallowing. Reed might be right about the minister. Any savvy sailor would have turned back, would have come along the north shore with the northeast wind, to head back down to the village harbor. But the *Tub* was plainly aiming to come around the east side. George Kinray seemed to be headed for the South Beach pier, probably. That would take expert handling today, especially when they were by Dickens Rocks.

That was a cruel finger of huge, sharp-cut boulders that had poked holes in the ribs of many an unwary craft in just such a no'-theaster.

Well, the older boys on board the *Tub* were first-rate seamen, and the boat was well out. He guessed she'd be okay if they kept the wind from blowing her closer to shore.

But the sheriff reached for his radio. Wouldn't do any harm to have the Coast Guard on Chatham keep an eye out for the *Tub* in case of trouble.

Amos Tarbell drove along as he radioed. Even in the cloudy day now, the Ridge was beautiful in his eyes. The sun was filtering a brown-orange color through the clouds, and the spreads of trees stood bronze in the unusual light. Almost the color of the cockroaches. The man didn't want the image, but it persisted. He tried to think instead of how the trees needed rain, but all he saw was the army of insects, that incredible mob of cockroaches that had chased after him and Ben and Russ at the grove. It was hard to believe he wouldn't wake up and find he had dreamed it all.

Despite the wind and the now glowering sky—though still no rain—the usual High Ridge serenity was all around him. The trees—beginning to whip about—now blocked his view of the ocean, but always up here he had the sense of the sea, as well as the stretching sky. There was a sense of great spaces extending all about. It increased the feeling of isolation of tiny Yarkie in the midst of the ocean. In a storm like the one brewing now, the land seemed even more precious to him—safe harbor, home. It would be that way again! he vowed.

The Laidlaw place was lovely, chalk-white against the storm-darkened pitch pine. It made a landscape out of a Wyeth painting, Tarbell thought, though today the scene was somehow disturbing. The white railing circling the widow's walk atop the house seemed more like skeletal bone than wood.

Tarlell shook his head impatiently. It was no time for woolgathering or omen-spooking. He told himself there was every reason to be on edge, but even the eerie bronze color bathing High Ridge was no cause for him, of all people, to get his heart thumping like a kid scared by a Halloween witch.

He put his mind instead to the Laidlaws, as he turned into their driveway. They had been on Yarkie for only fifteen years, which made them newcomers. But they helped the local charities and, more important, they never pretended to belong. That made them welcome. A paradox, the sheriff smiled to himself. Typically Yarkie.

He sat for a moment eyeing the house the Laidlaws rented from Stephen Scott. Then he knocked on the gracious white door politely. Tact and diplomacy. Get them out without scaring them. No answer. He tried the knob. Inside, the house was as quiet as it was cool. The polished bannister post sported its ivory "mortgage button" to proclaim that this house was owed to no bank. He wondered if that custom existed in other parts of the country.

He called upstairs. No answer. He sniffed. No smell of cooking, either. They might have driven to town for broiled fish at Elvira Soaras's cafe—Craig's mother cooked the tastiest meal anywhere on Cape Cod.

Outside, the sheriff paused for a moment, looking from the empty garage across the spreading lawn to the elegance of the building—the fantail window over the door, the Greek pilasters, all the trimming done with craftsmen's passion for perfect detail. It was a waste of breath to say they didn't build them that way anymore. And this lawn that generations of Scotts had tended. It wasn't easy to grow this lush a green carpet around a Yarkie house in the salt air. The gardener had done well with the flowers, too.

Portulacas, and the pink petunias like his own wife favored, and hollyhocks, with columbine and daffodils. The plants seemed to be opening in expectation of the promised rain. The colors of the petals seemed somehow brighter in the dark day than they did in bright sun. Another paradox, but it was the contrast, he supposed.

The wind was blowing leaves off the elm trees almost as if it were already fall. Well, August did bring autumn pretty early up here, especially in a long dry spell.

At the loveliness of the spot, anger shook Amos Tartell. This beauty and the decent people who lived in it should not be at the threat the scientists were talking about! Rampaging cockroach armies on Yarkie!

At the edge of the garage wall a motion caught his eye. His heart turned over. *One of them?* It disappeared around the corner. Tarbell tiptoed after, holding his breath, squinting at the cement floor. *There!* A cockroach at least five inches long, like a loathsome living cigar, was vibrating its antennae up at him. Violent hatred churned in the officer. He remembered what the scientists had said about these bugs not having emotions, but this lurking roach seemed to be daring him, even taunting him. Along with its acrid odor, he took in a maliciousness from the creature that iced his blood.

Tarbell looked around alertly. Was this a vagrant, or were there others? No, this bastard seemed alone.

In a reflex of his own, the man hopped forward. He landed on the roach with all his weight. Even through his thick sole, he felt the shell cracking and smashing. It was a noise as soul-satisfying to him as it was abhorrent. In a cursing fury, the man kept turning his shoe on the floor, wanting to grind the creature out of existence.

When finally Amos Tarbell looked down, he glared at splinters of shell flattened in a disgusting mash of dirty liquid and innards.

Disgusting. Like the odor of the dead cockroach, stronger now. The smell. Tarbell recalled what the scientists had said about the phero-somethings that were signals among them. This acidy stink might be a cockroach SOS to muster the tribe. He'd better get the hell out anyway. He wiped the bottom of his shoe furiously on the grass, kicking back and forth. He hurried to the police car.

He drove off with a last, grimacing glance at the large circular stain the huge cockroach had made. Good! He swore. No stinking lousy *cockroaches* were going to beat *people*, no matter how damn smart or "mutated" or whatever else the hell those miserable bugs thought they were! Craig would be bringing the dry-ice extinguishers soon, and they'd sweep the woods with all of Yarkie's volunteer firemen. They'd find the nest and destroy it before this day was over!

To his horror, Amos Tarbell felt a stab of pain on the calf of his leg. "What the hell!" he snorted. He jammed on the brakes, flung the door open and yanked up his trouser leg. There, like a leech, was a great roach clinging to his skin and sucking his blood. With a snarl, the sheriff plucked it off and flung it as far as he could—but immediately sorry. He should have stomped it, like the other one, instead of letting it live to attack someone else!

The thought came to him that it might be even more important than anyone had thought to get to the Laidlaws *fast*. Tarbell started to swing into the driver's seat, but stopped. His keen eyes searched the car interior. There had been one scurvy bastard waiting to ambush him. You couldn't take any chances with these sly bugs. You had to be as careful as they were cunning!

The man saw nothing now. The two roaches had probably been just stays, after all. He waited a moment, searching again, then got in the car warily, and drove off. But his eyes kept sweeping the interior, so that he almost slammed into the big elm tree where the road curved to the Laidlaw place.

FOUR

Russell Homer landed on the dump beach sooner and harder than he had intended. A surge of wind and twist of wave had caught his boat and spun it around like a cork, literally catapulting it out of the sea onto the sand. It landed a long way above the water line. Homer hopped out, unhurt, but worried that the impact might have sprung the boards. He didn't see how he was going to launch the boat again by himself, and feared that even if he could, the riptide he now saw running would capsize him in a second.

But he had to try to keep his pledge, no matter how difficult or dangerous. Without further thought, Homer grabbed the metal can and shovel he had prepared in the boat. His eyes fell on his old jalopy, but his heart dropped again. No help as a way out. The automobile was on the other side of the dump, and with the cockroaches and rats still in the heap, he'd never make it across alive.

And the huge roaches were there, all right! Suddenly, the surface of the garbage was alive with them. No rats, Homer noticed. The rodents had apparently been eaten or driven out—just as the woods, come to think of it, now showed no sign of the island's deer and other animals. He must remember to tell that to the Harvard professors.

Homer set up his metal can, preparing the cover for a quick closing. The son of a bitch roach giants were facing him as if daring him to approach. Their odor, mixed with the reek of the dump, was choking him. He had come away too fast to remember the nose mask he usually wore at work. Before the man's startled and dread-filled eyes, the roach population began to merge into a single shape. The carapaces, looking like a fused metal shield in the graying afternoon, seemed to form one huge surface, like a broad exo-skeleton of a single organism. The form flowed into a wide circle, and Homer could not help thinking that it was like a drilling band on a football field at halftime, especially when—as if at a baton signal—lines of roaches began to radiate out from the central body. No majorettes now, Homer thought with a shudder. These were tentacles of death coming after him.

The roach-creature seemed exactly like an octopus now. From its thick core, a dozen "tentacles" were dipping and soughing over the tin cans, broken bottles, raw refuse. They were reaching for him, moving menacingly over the heap. Russell Homer realized with a jolt of new terror that the creature had an intention as purposeful as if it contained the "brain" the scientists had described. It was as if he could read its "mind"—it "planned" to back him to the sea where he could no longer escape, and then it would wind its suffocating "arms" around his throat and choke him to death. It would break his ribs, suck his blood just as an octopus would. And, according to the scientists, the roach teeth would even grind up his bones, leaving no evidence . . .

Russell Homer sprang for his shovel. In seconds, he had his can half-filled with garbage containing scores of the great roaches. He clamped the cover over the mess, and stood alertly searching for an escape route.

The "octopus" began to move at him faster. The young man swallowed with bitterness and fresh terror. Was he really trapped? He realized that, much as he didn't want to die, and certainly not this way, his deeper pain was that he would be letting his friends down. Yarkie had been good to him when he needed help. This would have been one way to repay. But with his usual bungling, he had not prepared well enough in advance, had not planned against the contingencies. Damn the storm. Damn the boat for not having stronger engines. Damn the—

The man stopped wasting energy on his cursing. He could see an expectant shiver run along the whole body of roaches as the leaders' antennae went into a frenzied wiggling. They were signaling, it was plain. *More meat, more fresh blood here*—come and get this stupid prey that had stumbled so obligingly into their power.

The central mass of the roaches heaved, and the fattening tentacles swished back and forth over the garbage faster now. Homer was sure he would have felt their fanning of the air if it weren't for the louder noise of the wind and new thunder in the waves pounding the beach behind him.

One advancing roach tentacle had him backed all the way to the water. It gave Homer the idea that he might be safe after all. Roaches could not survive even shallow water. He might be able to run along the beach in the water until there was a chance to break away. He held the can to his chest stubbornly and took off, racing desperately and awkwardly with his burden against the sucking of the sand and water.

And all hope was slammed out of him by a battering wave he did not see. It came surging out of the storm and knocked him face-forward on the shore. The insects raced for him at once, alerted by the thud of his body. As he lay on the wet sand, half-stunned for an instant, he saw them inches from his nose. Their little eyes were balefully on him. Their mandibles were like a sharpening of knives as they twitched forward seeking his flesh. Their antennae, reaching, reaching, reaching, seemed like the fangs of snakes ready to stab poison into his face.

Homer was on his feet and plowing along the beach, still holding desperately to the can. The roach tentacles switched about madly, cheated, but his pounding feet told the "octopus" where he was. The great roach body started after the man with remarkable speed of its own. Loaded with the heavy can, it was hard to outdistance the roaches despite his athletic strength. He thought of abandoning the can, but if he dropped it, he might as well not return at all.

Luck was on Russell Homer's side. He had forgotten about the Yarkie bulldozer. It was standing like a hulking, patient animal of burden where he had left it—could it have been only yesterday morning? But Homer saw that he was not yet out of danger. As if the cockroaches realized now that he had a means of escape, many of them left off crawling and spread wings to fly. The strong winds made it difficult for them to reach the man, gave him more time in the savage, deadly contest. Homer leaped to his bulldozer seat just as a flying roach made for his right eye. He batted it away, and another. He had a moment to start the motor, disregarding a jabbing sting in his left cheek. He thanked God for the reliability of the powerful engine. The explosions frightened off other flying cockroaches that had started to circle his head. With one hand, Russell Homer plucked the clinging roach off his face. With his other he ground the gear shift into low. There was a stab in the palm of his hand. A giant roach was on the gear knob. It had brought blood, but he uttered a happy shout in his vindictiveness—he had smashed it dead.

He was far from home free yet. Flying roaches resumed their attack. Russell Homer poured the power to the great machine, and it lumbered blindly over the garbage pile while he squeezed his eyes shut and clamped both hands over his face. The stings and bites didn't matter. He had the specimens and the garbage for laboratory analysis. He had been able to lift the can into the bulldozer scoop, and it was riding safely in front of him now. Lest it roll out, he wanted to lift the scoop higher, but reaching for the control would mean risking half of his face. He could feel the roaches climbing all over his hands. It was a chance he had to take. With a flashing motion, he hit the scoop lever and heard the hydraulic piston go to work.

The can was lifted safely, and Homer let out a cry of victory—only to swallow it as the bulldozer began to stall. The extra power he had called on was stalling the motor; there had been no time for warming up. He worked the throttle and clutches with all his skill. If the machine died on him now, he was a goner for sure. Huge roaches were flying all about him; more and more were filling the air behind the trundling behemoth.

The motor sputtered again, and died. The machine halted. Homer's hands were soaked with dripping blood, his fingers slipped on the ignition key as he tried frenziedly to get the engine going. There was a sputtering, and his hope flared, but then silence except for the maddened hissing of the attackers all around him now.

Homer's raging temptation was to slam at the wheel and kick the throttle as if the bulldozer were alive and had purposely let him down. Instead, he murmured at the machine. It was a huge and hulking contraption, but he had always referred to it as his baby. He forced himself to work it gently, almost cooing to it, disregarding the roaches biting at his cheeks. Finally, pressing the accelerator tenderly, he brought the engine to life. Its new roar shook the whole machine, and the man could sense confusion in the swirling insects as the great coughing vibrations blasted the air. It came to Homer exultantly that for the roaches the noise and the diesel fumes pouring out now were what a savage cyclone would seem to a man caught in its funnel. The roach swarm veered away as Homer gingerly increased the power. He continued to keep his eyes glued shut against the insects still probing his face but he could feel the machine climbing up the garbage and he knew exactly where he was. Steering with one hand, Homer pulled away more of the avid, clinging insects. He could feel that he was tearing away bits of his own flesh with each roach he flung out of the cab. For the first time since he started the job, Russell Homer was glad for the stinking fumes the motor discharged. The thick smoke was blowing directly into the cab. It made him choke, but it kept the roaches at bay, and dazed the ones he was pulling off like ticks.

The bulldozer rode mightily over the garbage and started majestically down the far side of the heap. Wreathed in the engine exhaust, feeling no more pricks and bites, Homer dared a glimpse at his hands. He saw the blood and open bites, and felt sharp pain, but no roaches! His fingers flew to his cheeks, his ears, his hair. No roaches! He could thank God, too, for his beard. People had smiled at it, he knew, but today it had protected him.

The man looked back. No roaches were following the bulldozer as it clanked on to the road. The noise and the exhaust had apparently discouraged them. There was easier food around than a tough salt like Russell Homer, he crowed to himself, laughing aloud with relief and accomplishment. He sat like a lord on his yellow mount and shouted his joy as he steered the banging contraption toward the lighthouse. He could hear the metal can bouncing in the scoop, and knew it was safe. He had whacked the cover on so tight they'd need a crowbar to get it off! He had been needlessly reckless, Homer grinned to himself, but here he was rolling down the highroad bringing home the terrible bacon. The lighthouse was just ahead. He looked back at his boat. It was taking a beating. By the time he could get back to it, there might be nothing left. But it was worth it, the man told himself. He was keeping his promise!

FIVE

Deirdre and Tom Laidlaw had decided to walk the mile to the Tintons for their jeep instead of calling one of the Scott cabs that served Yarkie in the summer. The Tinton phone hadn't answered, and they wanted their car for shopping. The coming storm was threatening rain, but they didn't mind getting wet—it was part of the change of pace Yarkie meant to them.

In some ways they enjoyed the wind-blown days like this quite as much as the sunny mild ones. They liked the teeth of the wind, reminding of the sting of salt spray when they sailed. On idyllic Yarkie, it took the advent of foul weather to remind one that outside there was a world full of evil, crime, and catastrophe. Far away, for the summer, at least.

The couple walked toward the Tintons hand in hand. All winter long the demands of their separate jobs in publishing left them little time for each other, and the Yarkie weeks were a precious renewal. They took comfort in and from each other, and after thirty years of marriage found the quiet sharing as important as passion had once been.

Deirdre Laidlaw sniffed the air and wrinkled her aristocratic nose in distaste. "The wind must be coming off the dump today."

Tom Laidlaw agreed. "Awful stink." He ran his hand through his graying hair, and looked around with easy, blue eyes that held a deep appreciation of the woods. "Maybe it's that spray the firemen were warning us about earlier."

"What were they spraying against?"

"Tent caterpillars, maybe."

Deirdre nodded her handsome head. "Lots of them this year, aren't there?"

Her husband smiled at her fondly. "Wouldn't be Eden without some pain in the arse, would it?"

"Pain in the arse that the Tintons kept our car last night."

"I'm enjoying the walk."

"Notice, no birds, Tom," the woman said questioningly, stopping to listen.

"Isn't it always that way when a storm blows up?"

"I don't really know."

"I suppose we ought to notice things like that. It's the difference between really belonging and not."

She laughed, an attractive chuckle. "I don't mind being in between. Best of all possible worlds on both sides."

"I love you for your wisdom," her husband said, squeezing her arm.

"And here I thought it was for my wit."

"I like your tits, too."

"I said 'wits,'" she mock-scolded, and halted again, listening again. "Tom, the past couple of days, the birds have stopped all of a sudden, even though the weather's been perfect. I *have* noticed . . ."

"Elias Johnson and Stephen Scott will now give you the key to Yarkie Village."

The woman's usually cool face clouded over. "I'm not joking. It gives me a queasy sense that something's not quite right."

Tom Laidlaw was genuinely surprised. His wife was known for her equanimity. But he smiled and said, "Because you can't set your watch by the Yarkie birds?"

The woman took a deep breath and changed her mood. She doffed her tam-o'-shanter, and smiled back to her husband. "Because I'm a witch."

"I'll have a word with those birds, anyway," her husband promised.

They walked on in silence toward the Tinton place,

hearing distant summer thunder, and observing the sky flaring with lightning far out over the ocean.

"I hope it rains soon," Deirdre Laidlaw said. "Last night, Stephen said he'd seldom seen so long a dry spell.—I hope there's no trouble at the Tintons."

"Trouble?"

"I don't like their not answering their phone."

"They can be taking a walk, can't they?"

"Not with the hangover Harvey must be nursing this morning."

"Holier than thou . . . ? Not like you, dear."

"No," Deirdre Laidlaw said sincerely. "It's part of this feeling I have. I don't know. A sort of premonition . . ."

Her husband stopped and studied her questioningly from under lowered brows. "You're not given to that sort of nonsense, Dee."

Her frown was uneasy. "Must be the storm." Her shoulders shrugged as if without her volition. She forced a smile. "You know about weather changing the ionization in the air, and all that."

"We've been through storms before and your ionization never acted up this way . . ."

"Well, Harvey was so drunk, and Blanche was so upset . . ."

Tom Laidlaw laughed. "So you expect a scene of mayhem and murder at their house?"

"Oh, don't be silly, Tom." Her voice went vague, uncertain. "I just have a sense that there's some kind of trouble around . . ." There was puzzlement as well as worry in the eyes she turned to him. "It's the smell!" she said. Until she said the words she hadn't realized the truth of her statement. The repulsive scent brought out of the trees by the wind seemed aimed at her, touched some primal response of dread she could not identify or name. "Let's go back to the house!" she said suddenly.

"Hey," Tom Laidlaw said, "you're shaking!" Anxiety turned his mouth down. "I've never seen you like this, Dee!"

"I've never felt like this!" she said, with an annoyance addressed not at the man so much as at the strange feelings suddenly churning inwardly.

He spoke heartily. "We're almost there. I'll drive you down for coffee and one of Elvira's omelettes. Fix you right up!"

"I want to go home," his wife said softly. "I don't want to see the Tintons this morning!"

Tom Laidlaw's back went up. "You're being damn silly, Dee! The hell with the smell—something died in the woods, is all. No reason for hysterics, is it? You go on back if you want. I'm getting the jeep, and going to the cafe."

Deirdre Laidlaw uttered a deep sigh and put her hand on her husband's elbow. "I *am* being hysterical, aren't I? Sorry. I'm sure you're right about the stink. I keep forgetting that so much of Yarkie is really nature in the raw. We don't have to see the Tintons anyway, do we? Just get the car and leave."

"Exactly."

They walked on in silence. Deirdre Laidlaw said something under her breath.

"What?"

"I still wonder why they didn't answer the phone."

Tom Laidlaw's voice thickened with irritation. "Because they want to sleep late, or took off for Boston—how the hell do I know?"

There was challenge in his wife's turning face. "All I said was I hope there's no trouble there."

"What kind of trouble could there be?"

"That awful quarrel in front of everybody . . ."

"None of our damn business, eh?"

"It is when they keep our damn jeep," Deirdre Laidlaw said irritably.

"Well, there it is," her husband pointed ahead. "Safe and sound."

Their car was waiting under an elm tree, and the wind had driven leaves in a thick layer over the hood of the engine and the roof. "Leafed in," the woman laughed.

Deirdre Laidlaw got into the jeep on the passenger side, and tapped the driver's wheel with an unpainted fingernail. "Come on, then. I want that omelette you promised."

The man got in and slammed the door, liking the solid sound of the well-fitted metal. Then he asked his wife, "What's that?"

"What's what?"

Tom Laidlaw pointed to the floor beside the woman's shoe. A roach was resting there.

Deirdre Laidlaw said calmly, "Look at the *size* of that goddamn cockroach!"

Her husband made a flipping gesture with the back of his large, freckled hand. "Scrootch it out of here."

The woman screwed up her face. "You do it, hero mine!"

Her husband leaned across her lap.

"Don't get fresh." She slapped at his hand. "You won't respect me in the morning."

"Ouch!" Tom Laidlaw cried out, clutching his ear. He came up so suddenly he banged his head on the steering wheel. "What the hell!"

"My *God!*" Deirdre Laidlaw shrieked at the same time. Blood was running down the side of her husband's face and she saw an enormous cockroach, easily four inches long, disappearing, *disappearing* into her husband's right ear!

The woman swiveled to him with a gesture of help, but her hands remained frozen, with her fingers curved before his face as if she were holding an invisible bowl. She was looking at another huge roach biting into her husband's right eye.

In the next instant, she was screaming with a different horror. First there was a fluttering at her forehead like a large moth's wings; then an excruciating needle going through her face, a fire lasering into her skull.

While she could see out of one eye, Deirdre Laidlaw had to live with the inconceivable sight of great cockroaches coating her husband's face, a vicious, quivering crust of filth. Feeling blood on her own face, she knew the misshapen creatures were eating at her flesh just as she witnessed them shearing away her husband's nose. She did not want to die, but she was grateful for death's release from the horror.

SIX

Sheriff Amos Tarbell heard the cries before he saw the cars. What he witnessed as he swerved into the Tinton driveway hit him like a hammer, so that the police car skidded out of control and banged into a tree opposite the Laidlaw jeep. His head hit the wheel and he felt blood starting. He was too stunned even to reach for his handkerchief. He sat there with blood streaming onto his tan uniform, watching with bulging eyes the impossible spectacle of Deirdre and Tom Laidlaw being devoured by cockroaches.

Sitting upright in the jeep, the two looked like unnatural wax figures out of a horror museum. Their eyes were gone. They stared back at the sheriff from blank sockets from which gore was trickling. Right before his eyes, their skulls were being cleaned of muscle and flesh by a thousand scurrying bugs. Still-living shreds of their skin quivered with raw nerves, looked like white worms squirming over the bone-white of their scalped skulls.

The Laidlaws, before Sheriff Amos Tarbell's eyes, looked like two cadavers in an anatomy class held in hell. The bloodied bones made a gruesome tableau of skeletons driving a jeep.

The word "piranha" ribboned through Tarbell's brain like a red-hot wire. Clearly, these people had been taken by surprise, had been absolutely helpless, unable to defend themselves in any way . . .

So this was the vicious, the inconceivable, explanation of the island's mysterious disappearances! This was the meaning of Stephen's reluctance, his questioning about roaches eating leather belts, clothing, and the rest!

The sheriff was seeing it for himself now, understanding the fate of the missing Tintons, of Hildie, of her girls —and, by God, of those men off the ferry! This is what would have happened to himself, Dorset, and Homer if they had not escaped the insect army chasing them when they had the rabbit trap.

Bile was in the man's mouth, but this was no time to be sick. The sheriff clearly heard the clicking of the roaches' hard mandibles and teeth, the hissing of their tumbling battle to get at the human flesh. Above all, he heard the grinding of what he had been unable to believe when the scientists had described it—how insects like these roaches could eat into bone, chew through it, saw it and cleave it and splinter it. Could grind it into powder that they lapped up.

He was watching it happen! He wiped the blood that was dribbling into his own eyes. He batted a roach away from his face. He ground into reverse and shot the police car around, spraying gravel on two wheels.

The Laidlaws were beyond help, that was tragically plain. Before the demons got at him, he had to get to the lighthouse with his terrible discovery. The unspeakable theories of the Harvard scientists were proving correct! Yarkie Island might have to call in the Coast Guard, the National Guard, the whole damn United States Army to stamp out—to *try* to stamp out—the invasion of the murdering roaches.

HAVOC

ONE

Peter Hubbard was bent over a microscope when Elizabeth Carr came out of the kitchen into the laboratory. With the lunch things tidied up, Bonnie had gone to lie down for a rest. The Yarkie men were all off on their assignments. The expected storm was in higher gear, rattling the windows now, nearing full strength. The woman could see the driven sea beating at the shore outside. The waves had become threatening breakers, and the gale was whirling sand and leaves all around the creaking lighthouse. Sand was gritty on the floor in every room, sifting in through the cracks everywhere. But there was no rain yet.

Elizabeth asked, "Where's Wanda?"

Hubbard spoke without taking his eyes from the instrument. "She's phoning Chatham, trying to reach Craig. We need some special supplies." He explained no more. The harsh crescendo of the wind brought his head up. The building was machine-gunned with shells and stones whipped by the storm. He asked anxiously, "Can Craig get back in this weather?"

Elizabeth smiled confidently. "He's got the power under him and the know-how on top. This isn't half as bad as it sometimes gets. He'll be here, with whatever you asked for."

"You people are terrific," Peter Hubbard applauded

genuinely. Elizabeth noted that he included her among the Yarkie group. Well, he was right.

What the two scientists had already done with the long-unused room reflected their own special teamwork. Every kind of glass apparatus was set out neatly on the scrubbed tables. Liquids of different colors were boiling everywhere, sending curlicues of steam over the retorts and jars that rested on tripods above Bunsen burners. Tubing of glass and rubber twisted and turned in intricate patterns. From titration apparatus, which Elizabeth recognized from her sophomore lab work, colorless drops were falling slowly into a receptacle of liquid turning darker purple.

On shelves along one wall, empty flasks and cages awaited the specimens the scientists hoped the men would bring in.

Elizabeth returned Hubbard's praise. "You and Wanda have done a fantastic set-up here."

"We've got the reagents ready," the biologist commented. "We'll be able to analyze the poisons, for one thing." He gestured at some of the boiling flasks. "And Wanda is trying to determine the pheromonic possibilities . . ." Hubbard left his stool and approached Elizabeth. "We ought to have a talk, you and I."

Elizabeth looked away evasively. "About what?"

He smiled. "Something's wrong with *our* pheromones."

His manner disturbed the woman, and she moved to leave. "I don't want to interfere with your work."

He said promptly, "I'm talking about the freeze you've been giving me, Elizabeth."

"Freeze?"

"Aside from your travelogue about Yarkie last night, you've conspicuously managed to avoid a direct word."

"I'm sorry," she said. "I didn't mean to be unfriendly." But the coldness of her voice belied the sentiment. Elizabeth felt stiff and uncomfortable. The warmth in Peter

Hubbard's voice was confusing in a situation already too confused. She wished Wanda Lindstrom would come back into the lab. To keep the conversation impersonal, Elizabeth pointed to the roach specimen the biologists had taken from the rabbit and placed in a covered jar. "It's amazing, isn't it?"

The misbegotten bug was scuttling about, unpausing. Its antennae were straight up, like two trolley poles reaching for an invisible power line. The roach kept trying to climb up the side of the container. Sliding back, it sometimes landed on its back. Then its feet and antennae and mandibles went into a frenzy; its body arched in spasms of instinctual determination until, somehow, without any real purchase on the slippery glass, it regained its normal position. Shivers ran up the woman's spine. That damned thing will climb out of there yet! she thought with goose pimples.

"No," Peter Hubbard smiled grimly, watching her. "It won't manage. Don't worry."

"I'm worried about the *men*," Elizabeth told him. "Suppose they do find a nest. Won't they be in terrible danger?"

"I've given them specific instructions. They're not on 'search and destroy,'" he said. "They're on 'search and reconnaissance.'" He used the phrase from his Air Force service. "But what I want to tell you is how glad I am we had a chance to be together on the beach last night."

Surprised, Elizabeth turned away from the roach flask. She remained silent. Her heart was beating faster than she wanted it to.

"I thought about you for a long time—" Hubbard stopped and looked deeply into her gray eyes. "I'm glad I'm seeing you here, this way, instead of in your father's house."

Elizabeth was suddenly and unhappily conscious of how much she looked like a housemaid, hair tied up,

161

apron around her slacks. She knew what he meant. In Cambridge, she had been just Professor Carr's "kid." Now Peter Hubbard was seeing her for the first time as the woman she had become, a woman of her own mind and values.

His gaze was penetrating, and he was saying, "As a scientist I prefer things orderly, Liz. I don't like false theories cluttering up the place."

Elizabeth found herself more uncertain and perplexed. What was he driving at?

"Some people call me blunt," he smiled at her. "And especially right now we don't have time for beating around bushes, do we?"

Elizabeth nodded, though she wasn't sure what she was agreeing with.

Hubbard blew pipe smoke toward the flask holding the roach and watched the insect shake its antennae as its atmosphere thickened through the air holes in the cover. "So I would like to tidy up our relationship, yours and mine . . ."

"Do we have 'a relationship'?" Elizabeth let herself smile. She untied her apron and tossed it onto a chair. Her hands pushed back her long brown hair. She knew her cheeks were flushed, and suddenly she didn't mind.

The man brought her up with a frank, unexpected declaration. "Liz, I am not now nor have I ever been in love with Wanda Lindstrom!"

Elizabeth was shocked. His was a directness indeed, beyond any preparation or anticipation. He was demanding, "You have believed that, haven't you?"

Elizabeth Carr's head came up and she answered him with her own gathered force. "I have never considered it any of my business."

"Well, I would like to make it your business."

Elizabeth's heart raced anew as Peter Hubbard's words

flowered in her mind. He was adding, "We are going to see a lot of each other, not just here but when we get back to Cambridge." He was blowing smoke at the cockroach again. Elizabeth thought it was the damnedest way for a man and a woman to be reaching toward each other. "If you want to," he said quietly.

She did not hesitate. She could be as honest as he was. He was right. If she had misunderstood about Wanda Lindstrom, there wasn't enough time, or energy, in life itself for hypocrisy now. "I want to, Peter. I want to very much."

She hoped he would kiss her. She had feared he might in the moonlight the night before, but she would welcome it now. She was glad when he brought her to his chest, and she yielded in a quick confession of her long-suppressed feeling for him.

Peter Hubbard's lips on Elizabeth Carr's young mouth were firm and tender. His kiss stirred the woman in ways she had for years forbidden herself to imagine. Now it was real. Her own lips let the man know her emotion.

In their embrace, neither one heard the door open.

"Excuse me!" The door slammed shut before they could separate. It had been Wanda Lindstrom's voice, clearly shocked and distressed.

Hubbard kept his arm around Elizabeth. "It's all right, Liz. Wanda is a good friend and a good colleague, but she knows it's nothing more."

Elizabeth rubbed a finger over her mouth doubtfully. "This won't bother your work—?"

"Nothing will interfere with Wanda's work. It's one reason she's so great at it."

The door opened again. The biologist entered as if for the first time, except that her face was ashen. Business-like, she said to Hubbard, "I couldn't find Craig, but the police chief at Chatham will try to get the material we want. He'll reach Craig at the fire department with it."

"Good!" Hubbard said, equally businesslike. "Thank you."

Elizabeth hurried to the kitchen door, picking up her apron.

Dr. Lindstrom called after her quickly. "You don't have to leave, Elizabeth!"

But Elizabeth found herself deeply disquieted. She made an excuse. "I don't like being in the same room with that cockroach. It gives me the willies." Having made the statement, she realized it was more than an excuse. Every time she looked at the endlessly scurrying insect she felt a malign force emanating from the flask. Peter could say all he wanted to about the creatures being mindless automatons, but she intuited a power that would not rest until it had its way with them, all of them.

Wanda Lindstrom gave her a smile. "It won't get out, Elizabeth."

They were interrupted by the appearance of Elias Johnson, returning from the village. The noise of the wind and the blowing sand against the building had masked the sound of his engine pulling up. Taking off his mackintosh, he snorted, "Wish it would get to the rain! Damn wind blowing to tear your hair out, but those tarnation clouds won't let go!" He came to them rubbing his gnarled hands. "Anything new here?"

Hubbard answered crisply, "Yes, Elias. Wanda and I have done some more work on the specimen. It's no ordinary roach. We have got a mutation, without question. It's not one of those horror-movie inventions—these insects remain quite close to normal. The changes are well within the parameters of minor adaptive alterations, like the greater power in the leg and body muscles, the stronger mandibles and teeth. What really gives us concern is that these changes are coupled with a much more mature nervous system than anything we have ever seen in this or related species."

The old man sat down heavily, and passed his hand over his forehead. "Everything you said has been going around in my head over and over, but I still can't believe it."

Hubbard understood the man's difficulty in coming to grips with the extraordinary development. To impress him with the enormous number of biological "curiosities," he added another textbook fact, "You know, Elias, there are some ants with so strong a bite that if you try to pull them away, the ant's head will separate from its body before its teeth will let go!"

The old eyes widened. "Thunderation!"

Elizabeth gasped, "I never heard of that!"

The scientist said wryly, "African natives take advantage of it. When they're wounded, they get an ant to bite them to hold the flesh together."

With a sour smile, the old man said, "A living Band-Aid, eh?"

Wanda Lindstrom concluded for Hubbard, "People simply don't realize how inventive Nature has been through the millions of years of evolution."

Elias Johnson turned puzzled eyes to the scientists. "Could these big bastards be what you call 'communicating' with the regular cockroaches we have around the village?"

The woman looked to Hubbard. "*The Bratella germanica?*"

Johnson grunted, "Huh?"

Hubbard said, "That's the ordinary household cockroach. No, I don't think so . . ."

Johnson told him, "People are complaining about cockroaches running around in broad daylight."

Wanda Lindstrom frowned to Hubbard. "They *might* be sensing some of the new pheromones, Peter. They wouldn't quite connect up, but it could make them abnormally restless."

"Possibly . . ."

Elizabeth was impressed again by the immediate rapport between the two. There was a relationship that could not be denied.

Johnson said, "But the big buggers are out there in the woods! Miles away!"

The woman told him, "Pheromones can travel great distances. There's a female moth, for instance, that sends out just one hundred millionth of a gram—and you can't get much smaller than that. With it she can excite a billion males a mile away. Another species can reach as far as seventeen miles! Who says we humans are ahead of insects?" It was her way of telling Elizabeth that she understood the embrace she had witnessed. Elizabeth was relieved. The last thing she wanted was unnecessary tension in the lighthouse. The common problem was too pressing, the stakes too high. Right now a love triangle, if there was one, seemed of small importance.

A sharp clanging outside interrupted the group. There was a thumping, clattering, and grinding of heavy metal that shook the building. Through the window there came a whooping and shouting. The alarm in the room turned to quick laughter when they saw it was Russell Homer. He was in his yellow machine of triumph, his great bulldozer chariot, standing jauntily on the seat, waving his hat in circles of victory.

The group hurried out, cheering the man. He lowered the bulldozer scoop with the delicacy of a chef handling a soufflé. "There's a thousand of your specimens in there!" he crowed.

Inside, Peter Hubbard took over. "What I'm going to do," he instructed Wanda Lindstrom, "is punch one hole in the cover, so the roaches can get out only one at a time. You hold the trap jars over the hole, tightly."

"Be *careful!*" Elizabeth couldn't help blurting. The image of scuttling insects in the can was nightmarish.

There was a sudden lull in the wind beyond the windows, and the rattling of the giant cockroaches against the can could be plainly heard.

"Can I help?" Johnson wanted to know.

"Just stand by," Hubbard said tensely. "Wanda and I will handle this."

Before Peter Hubbard could take tools to the project, the roar of a wildly racing automobile stopped him. Brakes shrieked, a car door slammed, the lighthouse door was banged open, and Amos Tarbell pounded into the room. His face was ghostly. His big body was shaking like a boy's. He didn't know which of his terrible messages to tell first. "On my radio just now! The *Tub* is on the rocks! Off Dickens Point. They can't raise the Coast Guard station in the storm! *Call Chatham on the phone!*" The man's heavy voice broke. The news of the Laidlaws must wait.

Reed Brockshaw, coming in just behind the sheriff, turned to stone. His question was an unbelieving whisper, "The *Tub?*—The rocks off Dickens Point?"

Amos Tarbell nodded in misery, and turned to Elias Johnson. "Can we use your boat to get over there?"

"Sure! Craig has the Bertram, so we can take the *Jessica!* What are we waiting for?" The old man was limping to the door.

Reed Brockshaw cracked. He thundered at Johnson, "The *Jessica* will take an hour to get around the island in this storm!" He ran to his car. "We have to use the shortcut over High Ridge!"

Amos Tarbell grabbed at his old friend. "*You can't go through those woods, Reed!*"

"Get your hands off of me!"

"Those roaches are out there today! *I just saw them!*"

Reed beat at the sheriff with hard fists. "Damn the roaches! My kids are on that boat!"

Tarbell held on to him despite the painful blows. "The

roaches! They're all over everything in the woods! You'll never get through!"

"My KIDS!" the man kept yelling. He broke violently from the sheriff's grasp and darted to a pile of old flares Elizabeth and Bonnie had stacked neatly in a corner of the room. Good!—These were the Roman candle type, Brockshaw knew, not the fireworks rockets. He shouted at Amos Tarbell. "I'll use these. I'll get through!"

The sheriff pleaded as the man grabbed the flares like kindling. "These are awful old, Reed! They won't light!"

Tarbell desperately needed to tell Reed, tell them all, the horror he had just seen in the Laidlaw jeep. He needed to tell everyone that Yarkie was in more calamitous and gruesome danger than anyone had dreamed. He needed to set in motion the complete evacuation of High Ridge and every house anywhere near the trees. But this shipwreck emergency had to come first. He raced after Reed Brockshaw and tackled him. Brockshaw kicked out. Tarbell swung his own sea-hardened fists. The man had to be stopped, didn't realize the peril he was heading for.

His face bleeding from the sheriff's blows, Reed Brockshaw lowered his head like a football player and rammed his friend. The sheriff went sprawling. His large body struck the garbage can and knocked it over. It was only Peter Hubbard's reflex pouncing on the cover that kept the captive cockroaches from spilling out all over the laboratory.

By the time the dust of the confusion settled, Reed Brockshaw's car was burning rubber toward High Ridge and the shortcut he planned to take to Dickens Point.

The commotion in the laboratory kept the people from noticing how the introduction of the garbage can into the room had galvanized the roach in the glass jar. Its wings were buzzing frantically. It kept flying up against the glass cover. The lid held fast, which seemed to infuriate the insect more.

At the same time, a heavier odor seemed to be coming from the insect through the airholes in the flask. It was faint in the laboratory air, but with a definite scent of its own—vaguely caustic, intermixed with a loamy or even herbal aroma. Without realizing it, the people were taking it in with nervous exhalations of their own breath.

Had the people not been racing about in their own new urgency, they would have heard the sharp repeated cracking of the captive roach's shell on the glass, hitting the sides and the top harder and harder blows. Fortunately, the glass was shatterproof, and held.

TWO

When one of the *Tub's* ancient engines failed, George Kinray realized too late that even prayers would not save the boat from disaster on Dickens Rocks. The gale winds and the staggering waves were too powerful for the remaining motor. The minister did not have to tell the children to be quiet, to avoid panic as the slashing sea sluiced the deck. They were all experienced enough to know they were in dire trouble. Squinting against the salt spray, the older among them helped with the life jackets.

Using whatever power he could muster against the deck-washing waves and the beating winds, the minister desperately steered toward Dickens Cove. His hope was that the storm would beach the craft past the rocks. True, the tide was coming in fast, and there would be no beach at all in a little while, but with luck he would have time to get everyone off safely and into the nearby woods. Then the trek home would be familiar through the safety of the trees.

The curling combers had other plans for the *Tub*. Heavier and heavier seas broke mercilessly over the deck, threatening to sweep children overboard. The youngsters clung tightly to whatever was at hand, and to each other, in a chain of silent terror. A great sea would dance the ship up a heaving wave, only to chute it down with a timber-shaking thud in the trough between seas. The winds boiled up mountains of water that avalanched down on the *Tub*, surging across the children, and straining the human chain of small arms to the breaking point.

It was all the more terrible, the distraught minister wept inwardly, because not even the smallest of the clenched faces uttered the slightest whimper. These Yarkie children showed their inheritance of bravery, he saw with new admiration, and heartbreak. Kneeling in prayer, he watched the jagged rocks coming closer and closer, like iron shark jaws waiting to crunch them to bits. Even with life jackets, few children could survive the pounding seas and the erratic tides. They would almost certainly be swept out to eternity.

David Brockshaw clasped his sister, Kim, to him in an embrace so tight that it made her wince. But she did not make a noise. She saw the smile he had fixed on his lips, and took comfort from it, as she had been comforted by her father when he had lifted her to his chest in the woods. Inwardly, David was sick with fright. He had sailed this shore enough times with his father to know for certain that in this storm the crippled *Tub* would never make it to the beach. More clearly than the minister, he saw that their only hope was, paradoxically, to be wrecked on the line of rocks extending from the shore. Unless the *Tub* broke up at once, they ought to be able to climb on to the boulders, even though many of the lower rocks were already awash. The boy saw the minister calling frantically on the radio, and expected there would be help when they reached the beach and started through the forest.

The ripping, grinding crash of the *Tub* against the

outermost rocks sent children tumbling head over heels across the wet, listing decks. There were jolting cracks like pistol shots as brute waves pitched the ship up and thudded it down again and again. In the raging, egg-beater torrents, the old boat looked like a great horse lifting, rearing up on hind legs and crashing down furiously. Each time the *Tub* landed on the anvil of the boulders, great holes were ruptured in her groaning timbers and the whole boat creaked and shuddered through the shattering hull.

But the youngsters were agile, and trained to emergency. In a matter of seconds, senior boys had formed a body chain from the cracking ship to the solid rocks. Quickly they followed the youngest children, to help guide them over the slippery, sharp-edged ledges. The minister, searching the *Tub*, made sure everyone was safely off. He himself jumped to safety just as a rearing sea lifted the old boat and smashed her down with a final splitting of her worn and weary planks.

The children were washed by waves and spray as they made their way gingerly toward the strip of sand that promised sanctuary. Blasts of wind slammed and turned them. Some slid off the slippery surfaces into the deep turbulent waters, to be yanked back by strong companion arms.

By the time they neared the shore, none of the youngsters was without painful bruises and livid scratches. The sea water kept washing away the dripping blood, but David saw that Kim had a large open slash down one leg. He could not stop to stanch the flow. He needed a hand to help keep his own footing, and the other to clasp his sister's trembling little body as they fought their way along with the others. He tried to get Kim to drop the doll she had insisted on taking to the picnic, but she hugged it as tightly as he was hugging her.

Clambering and slipping over the uneven boulders, the

children, followed by the scarecrow figure of the minister, made a forlorn procession of disaster silhouetted against glowering clouds. With thunder and lightning splitting the sky and ocean, the children looked like pathetic puppets in a tragic storm painting.

Despite the hazards of the rocks, waves, and storm the whole party reached the shore. Jumping off the last rock onto the sand, George Kinray fell to his knees in a new prayer, of thanksgiving. The storm had carried them to the brink of death, but the same boulders that had wrecked their boat had been like a strong arm of the Lord stretched into the sea to shepherd them to solid ground.

The minister rose and assessed the situation. The wet children were shivering in the wind. First things first—Kinray sent a squad of older youths to gather wood. They couldn't make a fire in the trees because of the drought, but they could dry off nicely on the beach. He judged there was still time before the tide covered the strand entirely. Then they could make it home safely. The sheriff's office had acknowledged his SOS, so help was probably already on the way. The good Lord had indeed saved the day.

The minister watched with pride as his young charges scattered to find wood. Others, without being ordered or instructed, were digging a large hole in the sand, in which a fire could be built out of the wind. The children were beginning to smile, even laugh. The terror of the shipwreck had not taken them. They were sorry for the *Tub*, more than sorry. But they were safe, and that was what mattered to a sailor in the end.

When the older children had dug the pit, the younger children began to construct a sand wall around it. The minister, regarding them fondly, thought how typical it was of the young heart to be wracked with life-and-death suspense one moment and in another be resiliently building castles in the sand.

He would have a proud story to tell their parents, the minister thought, even though the day had brought disaster to the *Tub*—and, he considered grimly, to whatever reputation he might have hoped to earn as a good sailor in this community of seamen. He'd stick to his pulpit from now on, George Kinray decided, leaning against the wind on Dickens Beach in the ever-increasing storm.

THREE

Young Brockshaw started into the woods when he noticed that his sister was not in the group huddled around the minister. He looked about frantically. The girl was back on the rocks, on her hands and knees. The boy understood at once that she must have dropped her precious doll. Under his breath he muttered a curse he had heard from his father but would never dare say aloud. Voices were calling to him impatiently from the woods. The afternoon was growing steadily darker, the winds more furious. In the forest, it would be almost too dark to see. But Kim was climbing farther out on the boulders, unaware of her danger. The ocean was pouring in faster by the minute. Already it had engulfed some of the distant ledges they had traversed. A menacing wave towered above Kim and swept her half way along before she managed, with a birdlike cry of terror, to catch hold and save herself. She would not escape the next breaker already gathering its slashing height only yards from her.

David flung himself toward his sister without another moment's thought. He reached her just as a torrent of ocean avalanched over them both, crashing them to the hard surface, dragging them scratched and bruised until David caught a precarious hold and strained with all his young muscles to sustain it.

Filled with anger, he grabbed Kim roughly, and started her back to the others, not caring that she was crying he was hurting her.

Except that now he could not reach the others. In the minutes he had been on the rocks with Kim, his companions had come fleeing amuck out of the forest, empty-handed, wild-eyed pursued by an army of cockroaches.

David heard the hysterical before he saw the attackers. Totally unprepared, he did not understand what he was looking at even while he viewed the scene. The mind requires reference points, accustomed concepts; it cannot deal with something totally outside its experience, beyond its ken.

The carnage created its own experience in its incredible reality. Except at the foot of the rocks where David and Kim were standing, paralyzed with terror, the narrow beach was suddenly alive with giant cockroaches. They streamed out of the trees without stop. To David Brockshaw they looked like small tanks rumbling steadily on in their assault on the children.

George Kinray was rushing every which way, stamping, jumping and slipping on the roaches he crushed. The children were in a turmoil. As they perceived the terrible threat of the insect onslaught, they raced away from the roaches into the sea. They were driven, without thinking, by a primal, elementary certainty within: *The beach meant death now. The ocean held at least the promise of survival.*

But the tempest on the waters seemed in conspiracy with the insect storm rushing out of the forest onto the sand. Just as the last of the children splashed to seeming safety in the ocean, leaving only the minister in a kind of rear-guard action, a battering ram of a breaker roared in, shooting over the tops of the highest rocks, engulfing the children. It walloped them off their feet, and pulled them under in an overpowering, drowning maelstrom of colliding winds and tides.

Most of the drowned children were swept at once deeply out to sea, but the erratic waves tumbled some of the small, wracked bodies back on the sand. They lay still there. Like broken dolls, David Brockshaw thought dimly. His mind was reeling before the impossible sights. He tried to cover Kim's eyes, but his small sister stood as if hypnotized and he saw that no hand could ever erase from her young soul what had already carved it with unforgettable horror.

The minister, still trying to protect his charges, lost his balance and, arms waving wildly, slid down beside the bodies already sheeted with the invading, boundless creatures.

David Brockshaw saw the insects attack his friends, some snaking over the small corpses, others flying for their eyes. Stains of blood appeared on every face.

The rampaging attack had been so swift, so unreal, that no one in the Sunday School group had comprehended what was happening. It was as if life had abruptly presented a new element, beyond earth, air, fire, and water— an element of havoc beyond imagining, beyond the mind.

George Kinray again struggled to his feet, drawing on the superhuman power of his despair and guilt. He was already blind, with his cheeks stripped away. He was only a bleeding skull, but he kept trying to lift the drowned bodies away from the reach of the roaches. The children dropped from his arms when the insects gnawed through his tendons and bit through his bones. He fell again, into a new pool of his own gushing blood.

The beach was soon red everywhere. Crimson patches stained the sand darkly and rivulets of blood channeled through the sand to the sea. The spreading foam left by each rising wave was pink with the blood of the ravishment of the corpses in the unholy necropolis.

Still watching, his eyes glazed with panic, young Brockshaw saw he might have one chance to save himself and his sister. There was a narrow roach-free aisle from the rocks to the trees. He grabbed Kim, who uttered another cry of protest, and bounded headlong into the forest. When Kim tugged back, he had no choice but to slap her face. She howled louder, but he plunged on until, to his despair, he found he had run directly into a seething legion of oncoming roaches.

Without conscious thought, he boosted Kim up to a tree branch, and high-jumped after her. From the beach he could hear the earsplitting screams of the minister, but they were growing fewer and feebler. Cowering in the tree, he held on to Kim with all his strength. She was trembling as he was. He was quaking with his growing understanding. He had never heard of cockroaches attacking people. He had never heard of cockroaches as scary-big as these. He had never seen such gore. He had never seen anything killed besides fish.

And it seemed the roaches were strong enough to kill a full-grown man like the minister himself! The boy could understand the drownings, even accept them despite his bursting grief at the loss of his friends, because drowning was part of a world he knew. But he could not take in the roach scourge.

Shaking harder, David Brockshaw wondered whether these fearsome cockroaches could crawl up trees, could come after him and his sister.

He was answered too quickly by the terrifying sight of a file of the swollen insects marching steadily up the tree trunk toward him. He shoved Kim higher up, panting with fresh panic. Roaches were reaching his shoe. He could feel bites on his ankle. He kicked in a fury, only to see brown bodies—like funny little flying cigars!—aiming at Kim's white face, settling on her round cheeks. Her eyes widened in terror.

"Shut your eyes!" her brother shrieked. He had seen how the roaches went for the drowned. "Cover your eyes, Kim!"

Petrified, the girl obeyed. It was as if David were now her father and her only hope in this bad dream was to do exactly what he said.

But in raising her arms to her eyes, the girl lost her grip on the tree limb, and tumbled to the ground. She landed on her head, and David heard the sickening thud, and the snap of bones. A mass of cockroaches was on the crumpled little girl in an instant. David heard Kim whimpering and knew she wasn't dead. He leaped down from the tree, trying to scatter the roaches with his hands and feet. He stamped madly about, but there were too many to disperse.

The boy dropped his own body over his sister's, trying to shield her. The bloodthirsty insects crawled between them, now tearing and ripping at both juvenile bodies. Kim's silken corn hair was ropy with her blood and her brother's. Their empty-socketed eyes stared at each other face to frail face as they perished in this storm more horrible than the sea had ever hurled at Yarkie.

It was not a field of battle, only a rapine slaughter of innocents, because there had been no way to fight back.

FOUR

Reed Brockshaw screeched to a stop on High Ridge Road near the path to Dickens Point. There was no sound except the thundering storm, but the man imagined he could hear his children entreating him for help. From his car, he grabbed a handful of the flares he had taken from the lighthouse and made for the trees. Running as fast as he could, he tried to tell himself there was no serious danger. The *Tub* would be managed safely, one way or another. As for Tarbell's warnings of man-eating roaches in the woods, well, Amos had to be exaggerating. Anyway, if any of those insects came at him, he'd teach them a hot lesson.

The man slowed to catch his breath. He didn't want to get too winded. The climb was rougher than he remembered—well, he hadn't been this way since high school days. The leaves had certainly lumped up all around. The going was hard, almost like plowing through deep snow.

Why did he have a feeling as if animals were watching him come?

The brittle leaves. The sound of the leaves. What had the fellows told of their search for Sharky at the picnic grove? Those demon roaches had come out of the leaves, heading for the rabbit in the trap. Heading for the men themselves. All three of them wouldn't be blowing it up. Brockshaw halted. He might as well take heed. Stop, look, listen. And make sure of the flares. As Amos had said, they were pretty damn stale.

The man looked around, and saw nothing but the trees bending and shaking in what was now a full, howling gale. He listened harder, and heard nothing but echoing thunder rolling itself out in space over the sea. He could not see the ocean from the forest, but this sailor knew in his every breath how the storm would look and sound, and how it would frighten even Yarkie children, on the water.

Reed Brockshaw lit a match and carefully touched it to a flare. It sputtered and refused. Old in the lighthouse for years. His mind was jerking around like a fish on a line, he thought with annoyance. He needed to concentrate, but instead he was thinking how Elizabeth Carr and her friend had done such a great job of cleaning the musty old building. It reminded him of the way Doreen kept house. In the midst of the Yarkie forest, under the blowing storm, trying uselessly to light flare after stale flare, Reed Brockshaw was overtaken with a burst of love for his wife, for his way of life, for the cleanliness of his home, the orderliness of his island, his friends, the predictability of the future.

It made the intrusion of the alien cockroaches the more unbearable. He wished the damned flares would catch. He'd like to have one in his fist and see one of those damnation bugs. He'd gladly cook it to hell.

And he had his chance, all at once.

With a grunt of horror, Reed Brockshaw became aware that while he had been concentrating on matches and fuses, a file of the great roaches had emerged from the leaves only about twenty feet away, and was creeping toward him steadily now. The insects were coming on like a single machine driven by an invisible power source, almost as if they were on a conveyor belt. The roach antennae were stiff and straight, as if they were taking in their energy from an outside current. The leaves were crackling as more and more of the insects emerged out of some secret tunnel. Their hissing was like a soft whistling, a deadly harmony underneath the high pitch of the wind in the now-twisting trees.

The roach chittering was for his blood, Reed Brockshaw knew at once. It was almost as if the insects were whetting knives. He could hear a faint clicking that must be their teeth and mandibles. They were closing the distance quickly. In seconds it would be too late for him to turn back.

And his flares were still resisting the matches. Another try, and another match was blown out by a wind gust. The motions of the cockroaches fascinated him. Had someone —Russell?—said they looked like mechanical toys, harmless windup gewgaws—plastic imitations of the small crabs he played with when he was David's age?

But Brockshaw knew these were real, not toys. He'd

better get the hell back to his car or be quick with these matches *now!*

The roaches were hissing their warning closer and louder. Brockshaw was shivering with more than the storm's cold air. *This was what Amos and Ben and Russ had been trying to tell!* He owed them an apology for thinking they were laying it on. Watching this crawling, hissing, feral, clicking army marching at him now, the man could not doubt they could kill Sharky, or anything else they found in their path, including him.

He backed slowly away from the sinister formation to make one more effort at lighting a flare. The vibration of his step was all the roaches needed. The column seemed to twitch and shudder balefully—just the way a larger animal would crouch to spring. Insect wings quivered in the storm gloom. Could he make it back to his car, Brockshaw wondered in a heartstopping panic. Why had he waited so long? Why hadn't he heeded Tarbell's warning?

The miserable flare must catch now, or he was in unspeakable peril!

Fire sputtered in fingers he could not keep from trembling. The flame died, as if the hissing of the roaches had blown it out. Flinging the match away with disgust, Reed Brockshaw pivoted to run. A fluttering body struck his nose. Christ, they *were* flying! Now he couldn't get away!

With a cough of desperation, the man steadied himself. The flying roach was stinging his forehead, and he wanted to slap it away before it got to his eyes, but that would end his one last chance. Gnawing his lip, he struck another match.

The flare caught!

The hot swoosh of crimson-orange flame burst from the stick like a great chorus singing hallelujah! The flame apparently startled the roach on his head. It loosened its grip and dropped away. Reed brushed the back of his hand to his forehead and saw blood on it. He would surely have been a goner if the flare had failed. He aimed the flame at the roach battalion, and cried out with pure joy when the column broke up in disorder, with roaches scattering into the leaves for their own lives.

Good! He wished they wouldn't be rushing to hide, would stay and give him the chance he wanted, to burn them all to ashes. But he had other business! He headed for the shore again. But he had to stop once more; this time to stamp out little blazes his flare had started in the dry brush. He looked up. All this storm and no damn rain! It often happened that way, but those clouds were black bags swollen with a torrent. They had to let go some time, he thought angrily as he pushed on to the Point.

He was nearing the eastern edge of the woods now. He could see the sand dunes from which he would look down on the shore—find his children who, he was certain, would be safely on land with all the others safe and sound too.

Reed Brockshaw wanted Kim and David in his arms more than he had ever yearned for anything in his life.

No more roaches stopped the man. He burst out of the woods at just the spot he figured he would be. There was the one familiar high dune just before him. He started to climb it. The loose sand gave way under his eager feet, and he slipped back. He lunged upward, grabbing at the tall Phragmites grass that grew reed-like on this side of the island. He pulled himself up to the top of the dune, and could see immediately the wreck of the *Tub* against the outer Dickens Rocks. The boat was listing badly, and visibly breaking up as the unrelenting waves pounded it against the immovable boulders.

The sight that met him when he turned his eyes to the beach drilled Reed Brockshaw's brain and sucked out his sanity.

His first impression was that there was nothing on the

beach but some kind of foreign brown seaweed washed ashore by the storm. The man's eyes lifted again to the *Tub*. The kids could still be on her, but he guessed that George Kinray would have had them climb the chain of rocks to the shore. The *Tub* was too broken up for the minister to risk keeping his charges on board.

The group had come off, Reed Brockshaw's churning mind told him, and they were somewhere in the woods now enjoying their picnic after all. It was smart of the minister to get the children off the beach quickly, because the tide came in so fast here. At least the man had learned that much.

The father's eyes were drawn to the beach once more. Dazed, he felt the truth torrenting over him, like waves sweeping over a drowning man.

The children were not in the woods.

There was no picnic party.

No one was on the *Tub*.

Those who had not drowned and been buried by the sea, were below him, their bodies on the beach.

His mind sizzled with the terrible, incomprehensible question that was at the same time an accursed certainty.

He was not looking at seaweed. That brown spreading blanket, so dense that not a grain of sand showed, was not seaweed but a living mass of insects. It was the enemy, the cockroaches. It was a living carpet of the barbarian roaches and they were feeding.

His eyes closed against the sight, but there was a bright flame inside his head that lit up what had taken place, as plainly as if he were watching a film: He could imagine children coming off the breaking ship, struggling along the rocks. Reaching shore, they romped and jumped all over the beach in their happiness and relief at being safe and sound. The vibrations signaled their presence to the roving roaches. He could only hope there had been a mass drowning first. It would be at least more natural.

It came to Brockshaw that his own Kim and David lay there savaged, buried alive, or dead already, beneath the cover of filth!

The father's cry of anguish was an animal's roar. It defeated the thunder that crashed over the scene, and the lightning that eerily lit the gory carnage. It was the eruption of the man's exploding brain, the sound of a soul's dynamite blasting every nerve, leaving nothing but the echo of Reed Brockshaw's breaking apart. There was no way a man could witness the abomination and continue human.

The man beat at his face with his fists, he tore at his cheeks with his nails. In his unspeakable grief and fury he did not want to have a face. He did not want to belong to any world in which this torment could happen.

The insects were insatiable over the bodies. The bugs were red with human blood. Their shells gleamed in the lightning flashes with the slime of their destruction. To the funereal pounding of the waves rising higher on the shore, lightning kept disclosing more and more horror—lacerated flesh, severed limbs, a child's head rolling to the water's edge, being lifted by a wave and carried ghoulishly away.

Pieces and flakes of skeletons were floating on the sea now. The shore was a viscid spread of inert refuse, a roach-turbulent repository of misery beyond agony.

There was no way for a mind to encompass the atrocity. It was the excrescence of Nature gone evil. Evil beyond barbarism, beyond cruelty. It was deed beyond excoriation, curse or damnation. It was Damnation itself.

It was an apocalypse of Nature's mindless enormity, and Reed Brockshaw's own Gethsemane.

Fish would feed on strange fruit this day.

Reed Brockshaw gnashed his teeth and wailed.

The incoming tide was reaching for more of the mangled bodies. Each lashing wave carried more of the carnage out to sea as it broke over the roach-encrusted shore. The insects near the red-foaming water line began to scramble for their own safety. Roaches nearer the trees paused in their abysmal repast to test the charged air, receiving sudden signals of alarm. Their antennae marked acute danger and they started away from the children's corpses, scurrying for the dark dry safety of the trees.

Reed Brockshaw's unutterable anguish pulled the corners of his mouth back into a plastic grin of death. He was beyond mourning, he wanted only vengeance and requital. He lit a flare. His thumping heart knew what he planned. His delirium led him striding off the dune down to the beach, boldly stamping into the torrent of roaches now fleeing the oncoming ocean. Roach leaders made for him at once. Their antennae went high, an arrogance of superiority—how did this Enemy dare to come among them, they who could butcher him in moments! The insect teeth clicked, their mandibles scissored, they hissed and puffed new commands to attack, slaughter, devour.

They waited menacingly for Brockshaw . . .

The man understood, and laughed, and bellowed his maledictions with his first thrust of the flare at their malignant bodies. The flare sent the cockroaches scuttling crazily, their bodies bouncing in the fire, as if they were popping in a hot pan.

Reed Brockshaw laughed insanely at the gratifying debacle. He swept his fiery torch around as if he were scything a field. Circle after circle of burning roach bodies curled and twitched and burst in the fierce immolation.

Soon the man realized he could not get all the roaches while on the beach, and he wanted them *all*, every killer of them! And, ah, he could be as cunning as they! They would follow him into the woods, because the ocean was chasing them, and because he was more food, and because he had attacked them. Whatever drew or drove them, the insects flocked after him into the trees. Brockshaw was jubilant as he saw them filling the earth behind him, sheets and sheets of cockroaches, a pouring cascade of cockroaches filling the forest floor after him.

Brockshaw paid no attention to the lacerations on his feet, the roaches now sucking blood from the deep bites on his ankles. He rejoiced, knowing his intention. He was impatient, but he forced the time. He wanted them all in his power, every villainous murderer wet with the blood of the drowned children on that beach of horror. He turned to wait for them. He held the flare before his face, though the light hurt his eyes. He fended off the roaches that flew at his head. He kept stamping and shouting in invitation. He laughed. They thought *they* were the attacker! Hah! They'd see! Soon now! He slapped more flying roaches away. They weren't going to blind him, not yet! He wanted to *see*, to have the bursting joy of witnessing what he was about to accomplish.

Reed Brockshaw shook his head madly from side to side to splatter his own blood out to the roaches to make them more avaricious for him, to keep them signaling for more of their brothers to hasten to the new feast where he stood in the forest.

Words jostled and echoed in his head. He heard the Harvard man saying you couldn't hate the cockroaches any more than you could hate a runaway locomotive. *Wrong*, Reed Brockshaw snarled. It might be true that Mother Nature was a Crazy Old Lady with evil appetites, who programmed her bastard robots, but to him the cockroaches were palpable enemies, personal enemies, despicable enemies he was to kill with his own hands. He wished they were man-size so he could grip them in his fingers and choke them to death. He wanted to hear them wheeze and cry out, hear their dying moans as if pleading for mercy . . .

No, these brown-black, hard-shelled crawling and flying scum were no impersonal forces of nature to him. They were criminals, murderers, worse. They had butchered his children. They would pay! Intolerable that these little beasts should have made his innocent children suffer as they must have in that slaughterhouse on the shore!

Brockshaw laughed maniacally again. The cockroaches, in their tumbling droves coming through the leaves, expected to get him because his torch could kill only a few thousand and they were millions. In a moment now they would learn that for all their "mutation" and fancy ganglia, they were no match for a human brain and its cleverness.

The man swept the forest with his eyes. As far as he could see there were cockroaches coming. They were like a filthy, moving scab on the earth. They covered trees and leaves like disgusting, shuddering berries of brown and black. Their wings buzzed a hellish threat through the woods. He knew they would launch a concerted attack at him any moment. It was time, it was the time, the final moment for his plan, his purpose, and resolve.

Reed Brockshaw stretched out the flare and deliberately held the searing flame to a dry tree branch on his right. He whirled and did the same on his left. He circled into the brush, running and setting fire everywhere.

The woods sparked, ignited, exploded. Flames shot up furiously. The conflagration was fed by the storm winds and engulfed the area in moments. There was a cascade of firecracker bursts as the fire popped to the tops of the trees and raced down into the sere leaves. The blaze ran along the ground like a pouring torrent of molten death.

From the cockroaches there was a spitting and chittering and scraping as their bodies caught and fried. Their cooked insides set up a staccato sputtering like hot grease as the forest became a bizarre griddle, an exploding stove, a volcanic furnace. Thick, stinking smoke rose up into the black skies over the inferno.

Reed Brockshaw crumpled to the ground. His hair and clothes were afire. Maddened roaches were feeding on him even as they burned. Deranged, and choking in the smoke of his torment, he felt not drowning in hell's lake of fire but rising with the smoke of the trees and the dying cockroaches to the heaven that, something in him rejoiced, was waiting, clear and cool and beautiful, with his children, above the horrendous turmoil below.

The forest fire burned higher. The clouds of the man's self-cremation rose blacker than the storm sky to signal catastrophe to the people on Yarkie Island.

In the Nest, the atmosphere was dense not only with the acridity of caustic smoke, but with a kind of nervousness that had all the insects quivering. Sometimes housewives see cockroaches "dancing" after an application of the insecticide pyrethrum. It is a death dance, to be sure, but a frenzy of motion while it lasts, caused by the chemical-nervous reaction of the insects. Now there was something delivering an unclear but powerfully disturbing message: *Enemy outside has exterminated whole armies of our Nest.*

The Dome shook with spasms of preternatural energy, trying to comprehend fire and the death it had brought, interrupting an innocent feast of the band of insects near the water.

FIVE

The evacuation of Yarkie ordered an hour later by the selectmen and the sheriff's office was quiet and orderly.

People with their necessary luggage boarded the ferries called over from Chatham. All were silent and stunned, understanding the danger from the raging forest fire on High Ridge. The volunteer firemen were up on the Ridge battling the blaze, helped by the rain that had finally come down. But there were still too many flare-ups for safety, and with the storm still blowing, firebrands could land on homes almost anywhere.

More, there was a funereal mood among the people. Almost everyone was in some way related to the children who had gone on the Sunday School picnic, and there had been no word about the *Tub*. The spreading gossip was that the children had landed along the east shore and gone into the woods for their party. They might have been caught then by the fire the lightning had started. The people could get no answers to their heartsick questions from the stone-faced village officials.

Elias Johnson, Amos Tarbell, Stephen Scott, Ben Dorset, Russell Homer knew all too well what had happened. They had been coming around Dickens Point on the *Jessica* when the smoke billowed up on High Ridge. Johnson drew every ounce of power out of his massive engines. The men saw the *Tub* at once and, through their glasses, clearly made out what was left of the beach as the tide swept almost to the dunes marking high water. The torn bodies and skeletal bones of the drowned were all too clearly visible. Sickened beyond ability to speak, the men on the *Jessica* did not have to ask what was responsible for the wholesale ravaging of the wreck's victims.

They could not look at each other, could not trust themselves to speak. In the presence of so overwhelming a tragedy, each man withdrew into himself, soul-shriveled.

Stephen Scott managed to whisper to Elias Johnson, wet-eyed, "Ought we try to get them off?"

The old man stood as if deaf. In all his years at sea he

had faced nothing as horrible as this carnage. He had watched grim-faced as sharks had amputated men's limbs. He had lost friends overboard to beating storms. He had had to bring the sorrowful messages of lost husbands and fathers and sons to weeping widows and puzzled children. It had been harrowing and painful, but within his comprehension. This scene of obscene insect debauchery—he could call it nothing else—emptied him of all spirit.

But he was the captain of this craft, and he was in charge. The decision was his and he made it without hesitation. "No!" he told Stephen Scott. "For God's sake, let it be!"

"But—" The selectman made a gesture of pleading toward the shore. Even the pitiful remains deserved whatever decent Christian burial could be arranged.

Johnson read his thought and shook his head sorrowfully. "Stephen, by the time we tried to get in there, the tide will have the whole beach." His voice broke. *"But I wouldn't bring them home even if we could!"* The old man's eyes were wet as he watched the waves scour the shore, lifting more of the broken bodies out to sea each time. "I take it as a blessing." Let Nature cleanse what Nature had fouled.

Stephen Scott bowed his head and closed his eyes in his own silent prayer. Elias was right. Let the sea take what remained of the roach-desecrated children. The tides here would carry them away from shore eastward past the "cold wall"—the waters between the Cape and the Gulf Stream—and the Stream would mercifully bury the innocents in the deep forever. Let the parents never know the truth. Let all believe no one had been able to get ashore from the wrecked *Tub.* Everyone knew there were perilous riptides along this shore, especially when the sea was coming in, as now, during a nor'easter. Yarkie would be filled with lasting sorrow, but the people would suffer drowning easier than the unbearable truth.

Scott nodded to Elias Johnson. They were both sure the other witnesses with them would not disagree.

SIX

Amos Tarbell let his binoculars drop heavily to his chest from his big hands. He made no effort to hide his sobs. "I was in Vietnam and God knows I never saw anything as awful as this!"

Russell Homer kept his glasses to his eyes. He said in a thready voice, "I wonder how Reed is making out."

Ben Dorset's jaws were twitching with his effort to keep his knees from buckling. "I am praying to the good God that the fire kept Reed away before he could ever see that beach . . ."

"Amen," the others said, as the big deputy broke into heaving tears.

SEARCH

ONE

Craig Soaras had returned from his Chatham trip too late for his cargo of dry-ice extinguishers to help the fire department with the High Ridge blaze. The same fierce seas that had scoured the east shore of the dead children had slowed even Stephen Scott's yacht. By the time Craig reached the laboratory, most of the High Ridge fire was out, with volunteers standing by for possible flare-ups.

The volunteers and the group in the lighthouse—who had come to think of themselves as a Task Force—were the only ones left on Yarkie. Even Stephen Scott had agreed that evacuation was imperative. The forest conflagration proved an invaluable reason and excuse, without requiring further explanations to either the people or the ferries hastily summoned from Chatham.

In the laboratory, the scientists were plainly into some kind of experiment with the teeming cockroaches taken from Russell Homer's garbage retrieval. The roach removed from the sacrificed rabbit remained alone in its original flask. The jar next to it held two roaches from the dump; the next, three; then six; then scores of the insects crowded into other containers. All of this series were without food. In matching flasks on a second shelf, there were beds of garbage for the insects to eat. The idea, Peter Hubbard explained, was to learn how long the roaches would go without cannibalizing each other.

The men regarded the crawling creatures with new loathing and virulence. These were no longer just insects, monstrous as might be. They were The Enemy now—barbaric, vicious, and abominable predators. Their horde was to be searched out, discovered, and destroyed to the last diabolical miscreation, no matter what the danger or risk. Otherwise Yarkie would be surrendered to this incredible malevolence.

Elizabeth and Bonnie had not been told of Dickens Beach. Instead, Elias Johnson had a tragic enough story —the loss of the *Tub* with all aboard. It was this appalling report to which the women attributed the new unstrung mood they felt in the Yarkie men and the Harvard couple. Although they had all been grim enough before, there had been some interplay—an occasional smile, a personal exchange. Now the men sat as if nailed to their chairs. Every face was tight and feverish. Eyes were shielded, evasive. Heads were bent, with gazes downcast to the floor. Elizabeth supposed it was the agony of the wreck and the battling of the forest fire that left the men so dramatically different from their usual steadiness.

But she had a suspicion that something else might have occurred, especially when her grandfather suggested that she and Bonnie leave the group to prepare supper. Elizabeth's watch said four in the afternoon, far too early. She was about to ask what he was concealing when she saw the sternness in his eyes. She led Bonnie out at once. She would ask Peter later.

With Wanda Lindstrom standing pale at his side, Peter Hubbard asked Johnson, "None of the firemen reported any roaches?"

"That's right."

The scientist rubbed his cheek with the now familiar gesture. "Well, the forest fire obviously got the roaches that killed the children, and the rest of the colony are probably hiding in their nest. The fire would have triggered their alarm chemical over the whole area, and it will take time to dissipate."

Johnson said, "You say they're hiding in their nest. Now you are sure we're talking about 'a colony'?"

The woman answered him. "Everything points that way. After that terrible beach disaster, I have to say we are not dealing with individual insects. I believe these roaches have definitely mutated in the direction of the ants and termites Dr. Hubbard and I have tried to tell you about. They seem definitely organized, and definitely communicating as an integrated group . . ."

Hubbard said carefully, "We certainly have to proceed on the basis that there is some center of control." He indicated the roaches in the jars. "Look here. You can see for yourself a revealing pattern of uncommon behavior."

The men turned baleful eyes on the insects.

"First, even in the jars where they have room, they are huddled together. That's unusual for cockroaches, which are normally loners." Hubbard pointed to the largest jar holding many scores of roaches. "And here we see them resting layer upon layer, the way Dr. Lindstrom said they might."

"But most important," the woman said forcefully, "notice how every single flask shows the roaches congregated in one corner! The *same* corner!"

"And watch this!" Hubbard rotated a jar. The roaches scurried across to the corner opposite their original resting place. The men gulped in wonder. Hubbard declared, "These roaches are definitely getting pheromone signals through the air holes of these flasks. *And* those chemical signals are definitely coming from one direction!"

"A nest?" Amos Tarbell ventured.

"That's my bet," Peter Hubbard said flatly.

"The dump!" Russell Homer gasped. "They're pointing to the dump!"

"Or a hundred other places out that general direction," Elias Johnson corrected him dryly. But he went on, "Seems to me the only sensible thing is to check out the dump, and the sooner the better."

"And get *ourselves* torn apart?' Stephen Scott rasped.

The old man kept himself calm. "Now look. It's only around four o'clock, and it stays light until nearly nine. We dress as tight as we can—diving suits or whatever you have in your warehouse, Stephen. We wear snorkeling goggles. We take these dry-ice extinguishers Craig has brought." Johnson lifted the red hose of one of the fire tanks, and petted the plastic black horn that hung like a narrow megaphone at the end of the tube. A trigger on the top handle of the extinguisher shot the carbon dioxide through this horn, where the chemical turned to dry ice on contact with the air. Firemen used this equipment specifically for oil and electric fires, where water would only make things worse. The old man continued, "We take guns along, and we take flares." He looked over at Peter Hubbard steadily. "And we go hunting."

The scientist met his eyes as steadily and answered as quietly, "We go hunting." He had his own fury. He prayed silently the children *had* been drowned first.

"No 'search and reconnaissance,' " Elias Johnson bit the words out. "Search and *destroy!*"

The scientist understood, and nodded, but said, "Depending on what we find."

The men rose, ready, fierce. Hubbard held them. "Before we try the dump area, I would like to look at Dickens Beach . . ."

Johnson told him brusquely, "It's under water now!" Under his breath he added, "Thank God."

Hubbard said, "I mean the woods where the roaches came out. We might see where they tunneled . . ."

"There *are* tunnels around Dickens Rocks!" It was

Elizabeth, who had obviously been listening at the kitchen door. Excitedly, she said, "If you're going, I'm coming. I know those woods better than any of you!" Behind her, Bonnie blurted, "Hey, you aren't leaving me here alone with these cockroaches!" She grabbed her own raincoat and followed Elizabeth who was getting into her gear as the men started out of the laboratory.

Amos Tarbell held back a moment. He had been tempted to advise a delay. Everyone was strained and exhausted, physically and emotionally. But old Elias was right again. Now more than ever they all wanted and needed to get after the sons of bitches. The sheriff shook his fist at the jars of brown, skittering insects lining the laboratory shelves. The roaches seemed to be staring at him with eyes as malignant as his. "Gonna get every one of you miserable damnations!" he pledged in a spasm of frustration. Tight-mouthed, he silently pledged that by the time he and his friends were done there would be no nest of the demon marauders left on Yarkie to plunder its children or anyone else ever again.

When the humans left the laboratory, the roach antennae went into a paroxysm, flailing and curving in what could only be a frenzy of attempted communication.

TWO

The fire above Dickens Beach had burned away the leaves in the forest, and it was easy to clear the ashes off the trails with a scuff of a boot. The Task Force split into groups. Elizabeth and Bonnie went with Peter Hubbard, Wanda Lindstrom, and Elias Johnson. Craig Soaras was following Amos Tarbell and Ben Dorset, while Russell Homer brought up their rear. They went through the charred woods alertly, but nothing moved. Hubbard was right.

The roaches were burned to gray powder indistinguishable from the ashes of the leaves and branches.

Or they were in total hiding.

Once again the forest closed around a weird-looking procession. Where Amos, Ben, and Russell had worn yellow oilskins when they set the rabbit trap, these figures were in body-hugging diving suits. They seemed swimmers slowly advancing in an underwater grotto, heads turning constantly, on the lookout for shark shadows. They had to be careful not only of possible roach attackers, but of smoldering embers that lay beneath the ashes. The rain had been welcome, but the storm had blown the heaviest clouds off without a real local soaking. Fire could still explode.

Like a diver, Elizabeth tapped Hubbard's rubber shoulder, and pointed away from the track he was entering. Despite the somberness of their mission, the man nearly smiled at the picture she made. Beneath the diving goggles, the woman's lovely lips were moving like a fish's as she spoke. "I remember when I was a kid, there was an open ditch along here." She indicated the direction of the dump.

Hubbard aimed his flashlight at the earth. The lingering smoke of the forest fire and the darkness of the sky above made it hard to see clearly, but the outlines of a depression were visible. Elizabeth was right. The trench would never have been noticed before the fire because leaves would have filled it in. The scientist knelt quickly. This could be a major insect trail, possibly leading to a nest! He brushed leaves away with an impatient gloved hand. He came upright with an exclamation and held his find high for the others to share. He was holding a handful of broken cockroach shells. They were charred but had not burned completely. He said grimly, "The roaches were definitely along this way!"

He called the others at once. They joined forces to follow the trail now clear on the forest floor. Spirits rose. They might be getting somewhere at last! The column of pursuers moved faster despite the awkwardness of their protective dress.

THREE

Amos Tarbell moved up alongside Peter Hubbard. "I suppose we can burn them out once and for all . . . ?"

"Let's find them first."

Tarbell said, "But we ought to go back for gasoline, kerosene now . . . ?"

Johnson overheard and intervened. "Amos, you aren't thinking. These woods are still hot. You'd blow us all to hell."

Hubbard counseled the sheriff. "Amos, there'll be time. If I'm right, those cockroaches are so scared they aren't going to move out of their nest for days."

The sheriff was insistent. "Craig and Ben have the dry ice with us. We have the flares. We could freeze them or fry them *right now!*" He let his imagination jump ahead, overlooking the fact that they had not yet even found a roach retreat. He wanted to see the insects burn, freeze, go up in smoke, melt in a great combustion of death. He hoped they would make noises, squeal or shriek or whistle in agony. It would help drown the cries of the children he kept imagining in his head.

Wanda Lindstrom said to the sheriff patiently, "We talked about this before. If I'm right about the way they cluster, fire would get only the top layers. Most of the brood would get clean away."

The man's anger would not let him rest. "We'd have them trapped, wouldn't we?" he argued.

"No," she told him, with an edge of impatience. "They would have many tunnels in and out. We would only defeat our own purpose!"

Peter Hubbard confirmed, "There would be too many left. I did think of gasoline, of course, but it's far too dangerous today, and wouldn't do the job anyway . . ."

The sheriff remained upset. "Then what did we bring all this stuff for?"

"For protection!" Elias Johnson was irritated. "Now quit fussing, Amos. This isn't easy for anybody . . ."

As the group resumed its slow hunt, none of them realized that a few steps into the opposite trail would have brought them to the burned skeleton of a man. In the instance, it did not matter to either Reed Brockshaw or his friends that it would be days before his remains were discovered.

It took only minutes more, however, for the group to discover they were on a false trail. Whatever purpose the trench had once served, it now ran into a dead end at a great boulder. The men dug far enough around to see that the trail went nowhere.

Elizabeth spoke with sudden spirit. "Peter, I remember a deep kettle hole somewhere out this way. They might be nesting there!"

Elias Johnson's head came around hopefully. "Liz, I think you have got an idea!"

Amos Tarbell's vexed face uncreased. "I remember that one, Liz! My father had it boarded over when I nearly fell in myself!" The sheriff grabbed his shovel and started away.

Elizabeth stopped him. "Not that way, Amos! The hole I mean is out behind the Cannon place."

Tarbell accepted the correction, and the dogged procession resumed. In minutes, the Cannon house was visible in its clearing through the fire-denuded trees. To Peter Hubbard, seeing the mansion for the first time, the building was stern-looking. Its windows were small—harking back to glass taxes in the colonies?—and seemed to be disapproving the strangely-costumed parade emerging out of the trees.

Elizabeth went directly to a small mound of earth. No one needed to be told to be quiet. Breaths were held as the sheriff tiptoed behind the woman. They both kneeled carefully. And both nodded.

Elizabeth whispered excitedly to Peter Hubbard as he came up to her. "*We've got it!*"

Hubbard looked around with sharp eyes. There were moulted cockroach shells in the grass. His heart raced, and he motioned the others back. His own whisper carried in the air. "If the roaches are down here, this is going to be extremely dangerous. I want just Amos with me!"

The others moved cautiously to the Cannon house, stepping as lightly as possible. Everyone understood. Beneath the earth-covered old planks might be the crucible of the Yarkie horror. They knew its power, the speed with which it could strike, the implacability of its deadliness. Hubbard was whispering to the sheriff, "We just want enough of a crack for a fast look down." He signaled Craig Soaras to join them. "Craig, you cover both of us with the dry ice. Use it fast if you see *anything!*"

"Don't worry about that . . ." The dark Portuguese face was iron.

On his knees, the sheriff was quietly pressing against a thick board, now visible under his gloved hand. "Just the way I remembered!" he murmured to Hubbard.

It was a greater strain to try to nudge the board silently than if he could put all his muscle to it. The half-buried wood yielded slightly.

"I'll hit them with my flashlight," Hubbard said to his two assistants. "It should stun them a split second, but only for a second and then they'll be coming right after us. We get out *fast!*"

The men nodded.

Amos Tarbell bent to his job again. The whole area seemed suspended in apprehension. There was an eerie lull in the wind. Behind the tense people, the forest lifted scorched spars to the air. The clouds were so low that the leafless tree seemed to be spiking down from the sky, crazily grown upside down. It seemed appropriate enough to the group. Everything on Yarkie had been somersaulted on its head in these two incredible days.

Without warning, the wind whipped up again. It howled through the bare trees like a wounded beast. The nerve-shattering noise punctuated the apprehension of the three men at the kettle hole and the uneasy eyes riveted on them. The searchers were frightened to their depths, yet at the same time elated. If the roach nest *was* below, this moment would be among the most important of their lives. For who knew what might yet happen if these mutant insects were not destroyed?

Peter Hubbard's jaws were clenching and unclenching as he admitted his anxiety to himself. He found it hard to fill his lungs, and it was not the constraint of his black rubber suit that was making him sweat in torrents. The responsibility was his in the end. The man's eyes were hot marbles as he waited above the kneeling sheriff, wishing the man would hurry, but glad he was being slow and careful. Tarbell was shrewd, all right. He was making no more noise than a passing animal might in stepping over the mound—sounds the creatures below would accept as unalarming.

If there were creatures below . . .

The scientist became physically itchy in his craving to know.

The sheriff bent his ear to the plank.

"Hear anything?" Hubbard inquired in an urgent whisper.

The sheriff shook his head doubtfully and looked up. "I've got a crack here, Peter! Do you need more?"

Hubbard checked, and said, "Can you give me a half-inch?"

He was shivering. The crack so far was too small to let in a useful beam of light, and he had seen only blackness through the slit. But a terrible stink of death and rotting food had assailed his nose, and the acrid roach smell was unmistakable. Nothing else in the world smelled like cockroaches.

So the giant killer roaches were down in this kettle hole! Bless Elizabeth Carr for remembering!

He would confirm it in a moment. Hubbard held up his fingers in a new, tense warning for silence. His gesture said plainly, *"This may be it!"* The watchers tensed. It was a bone-chilling moment. No one moved or breathed. Hubbard nodded to Amos Tarbell.

Under the sheriff's straining hands the board over the kettle hole moved a little more. Tarbell stopped and waited, listening for any disturbance below. Hubbard signaled him to go on. The board moved again, visibly a full quarter of an inch.

"Now!" Hubbard clipped to the two men. Craig Soaras put his finger on the dry-ice trigger. Amos Tarbell cocked his gun. Both men were crouching protectively beside the scientist.

Peter Hubbard flashed his light into the stench coming up from the kettle hole. He wanted the first sight of the roach den. But the moment burst his tension like air out of a broken balloon. The circling beam of his flashlight showed no motion below. There was no hissing, no sound. There were no roaches.

Hubbard stamped on the boards with anger and exasperation. The group gawked at him in amazement. They had never seen the scientist agitated before. He shouted at them all as if they were responsible for the failure. *"They did use it!"* he cried out. He bent over and heaved all the planks off the kettle hole. *"Look at that!"*

The others came running from the Cannon house. Pair after pair of curious eyes saw the glint of a mound of cockroach shells in Hubbard's rotating flashlight. The pile seemed feet thick, spread widely.

The people held their breath against the stink.

Wanda Lindstrom was saying;, "They shed their exoskeletons as they grow. Usually they eat the remains, but these roaches have had so much other food—"

She did not have to go on. The stench told the story. The sickened eyes were looking into a cavern of death. The people could see chambers cut into the sides of the pit. The niches were loaded with chunks of maggoty meat, broken limbs, internal organs, cracked skulls from which the brains had been sucked.

Rat skulls.

Human skulls!

This pit was not just a nest, it was a cemetery, hellish catacombs of ultimate foulness.

Gagging and choking, the people moved haggardly away. As they left, Peter Hubbard grunted, defeated, "We've missed them!"

Soaras asked glumly, "Was it the forest fire that chased them?"

"I don't know," the scientist gritted. He sat down heavily, wishing he could yank off the constraining suit, wishing he had never heard of Yarkie. But he had to share whatever little he did know. "There doesn't seem to be any fresh moulting, so they probably left some time ago. That hole probably became too small for them as the colony kept growing . . ."

Wanda Lindstrom observed, "But they didn't take their stores along . . ."

Hubbard answered, "They kept finding plenty of fresh food, unfortunately."

Amos Tarbell was walking in a circle, eyes hard on the ground. "Wouldn't they leave some sign, some track?"

"I doubt they'd travel on the surface," Hubbard said. "Not if they have a tunnel down there under that mess."

Tarbell's face crumpled in sheer disgust. "You mean somebody has to go down there to see?"

"If we want to be sure."

The sheriff uttered a sigh of concession. "Okay, somebody go get me a rope."

Peter Hubbard regarded Amos Tarbell with new respect. There were many forms of bravery. This task was worse than Hercules cleaning the Augean stables, and the sheriff was taking it to be the responsibility of his badge.

Elias Johnson stepped forward, putting a hand of comfort on his friend's shoulder. "Before you need to do that, Amos, there's another place we might check. What about that old pirate cave between the dump and Dickens Point? You know the one . . ."

Life came back into all the Yarkie faces. "Hey! Could be!"

"Well, let's go see!" Russell Homer started running as fast as he could.

An explosion of flame in the trees blasted him back. The return of the blustering storm winds had fanned hidden embers to a new blaze. In only a moment, there was a wall of percussive, roaring fire, impenetrable, between the group and the cave Johnson had recollected.

The new home of the killers, if it was out there at all, would have to wait.

Racing back to the road, Craig Soaras grabbed at the sheriff's radio to call out the volunteer firemen again. Among the Task Force there was a quick council. Russell Homer wanted to stay and use their carbon dioxide tanks on the new fire. Ben Dorset scoffed, without regard for the presence of the women, "Might as well piss on it!" The fresh blazes had raced up the trees, which had hardly been moistened by the sparse earlier rainfall. Fire was leaping higher than a three-story house. Johnson gave quick orders, mindful of how puzzling the diving outfits would be to the firemen, who had been told nothing of the roaches. "Back to the lighthouse and change! Then we can come up again and lend a hand!" the captain commanded.

FOUR

When the haggard group entered the lighthouse, the telephone was ringing insistently. Amos Tarbell ran for it, and handed it over to Johnson. "It's the Coast Guard, Elias. Commander Schweitzer wants to talk to you."

Johnson took the instrument quickly. Schweitzer was an old friend, one of the savviest sailors on the Coast, a gold braid man all around.

The officer reported that his Coast Guard ship had checked the *Tub* and couldn't do anything for it in the storm. Nobody seemed to be aboard. The passengers must have made it safely to shore—or it was possible that all hands had been lost.

Johnson nodded as he listened, then said only that he would give the appropriate officials a full report on the *Tub* as soon as he could.

When the commander asked if Yarkie wanted Coast Guard help with the forest fire they could see from their ship, Elias Johnson thanked him but said they had enough men to handle it. He agreed with Scott that at this point there was no need to broadcast the roach problem.

FIVE

Peter Hubbard motioned privately to Wanda Lindstrom, arid they moved to a corner of the laboratory, whispering. Elizabeth noticed, but went to the kitchen to put up coffee. They could all use a hot brew.

Hubbard was telling his colleague he thought the new circumstances called for the "Plan B" which the two of them had prepared. It involved risks and it might not work at all, so there was no sense telling any of the others, Hubbard urged. It would be premature and cruel to arouse hopes in these people who had already suffered too many setbacks.

Wanda Lindstrom agreed. Making sure they were alone, Hubbard went to the carton that Craig Soaras had received specially from the Chatham police chief that morning. The scientist tore open the red container. A small red box in heavy packing lay safely inside. Its warning label seemed to stare back at Peter Hubbard.

The scientist nodded to Wanda Lindstrom. Assuming the storm and the fire would be over by the next morning, they could put the plan into action then.

CLASH

ONE

Johnson joined the men changing their clothes. From the distance they heard the wailing sirens of the Chemical Engine and the Hook & Ladder Truck speeding to High Ridge. The pulsing sound still stirred the blood, though the evacuation had left nobody to warn, and the volunteers' mission would be one of containment only. They would wet down threatened houses, and pray hard for a bigger rain. Mostly, the fire would have to burn itself out.

The men in the lighthouse were at last voicing a question each had held silently. They had wondered from the start where Reed Brockshaw was. No one really knew, but the sheriff believed he had caught a glimpse of the man going off on one of the evacuation ferries. Heads nodded all around. It would make sense. Reed wouldn't want to leave his wife, Doreen, alone with the children missing.

As the men set out to join the fire companies, Peter Hubbard asked Johnson, "No sense in my coming along, is there? I think Wanda and I ought to get on with our work here."

Johnson approved firmly, and turned to kiss his granddaughter with dry lips. "Nothing you and Bonnie can do up there, either. We'll be hungry when we come down."

Elizabeth managed a wan smile. "Guess I'll major in cooking next semester."

Bonnie joined Elizabeth in her small attempt to lighten the gloom. "Advanced Dishwashing for me." She saw Craig Soaras glance at her appreciatively, and she let him see her lips soften for him.

When the men were gone, Elizabeth watched Peter Hubbard and Wanda Lindstrom carefully placing the little red box in a corner. It seemed extremely heavy for its size. She could not restrain her curiosity. "What's in that, Peter?"

He answered without turning. "Something Wanda and I may need to use." There was a sharp tone as he added, "You and Bonnie please stay away from it."

Elizabeth flushed at what she took to be a rebuke. Peter should know she would never interfere with any lab procedure. His reply had reminded her again that it was Wanda Lindstrom and not she who was his partner. She flounced toward the kitchen. He didn't have to rub it in! she thought. And softened at once, understanding that her quick irritation wasn't directed at him, but at the bleakness descended on her beloved island.

Opening the kitchen door, Elizabeth gasped in dismay. The storm had blown a stone through the window. Wind was funneling in, scattering papers, rattling dishes. Bonnie hopped to help Elizabeth plug the hole as best they could with dishrags. "We'd better check the other rooms!" Elizabeth suggested. "The shape this building is in, it'll fall over if the wind gets any worse."

"Can't be any worse than this!" To Bonnie, it looked as if the gale was literally tilting the entire beach, blowing a wall of sand so dense she could hardly make out the sea beyond. The waves seemed to tower to the thundering sky. The woman gulped in amazement. "My God! Those waves must be fifty feet high!"

Elizabeth squinted through the window. "Twenty-five, for sure. They don't get much more than that."

"High enough for me!"

"It's what sailors call the long fetch, you see." Elizabeth was surprised to see Bonnie nod knowledgeably.

Bonnie smiled, pleased. "Craig explained how the sea builds up for thousands of miles coming out of the northeast with no interruption." Bonnie moved from the window. "Glad I'm not out in that!"

Starting to straighten the kitchen, Elizabeth said, "I was caught in worse with my grandfather when I was a kid."

"What happened?"

"We got wet."

"How come it can storm this way and not be raining, Liz?"

"It squalls," Elizabeth told Bonnie. She pointed to a black area of sea and sky in the distance. "Over there it's coming down to drown fishes!"

Bonnie sighed. "I thought I liked the seashore, but not this, honey. Craig tells me there's sharks all over the place, too, especially off the east side . . ."

"Mako and stuff, yes. You always have to be careful." Elizabeth saw her friend's genuine worry. "You should have gone to Chatham with the others, Bonnie."

"No way. The men need us here. It's just the storm has me jittery."

"No, I mean, this trouble we're having, it isn't really your concern."

"Hey! I'm with you, Liz!"

"I only mean there's no reason for you to expose yourself to danger."

"I'm not in any danger." Bonnie's lovely, strong chin came up and she said with confidence, "Peter and Wanda will work it out, I'm sure. I just think everyone is so wonderfully brave, like the way they're plowing into the forest fire up there . . ."

Elizabeth said thoughtfully, "You're talking about men

who have been to sea, Bonnie. It separates the men from the boys. They can't afford to treat anything as an 'emergency'—they have to be cool every moment, know exactly what to do and *not* to do. The ocean can be a lot rougher than this, you know. Sometimes, with the wind blowing one way and the tides running differently, even the waves don't know where they're going! *That* takes sailing!"

Bonnie allowed herself a small, confessing grin. "I never dreamed I'd be interested in a fisherman . . ." She added self-consciously, "Of course, I mean just as a friend."

Elizabeth smiled to herself. Storms were unpredictable and so were people. If Bonnie liked Craig Soaras, so much the better for both of them.

Checking the floor above, the women found another broken window and leaned loose boards against the opening. It did little good. The wind kept blowing sand all over the room, but no one was using it so it made little difference.

When there was no more they could do, Elizabeth started down to the kitchen. "Vegetable-peeling time, I'm afraid."

Bonnie said, "I'll tell you a secret, Liz, I love cooking."

Elizabeth Carr laughed, a welcome bright sound. "Don't ever tell my mother, but I do, too."

Bonnie said in a teasing tone, "And don't think I didn't notice the way you gave Peter Hubbard the best parts of that fish chowder, friend."

Elizabeth responded lightly, not wanting to be drawn into the circling confusions in her own mind. "Why, of course, Bonnie. It's an old Yarkie custom to give a visiting scientist the red carpet treatment."

"Don't get me wrong," Bonnie added at once. "I think he's absolutely super."

Elizabeth made herself shrug. "Yes, my father—and Wanda Lindstrom—think the world of him."

TWO

In the laboratory room, Peter Hubbard and Wanda Lindstrom were making new dissections. Their gleaming steel scalpels clicked on cold glass slides as they worked with silent efficiency amid the bubbling flasks and other apparatus.

There was a clicking from a roach container. Hubbard murmured, "I wish you had gotten the screw-top jars."

"I know," Wanda Lindstrom said. And defensively, "The stockroom sent up the wrong cartons, and I'd have missed the plane if I'd waited."

Hubbard glanced across the table with a quick, friendly expression. He knew how sensitive his associate was beneath her cool exterior. "I'm not scolding, Wanda. Just a bit worried whether the covers will hold those brutes." He scrutinized the jars on the improvised shelves. The roaches were abnormally active. In the daytime, under the bright lights that Craig Soaras had rigged up, these nocturnal creatures should be sluggish, motionless. Instead, they were scuttling and scooting around the glass cages energetically. Hubbard wondered whether they might be receiving a pheromonic summons from the central domicile—asking where they were, calling them home. Might the group be so well-knit, might their communications be so advanced?

Wanda Lindstrom was answering his concern. "I've checked every cover, Peter. Absolutely tight, and too heavy even for these beasts. The lips go down a full half-inch."

Hubbard frowned. "But not ground glass."

The woman said firmly, "Any cockroach that can beat those covers deserves to get out!"

The scientist smiled at her. "Not near me, please!"

She was mollified a little, and admitted, "I'd feel safer with the screw tops, myself."

They returned to their silent examination of the roach carcasses before them. After a full hour, Wanda Lindstrom straightened. She rubbed the back of her neck, wincing. "My neck's killing me again, Peter. One of your better massages, please?"

"My pleasure." Hubbard put down his scalpel. His strong fingers went familiarly to her neck, and he pressed gently into the stiffened muscles.

The woman sighed with pleasure, but spoke of their work. "Do you notice a decided enlargement of the Malpighian tubules, in both the male and female roaches?" Her eyes closed blissfully.

Continuing the massage, Hubbard said, "Yes. I've been thinking about that. They may be using the excretory system rather than other glands to send out the phero-monic signals."

There was another sigh of relieved tension from the woman. "It's a real possibility, I'd say."

His fingers pressed harder. "We'd need more powerful microscopes to be sure."

"M-m-m!—It doesn't really matter, though. I mean, we've established an unusual number of pheromonic chemicals already." Dr. Lindstrom opened her eyes and indicated the apparatus containing the variety of chemical tests proceeding all around them. She turned to face him, eyes closed again. She sighed deeply. "Oh, that's good, Peter . . ."

The man rotated his fingers into her shoulders. Her head bent closer toward his chest. Peter Hubbard smelled the woman's hair beneath his nose. It held a trace of sweet perfume. His mind went back to the one time, after Christmas drinks at a faculty party, when he had taken her home and they had almost—

The man concentrated on the massage. The neck muscles were stiff as a board. Elizabeth Carr, he mused, would be soft and yielding under his touch. He was glad for the break in the dissection, and he let his thoughts spiral. Women should be soft. He was old-fashioned about that.

Wanda Lindstrom looked up with misty eyes. "You always make me feel like purring."

"Long practice, after all," Hubbard laughed companionably.

What the woman said came as a surprise to him. "I like Elizabeth Carr." In the hovering silence that followed, an explanation seemed necessary, a word to indicate she was making no personal comment about Peter Hubbard's relationships with anyone else in the world. "I mean, whenever I've seen her in Cambridge, she seemed—oh, a princess character. Here she's been cleaning like a housemaid, peeling potatoes without a fuss."

"You've had her wrong. She is good people," Peter Hubbard said, dropping his hands.

Wanda Lindstrom returned to her place, her voice quickly clinical again. "I've dissected out the brain and ganglia on this specimen. I suspect a high order of neuronal function. I'd guess we'll find noradrenaline, adrenaline, and neurosecretory cells with granules making kinetic metabolic hormones . . ."

Hubbard responded in the same business-like tone: "Morphogenetic controls on growth and development, abnormally advanced. Yes." He studied his own specimen. "I would say these roaches can do damn near everything but *think!*" He paused, then declared, "And maybe even that, in their own way . . ."

"Well, I wouldn't go quite that far," the woman considered.

The two scientists became so absorbed in their dialogue that they did not observe what was happening on a shelf behind them. Had they been looking at the container set aside for the largest group of roaches, they would have witnessed a remarkable feat. An ingenious escape effort was under way. It was an effort requiring the kind of "thinking" Peter Hubbard had just anticipated—a plan requiring common purpose, common effort in an amazing way.

The scientists were sincere and correct in their caution against anthropomorphism, but both Peter and Wanda had themselves described insect colonies acting with seeming intelligence, and an intercommunication that paralleled some human behavior. Wanda Lindstrom would have been reminded instantly of the time she had watched ants cross a water obstacle by forming a bridge of individual insects. It was a living construction, with one ant crawling on top of another and clinging to the preceding body while another ant repeated the process. The linkage of clasped forms became the core of reinforcing strands of ants, until it was strong enough for the whole tribe to use as a span.

Similarly, rats were known to ascend out of deep holes by forming a ladder of their bodies.

The Yarkie roaches in the specimen jar were now engineering just such a ladder device. They were at the last inch up the side of the jar, reaching toward the glass cover. Although the lid was tight, the roaches atop the living ladder were beginning to loosen it little by little. Whatever their drive, the comparative effort among men would have been superhuman. The insects worked silently, as if fearing that any noise would attract attention from their huge white Enemies across the room.

Then it somehow became clear to the roaches that a single ladder could only tilt the lid, making it stick harder on the opposite side. Promptly, a second ladder was started at the other end. Finally, together, the leading cockroaches

—ones with the strongest heads, apparently—lifted in concert.

And the lid moved up, evenly.

It moved only a fraction of an inch each time, but with primordial patience the monster insects continued the task—until their combined strength and cunning actually raised the glass cover sufficiently.

But their intelligence, if such it was, did not foresee that their success would bring a shattering noise.

Hubbard and Lindstrom took in the threat in a moment. A great cockroach with a five-inch wing expanse was already flying at the man's eyes. Hubbard ducked in the nick of time, and Wanda Lindstrom batted the roach to the floor where she ground it savagely under her heel.

Other roaches were crawling up the living ladders and scrambling out of captivity. Not all were the flying type. They sat on the open shelf sifting the air for the scent of the Enemy. Hubbard shouted to the horrified woman to escape out of the room. He himself rushed for another lid.

A flying roach landed squarely on Peter Hubbard's nose. Without thinking, he smashed his face hard with his open palm. It killed the roach, but squirted its smashed innards over his cheeks, sending a stinging chemical into his eyes. He stood stunned, temporarily blinded, unable to defend himself against the roach threats now coming more fiercely from the opened glass container.

Wanda Lindstrom saw there were only moments to act before the full scores of roaches sallied out of the jar and set upon them both. She shoved Hubbard out of her way to rush to a steaming kettle nearby, and dashed back with it to the shelf, pouring the boiling chemical on the roaches crawling and hopping about. Watching them shrivel, she did not notice when two huge roaches, as if teamed, winged up and struck at her eyes. The woman shrieked with the abrupt pain and, in the shock of the assault, dropped the utensil. Scalding liquid skinned her feet in an instant.

Peter Hubbard, wiping out his eyes, leaped to help his besieged colleague. Roaches were already tearing at her blistering legs, their mandibles peeling off the burned flesh easily, their teeth avidly chewing the soft, blood-oozing tissues. Wanda Lindstrom slumped to the floor, moaning. Dropping beside her, Hubbard tried to pick away the storming cockroaches. He smashed a few, but many clung to the running wounds. For the moment, the gorging insects disregarded the man; the open flesh was easier to get at, and they were hungry after their long fast.

Wanda Lindstrom cried at him indistinctly, "It's too late, Peter! Don't let them get *you!*"

He still tried to aid her. The insect bodies became a moving blotch over her face. Hubbard tried to keep the roaches off, but he saw one already crawling up into her nose, others violating her ears, and both her eyes had been taken at the first assault. The woman kicked Hubbard away with her burned, torn feet. "Get *out*, Peter!" Her scream gurgled through globs of blood streaking her chin, running down her throat into the cleft between her breasts. The white lab coat was smeared crimson. He saw she was right.

Peter Hubbard started to fumble his way out, but was overcome with nausea. As he helplessly vomited, he thought how it was one thing to examine a chewed dog ear under a microscope, to hear of the abomination on Dickens Point, but it was intolerable to watch his companion choking to death because cockroaches were crammed in her nose and throat. It was one thing to dissect an insect-lacerated rabbit and another to see these scurfy roaches drill into the body of his dear and cherished friend, Wanda Lindstrom.

Wanda could have escaped, Hubbard considered bitterly as he bent again in his vomiting. She could easily have made it to the door when that one roach had landed on his face. But she had stayed in the lab, gone for the boiling liquid, consciously risked her life to save him.

And he had been unable to save her. She lay still now, mercifully fainted or, better, quiet in the clemency of death.

Now, Hubbard realized abruptly, roaches were lurching toward him, attracted by the stink of his sickness. He had to save himself! He was Yarkie's one hope for now. He looked about desperately for the dry-ice tanks, then realized that in the haste of the men, the weapons had been left in the kitchen shed. Could he get out at all?

Not if the roaches could help it!

They had sensed him again. Through his still-fogged eyes, he could make out hazy forms crawling toward his shoes. Sickeningly, there were new wings fanning around his head. With his hands up, Hubbard made for the door. With only half-vision, he stumbled into a crate from which Wanda had been taking fresh apparatus. He tripped. As he flung his arms out to regain his balance, the flailing kept the flying roaches from him. He stamped at others on the floor, and slid frighteningly on the slippery mess they made, almost going down.

He grabbed a table, clung to it, breathing heavily, wishing his eyes would clear. He needed to get to the sink and water. But if he stumbled or skidded again he might fall, and if he fell they would be over him in an instant.

The kitchen door flew open. After hearing the commotion in the laboratory, it had taken Elizabeth minutes to free a carbon dioxide extinguisher from the packs tied in the shed. She had realized at once what must have happened. Now she burst into the room with the black tank nozzle held out like a gun, her legs apart, ready to let loose a dry-ice bombardment.

She took in the scene immediately, and pressed the trigger violently. The white, freezing stream blasted onto the roaches circling the floor threatening Hubbard.

Elizabeth Carr had no time for the revulsion that wrenched her insides when she saw Wanda Lindstrom, with cockroaches invading the bloodied corpse. She turned the spray on the bugs with new imprecations. She saw the woman was gone, the dry ice could do her no harm now. As the insects died, Elizabeth heard herself shrilling, "Come on, you spawn of hell! Just come after me, damn you!"

Behind her came Bonnie's uncertain voice. "What's *happening*, Liz?"

Elizabeth screamed hoarsely, "Get *out*, Bonnie! Close the goddamn door!"

But Bonnie was beside her friend, pulling away a roach that had reached Elizabeth's ear. The black woman warned frantically, "They're getting at *you*, Liz!"

Peter Hubbard was at the lab sink, furiously trying to get his eyes clear. But water seemed to have been a mistake. Whatever chemical the roach had left on his face made an acid that blurred his vision rather than clearing it. He had to stand by helplessly while the two women were trying to fight off the insects.

Bonnie Taylor went down on her knees in a reflex of fury, and was chopping at every roach within reach with the kitchen knife she held in her hand. With each hacking blow she gave out a loud grunt of satisfaction as the sharp blade slashed giant roaches into pieces. She shuddered in new horror when she saw both pieces of a roach body continue to scuttle about for a moment after being sliced apart.

Peter Hubbard blinked his eyes hard, willing them to recover. Thankfully, the effects of the chemical began to wear off. He still could not see clearly, but at least could make out the figures of Elizabeth and Bonnie, and saw the furious contest they were in. There were still scores of roaches attacking, each one a hideous threat of blindness and worse.

Hubbard grabbed Bonnie from her knees. "Get two more of the tanks, *fast!*" She obeyed swiftly. To Elizabeth, Hubbard barked anxiously, "Are you all right, Liz?"

"A few bites, but okay, I think!" Elizabeth panted. "You?"

For answer, the man grabbed the tank from her. "Give me that and get back inside with Bonnie!"

Elizabeth handed the tank over. As it left her hands, she was seized with a tremor. The ordeal had stimulated her to physical action equal to her fury. Now horror took over, searing every last nerve. The tears came as she took in Wanda Lindstrom's ravaged face—that beautiful face ripped like a rag—and the stare of the blank eye sockets. Bright, intelligent, caring human eyes only minutes ago!

Elizabeth ran for the kitchen to help Bonnie bring more tanks. But the floor was slippery now with melting dry ice as well as gore, and she lost her balance. She landed on her buttocks with a bump that drove the wind out of her.

Hubbard cried out, aiming his tank near her, "Hurry *up!* Get into the kitchen!" He saw insects circling her fallen body at once. They were too close to Elizabeth to permit the use of the tank.

Crawling on her knees, in her panic the woman kept slipping and sliding like a clown. But it was not funny in any way. Sheer terror was on her face as she saw three great roaches nipping at her ankle, the blood spreading quickly on her skin.

"Peter!" Her voice came out as a croak of despair rather than a cry for help.

Hubbard dropped his tank and stepped carefully to Elizabeth. Disregarding the danger to himself, he deliberately picked off the attacking roaches, one by one. They punctured his fingers and drew his blood, but he did not stop.

Bonnie came in again, joining the laboratory battle. "Throw those bugs right here!" she yelled. "I'll squirt the motherfuckers to death!"

Peter Hubbard was as human as any of them. When he had lifted Elizabeth safely to her feet, he carefully placed each roach where he could stamp on it with his heavy boot. He wanted the personal revenge of hearing their fat bodies pop and break under his foot. It could not help Wanda Lindstrom, or the other victims, but it could express the surging hatred he felt for these harpies, these scum of Nature. It was not a scientist's reaction; it was a man's.

He guided Elizabeth gently while Bonnie covered them both with her tank. In the kitchen, Hubbard cleansed the woman's bites, then left Bonnie with Elizabeth and went back into the laboratory for his grim, necessary task. With dry-ice flowing, he killed every escaped roach he could see. At Wanda Lindstrom's body, he iced to death every brown-black insect that was violating the woman. His face was a mask of primitive malevolence.

When nothing more moved near Wanda Lindstrom, he knelt to roll the body over. As he suspected there were still roaches at work, eating at her back, masticating her flesh. With his jaws biting until his teeth hurt, Hubbard ragingly sprayed the dry ice to murder them all. Finally, every insect was belly up, legs stiff wires in death. Wanda Lindstrom's enemies were frozen and gone.

Peter Hubbard searched the room thoroughly for any other possible loose insects. He saw none he hadn't killed. He found gripper's tape in a carton and strongly sealed the lids of every remaining specimen jar—the bloody pariahs would not repeat their escape. As he worked grimly on, he thought he should have been a theologian rather than a biologist. Maybe then he would understand how Nature, or God, or Whatever could create this blind vicious hunger to so wretchedly destroy a woman like Wanda Lindstrom.

Looking down, above the torn body, the dry-ice tank hanging from his weary hand, the scientist cried for her, for all of them.

THREE

There would be grief later on at the memorial services for Wanda Lindstrom held in Cambridge, but nothing then would match the outpouring of sorrow of the Yarkie men returning from High Ridge that night after the laboratory debacle. With the help of new rain, the second flare-up of fire in the woods had been controlled without too much difficulty. Now the men shared the bitterness of fellow soldiers beside a fallen comrade.

This woman, so different from all of them, had come to aid Yarkie, and she had helped generously, without the reserve that might have been expected. She had not needed to trek to the kettle hole searching for the roaches with them. She had not needed to work so arduously in the lab. She had not needed to respond so immediately to Hubbard's summons in the first place. Far from being cold or distant, she had stood with them shoulder to shoulder. And from what they learned now, she had just sacrificed her life to save Peter Hubbard's. The Yarkie men gave Wanda Lindstrom their highest accolade—she was "top-notch crew."

At times like this the least said among them, the best. The sheriff quietly asked Craig to make a coffin. Meantime, Elizabeth and Bonnie had, with aching tenderness, wrapped the woman's broken body in old curtains. The shroud was not clean, but it covered the terrible sight. The men, as if in a funeral procession, reverently carried the body to the empty second-floor room and laid it on the sandy floor until the officials could decide how to handle the matter the next morning.

When Elizabeth called the Task Force to dinner, they ate without appetite. In the general quiet, they became conscious of the noisy way Russell Homer stowed away his food. He didn't slurp, but he bent over his plate and sucked food into his mouth, swallowing with an audible gulp. It was a little irritating, but at the same time somehow comforting, a reminder of normal Yarkie days when there was nothing more troublesome to be worrying about than one's manners and what herbs to put in a fish chowder.

FOUR

That night on their side-by-side cots, Elizabeth and Bonnie were dismally aware of the missing bed. It had been moved into Peter Hubbard's room for Elias Johnson to use. With families gone off the island, the other men remained in the lighthouse for an early start to hunt the roach nest at daybreak. They were in sleeping bags on the laboratory floor, except for Ben Dorset who was spending the night with the volunteers in the firehouse. Stephen Scott was in his own home, feeling ill, he said.

The overall plan was clear and agreed. With dawn, they could scout the pirate cave Elias Johnson had mentioned that afternoon. Assuming the woodland would be cooled by the rain that had fallen on and off, the forest should be safe enough for bringing in cans of gasoline. If they found the nest, Peter Hubbard would use carbon dioxide—in gaseous form—to immobilize the insects while he studied them. Then the flame would put an end to the scourge.

Hubbard believed that most if not all of the roach armies would have swarmed back to their hub, especially after the disturbance of the forest fires. If there were individual strays, they could be dealt with in time, probably with baited traps.

On the other hand, if the nest was not discovered, then Elias Johnson was to call in the U.S. Public Health Service. Officials would have to be advised of Wanda Lindstrom's body and of the mysterious disappearances on the island. It was going to be a tangled nightmare of red tape, Johnson thought as he turned on his cot with a sigh of despondency.

Peter Hubbard had remained silent about "Plan B." Time enough to interpose it if it became necessary. It would have been a little easier with Wanda's help, but he could manage it alone.

Bonnie Taylor murmured to her friend, "Get a good night's sleep. Things will look brighter in the morning. That's what my mother always said, and she was always wrong."

Elizabeth Carr could not sleep. Wanda Lindstrom's gashed face stayed in her mind. Elizabeth was weeping for the woman with an honest, open grief that wracked her body and mind. These were tears of self-knowledge, too. All at once, the daughter of Jessica and Richard Carr saw herself not with her own self-centered eyes but with the judgment of a world outside. What a long way she had to go before she could match Wanda Lindstrom's self-sufficiency, and the value of the woman's work! And what a long way to be worthy of Peter Hubbard in the way Wanda Lindstrom had been.

For the first time in her life Elizabeth Carr, lying on a bumpy mattress in a wind-leaking lighthouse on a roach-infested island, was led to take stock of her weaknesses and failings instead of basking in her taken-for-granted strengths and blessings—her family's wealth, her own good looks and innate brains and charm. They were a heritage, not earned. She had never really applied herself fully at school. She resolved strongly that in her senior year and her graduate work thereafter she would stretch herself. It would be a way of remembering Wanda Lindstrom for giving her life for Peter Hubbard. Who, Elizabeth considered palely, had very nearly sacrificed his own life for her!

She could not keep her eyes closed. A lemon moon was out after the storm, shining through the window over Bonnie's blanketed shoulder. The rain was gone, the wind and waves were easing off. Elizabeth raised herself on an elbow. How lovely things could be. The sand was a curious lavender hue and the sea a contrasting pewter color in the yellowish moonlight.

Bonnie's dark face against this strange combination of night colors was even more beautiful than ordinarily. Egyptian princess? She had a nobility. And Craig had his own, of the sea itself . . .

The woman's musings were interrupted by a faint clicking sound from outside. She put it to loose boards. This lighthouse's walls would be flapping like seagulls in the next big blow, she groused. Elizabeth dropped back to her lumpy pillow, and closed her ears against the sound. With the men leaving at dawn, she'd have to be up unearthly early to put the coffee to the kettle . . .

FIVE

In the New Place of dark, warmth and rechambered food stores, an irritating odor was thickening the air and creating disquiet and restlessness. Around the pulsing central Dome of the Nest, the creatures stirred and fanned the gloom with their antennae.

The smoke seeping in from the forest fires was not the only cause of the community agitation. Their spiracles had known such a stinging from time to time when they were back in the dump. Now it came along with a confusion of signals, difficult to sort out, baffling to decision. The murky air carried urgent roach calls as well as the smoke. Some of the roach signals were clear, such as alarm and urgency, but there was something else—something the straining sensories in the Nest could not take in or use for action. As a result, contradictory emanations were coming from the Dome in the center. The disarray was making some of the insects wild, leading them to sudden cannibalistic assaults on neighbors.

Many of the layers of roaches lay quiet, however. Most waited torpidly for some clear stimulus of hunger, thirst, sex, alarm.

Suddenly, the Dome ceased its uneasy pulsations. The Nest grew quiet, silent, motionless. Not an antenna stirred. As suddenly again, the Dome heaved, shuddering so violently that many layers of roaches were displaced. The disturbing message from outside had finally been deciphered! ... Roaches outside were captives ... They were relaying not only their own call for help, but an urgent message ... *"The Nest itself was threatened...* Large animals were seeking the Nest, to destroy the Colony ..."

Defend! Defend!

The Dome heaved violently: *Send out the fighters! ...* Follow the scent, and *attack! ...* Launch another raid! Besiege and storm the Enemy!

The central Dome spasmed again, and great roaches raced up the exit tunnels after their captains who had rushed to the front. Something magnetic in the Yarkie night was now tiding the roaches irresistibly—urging, requiring, dominating. It had to be responded to by each insect. It had to be fulfilled, as stomachs needed food, as wombs needed sperm. *Survival was at stake!* ... Kill! Destroy whatever was inimical! ... Strike first! Strike and protect! ... March! Strike! ... Protect the Colony! At all cost!

Layer after layer of the great roaches peeled off the Dome. Roach platoons formed up quickly in orderly fashion, multiplying into battalions, with designated commanders in charge. Thousands upon thousands of the roaches hastened out through the freshly dug tunnels until the only insects left in the Nest were the egg-laying females—who were depositing their oöthecae early because of the disturbance—and the palace guard around the Dome, which, having completed its commands, now subsided into a slow rhythmic pulsing.

The guard roaches, in thousands surrounding the Dome, were truly mammoth insects—as much as eight inches long and well over an inch around, with mandibles and teeth as viciously dangerous as any jungle animal. The huge mouths and sawteeth could chop through bone as easily as pulp. These were literally the killer sharks of the Colony, especially bred and programmed to be the royal protectors. They circled in an endless, fearsome procession of deadly intent around and around the Throne of the Roach Society.

SIX

The roach commanders led the advancing fighter horde confidently through the forest as the signal odor grew stronger and more intense, a funnel of pheromones narrowing toward the lighthouse. The slithering roach formations looked like great snakes sliding through the ashes of the forest fire. These were sinister reptiles with endless bodies, reaching out of the Medusa's head of the Dome in the Nest.

Nearing the edge of the trees and the open space of the lighthouse beach, the phalanx was halted. Scouts were dispatched. They hurried away, keeping to the clumps of dune grass that were almost phosphorescently gray-green in the now-fading moonlight. The vulnerability of the open space must be risked. The messages coming from the Great White Tree ahead of them were more urgent than ever. Their swiftness was on their side. If the Enemy spotted them, they would still be strong in combat, for they would strike at the huge Tree from every arc.

The scouts raced back to the main body. They tattooed a new message: The easiest prey was not on the level from which the roach signals were coming, but from a space above. Easy to reach, easy climbing. And no signs of counterattack, no Enemy lurking. Quietness everywhere, little sounds only, unfrightening, no threatening vibrations.

As the roach troops moved out of the shadows of the trees, the beach seemed to quiver and come alive. It was as if the grains of sand took on life and motion, rolling toward the lighthouse and starting to climb the white exterior. The climbing insects were like a rising brown wash on the walls.

Up and under the loose shingles of the lighthouse, roaches crawled easily, easily found the broken window of the room where Wanda Lindstrom's body lay. Inside, the insects jostled each other in their haste to enjoy this new human repast. Their shells clicked against each other as they quarreled for position at the feast. The cockroaches were hungry now. In changing nests, it had been necessary to leave much food behind, and the transferred supplies had gone first to the Dome and the palace guards, with the females next. These fighters and workers had been waiting their turn. In their greed now, they began to exchange loud droning hisses warning each other off as they snatched at the corpse's flesh before them.

The noises of the scuttling, clicking, and puffing came down the open staircase to the room where Elizabeth Carr and Bonnie Taylor were sleeping. It was Elizabeth in her restiveness who heard it first. She nudged Bonnie with a terrified whisper, *"Something is upstairs!"* Half-asleep, she almost imagined Wanda Lindstrom's ghost coming down the steps.

But the women both knew at once what the "something" was. Bonnie came bolt upright. The hissing noise pierced her ears like a branding iron. She would never forget the terrible sound that had drawn Sharky to his death. "My God, the roaches are *here!*"

Both women had the same horrifying thought—the insects had found Wanda Lindstrom and were at her body. From the loudness and scuffling, it was clear that this invasion of the lighthouse was not just strays or a small group but a multitude of ghouls.

Despite the horror upstairs, the women were thankful. At least they had a chance to warn the others and to escape.

Grabbing clothes blindly, the two dashed into the men's dormitory. They took care to be as quiet as possible. They were veterans of roachmanship now, Elizabeth thought wryly. They knew too well that they must avoid sending vibration signals of their own to the invaders.

Elizabeth whispered to awaken Peter Hubbard, as Bonnie did to Craig Soaras. Hubbard jumped off his bed wearing pajamas. Craig leaped up stark naked. It was no time to be embarrassed. The men ducked for their clothes, waking Elias Johnson, Russell Homer and Amos Tarbell.

The sheriff directed, "Everybody grab a tank and get outside to the cars! We'll be able to freeze them off if they come after us."

Peter Hubbard handed a specimen jar to Russell Homer. *"Save this one!"* He himself ran for the red box in the corner.

At that moment, before anyone could reach the door,

the ceiling gave way, blocking the exit. It was the rot of the old wood, newly strained by the storm.

Avalanching with the debris, with Wanda Lindstrom's doubly ravaged body, with the dust, and the sand, came a cascade of the deadly cockroaches. For a moment, the falling insects were as stupefied as the humans, but they immediately scuttled to reorganize into attacking formations. A fresh imperative knit them quickly into a new army against the humans. It was almost as if the roach leaders had raised flags and pennants proclaiming these humans the Enemy they had been dispatched to fight and destroy. The Dome had not sent them for the corpse higher up. That had been an accident, a diversion they should not have allowed themselves. Now they were in harmony with each other and with the Dome again. They knew where the signals had come from—their fellow roaches, captive in the jars on the shelves! The signals from their maddened brothers were overwhelming now—not only the call for assistance, but the companion message: Protect the Nest! . . . Destroy the Enemy!

The invisible pheromonic surges were sweeping the air powerfully between the Nest and the room: March! Kill! Protect! . . . Consume the Enemy, that it will not consume the Nest!

The exchange of the vibrating insect messages—like a grim parody of radio waves traversing space—gave the beleaguered people the moment they needed to open their own attack on the insects. From the kitchen, Ben Dorset and Craig Soaras passed the deadly dry-ice extinguishers into the debris-filled laboratory. The black horns of the tanks began to spurt carbon dioxide. The ice vapor formed everywhere over the roach brigades in lethal, exterminating streams.

Amos Tarbell was shouting, "The back window! Quick!" Holding the tanks like flame throwers, the people backed hastily from the ever-advancing roach battalions. Tarbell yelled again. "Elizabeth! Bonnie! Go on out while we cover you!"

To the sheriff's amazement, Peter Hubbard was pushing Elizabeth aside to get out first. Amos Tarbell would have bet the man was no coward, but now he was showing his colors! *Bastard!* What the hell was so precious in the red box? Why didn't he leave it and get the hell out of the way?

Antipathy for the scientist was swept from the sheriff's mind when he saw a flying roach go for Hubbard's neck. The avid insect had already pinched up flesh in its mandibles and slashed a deep wound, sucking blood. Holding on to the red box, Hubbard could not use his hands to defend himself. Tarbell thought of going to his aid, but he had to use his tank to defend his own position; and roaches were threatening all around the others.

Elizabeth heard Hubbard's gasp of pain. She darted to him, her fingers reaching for the roach. He yelled at her furiously, "Don't touch it!" She disregarded his warning and yanked at the insect with all her hatred. Sickeningly, its body came off in her hand, while its head remained obscenely fastened on Peter Hubbard's neck. Shuddering, Elizabeth remembered his telling of ants that acted the same.

The sheriff was ordering her angrily to climb out through the window. She was just in time to turn her tank on a rush of roaches coming at her bare feet from one side. Elizabeth splashed them with a furious jerk of the tank, and bobbed her head in deep satisfaction as the vapor immobilized them. Filth! she cried to herself. Die! *Die!*

Tarbell saw Hubbard still awkwardly blocking the window. He bellowed furiously, "Let the women out, damn it!" Peter Hubbard heard the accusation of cowardice in the man's shout.

The sheriff swore in his rage. Something was going

on he did not understand, and had no time to consider further. Roaches were closing in on him from all sides. He had to spin like a top, spraying a fast and widening circle to keep the slithering fiends at bay.

Behind him, he heard another cry of alarm. A flying roach was attacking Bonnie Taylor's face. Craig Soaras trained his extinguisher her way before realizing he could not spray the dry ice without injuring the woman herself. He dropped the tank to rush to her side. The roach came off in his hand. Thankfully he saw only a small spot of crimson on her dark cheek. Her eyes were safe. "Craig," she moaned. Just his name, but in it he heard not only her gratitude for his risk but a tenderness he had not dared to dream about.

In the moment Soaras stood beside Bonnie Taylor without his protective tank, a quick crescent of the cockroaches got at his feet. They struck as a gang, as if at one command, so that the man had no time to regain his tank. He gagged with the pain of the knife-like incisions. Desperate, Bonnie made a precipitate decision and triggered carbon dioxide at his feet. He might be hurt by the dry ice, but the roaches were worse.

As if maddened by Bonnie's attack after tasting Craig's blood, a flight of roaches zoomed at his unprotected head. They were like small savage bats arrowing toward his eyes. There was no way Bonnie could help without blinding him or killing him with her dry ice. His own flailing arms could not keep off all the swarm.

In torment, Bonnie watched helplessly as more insects landed on Craig's head. One rested obscenely on his mustache, lifting its body as if to crow cockily. Its companions had already started their terrible destruction of eyes and flesh. One huge roach aimed for and reached Craig Soaras's jugular. His blood spurted onto Bonnie Taylor's arm as she tried to come to his rescue.

The woman took the man's dying agony into herself. His groans of pain were hers as he kept trying to yank the clinging insects off his skin, out of his ears, away from his clenched mouth. Bonnie wanted to embrace the man, tell her love, hold him for the life they could never now have together.

She could not move to save him, or herself. She was paralyzed with the horror of his murder as the killer roaches took his face to pieces before her eyes. Her own dry ice tank dropped from her fingers in her anguished defeat. She prayed that the roaches would end her too, and fast. She hardly heard Elizabeth Carr screaming, "Come out, Bonnie! *Hurry!*"

Amos Tarbell stamped to Bonnie with his tank spraying roach death fiercely. He kept the killers away from the woman, but she was blind with her loss, with the devastation of the impossible raid. Not her flesh but her mind and heart were being despoiled.

The sheriff tried to pull the woman to the window where the others were now outside, reaching in to help). Hampered by his tank, he could not get hold of her and she remained rooted, staring at the insects now covering Craig Soaras's still-twitching muscles. Tarbell kicked the woman's legs to make her move. She looked up from the dying man on the floor. Tarbell could see that he was a stranger to her. Her eyes were a zombie's. But she started to the window. With Tarbell's tank protecting them both, they reached the eager, outstretched hands of their friends. Tarbell kept triggering the killing spray at the oncoming marauders, overcome with his own loathing and fury. To him the formation of the roach heads, their eyes, mandibles, mouths, gave them the appearance of laughing monsters—monstrosities mocking all the humans! This, he thought, was what the demons of Hell must really look like: *Roaches!* Satan himself a deformed, giant roach!

The sheriff heard Elias Johnson calling desperately for him to leave. "Amos! We want to burn the place fast, while they're all inside!"

The sheriff gave the nearest roaches one more deadly shot of his dry ice, and leaped through the window head first, heedless of the jagged glass. He jumped to his feet to help Johnson, Homer, and Hubbard as soon as he understood what they were up to. They were stationing themselves around the lighthouse, carrying gasoline cans.

"All at once!" Elias Johnson cried. *"Splash her now!"* Johnson lit a flare and threw it into the lighthouse. The explosions of orange-red flame showed droves of cockroaches crawling out on the window frames coming after the people. The blaze caught them. Some were soaked with gasoline and split open with a hard percussion that had the Yarkie men cheering. To them, the flaring up of the roach legion was a burning flag of revenge, a fire banner of reprisal and retaliation. The conflagration stirred a sediment of savagery in them they did not know they owned.

Cries of triumph came from Johnson, Tarbell, and Homer. Elias Johnson's eyes were fiery orbs of his own wrath. Let this burning lighthouse and the incarceration of the roaches avenge the murders of Craig Soaras and Wanda Lindstrom, of everyone the killers had slaughtered and bereaved. The old man watched with a dark, unhidden exultation as the gasoline explosions ripped the building. Now the lighthouse was a different kind of beacon light, he thought truculently—now it was a marker of a different kind of succor and salvation for beleaguered people.

They were wiping out the insects.

SEVEN

Leaving the flaming tower behind, in Johnson's car speeding for the village, Bonnie Taylor was sobbing wretchedly in Elizabeth Carr's arms.

Peter Hubbard and Russell Homer were riding with the sheriff. In the long silence among them, it came to Amos Tarbell that if Hubbard had tried to escape first, he had a reason. The man was no coward. As if to let the scientist know he did not misunderstand, he made conversation. "You think we got all the roaches in there?"

Peter Hubbard did not open his tired eyes. He was sick to death of the insects' saturnalias of blood, of Wanda Lindstrom's heartbreaking sacrifice, of the mindless annihilation of Craig Soaras, of all the lives pillaged by the Yarkie miscreations. It was a burden he had accepted as correctly belonging on his shoulders, but it had grown too heavy with terror and death, and he felt he was sagging under it. But he knew, too, that he must keep himself strong. At this point he was truly the only one who could help Yarkie before the killer insects became uncontainable. His reserve plan had a chance of succeeding. No matter how exhausted he was, he had to set it in motion. The scientist hugged the heavy red box to his chest, and glared at the roach container he was steadying between his feet on the floor of the car. His plan required both what was in the box and in the container . . .

The sheriff was repeating the question.

"No," Hubbard had to answer. "If the roaches are organized the way I now believe, we will have burned up many of their fighters, maybe most of them. But the infestation still comes from a core on the island. I'm convinced of that absolutely. Until we get that core, this will go on and on."

Russell Homer said under his breath, "Jesus Christ, I don't know how much more I can take."

"Me, too," the sheriff admitted honestly.

Peter Hubbard fell silent. It was necessary to think through once more the details of the next step he intended in this escalating battle against the killer cockroaches. What exactly were its chances of working? What were its risks?

There would be time enough to tell the others of "Plan B" after they had all taken some breakfast, and after he had primed his "secret weapon."

They were lucky the Chatham police chief had been able to get his hands on what the plan required. And lucky that Craig Soaras had been able to bring it back to Yarkie without incident.

The thought of Craig Soaras made Peter Hubbard even more determined to succeed. How refreshing it was to enter a world where honesty and decency were the order of the day. Oh, not that Yarkie was a paradise of angels. Of course these people had their faults, like everyone else. Yet their way of life was still based solidly on old, proven truths of getting along through mutual respect and tolerance. They wanted no handouts, no "free lunch."

Hubbard smiled to himself wryly. He knew he was drastically simplifying problems of enormous complexity. As a scientist he chided himself for doing so, but in his head he found himself believing, perhaps childishly, that the woes of the country would be much reduced if everyone was like Craig Soaras and his fellows.

COUNTERATTACK

ONE

The bedraggled, half-clothed group arrived at the Johnson house as dawn began to show the promise of a clear day. Their spirits did not match the lightening sky. Nature was a hypocrite. The arching sky was an inviting, cerulean innocence—"heaven" above. It was hard to remember the glowering blackness of yesterday's storm. And harder to remember that the innocent morning somewhere harbored the murderous insects imperiling Yarkie.

Peter Hubbard was concentrating on the Johnson living room, trying to clear his mind of the tragedies at the lighthouse. Elizabeth looked young and fragile in the skimpy cotton bathrobe in which she had escaped. She was going around refilling coffee mugs. The man thought how much the room's simple elegance mirrored the character of the granddaughter who had come out of it.

The chamber was large and square, paneled in pine. The fireplace was of wood, not marble, and it had a wooden mantel, a business-like shelf without fuss or ornament. It was painted clean enamel white, in quiet contrast to the pewter-gray walls.

Cupboards held an assortment of milk glass behind square panes. Priceless pieces, Hubbard supposed. Yet, the chairs and sofas had a no-nonsense, homespun look —maple and walnut mixed unfashionably, with seats cushioned in faintly patterned muslins, for utility not show.

The more dramatic contrast was a museum-quality collection of treasures brought home over generations of overseas sailing and trading. As in other Yarkie homes, the Johnson sideboard held lacquer boxes of Chinese black and gold, along with carvings of ivory and alabaster. A gold-leafed Buddha head commanded one corner of the room on a fluted column of black marble. A Japanese screen of soft golds and browns brought a distant landscape of rising mists into the New England room.

These were lush notes against the basic austerity; yet nothing seemed incongruous or out of place, for everything reflected the actual experience of the people who had lived for so many years in this house, on this island. In the same way, Peter Hubbard mused, Elizabeth Carr held an exotic romantic appeal behind the sober gray of her straight New England gaze. She had grown into an arresting woman; and there was no incongruity, either, in the ardor he saw along with the intelligence in her deep-set eyes.

Elias Johnson began the necessary discussion. "One thing bothering me is whether we ought to tell the fellows in the firehouse what has been going on."

Stephen Scott, who had been called to the meeting, surrendered drearily. "I don't see how we can keep it from them anymore."

Peter Hubbard disagreed. The men listened to him with quick respect. He had to be their leader now, not Johnson or Scott or the sheriff. He said, through the weariness and distress that creased his gaunt face, "I'd like to wait until we try one more way of getting at the heart of this. It's a strategy I worked out with Dr. Lindstrom."

The man's voice broke on the name of his slaughtered colleague. Elizabeth Carr was wrenched at his obvious desolation. There was no way she could console him. She could only offer the compassion and support of her new understanding, and pray that his "strategy" would bring them all new hope against hope. The only consolation for any of them would be the total destruction of the infernal nest, the utter extermination of the raging insects.

Peter Hubbard was going on slowly, weightily. "I haven't talked about this before because it introduces a new kind of risk." His voice grew louder and blunt as he disclosed his plan. "It involves the use of radioactive material."

The silence of the group's response was a measure of their unpreparedness.

Hubbard lifted the small red box he had not let out of his grasp. "That's what I have in this box—a radioactive liquid." He said quickly, "I can assure you that the amounts to be used are very small, and will be no real threat to any of us."

The staggered sheriff asked, "You mean, Peter, you're going to put radioactive stuff in the nest when we find it?"

"No. To exterminate them that way would require a quantity that might be dangerous, and could be spread all over the island if we weren't entirely successful." He paused, and resumed, "My thought is quite different." He tapped the red box. "I plan to use this radioactivity to help us locate the nest . . ."

"How in the world—?" Stephen Scott began. The others shushed him, keen to hear the scientist.

"To explain it briefly, I am going to mix a radioactive salt with food for these roaches here." Hubbard put a finger on the taped lid of the jar he had saved from the lighthouse laboratory. "I have purposely kept these devils hungry." He eyed them narrowly. They were hyperactive, though it was morning. He judged they were ready for what he had in mind. "After these specimens have eaten radioactive food, I can follow them with a small Geiger counter I have here. My expectation is that they will head straight for their home base . . ."

"Ingenious!" Elizabeth applauded.

Amos Tarbell asked a sensible question. "How do you know what these damn things will do when you set them free? They might just as easily go for you!"

"Well, look here," the scientist reminded the group. "These fellows are in one corner with their heads pointing one way, just as we saw in the laboratory." He rotated the jar as had been done the day before, and the roaches raced across to resume their compass-pointing pattern. "After all the disturbances at the colony—forest fires, the loss of the fighter roaches we burned last night—I believe these roaches here are 'magnetized.' That is, I think the air is carrying unusually heavy pheromones pulling all the strays back to the base."

"My God, it's uncanny," Bonnie Taylor murmured.

Hubbard continued. "They have to regroup, as we would put it. I'd almost say they're 'rethinking' their position."

Elias Johnson whacked his thigh enthusiastically. "And we follow them right to the hellhole!" Spirits began to rise. "But if the radioactivity is going to be as weak as you say, Peter, how will it destroy the whole population?"

"It won't!" Hubbard spoke forcefully. "I do have a plan to get rid of them, *but let me make it plain right now that no one is going to destroy the nest until I have a chance to study what's down there and take pictures and recover specimens for the university.*"

Protest came from Elizabeth. "How can you do that without getting killed!"

Peter Hubbard gave her a pale smile. "That is my problem, then, isn't it?"

Amos Tarbell thought again he needed to apologize for ever thinking this man a coward.

Hubbard was adding, "As soon as we're ready to go, I'd like Amos and Russell to back me up with the dry-ice tanks. I'll feed these roaches our poison, take them into the woods in this jar, and let them go up there."

The sheriff spoke in an admiring tone. "You're taking a hell of a chance, Peter!"

"It's the only way," the scientist answered resolutely. He turned a stern face to the flask containing the experimental roaches. His determined thought was—*you traitors are going to lead me right to Big Daddy, aren't you?*

Peter Hubbard understood fully that the only concern of his companions was the destruction of the roach nest. They could not realize the scientific significance of the fantastic discovery he expected was awaiting him somewhere in the Yarkie woods. It would indeed be a major moment for modern biology. If only half of what he suspected was true, there were lessons to be learned in phylogeny, in biochemistry, in the evolution of the nervous system, in insect sociobiology, and more.

Unfortunately, the scientist reflected, he could see no possible way of either containing the Nest, or salvaging it. Something might yet occur to him, but for the present he would have to be satisfied with his current plan simply to take out as many significant specimens as he could.

Hubbard did not see Elizabeth Carr's admiring eyes on him. She would have liked to reach out and touch him, but the shadow of Wanda Lindstrom's death stayed her hand. It was not a time for sentiment.

Amos Tarbell was asking, "Peter, what if you let them loose and they get away from you in the leaves or wherever the hell? They're damn slick and sly."

"Precisely. The Geiger should pick them up. I expect they'll be laying down trail signal—including the radio-activity—all the way." Hubbard did not deny himself the tingle of nonscientific pleasure he felt at the thought that the roaches' own adaptive mechanisms would be working against them this time.

Stephen Scott held his mug out to Elizabeth for more coffee. "If it will get the cockroaches, I'm all for it! I think it's a brilliant idea, Peter!" he praised.

"We have another positive element going for us," the biologist said. "Remember about trophallaxis?—the way one insect regurgitates its stomach contents to feed another, and so on all around a colony? I think these roaches sometimes follow that behavior. If so, our messengers will soon be sharing their radioactivity with all their brothers and sisters. It might take twenty-four hours to contaminate the whole group, but that would give us a broader signal on the Geiger counter if I should somehow miss the trail of these particular fellows."

"And help track down strays, too!" the sheriff appreciated.

"Brilliant!" Elizabeth applauded again. The others haggardly smiled their appreciation as Peter Hubbard rose to put his strategy into action.

TWO

If the cockroach enclave had indeed been the higher-order vertebrate it resembled in many ways, the Colony could now be thought of as nursing its wounds in its lair after losing a bloody jungle battle.

The viscid Dome in the inky murkiness of the Nest was throbbing erratically with unfamiliar nerve currents. The organism's unease was only partly due to the strangeness of the recently moved domicile. The discomposure was deeper. *The group was incomplete.* It was as if an animal like a wolf had lost a limb. No blood flowed out here, but the missing layers of weight, of motion and odor and sound, were somehow akin to an open wound.

The disturbance, an inchoate inner distress, took the

form of tiny sparks of neural electricity that ran irritatingly along the roaches' ganglia: Why hadn't the fellow colonists returned from the battle to which the Dome had sent them? Where were the fighters who had the mission of keeping Enemy away from the retreat?

The huge roaches of the royal guard raced about in a frenzied oscillation, stirring the air of the rancid nest. New surges were issuing through the heavy atmosphere of the cave from the center palpitating cluster, but as yet they did not form into obeyable stimuli. They only increased the vexedness that was leading roach to pinch at roach, females to gobble their eggs as they laid them, and some of the royal guard, even, to jostle and jab irritably at each other. This was conduct never before experienced in this roach domain.

THREE

In the brightening morning, in the woods beyond the Cannon place, the Geiger counter was ticking steadily and reassuringly in Peter Hubbard's hand. This tracing gave him a solid sense of gratification. He had always admired inventors, people who saw into difficult problems and unknotted their solutions. The devising of laboratory experiments tapped the same kind of resourcefulness, but this roach hunt was unique. Hubbard's glow came from the success of an idea that might not have worked at all. Now it was the promise of a successful mission of discovery and, yes, revenge.

A few yards behind the scientist, Amos Tarbell and Russell Homer came vigilantly, carrying the tank weapons against possible surprise. The three men were again wearing the clumsy diving suits for protection. It made it difficult to move as softly as Hubbard wished. Hearing the ticking of the Geiger counter, the sheriff and the young man were lost in admiration of the scientist. Privately, they had wondered how the trick could work. But the contaminated roaches had set off without hesitation just as Peter Hubbard had predicted. These bugs were more interested in nesting than in seeking to attack anyone.

Hubbard had reemphasized that he was out only to discover the nest. When found, they would wait to demolish it. For one thing, it was his obligation to study what he could before its destruction. For another, it would be wise to give the home center at least another day to call in the stray roaches around the island.

At a sharp signal from the scientist, Amos and Russell jerked to a stop. Apparently the roaches had halted! Was it the nest!—or were the insects themselves confused? There was still a considerable smell of smoke among the stark, burned trees. It could be misleading them.

Hubbard dropped his hand and turned in a new direction, heading back toward the Cannon house. The men followed obediently in silence, their eyes turning constantly on guard against possible crawlers.

At the Cannon picket fence, Hubbard halted again. He pointed toward the cemetery plot beyond the Cannon barn, and started to climb over the fence.

Beneath his goggles, the sheriff whispered excitedly to Homer, "The nest is in the Cannon graveyard! *The roaches are in the graves!*"

Russell Homer shuddered. "Christ!" he moaned. "That would be just like it, wouldn't you know!"

But the Geiger tracker went suddenly silent. Peter Hubbard looked around unhappily. Had he lost the insects after all? He stuck the counter out at arm's length and revolved a full circle. Nothing. The sheriff and Homer watched with disappointed expressions. In their hearts they had somehow expected this to fail. The pariah bugs were proving too smart for even the smartest of them!

But when Hubbard retraced his steps to the fence and tried the ground on his knees, the faint ticking began once more. He did not stop to question what had caused the diversion, but signaled quickly to the others to continue the strange chase. They came on with renewed confidence.

The sheriff saw that they were taking a course between the dump and Dickens Point. He whispered to Homer, "Out that way's the pirate cave we talked about!"

"It'd be all overgrown now."

"Sh-sh!" Hubbard was motioning for them to approach him. He had left the forest and moved down a small incline to a sandy ledge. The three men stood on a plateau about six feet wide that dropped to another earthen ledge about four feet below. That platform, in turn, extended some three feet before dipping into high sand dunes bordering the step-like formation.

Peter Hubbard's face became flushed. The Geiger counter was louder and clearer than before. "They've gone down here!" Hubbard said with certainty. *"Right here!"*

"You mean this is *it?*" Russell Homer gulped. It was hard, almost impossible, to believe that the terrible search was over, that the danger might be beneath their feet, vulnerable to their own powers of destruction.

"Hallelujah, goddamn!" exploded Amos Tarbell. Could the Judas roaches have led them to the answer Yarkie needed so critically! Peter Hubbard was a genius!—Unless. Unless this too turned out a dry hole, with the diabolical insects fooling them again . . .

There was a whispered exclamation from Russell Homer as Hubbard kept checking the Geiger instrument. "Look down there!" On the ledge below, the three men viewed what no human eyes had ever beheld. It was a brute roach as large as a good-size crab, with mandibles as ferocious looking. The scientist bent carefully and showed the others a hole from which it had emerged. The opening was an inch in diameter, barely large enough for the misshapen insect to squeeze through.

Another of the giants appeared out of the opening, and a third. The gargantuans rotated their big ugly heads like combatants seeking their opponents. Their leathery antennae whipped the air toward the men, like fighters shaking challenging fists. Their thick shells on their overgrown bodies shone like gladiators' shields in the early sun. Their folded wings—seeming as large as bats' to the men looking down—reflected an ominous metallic iridescence in the daylight.

Christ, the sheriff thought, if those buzzards ever fly at us we're gone no matter what we're wearing! He turned his dry-ice nozzle cautiously in their direction.

Hubbard clamped his arm. "No, Amos! If they're disturbed, we may lose the whole nest again! These are obviously sentries. Let's get out of here!" The scientist tread softly away, trying to set up the least possible vibration.

FOUR

The final strategy of the human counterattack against the Yarkie invaders evolved naturally enough, Hubbard considered. Now that he grasped the basic structure of the roaches' retreat, he could calculate tactics with some assurance. He had the two objectives, plainly: For Yarkie, to wipe out the threat of this mutated species. For science, to study the colony, its organization, and to preserve the leaders he was convinced he would discover at the heart of the cave, as a queen bee is the heart of a hive.

Back in Elias Johnson's living room, Hubbard told the group how he planned to accomplish both purposes. They had enough gasoline and flares to destroy the vermin in the end, but his necessary scientific investigation required the carbon dioxide strategy first. His plan called for piping auto engine exhaust into the Nest. It would quiet the roaches without killing them. After his studies and photos, the Nest could be fired. In any case, there was no hurry —they still wanted time for strays to get back.

Bonnie wanted to know why the colony would not attack them again, the way it had assaulted the lighthouse.

Hubbard answered with absolute conviction. "For one thing, they're no longer receiving the alarm signals they were getting from the roaches in our laboratory. For another, they are scared, if we can use the word. They certainly sense something has gone wrong. The fighter corps hasn't come back, and they 'know' it. I am assuming the colony right now is like a turtle pulling in its head until it feels it's safe to reconnoiter again."

"Suppose you're wrong, Hubbard?" It was Stephen Scott. "My advice is to get right on out there now and burn their unholy guts out! Right now! Let's vote on that!"

Peter Hubbard was quick as a sword. *"Nobody touches that nest until I study it and give permission!"*

Scott argued back, "On this island we do things by vote, young man!"

Hubbard's eyes went stormy. "Don't lecture me, Mr. Scott! You will not interfere with my doing my job as a biologist!"

"At our expense . . . ?" Scott flashed.

Elias Johnson thundered, "Oh, shut up, Scott! You know what we owe Dr. Hubbard! I wouldn't blame him if he turned his back and let us sweat in our own juice, the way you're going on!"

Amos Tarbell said firmly to the important islander, "We will do this Dr. Hubbard's way!" The scientists had certainly paid their dues—including a life.

Scott snapped frostily, "And you won't be sheriff on Yarkie long after that!"

Elias Johnson laughed aloud. "Scott, how'd you like for me personally to throw you into that den of roaches!"

But Scott would not be diverted. "I say, see 'em, kill 'em! Talk biology later!"

Elizabeth Carr stepped to the fat man, her eyes blazing. "You, sir, are an unmitigated fathead! Now please sit down and be quiet or leave this house!"

Disconcerted, Scott fumed, "Mind your place, Elizabeth! Your grandfather has something to say about that!"

Elias Johnson shrugged, smiling. "You heard my granddaughter, old friend."

As Scott subsided, Johnson told Peter Hubbard they did indeed understand his requirement before the nest was annihilated. Then he added with an honest frown, "Peter, you've been throwing some heavy stuff at us about this social organization and mutation. I have to say I still don't get it how a bunch of dumb cockroaches join together and suddenly become what you call a colony." He showed an uneven smile, confessing, "To admit it, I've never really understood about ants and termites and those broods, either."

Stephen Scott tried to get back on Johnson's right side by nodding vigorous agreement with the questions. "The whole thing seems damned unnatural to me," he harrumphed obstreperously.

Hubbard answered the continuing incredulity. "On the contrary," he said to Scott, "it is the most natural phenomenon in the world, the base of all evolution." He paused, and saw them waiting for more of an explanation. It was, after all, hard to accept that "dumb cockroaches" *could* act in concert as cleverly as these had done.

He earnestly wanted them to understand. "You all know that life began with single cell organisms. Way back, some of those cells joined together, making a kind of commune of individuals. We call that a eucaryotic cell. These cells didn't just cluster like a bunch of grapes—they developed adaptations for different jobs. Some units specialized in gathering food, others in digesting it, others in excretion, locomotion, reproduction, and so forth. Some cells provided a protective skin around the whole group. The process grew more complex through the eons . . ."

Elizabeth interposed, "Right on up to the human body . . ."

"In a way, yes. But in considering a species like termites —or these Yarkie roaches—we're not talking about *cells* getting together, we're talking about separate individual insects forming themselves into a social organism—a group that operates *as if* it were actually one unity."

The scientist paused and measured his listeners. What he was about to add would certainly meet with new, deep skepticism. But it was his considered conclusion as a trained biologist. "I am saying," he told them deliberately, "that the Yarkie roaches are being directed by what I can only describe as a brain."

Russell Homer's forehead was strained with his wish to learn, but he could not hold back his scoffing interruption, "A *brain* like *ours* . . . ?"

Hubbard declared, "When we open that nest tomorrow, we are going to find the mutation of a whole group of insects—an evolutionary change that has welded together a community. We are going to see, in effect, yes, a brain —but not a system like ours. No, this brain will be using individual insects as its arms, legs, eyes . . .

"I can visualize this brain made of millions of 'nerve roaches,' in actual physical and chemical contact, the way our own individual brain cells are. The anatomy of this 'colony brain' would be similar to the neurons and dendrites of our higher nervous systems. In their multitude

247

of numbers, they could even begin to approximate the cortical richness of higher animals. And they might well be using all the kinds of chemicals our own brains use to carry nerve messages from one cell to another across the synapses.

"I don't mean to be too technical, but I want you to realize this possibility is very real and not at all farfetched."

Amos Tarbell breathed, "Maybe not to you . . ."

"Obviously, the 'brain cells' of this roach colony would be primitive, but there could be much more 'intelligence' than we might otherwise expect—with the central brain telling the specialized cockroaches what to do in much the way my brain tells my hand to move and my head to turn, and so on."

Stephen Scott demanded testily, "You say this has happened *before* in biology?"

"In parallel ways, many times. Let me remind you of what you learned in high school biology, or can see in the natural history museums. After the Protozoa, which lived as isolated single cells, there began to be *clusters* called Phytomastigophores, and Rhizopodea, and the Ciliata.

"The sponges, Hydrozea, are similar, showing first steps toward a differentiation of functions.

"Another step up the ladder brought even clearer specialization, in the Mesozoa. In this stage, a single layer of cells became surrounded by units whose sole function was reproduction."

Hubbard paused. His listeners were not bored or put off by the Latin names. Their eyes were bright and their ears open, because he was talking about their own lives, not book texts. The scientist saw their eyes on him, and he understood that they did not want him to talk down to them.

"Going on, then, a two-layer organism evolved, called Cnidaria. The reason for such banding together is obvious in terms of survival. When they bind together, cells have greater protection against the environment. They find food more easily. They fend off enemies.

"How do they get together in the first place? One theory is that individual cells congregate in one spot because of a concentration of a common food—certain bacteria, for example. We see something of this in a higher form like the ladybird beetles. They're usually loners, but sometimes in autumn a group will be attracted to a certain bush where they feed on aphids, and then they sometimes continue as a combined group after that. They form a colony held together by chemical attractants and tactile stimuli . . .

"You folks, particularly, know the ocean's Portuguese man-of-war . . ." Heads inclined in agreement, glad to be hearing a familiar name. "In these forms, several types of individuals get together to divide life functions in a crude way. In the man-of-war, this division of labor is actually controlled by a primitive nervous system—a 'nerve net,' it's called. I am saying the Yarkie roaches may have the same morphology . . ."

Elizabeth's voice came across the room, clear and accepting. "You mean it really wouldn't be all that unusual if the roaches coming out of a single colony were controlled by a master brain! Not beyond a natural phenomenon!"

"Exactly," Hubbard said. "And now you can see why I'm so anxious not to destroy anything before examining and studying this major biological possibility."

Elias Johnson shook his large head, saying with a rueful smile, "There is something indecent in learning such important matters for the first time at my age."

Stephen Scott's expression said he would not believe a word of the folderol. The notion was crazier than the astronomy stuff about black holes and four dimensions spouted by the Harvard types. Any man knew that bugs didn't have "brains," and nothing this professor said would make him credit it!

The sheriff spoke, more to himself than to others. "Why Yarkie?"

Peter Hubbard heard him. "Who knows? You have a quiet island. The dump would be a great starting place . . ." He held his voice level. "As Dr. Lindstrom and I explained at the beginning, chemical variations can start a mutation. I mentioned 'ENU.' There are DNA changes that alter amino acid sequences. Some biologists have mapped the development of the races entirely on the basis of the amino acid changes in a basic life substance known as the cytochrome c molecule."

Russell Homer's chest swelled. This was like being in a Harvard classroom!

Amos Tarbell was frowning. The scientist was way over his head now. He said so forthrightly.

Hubbard gave them all a friendly, understanding smile. "I have gone deeper than I intended, though this is still just on the surface of what biology knows today."

"The point is," Elizabeth repeated, "there is absolutely nothing impossible about there being a roach world in that cave not too terribly different from ours."

"That," said Bonnie Taylor unhappily, "is a terribly spooky thought!"

Stephen Scott made his pronouncement. "Well, natural or not, we get rid of those damned things tomorrow!"

Amos Tarbell grunted, "What if we don't?" Having experienced the carnage of the past two days, he wasn't at all sure they were entirely over the hill.

Elias Johnson stared at the sheriff. "If we don't get rid of them, Amos, we give Yarkie to the Navy for target practice!"

FIVE

Despite Hubbard's assurances that the Yarkie cockroaches would not likely leave their nest, no one slept easily that night. Elizabeth made up a bed for the scientist in a Johnson guest room. The other men went to their homes, half missing the camaradie of the lighthouse hours, fearful though the experience had turned out. The night did pass without incident, and they were all grateful for an uninterrupted, if fitful rest.

Alertly the next morning, Hubbard presented his briefing, concisely and candidly. The group in the Johnson living room was now enlarged by the contingent of some twenty volunteer firemen. The latter had been standing by in the village, with growing irritation at official silence and mystery. In the now-crowded room, it was difficult for the men to absorb the weird story the Harvard scientist was telling, but they could see from their Yarkie neighbors —all men they respected—that the impossible-sounding cockroach incursions on the island were true. Along with the Task Force, the volunteers listened closely to Peter Hubbard's instructions.

He told them, "My scheme is to introduce carbon dioxide vapor into the nest. There is already an opening on the bottom we can use. At the same time, we will prepare a small hole in the ceiling, and send more vapor down from the top. In this way, we have the best chance of immobilizing all the layers in the nest before they have a chance to escape through the tunnels they undoubtedly have.

"I will then have my own chance to examine the colony. Amos tells me the top of the cave is soft shale, so there should be no trouble removing the ceiling. I will go down into the nest, take my photos and make my studies—"

Elizabeth could not restrain a cry. *"Down in the nest?* That's terribly risky, isn't it, Peter?"

"Mr. Scott is lending me full diving regalia," Hubbard told her. "I'll be safe enough." He turned back to the others. "After I am through, you men will come on with the gasoline and start the fire. Some of you will be standing guard nearby with dry-ice tanks. Amos will station others back to spray any roaches that may get out."

A beefy volunteer asked cantankerously, "Hey, isn't carbon dioxide dangerous? Why not use just the regular roach stuff?"

Hubbard answered patiently, "Two reasons. I don't know whether, or how, pesticides like boric acid, chlordane, pyrethrum, or sodium fluoride will work on this species of roaches. More important, all of them take time, and we want to be in and out of that cave damn fast."

The volunteer demanded again, "If carbon dioxide's the best, why don't we use it all the time?"

Russell Homer replied in a superior tone, offended that such a silly question should be put to a man like Dr. Peter Hubbard, "We'd knock ourselves out! Can't you figure that out?"

Hubbard explained further. "The gas is just for knocking them out for a while, you see." The man withdrew with reddened face. The scientist said, "The only danger I see is in our approaching the nest. We know there are guard roaches, and they are big and murderously dangerous, I promise you."

A husky man scoffed. "I haven't seen a damn ol' cockroach yet could scare *me!*" To him and many of his company the reports of the morning were clear exaggerations, old-maid's lollygagging over some damn nuisance water bugs.

Amos Tarbell answered for Hubbard, with a grim smile. "You fellows will change your mind! Just take your orders from Dr. Hubbard here, and you'll be all right."

The scientist moved the sheriff aside. "Amos, when you shear off the top of the nest for me, the trick will be not to drop too much dirt inside."

The sheriff told him, "I understand. Should be okay —shale there—should come away clean."

"Then we're all set," Dr. Peter Hubbard said finally.

As the group left to dress and gather equipment, Elizabeth asked Hubbard worriedly, "Do you really have to go down into the roaches, Peter? Wouldn't pictures be enough?"

The man's face went taut with his inner scholarly excitement and determination. "Liz, this is a fantastic opportunity to view a colony mutation at first hand. It's something scientists everywhere need to know about! What I really regret is that the nest does have to be burned for the sake of the island. The least I can do is make the fullest examination and report possible."

"What if the carbon dioxide doesn't get all of them?" she persisted. "We know how powerful they are, whatever you're wearing!"

"If there's trouble, I'll have a rope around me so the men can pull me right out."

She tried again. "Why not use something like chloroform?"

Hubbard found it easy to be patient with Elizabeth, and answered her quietly. "Wanda and I had discussed it, and there are two negative reasons. Chloroform could possibly work on our protective clothing and, more important, it would kill the roaches before I had any chance to take any alive."

"I wish you wouldn't do it!" Liz's eyes were moist. Bonnie had been in love with Craig only for hours; she had loved this man for years.

"You know that I must," he said simply, and pressed her shoulders with a tender message they both understood.

SIX

"Operation Extermination," as the Yarkie men quickly labeled the venture, went more easily than even Peter Hubbard had hoped. Only a few of the vicious roaches were visible when the group reached the cave. The huge insects were dispatched with the dry ice, but not before even the most skeptical of the firemen became frightened and shaken believers.

Proceeding by Hubbard's scheme, a hole was quickly drilled in the ceiling of the nest, and the hoses from car exhausts were inserted simultaneously. The vapors penetrated and spread as Hubbard planned. Elizabeth and Bonnie, standing at a considerable distance away with the firemen holding gasoline tanks, watched tensely, exchanging anxious looks.

From the firemen on guard, there were puffs of the dry ice. Where tunnel exits did bring a few furtive roaches trying for the surface, they were readily managed.

Men trained in the use of salvage tools had no difficulty shearing away the ceiling of the roach cave. Watching them enlarge the opening with their poles and hooks, Hubbard felt as if he were in an operating room where surgeons were removing the top of a skull. His heart was palpitating with the expectation of the discovery he anticipated. If his hypothesis was correct, he was about to bear personal witness to *the actual fusion of individual insects into a multi-individual organism analagous to a vertebrate brain!*

It was time. A hush fell over all the people on the scene. There was little breeze and only a few bird calls in the burned, leafless trees. It was almost as if the massive dose of carbon dioxide put the whole world to sleep—as the roaches seemed to be motionlessly asleep, or dead, when

Peter Hubbard looked down and signaled Amos Tarbell and Ben Dorset to lower him into the nest's darkness without disturbing the great roach mound he saw in the center. It was *"the brain,"* he was certain.

Elizabeth bit her lip and held her breath as the man disappeared into the hole. Pirates, or someone, had indeed cut out a great hidden cave in the eastern ridge. It was some eight feet deep to the floor. Despite the clumsiness of his protective suit and the diving helmet he decided to wear, Hubbard was able to see all around the walls. His flashlight picked out storage chambers everywhere. As in the earlier, abandoned nest, the insect larder was grisly with gaping skulls of both animals and men, broken bones of young and old, and maggots anesthetized to motionlessness on lumps of flesh that could only be from the children off the *Tub*.

Shuddering with aversion, Peter Hubbard was glad his mask spared him the effluvium of the cavernous death surrounding him. The redolence would strike at a man like a dynamite explosion.

The scientist scanned the cave impatiently. Only a few of the roaches showed any movement, a wiggling antennae here and there, an isolated flurry of wire legs in an insect's weak throes. Hubbard knelt in a splashing of roach bodies to examine the centric mass. With one gloved hand directing his flashlight, his fingers swept aside the confusion of gassed insects shielding the omphalos.

And there it was!

The "brain" existed precisely as Peter Hubbard had imagined it would be! Incredibly and fantastically, in its own way it was awesomely and wonderfully there before his eyes. The integument covering the mound protectively was partially transparent, so he could mark the gross anatomy of the structure before even making his planned incision.

The rise itself was three full feet at the center, and it was five or six feet in diameter. The covering was, Hubbard noted, morphologically like the *dura mater* between the human brain and the bone of the skull. Beneath the membrane lay the brain cells, and he saw at once that they were very different from the huge roaches with which they had been dealing outside. These were very small insects, smaller than the usual house roach, not more than a quarter of an inch long.

Not unexpected! The human brain has billions of cells. The roach's brain cells could not be the size of the rest of the colony or there would be no room for anything, including itself. These thoughts flashed through Hubbard's mind as he pierced the membrane to take a sample of the liquid within. Stoppering the test tube, he bet himself that the clear liquid would contain some form of acetylcholine—the chemical, localized in little sacs at the ends of neurons, that conducted impulses across the synaptic cleft in vertebrate systems.

Hubbard had trouble steadying his hands in his uncontainable excitement as he painstakingly cut away a full section of the dome roaches—the "roach cerebrum," he thought elatedly. He could predict what his later dissection and analysis of the unprecedented body would show. He would find that these tiny roaches were actually adapted in two separate ways to receive and discharge nervous impulses. Some of the bodies, he was sure, would be acting as postsynaptic receptor cells, structured to receive chemical-electrical impulses across the synapse, while other of the roach bodies would be presynaptic—the transmitters. Microscopic examination would show these to have the spherical vessels that discharged the transmission chemical initiating action. The latest work in this field was being done in San Francisco, and he would rush some of his bizarre specimens there.

His improbable-sounding hypothesis was proving one hundred percent correct, incredible though it had seemed even to him at first. He regretted only that Wanda Lindstrom had not lived to share this transfixing discovery with him.

Keenly, Hubbard stripped away more of the cover. Some of the brain-cell roaches were still twitching, having been partially protected from the anesthetic vapors. But these little insects posed no physical danger. For one thing, they were not free. As he had suspected, the roach bodies were fastened together, antennae to antennae, like the wired component units of a computer. They had only tiny, seemingly vestigial mandibles. These bodies were clearly not designed for fighting or food gathering or reproduction or locomotion. Only for "thinking!"

The oozing liquid bathing the cells also contained their food supply, Hubbard reasoned. There were signs all around that nurse roaches, feeding off the larder brought in by the foragers, regurgitated their stomach contents into the dome's fluid—an adaptation of trophallaxis done on a community rather than individual-to-individual basis. The brain would literally be bathed in food! Ingenious Nature again!

Unfortunately, there was no way this biological freak could be preserved in its entirety for the world to study. Hubbard signaled for his camera to be lowered, and began to take flash pictures. At least there would be this photo record of the incredible mutation on Yarkie Island. Science would ponder it for many a year.

His concentration was so tightly focused that Hubbard did not notice a weaving line of guard roaches coming toward him, emerging from one of the larders. They prowled like hunting animals stalking. They were dazed by the penetrating fumes in the nest, but unlike its soporific effect on most of the insects it was having a paradoxic reaction in these mutants. As happens with some humans, their nervous systems had been jolted into activity by the anesthesia.

Hubbard was finding the heavy diving gloves a nuisance as he clicked picture after picture. He managed to draw off the glove from his right hand, and returned with new satisfaction to his record-making.

He saw the blood on his hand before he felt the incisions that were already needling down to the bone. Huge mouths were gnawing at his fingertips before he realized what was happening. He could not loosen the great mandibles without dropping the camera, and that, to him, was unthinkable.

Looking up for help, he saw the top of the nest rimmed with horrified faces. He saw mouths working, but his helmet had cut off the sound of their warning cries.

With his gloved hand, Hubbard tried to defend against the roaches eating at his right-hand fingers. He could not manage. He flung his hands upward in a frantic gesture of despair, while gripping the camera fiercely. Another rope fell before him. He could use only his left hand, but his plight lent it power. His grip held his weight as the men above started to pull him slowly out of the pit.

Halfway out, Hubbard felt himself slipping. Involuntarily, he made a grab for the rope with his right hand. All it did was smear the strand with his blood, making it more slippery. He felt himself going down. His left hand was unable to clutch firmly. In a moment, he would be dropping back into the brain mass. He would be half-buried in it, helpless, and the attack roaches could gnaw his vulnerable wrist under his suit. One opening was all they needed. It was his turn to be annihilated by the brood he had been battling!

But strong hands were reaching down and grabbing Hubbard under the shoulders. He was yanked to the surface. Sprawled on the ground, he tried not to cry out with the agony of his lacerated hand. He dared not look at the damage to his fingers. The sheriff was pouring antiseptic directly on still-chewing roaches.

Firemen lifted Hubbard to the seat of the fire truck. Elizabeth helped them get his helmet off. She quickly opened a first aid kit to bandage his lacerated hand, and found with infinite relief that the injury was not as severe as it had seemed. The exhaust gas had evidently weakened the jaw muscles of even the monster insects. Otherwise, their bites would have been deeper and more massive.

Hubbard saw Elizabeth expertly tightening a tourniquet above his wrist. Through his pain, he noticed with new respect that the woman was dealing with his raw wounds without the slightest flinching, and her touch was soft and comforting.

Bonnie Taylor was nearby, watching the two in a terrible, suppressed anguish. The sight of Peter Hubbard's blood smearing the ground brought back the butchery of Craig Soaras. In her mind's eye, she again saw Craig fall amid the roaches, saw the killers tearing away at the lips she had wanted. Death had kissed them first, death out of this evil cavern where men, themselves looking like robot creatures in their masks and rubber suits, were now pouring gasoline down on the roach pile.

Bonnie's hate burst in her breast. With a shriek of outrage, she grabbed a can of gasoline and dashed to the opened roach nest. For one moment she stared into the sullen shadow of the deep hole. There were the predators, her enemies, every stinking one! The murderers of Craig Soaras! Many, she could see, were now creeping about, coming alive, surviving yet to rampage and maim again. Bonnie terribly needed to be with the first to pour the fuel on those crawling beasts, the first to set the devilish hiding place afire, the first to see the insects consumed, burned,

burned, burned, and hear their roach squeaks of agony, watch their dirty bodies singe and sizzle and turn to blobs.

The weighty container slipped from her slim, perspiring hands. In grabbing for it, the woman's feet came out from under her on the loosened earth. Spikes of new terror ripped her insides as she slid down the yawning hole. She saw herself falling in, buried alive beneath the insect filth. She, too, would die in bloody pieces in the foul roach mouths! Bonnie Taylor fainted, and did not know she was being pulled to safety by the sheriff and his men.

When she was safe and recovered, Tarbell signaled firemen to come forward with more gasoline.

The cresting explosion sent flames geysering out of the nest, destroying everything within.

The Yarkie men pounded each other on their rubber-suited backs, jumping about and shouting jubilantly in the ultimate victory.

Bonnie watched the blaze with glaring eyes of malice and detestation. Lines from Shakespeare seethed through her mind: ". . . and entrails feed the sacrificing fire. Whose smoke, like incense, doth perfume the sky." To the others, the incinerating fire might be the foulest stink in the world, but to her the smoke of the roach entrails was a perfume, an incense of revenge and vengeance sweet to her nostrils, though too late, too late, too late . . .

SEVEN

The column of smoke marked the immolation of the fearsome Yarkie misbegotten. It was the funeral pyre of demonic creatures, mutations that turned out evil dissonances in the hidden mysteries of evolution—"dissonances" at least to humans, Peter Hubbard thought.

On his feet, with his bandaged hand on Elizabeth Carr's

arm, the scientist watched with a swelling of regret as well as abhorrence as The Nest went up. The threat had to be demolished, as he had acknowledged. Yet, the natural power that had created this roach colony was an imperial force beyond Man's right and wrong.

After all, as he taught his classes, there are a billion billion insects on earth, nearly a billion for each human. Mass extinctions occurred in Nature—like the close of the Cretaceous period, when death came to dinosaurs, plankton, ammonites, and other forms of life. Theories included disease, copper poisoning of oceans, climatic upheavals, even asteroid collisions with earth.

Maybe, a scientist had to consider—maybe Nature had created destructive creatures like these roaches precisely to start wiping out the world as it had come to be. Maybe Nature wanted a clean slate, to destroy what Man had become and done to the earth. Maybe the roach hunger which he, as a man, so readily deplored as "feral" was in more universal fact Nature's yearning to start over.

There was a point of view from which he himself had undertaken a terrible responsibility in this destruction. To humans, this roach mutation was intolerable. But for a naturalist, it was superficial to view the creatures simply as vile. He himself had lectured the Yarkie people that the insects had acted out of their inner essence, not from "malice" or "enmity" or "malevolence." So, a cancer on Yarkie, yes—from the human point of view; but from Nature's view—who could know?

Hubbard wanted to share his thoughts with the woman standing beside him. He took in her grace and beauty with new gratitude for the warmth he felt from her and toward her. That was Nature, too. But he knew she would not want to hear his speculations, not yet. She did not have his training, his objectivity. She would not be wondering, as he was wondering, whether this mutation of cockroaches was a form of Nature's own antennae stitching the air of infinite time in search of new organic forms, new expressions of the life force.

He could not still his mind and its agnosticism.

The purposes of life, their own and all the plants and animals on earth, were beyond a man's understanding. Who should say how far Man's dominion properly extended? It was an essential riddle of both biology and theology: In the contentions of the species, did Man have the unlimited, absolute right to assume he was the lord of the earth, that *his* well-being was paramount and unqualified?

In human laws, there was the canon stated by Justice Oliver Wendell Holmes: *Your right to swing your cane ends where my nose begins.* Did mankind have a God-given right to swing its cane regardless of the noses of any other living beings? But then there was the vice versa of it and, inwardly, watching the cremation of the roaches, the scientist had to admit his own, primeval enjoyment of the sounds of the insect bodies sputtering in the flames to oblivion. Whatever his rationalizations, people simply could not tolerate such a colony of butchers in their midst. Intent was irrelevant.

In a nutshell, Peter Hubbard concluded grimly, if Nature's rule was indeed the survival of the fittest, men did have a natural right to impose their intelligence against these challengers.

And so the scientist joined with Elizabeth and Bonnie and the Yarkie men as they expressed their loathing of the intruders with unrestrained cheers, hoots, and cries of triumph.

It was too bad, Hubbard thought, that Reed Brockshaw and Craig Soaras especially could not be with their Yarkie fellows to witness the victory they had now finally achieved. The Task Force had won in the end. The price had been high, the way perilous and troubled. It was more than right for eyes to be shining with achievement through their fatigue and tension.

Hubbard saw that even Bonnie's tears had ended. Her back was straight and her head was high as she watched the flames dying down. There was some consolation for her and for all the Yarkie victims in this fiery retaliation.

They could turn now to leave. The threat was past and gone, the suffering was over at last. Yarkie Island was finally free again.

VICTORY

ONE

Jubilance was tempered with sadness, sadness was brightened by hopefulness at the celebration that night in Elias Johnson's house. The captain prepared his special drink, a "switchel," to toast the Task Force that could now be disbanded. The generously filled mugs contained a mixture of rum, molasses and ginger-flavored water. It was a potion that sailors usually foreswore as being for landlubbers and sissies—but not when made with the extra dollops of rum Johnson poured in with a generous hand.

The captain toasted the group, ladies first: Elizabeth and Bonnie. Then Peter Hubbard and Amos Tarbell, Ben Dorset, Russell Homer, and Stephen Scott for supplying the special equipment they had needed. "Well, we got the scurvy lot!" were his words. "And the more credit to all of us for it!"

They drank heartily, and took more. By common consent, they put off the mourning they still had to do for what they and Yarkie had lost. Now was the hour to refill the cup of their triumph and supremacy. The old man did not hesitate to brim up Elizabeth's cup when she held it out again and again. Or Bonnie's, or Hubbard's, or the others'.

They exchanged yarns that had the men slapping their thighs and calling out, "Whacking good!" In one story,

Amos Tarbell used the word "mooncussin'" and had to explain it to Hubbard and Bonnie Taylor. Nowadays, it referred to nighttime scavenging on the beaches, people picking over the tide's flotsam and jetsam; but its origin was out of a time when people swung lanterns on dark nights to mislead ships. The wrecks could then be plundered. The trick couldn't work when the moon was out, so those nights the folks "cussed the light"—and now walking the beach with a lantern had become "mooncussin'."

Laughing now, Bonnie Taylor told how Elizabeth had fooled her into picking up a scallop, without warning her she'd get squirted. She knew about squirting clams, but not scallops.

Elizabeth's turn brought a poem for Peter Hubbard's edification. It was one that had so tickled Elizabeth's fancy she had memorized it from a book called "Cape Cod Pilot," a Federal Writers Project back in 1937. It was attributed to an Eva Tappan of Yarmouth, and went:

> "We drove the Indians out of the land
> But a dire revenge the Red Men planned;
> For they fastened a name to every nook
> And every schoolboy with a spelling book
> Will live to toil till his hair turns gray
> Before he can spell them the proper way."

Ben Dorset contributed the way old-timers confounded newcomers who tried to start lobstering. The natives would smile while the interlopers baited their traps with cut-up flounders, all correct. Then the old fellows would steal the lobster catch out of the traps and send them to the bottom with their concrete sinkers *after* removing the float. The newcomers never could find their traps again. "And," he chuckled, "the way you could tell when *they* became old-timers was when they started to do the same to the next batch of tenderfoot that came along to lobster their waters!"

Russell Homer nodded knowledgeably. "You have to get up mighty early after your lobster. When the breeze whips up the whitecaps, you can hardly see your floats at all." He grinned winningly. "I was always out when it was still ten-eleven blankets cold!"

Hubbard and Bonnie both looked at him with bemused smiles. "Ten-eleven blankets cold"—what a graphic way to describe the temperature. It would be a refreshing note on the television weather reports!

When the switchel was finished, it was time for the Task Force to break up. Separate groups formed with the goodnights. Elias Johnson and Stephen Scott considered how to bring the evacuees back to Yarkie, and which mainland officials to contact about the island's deaths. Amos Tarbell and Ben Dorset discussed assigning the two fire trucks to a continuing patrol on High Ridge in case pockets of fire might still flare up. Peter Hubbard talked to Russell Homer about sailing him with his specimens to Chatham the next morning for a flight back to Cambridge; except for his report, his project on Yarkie was now completed.

TWO

After her bath, Elizabeth was slipping on her flannelette nightgown—smiling to herself that it was only "a four-five blanket" night—when she heard the noise. It had not sounded in this house for a long time. Typing. Peter Hubbard at his report. The thought of his leaving in the morning was painful to her.

On impulse, Elizabeth opened her door and went across the hall. In the days this house was built, her conduct would have been unthinkable, but these prim walls too had to accept modern ways.

"If I'm not interrupting, I'd like to talk to you, Peter."

The man looked up from his papers and smiled. "I'm not typing too well with one hand, anyway. Come on in, Liz." Standing shyly in the doorway with her black hair wetly plastered on her head she looked like a mermaid out of her element.

And to Elizabeth, Peter Hubbard in his pajamas, seemed a sweet boy at bedtime rather than the Harvard instructor always in steady possession of himself.

He asked amiably, "What do you want to talk about?"

The woman said gravely, "I just took a long bath and a lot of questions kept bubbling into my head."

"Such as?"

"If you're too tired, we can talk tomorrow."

"You relax me," he smiled. "Go on."

"My question isn't relaxing," she said. "Do you really think all the roaches were back in that nest?"

"No. I've said there are bound to be strays. The volunteer firemen are watching, and they have the dry ice . . ."

"Aren't the strays just as dangerous?"

"No," he said again. "Without the central brain, they're just bugs, Liz. They're big and nasty and they can do some damage, but not in the organized way they did before."

"Won't they start another nest?"

The scientist regarded her doubtful expression soberly. "Not likely. This phenomenon was the result of a very unique combination of environmental and evolutionary forces. The odds are way against a repetition. We *did* destroy all the brain cells—that's the important thing." He added firmly. "Even if there should be a phylogenetic thrust again, it would take years and years."

"So you really don't see any more danger?"

"Isolated incidents, maybe. A general problem, no."

"The people here owe you a great deal, Peter."

"I'm glad your father sent me over."

"So am I." Elizabeth Carr looked at the man, her eyes clear windows. "I want to go back with you tomorrow," she said straightfowardly. It sounded as she hoped it would —honest, not bold; truthful, not brash.

He responded in kind. "I want you to, Liz. But your grandfather needs you here right now. This has been awfully rough on him."

"I know," Elizabeth squinted. "Peter, can you please put out that light?" The desk gooseneck was shining directly into her face. Hubbard obliged. The room sank into its shadows, illuminated only by the small lamp next to the double bed. Elizabeth Carr was standing between the lamp and Hubbard's eyes. The man grinned like a schoolboy. "I can see right through your nightgown, you know."

Her ingrained impulse was to duck, but her smiling eyes invited the man to enjoy her. "What do you see?" she openly teased.

He laughed back, "All the way to Chatham."

"Chatham? I thought biologists knew female anatomy."

"The difference between anatomy and life is amazing . . ." Hubbard got up from the desk, took a step toward Elizabeth, and stopped. "You had better go back to your room."

Elizabeth let her answer come from the rum in the switchels she had drunk. Giddily she whirled around, and her nightdress tightened around her body. "I feel wonderful!—Why do I frighten you?" She stopped so close to Hubbard she could feel his breath on her cheek. "I do frighten you, don't I, Peter?"

He said huskily, "Because I've been falling in love with you."

"That's not frightening, that's supercalediciouswhatever!" She followed him in her bare feet as he moved prudently away.

He answered, "You have had too many whatever you call those drinks."

"So do I think so! And I'm glad!" With one soft motion, Elizabeth went into the man's arms and was kissing him passionately on the lips. When she felt his answering embrace, she was sure beyond all doubt of her destiny with this man. Leaning her head against his chest, she murmured, "Peter, I have been in love with you for so terribly, terribly long." She reached up to stroke his face. Now he did need a shave. She enjoyed the sandpapery sensation, his skin real and masculine with the promise of his own passion.

He bent his head to her. "I have loved you for too short."

She gave him her lips without restraint. Their tongues played wetly in each other's mouth as they freed their hunger for their love.

Her hand went of its own accord to the hardness she felt rising against her body. Her moistness down there was as wet as her mouth, sweet with his kisses. She wanted, was glad at, his fingers seeking her other wetness gently, strokingly. She parted her legs a little to his hand. In a little while they turned together to the bed.

She lifted her nightgown off over her head and watched with a pounding heart his eyes take in all of her body and its heat.

He shed his pajamas and stood naked before her, with his aroused sex lifting to her own ardent gaze.

They were both panting when they lay back on the soft quilt. Elizabeth breathed against his cheek, then his mouth was on her nipple. The electricity of his tongue on her erotic flesh shot through Elizabeth's nerves to her center. It was an unexpected, galvanizing shock that arched her back and brought her thighs wide open for him. She had "made it" before, but she never felt anything like this torrent of sensation.

Sex swept over her and sent her spinning in a riptide of a discovered ocean without end. Her body surged like a breaking wave itself, a curling spume and lacy foam of sheer, breath-catching delight. Peter Hubbard's sex pressed between her legs and she spread herself wider, welcoming, wanting, lusting for him now. She felt Peter Hubbard enter her body. He was full and strong and straight. She uttered one small cry which gave way in a moment to a gasp of ecstasy.

She held him fast inside of her as the deck of her life listed in the sudden storm of emotions she had never sailed before. She clung to him harder as her body became a skimming craft on swelling seas. She rose and fell, bobbed and turned and wheeled and heeled. She was a ship running before the wind of love; she was its sails; he was its keel. She was a bird; he was its wings.

Then suddenly she was the wind itself, and scudding clouds filled up with thunder and with the lightning he was charging up in her, and charging up in her. Until she could contain it no longer. Like a storm sky she split, the thunder crashed out of her and the burst of her orgasm shook the world.

They came crashing to release together, both riven to the core. Then the tempest passed, easing, easing at last to let their hearts clear and quiet in the fading wind, quieted to deep-breathing in a sleepy peace in each other's arms.

Elizabeth Carr woke later and stirred against Peter Hubbard. He tightened his hold on her warm flesh. "Where are you going?"

"Nowhere."

He rubbed his eyes like someone coming out of a dream. He looked at her with eyes that could not believe

Elizabeth Carr was lying beside him. He stated, "You have to go in to Bonnie."

"No." She lifted herself on an elbow. "She guesses where I am, Peter. She knows how I've felt about you." Sudden tears spilled out. "Poor Bonnie. She was truly falling in love with Craig Soaras, I know."

"I guessed," he nodded slowly.

It came to Elizabeth Carr in that moment how right it was for her to have come to Peter Hubbard's bed. Bonnie had lost the lifetime of happiness she might have known —lost it so suddenly, so meaninglessly, so uselessly.

Elizabeth counted the blessings of her own discovered love, not stolen like Bonnie's.

It came to Elizabeth Carr that what she felt was what men and women in wartime had known. With death all around, you grasp what you can of life. She and Peter had been in a war together; they could have been killed as wantonly as Wanda Lindstrom, as Craig Soaras, she could as easily be as bereaved as Bonnie. She understood what had given her the courage to cross the hall.

But it was not a time for thinking. Peter was pulling her nakedness to his own ready body, wonderfully importunate again.

THREE

In the morning, Elizabeth knew again why she loved and respected her grandfather as she did. He was passing in the hall when she came out of Peter Hubbard's room in her nightgown. He let no question show in his eyes and his greeting was an unstrained, casual "Good morning, Liz." When Elizabeth stood on tiptoe to kiss his leathery cheek, he added with an approving chuckle, "I want the wedding right here, in this house!"

Larking, Elizabeth pretended innocence. "What on earth are you talking about, Elias?"

He winked. "A nose that can smell weather off to Greenland can smell a wedding cake baking in its own kitchen."

"The biggest cake we can find!" It was Peter Hubbard, dressed and smiling. He was carrying the flask with the roaches to be brought to the Harvard laboratories.

Elias Johnson said in the same breath, "Congratulations, and if you're going to drop that goshdarn jar, Peter, wait till you're back in Cambridge, will you?"

Elizabeth uttered a small cry of disbelief. "Peter! Look at the way those roaches are all huddled in the right hand corner! *It's as if they're still getting signals from somewhere!*"

The scientist's eyes followed hers, but he remained calm. "Good observation, Liz. But I'd say this is just a habit pattern now, an imprint. They couldn't be getting signals from the nest after the way we burned it out."

"Might some pheromone signals still be in the air?"

"That's possible, but doubtful by now, I'd say."

Elias Johnson's eyes lost their merriment. He said with immediate concern, "Peter, those bugs *are* aiming smack in the direction of that scurvy cave!"

Hubbard rotated the flask. His own expression revealed a moment of trepidation when the roaches skittered immediately to the opposite side. But he spoke his conviction, "I double-checked the nest before we left, you know that. The brain is absolutely gone. At worst, Elizabeth may be right about a scent still in the atmosphere."

The scientist set the flask down carefully on a chest against the wall. The restless cockroaches looked even more grotesque seen between two priceless T'ang Dynasty bowls.

The three humans eyed the insect survivors. Elizabeth accepted Peter Hubbard's conclusion. Elias Johnson hesitated, uncertain, but had no choice. "Well," he said gruffly, "if you city slickers are all going back to Cambridge today, we better get ourselves a move on."

FOUR

While Elizabeth Carr was dressing, Captain Johnson and Peter Hubbard drove to the village. Johnson had to start the official wheels turning at the town hall. At the *Jessica's* dock, Hubbard checked the now-crated specimens he was taking. Ben Dorset stowed them on board for the crossing to Chatham. Hubbard was surprised to see Bonnie Taylor sitting quietly at the bow of the boat, taking in the bustling harbor. She didn't turn to him, and he did not intrude, aware that the woman preferred being alone. Patience was her balm now.

The man realized afresh how providential it was that he and Elizabeth Carr had met again, and would, God still willing, have their lifetimes together.

Back at the Johnson house, Elizabeth, making her breakfast, was pleased to be alone, too. It came to her that she had scarcely had a moment to herself for the past four days. Could this be only the fifth morning since a carefree Bonnie had so gaily taken Sharky off for a picnic on High Ridge? The nightmare hours since would always seem an eternity to her, an interval out of normal life, like something heard that could not have been real, could not have been experienced.

But it was real, of course. So many people bereft. And the awful, irrefutable evidence Peter was carrying for the scientific world to study and marvel at—while Yarkie mourned.

Fragrant coffee was on the stove, eggs were frying in butter—a diet-defying treat. Elizabeth was starving. She smiled smugly to herself—her hunger wasn't due to the switchels of the night before, it was the voyage of love she had taken with the man she could claim now. As the omelette sent its mouth-watering odors through the kitchen, Elizabeth thought with delight that making love with Peter would always be like their first magic last night, no matter how long they lived.

Elizabeth wiped her plate clean with extra toast, and laughed at herself. If the bliss of sex with Peter did this to her appetite, she would have to cut down on one or the other. It would be food! she promised herself fervently.

After breakfast she wanted to walk, to walk by herself, to go along paths she had known so intimately as a child. She knew in her heart that though she would return for visits, this morning was her farewell to "grampa's island." Elizabeth started up the old dirt road leading from her grandfather's house to High Ridge. As she went from the village up the curving incline, she heard birds singing again. Things were returning to normal. The trees, unfortunately, would take years, but there might even be an ecological silver lining, Elizabeth considered. With the old trees burned, new growth would have more room and encouragement to flourish.

Meantime along her way there were the familiar and beloved old friends. There was the poverty grass, so named because it grew only in poor soil. It was usually found on the dunes, but there were patches of it here and there around the island, a welcoming mossy carpet of silver green. From nearby houses along the lanes she passed came the distinctive fragrance of boxwood. There was the crisp bayberry plant, too, its berries a gray-green color that glistened to gold although the sky was cloudy again this morning.

On the path, Elizabeth saw a beautiful conch shell. Some child must have dropped it, perhaps when the people had hurried to the evacuation ferries. She tried to shake that thought out of her head. They would be coming home soon, it would do no one any good to dwell on what had happened. Picking up the conch, Elizabeth smiled as it reminded her of the captain telling how he and his fellows had used these shells as horns when they were young fishermen out in dories blowing signals to the mother ship.

The pink lavender of beach peas invited Elizabeth Carr, and among nearby junipers she made out a flower whose name she had loved best as a child—the "pearly everlasting." She had thought that should be the name for the inside of oyster shells, which truly shone like pearls.

On her left, Elizabeth recognized the very same blueberry bushes from which she had so often come home with a happily smeared face. The fleabane plant was across the lane, supposed to keep away fleas—which she, thankfully, had never acquired.

Elizabeth stopped near the top of the climb to enjoy a stand of beach plums. How many times she had stood on this very spot, mouth and eyes wide in wonder at the sight in the flowering season. Their blooming had put to shame the celebrated Japanese cherry blossoms she later knew along the Potomac.

She turned at the top of the hill to look back down the path she had come, taking in gratefully the variegated flowers, the neat houses, the tidy village centering on the harbor. The sky was a stretched gray canvas, but the clouds were light and slow-moving this morning. The sea seemed calm. The well-known streets, stores, and landmarks were reminders of her childhood security on Yarkie. Tears came to Elizabeth Carr's eyes. How, how *could* the horror of the past days have happened amid this peace! Thank God it was all over.

FIVE

The New Place was quiet. There was much to be taken in, fresh ways to be dealt with. There was the strength of rebirth, but at the same time the weakness of lack of independent experience. There was little motion, some fluttering of antennae, but mostly it was a time to rest, to let new balances become established.

There were no outside disturbances to mar the quiet they needed for the resting and the development of their own world, now separate and separately driven.

The individuals in the New Colony were licking each other, as if the roaches were coated with some appetizing substance. Their antennae kept touching, and their bodies jostled softly together. In the effort to establish the necessary interconnections of the fresh society, some of the insects were even engaging in a form of anal trophallaxis, seen among certain termites. Nest-mates exchanged chemical symbionts by eating droplets discharged from a neighbor's anus.

The convergence was being directed by the Dome in the center of the new Nest. It was a smaller structure than its parent; as indeed, the members of this new branch of the roach colony tended to be smaller than their brothers in the pirate cave. Usually, with insects like bees, Nature sent the older group out to establish a new Nest. Here the development had been different—as with so many other aspects of the Yarkie Island mutation.

The Dome's signals grew stronger and clearer with each passing hour. Soon it would be time to make known this Colony's presence and assert its own, new territorial rights and appetites.

SIX

Elizabeth reached High Ridge Road just as the Hook &
Ladder truck came along on its assigned precautionary
patrol. It was a brand new vehicle, acquired by Yarkie as
new homes rose on the island. In its red and gold majesty,
the engine was the pride of the village and its crew. Its
aluminum aerial ladder always shone brilliantly, polished
by devoted and caring hands every day.

The volunteer firemen stood vigilantly on the running
boards, at the ready, wearing their high boots, rubber
coats and fire helmets. They looked like warrior heroes
on some gleaming chariot, Elizabeth thought. And they
were heroes. Elizabeth knew how long and faithfully the
men trained, and how many perilous times they selflessly
risked their own limbs and lives to save life and property
on the island. She remembered her grandfather jumping
into his clothes any hour of the night to answer a fire call.
It was a canard that volunteers were mostly drinking beer
and marching in parades.

With a sudden catch in her throat, Elizabeth made
out Peter Hubbard sitting on the high front seat with the
proud driver. He was dressed as a fireman, ready to help
if they spotted a maverick burst of flame—or a patch of
maverick roaches.

It came to the woman that the scientist fit right in with
these fishermen, sailors, carpenters, boat builders. Character made its own brotherhood.

Elizabeth had never felt more set up than as she waved
brightly to the man she loved among the men who had
been her friends since girlhood. But she was glad the
truck did not stop; it was still a time to be alone with her
thoughts. She struck out in the opposite direction toward

the Cannon place, knowing what she wanted to do there. It would be time enough to join Peter when the fire truck returned on its reverse patrol.

A smile brightened the woman's lips. She would join Peter on the front seat of the engine, and it would be like the annual Fourth of July parade in town. She might even clang the bell as she had done when she was a girl. It was forbidden usually, but her grandfather had been the chief then, and no one on Yarkie Island to tell a Johnson nay.

The brightness faded when Elizabeth came to the Cannons' fence. Before her stood the solid house with its hand-split shingles, reflecting in its elegance and charm what the island people called "snug fortune." But Hildie was gone, and her girls. So horribly gone. There had been no "snug fortune" for them against Nature's capricious perfidy. Well, many Cannons had been lost in other natural disasters, Elizabeth told herself. Maybe it would help all the living to think of the Yarkie roaches as a natural calamity—a hurricane that swamped boats, drowned men, and tumbled trees. That is what the roaches had been—elemental havoc. She thanked God again that they were gone!

Elizabeth proceeded into the Cannon graveyard—what old Cape Codders called the "eternity acres."

Her great grandmother had been a Cannon. Delilah Cannon Johnson. To a five-year-old girl, the then-ninety-year-old lady had been a fairy queen.

Meandering among the family gravestones, Elizabeth was struck again by how many infants had died of diseases that could now be easily treated. The world had made some "progress," after all, she thought. But nothing would have helped the young men lost at sea. It always amazed Elizabeth that so many had been full masters of vessels on long voyages at the early ages of twenty-one and younger, as the markers told laconically.

Elizabeth Carr bowed her head at the gravestones of Delilah Cannon Johnson and Ezekial Scott Johnson. She wanted these two good people of her girlhood to know she was entering a new stage of life, and that she would take her marriage to Peter Hubbard as sacredly as they had taken theirs. She would enjoy modern freedoms in other ways, but in this she would hold with them.

SEVEN

Standing in the "eternity acres," the woman suddenly became aware that birds were no longer singing. In the unnatural silence, there began a soft susurration from the high grass around the stones. Elizabeth's head came up. Her eyes blinked with disbelief.

A moment later the air brought a clear swishing noise. The emanation was all too familiar. Inwardly, Elizabeth Carr crumbled. It was not her imagination! The buzzing sound was too plain, and she could now see a visible disturbance in the leaves piled along the cemetery fence. Her heart exploded. Elizabeth knew beyond hope that her alarm was not an invention of lingering hysteria. *Killer cockroaches were still roaming Yarkie*, and they were coming on again! *For her!*

Somewhere—and nearby!—a band of the creatures had hidden, had escaped the nest's destruction! Peter Hubbard had been too sanguine! The insects in the jar that morning *had* been warnings! The admonition had been disregarded at their peril—her peril now!

Elizabeth forced herself to concentrate on the shifting perturbation in the leaves and the grass. She was right! The surfaces were in motion though there was no breeze!

Yes! The well-known, disgusting brown shapes were emerging before her stricken eyes. She saw the weaving antennae and the brown-black bodies by new thousands on their wire-flexing feet, and the ugly mandibles reaching viciously, and the sawteeth mouths clicking in savage, seeking hunger, all as horribly as before!

Elizabeth stampeded to the Cannon house. She prayed the kitchen door would be open for sanctuary. The hideous roach pack was scrabbling after her with terrifying swiftness.

In her panic, Elizabeth tripped on the groove that most Yarkie homes chipped into the threshold stone to run rain off. The channel caught her toe and sent her stumbling so that she banged her head on the kitchen door. Dazed, she grabbed for the knob. If it did not turn, she was a goner. The roach mandibles would be at her feet in just moments.

Her heart plummeted as the door did not yield. Locked! Since when did Hildie lock her damnation doors? No time to think about that! With a muttered curse, Elizabeth saw the roach cadre making for her even faster. She might have just one more chance. She flew around to the buttery door. All Yarkie mansions had such a room or shed abutting the kitchen. In the old days, butter had been churned there; nowadays the space was used for potting plants, or as an extra pantry.

Elizabeth's fist hit the buttery door open. As she swung it hard behind her, she saw it had caught and crushed a handful of the leading roaches. She took a moment to breathe. The acid taint in the air outside was unmistakeable and sinister. She knew it would not be long before the marauders found a way into the house and were after her again. The revolting insects could squeeze even their obscenely large bodies through the narrowest of cracks. Any slight opening, any window ajar, and they would be upon her. She remembered the lighthouse.

Elizabeth's thoughts started to jump erratically. Part of her mind refused to accept what was happening—told her she was asleep in the safe Johnson house, dreaming out the nightmare of the past days. Part of her brain was crying out to Peter Hubbard, ironically damning the *human* limitations that provided her with speech instead of insect pheromones that could reach him over miles! Where was man's much-vaunted superiority!

The woman took hold of herself, forced herself to concentrate. The roach odor and the sounds of the killers scratching outside were making her panic, but she had to gather her wits, she scolded herself. Taking a deep breath, Elizabeth Carr hurried on through the kitchen. She noticed with wry surprise that even in her desperate state she loved the friendly smell of Hildie Cannon's crushed herbs on the floor. She was thankful for the momentary respite from the stench of the cockroaches.

The woman raced upstairs, only to see that one platoon of the insects was already climbing up the shingles outside. As had happened at the lighthouse, they were coating the side of the house brown like a huge living paintbrush —a crazy, upside-down painting of the walls with a living brush of cockroaches!

Elizabeth ran on in blind flight rather than by directed effort. If no room was safe, what did it matter? Wherever she turned, she was only postponing the inevitable. She searched for a weapon, anything. What could she use to stave them off? The iron poker beside the bedroom fireplace? Laughable, a mockery! If only this adversary were large enough to strike at! Elizabeth did not know that other victims had wished the same thing, wanting to grapple, to collide physically with the attacker, wishing it were a wild dog, a wolf. What, she moaned like the others who had been besieged, what could she do against the thousand, the million ravening insects coming after her blood?

She saw no fire extinguisher. She spotted a can of insect

spray on the dresser. Laughable, indeed! One measly can against the oncoming drove?

There was no way to blockade herself, no device to keep them off. To her horror, she saw the moving shadows on the window turn from what she had hoped were leaves into roach bodies. The hissing and clicking, the wheezing and puffing of the insects were loud with closing menace now. She searched wildly for a hiding place. There was none. No room was safe from them, no door could keep them out. She could only run, much good that would do!

Abruptly, though she did not know how they had entered, roaches were thick on the floor of the bedroom, skittering greedily for her. Elizabeth choked in silent misery as she huddled against a wall. Why hadn't she gone with Bonnie to the harbor? Why had she walked out alone? Why hadn't she joined Peter on the fire truck? Why hadn't Peter known there would surely be more than just stray roaches left!

With each whipping question, Elizabeth Carr ran again from the tide of insects now moving over the bedroom floor like dirty weed covering a beach. She bounded up a staircase to the Cannons' third-floor guest rooms. Thankfully, she saw she had gained a respite, though it would be short. For some reason, the roaches were not climbing as quickly now. It occurred to her they looked to be smaller bugs than the lighthouse army had been. Perhaps these were not as strong, being second-line troops since the best fighters had been decimated. But they were certainly as vicious looking, and the implacability of their avid search for human blood was morbidly the same.

Now at the top of the house, where could she run? Elizabeth saw she had trapped herself. She had been stupid in her panic, she flagellated herself—she should have taken a chance and jumped from a lower window. True, there were attackers all over the lawn, but most of the roaches were already in the house. Her leap might have scattered the laggards and she might have gotten away.

But the second-guessing was too late and futile now. There was only one possible hope of safety, and that exceedingly slim. Elizabeth made for what the Yarkie people called the "chicken ladder." In many of the old buildings, it went steeply to the attic and on to the widow walk atop the house.

In another moment, Elizabeth was out in the open. The salty air was welcome to her lungs. The roach smell didn't reach her here. Yet. If they found her and killed her, well, she preferred to die under the sky—now mockingly sunny and clear over Yarkie—than be devoured in the house.

She walked cautiously around the platform, testing its long-untrod boards. They sagged under her weight, worn as they were with generations of weather. She could only hope they would hold her and not drop her bodily into the roaches she knew were piling into the room below.

She stepped to the railing—what people still called the "running rigging," she didn't know why. She took care not to lean; the old railing would give way easily, she saw. If she dropped from this height, it would be broken bones and certain disaster. The cockroach mass would be over her before she could breathe. She could see the insects below like a viscous preternatural mucilage pasting heaps of leaves around the base of the house. The roaches were climbing up the walls, climbing slowly but without pause, up and up and up to the window ledges where some entered the rooms below but more kept climbing directly to the roof, as if they knew she was up on the widow walk, trapped, no way to fend them off, no way to stop them, no way to escape except to jump to her death to them, to the waiting mouths on the ground.

Elizabeth wailed aloud for her life. Her chin dropped to her chest in a physical acknowledgement of utter, visceral defeat. Now she wished only that she had a weapon to kill herself, to be spared the torture of being taken by the insects and eaten alive. Her horror enclosed the whole space of her life; it came to her that there was another meaning to "the fourth dimension." In addition to time and space there was a dimension of terror, a world of its own, for dying in.

Miraculously, the woman's wailing moan was answered by the sound of men's laughter. Around the curve of High Ridge Road rolled the Hook & Ladder truck. The men had been joking among themselves Elizabeth saw through her tears but they cracked-jumped to attention at her fierce scream for help.

EIGHT

The truck motor roared like an angry beast and the tires smoked as the heavy engine swerved into the Cannon driveway. In another instant, the company was stamping over the lawn at Peter Hubbard's direction, squirting dry ice everywhere. Without waiting, other men were setting the truck's hydraulic system to raise the aerial ladder toward the building. Their procedure was fast, every move precise; they were trained for pressure and emergency.

Elizabeth saw roaches squeezing under the crack in the roof door. She cried out for the firemen to hurry, but there was trouble maneuvering the ladder on the uneven grade of the lawn. It was taking time to adjust the hydraulic jacks that leveled the truck. Peter Hubbard was standing beside the fire engine looking up at Elizabeth. His face was livid with disbelief and self-fury.

More of the insects were finding their way to the woman's last perch. She went after them with an atavistic violence, crushing and mashing to death whatever her foot could find. Dimly but thankfully she recognized that at least none of these roaches seemed to be the flying type. They were not reaching her face or eyes, only trying to climb her legs—and coming too thickly for her to handle for long. She cried out in anguish to the firemen again.

Peter Hubbard broke from the truck and rushed to the now-extended ladder, which was beginning to rotate toward the roof railing. Hubbard lunged for the bottom rungs and started up. Firemen yelled at him and tried to pull him down. Despite his bandaged hand, he kept climbing desperately, while holding tightly to a dry-ice tank he had grabbed.

Burdened as he was, Hubbard kept slipping, once nearly fell off altogether. All he heard was Elizabeth's cry for help. He saw the insect swarm around her and realized the ladder would not close on the building in time. The only possible chance was to throw the tank across. It was heavy and his perch precarious on the swaying ladder. If the tank did not reach Elizabeth, she was doomed.

Holding tightly with his bandaged hand, Hubbard swung the clumsy fire extinguisher in an arc with all his muscle.

The tank hit the roof railing, teetered for a moment as the rotten wood broke, and started to drop away. Reaching with all her strength, Elizabeth managed to catch hold of the hose. The weight of the tank nearly pulled her off her platform, but she braced herself and managed to hang on. With the surging strength of ultimate desperation, she tugged the heavy extinguisher up toward the roof by its red tube, only to blink in terror as she saw the hose threatening to pull loose from the metal body. Taking the final chance that she might fall off the roof, Elizabeth made a lunge for the container itself. Her hands closed on it, and she grabbed it up to her chest like a salvaged child.

At once, she started the icy spray at the attacking roaches, making a circle of dead insects around her bleeding feet.

The very smallness of the trap she had led herself into proved a help now. The roaches were unable to converge on her from many directions. They could come only from the walls—which the firemen were now spraying heavily—or from under the roof door, which she could now control.

Relief and prayer tingled through Elizabeth, body and soul. She was still in deadly peril, but she had assistance and she could hold the roaches at bay until the rescue ladder touched. She could hear it bumping against the roof behind her, and she heard Peter calling her stoutly to its safety.

Elizabeth whirled from the door and dashed for Hubbard's outstretched arms where he stood atop the now steady ladder. A rotted plank snapped under her feet just as her fingers touched his. The woman found herself plummeting away. She tumbled and fell amid a concussion of broken boards, dirt, and avidly hissing roaches. Crashing to the floor below Elizabeth Carr struck her head so hard she almost fainted. She wished she had, for she felt the insect teeth going at her body at once. She covered her face hopelessly against the stinging bites.

Elizabeth knew she was beyond help. As a girl she had wondered how it would feel to drown—no other form of death had seemed real. Sometimes in bed she would hold her breath as if she were underwater and her life depended on it. Then she would suck in the life-giving air, drenched in sweat with the effort. She felt that way now, but knew it was the wetness of the insects on her skin, not her perspiration but her blood.

In the doom that was hers now, Elizabeth Carr had only one thought: She was sorry, not glad, for the night with

Peter Hubbard. To know how much she was losing made dying more intolerable and tragic.

Through her torment, Elizabeth thought she heard Peter's voice nearby. She could not look, dared not expose her eyes to the roaches she felt biting the back of her hands. With her last strength she cried out, "Don't come in here, Peter! It's too late! They'll only get you, too!"

A curtain drew down inside the woman's head, slowly at first, then more quickly into the sheer dark of nothingness.

As she submerged, there were fire bells and sirens in some receding distance. The bells were tolling her funeral. The sirens were all the mourners lamenting the tragic end of all the victims of Yarkie Island's unspeakable travail, and the end of Elizabeth Carr.

NINE

Elizabeth came to consciousness in her own bed in her grandfather's house. It took time for her eyes to focus. She wondered whether she was on the other side of life, but the sound of Peter Hubbard's anxious voice was no illusion, and her grandfather's hovering face was no mirage. There were no angels or devils, no harps or pitchforks, only the two beloved countenances, and dear Bonnie behind them, distraught.

"We have the doctor coming over from Chatham," Elias Johnson said as soon as he saw his granddaughter's eyes open.

"Oh, Liz!" Bonnie wept. "You're going to be all right!"

Peter Hubbard did not speak, only held her sore hands tenderly, and looked his love into her eyes.

Elizabeth found the strength to say, "I—I'm all right." Her voice sounded strange to her. It seemed underwater, coming from the bath of pain in which she was swimming.

She said no more. Her head hurt from her fall, her body was a mass of stinging needles—like the time she had stepped on sea urchins, she thought, only this was every inch of her skin, not just her feet and legs. She gave up talking, it was too difficult to form words.

But Hubbard saw the questions in her eyes, and knew she impatiently wanted answers.

He explained, in a soft voice. "We got to you in time, Liz, yes. And we got the damn things off you with lights."

The curiosity in the woman's face increased.

"You know the firemen have what they call Wheat Lights—portable but extremely powerful. To the roaches, it was almost like fire. They couldn't take the beams. They scattered the hell away."

"Thank God!" Elias Johnson muttered from the foot of the bed.

"We killed as many as we could get to," Hubbard went on. "We got you safely out, and I went on with some of the men to follow the roaches. They ran from our lights, directly into their nest . . ."

Elizabeth gasped, "Another *nest?*"

"You were right this morning, Liz! Those confounded roaches in the flask *were* pointing to another lair. I know just what happened . . ."

Bonnie interrupted Hubbard bringing coffee to the bed. She lifted Elizabeth's head to help her drink it.

The scientist went on, "It turns out the first nest wasn't large enough to hold the expanding colony. In the same way that a rival queen will appear in a crowded bee hive, a *rival brain* apparently developed or split off. The original tribe battled the others until they were driven out. The 'exiles' were the roaches that attacked you. They formed a new home base in the graveyard at the Cannon house. The graves provided convenient, ready-made excavations in which to start up the new community."

The coffee helped clear Elizabeth's head and throat. Her voice was still uncertain. "Then there could be other nests?"

"No! I am certain of that," Hubbard declared without qualification. "I don't even have to look, though we will as a precaution. You see, this has been exactly what ants and bees do. They spin off one new colony, not more. There isn't vigor enough for more, and here there certainly hasn't been enough time. In fact, one reason you survived is that these roaches from the new colony were weaker and slower than the older society—and hadn't yet fully developed the kind of brain that directed the original group. We're lucky to that extent."

Elizabeth needed to know, insistently if weakly, "But they're still out there?"

She saw both men shake their heads negatively.

"No," Hubbard stated again. "We fired the nest." He added sadly, "We had to burn the Cannon house, too, I'm afraid, but we had no choice."

Elizabeth took it unhappily. She recognized the necessity, knew it bitterly, but the house had meant so much to her as a child. To all of Yarkie it was a symbol of the wealth and security of the island.

Security? Not in the universe of Nature's whims, Elizabeth considered astringently. The reality of life was not lovely houses on High Ridge but earthquakes, tidal waves, cyclones, volcanoes, meteors, epidemics, massacres— mutated insects!

Elizabeth Carr groaned inwardly with her own confrontation of Nature's indifference to the individual. Now the Cannon house was gone, as Hildie and the girls were gone. *Sic transit gloria*, and all vanity. How grievously true we find those old clichés to be, the woman contemplated unhappily.

But she should be thankful that she herself was safe,

after giving herself up for lost. Peter Hubbard was her renewal in so many ways. It seemed she was to be granted the years she had thought were eternally gone. She, prayerfully, would never forget how closely death had come to ending it all. She would praise God—even while asking endlessly in the recesses of her soul how and why He came to create such evil. Job's never-answered question, she remembered as her tired eyes closed in welcome sleep again.

EPILOGUE

On the *Jessica* sailing spankingly to Chatham a week later, Bonnie Taylor was at the wheel under Captain Johnson's fond supervision. The woman's eyes were bright with the pleasure of handling the boat, but her mind would never be free of the remembrance of human vulnerability, and her heart never free of the soul-reaching smile of Craig Soaras.

Elizabeth Carr and Dr. Peter Hubbard stood aft watching the bowler-hat outline of Yarkie Island recede into the haze of the horizon. The sailing was pleasant, the ocean was as easy this day as it had been murderous during the northeaster. The open blue above seemed a lighter color than usual, as if the sky itself were drifting higher, upward into outer space.

Gazing back at Yarkie, the woman felt as if she were leaving another planet, returning to earth. It was a fearsome paradox that the island she had loved so deeply should now forever be an alien place.

Perhaps the harrowing memories would fade eventually, and Yarkie return in heart as in fact to the lovely oasis it had been with its fresh woods and pristine beaches. But now, though safe with Peter Hubbard's arm around her still-bandaged body, Elizabeth Carr shivered. As she faintly made out the bowler shape, she saw not High Ridge and its stately homes and bright flowers; she saw the slimy dome in the abominable cockroach cave, the detestable "brain" whose "cerebral cells" in the form of the tiny insects Peter was bringing back—oh, safely packed!—to Harvard.

The biologists of the world would come to understand what had transpired. They would bestow Latin names and learned theories to relate the freak cockroach colony to known natural developments. But for her the Yarkie aggressors would remain a black mystery of the impossible.

Elizabeth turned her back on the island in a gesture of finality. Her life was elsewhere. Secretly, she doubted whether she and Peter would even return for the wedding. She would do almost anything to please her grandfather, but there would be too many ghosts in that hall—the lost children off the *Tub*, Craig Soaras, Wanda Lindstrom, the Cannons, the Tintons, the Laidlaws, the unknowns. No, she wanted to dance at her wedding without tripping over phantoms, dance with the man holding her tightly and safely now.

She lifted her face for his kiss of promise. He gave it with a man's love as full as her own.

From the wheel beside Bonnie Taylor, Elias Johnson looked back at the two and wiped a moist eye with a rough wrist. "Keep her straight into the wind," he admonished Bonnie. "You're kicking up too much spray!"

The first faint sight of Chatham caught everyone's attention. Boston and Cambridge—the world—were close and real again. Life would resume.

None of the people on board saw the small blot that skittered on the *Jessica's* scrubbed deck for a split second before disappearing in a coil of Elias Johnson's neatly arranged rope.

Bigfoot! Killer Cockroaches! Sinister Nuns! Creepy Kids! Ancient Monsters!

COLLECT THEM ALL!

HUNGRY FOR MORE?

Learn about the Twisted History of '70s and '80s Horror Fiction

by Grady Hendrix

"Pure, demented delight."
—The New York Times
Book Review

Take a tour through the horror paperback novels of two iconic decades . . . if you dare. Page through dozens and dozens of amazing book covers featuring well-dressed skeletons, evil dolls, and knife-wielding killer crabs! Read shocking plot summaries that invoke devil worship, satanic children, and haunted real estate! Horror author and vintage paperback book collector Grady Hendrix offers killer commentary and witty insight on these trashy thrillers that tried so hard to be the next *Exorcist* or *Rosemary's Baby*.

- -

AVAILABLE WHEREVER BOOKS ARE SOLD.

Visit QuirkBooks.com for more information about
this book and other titles by Grady Hendrix.

QUIRK
BOOKS

CPSIA information can be obtained
at www.ICGtesting.com
Printed in the USA
FFHW020623050319
50865497-56276FF